Exposed . . .

"Ruby?"

Nate's voice was low, tentative. I swallowed, thinking how stupid I was, thinking that my mom might have actually come back, when I knew full well that everything she needed she'd taken with her. "I'll be done in a sec," I said to him, hating how my voice was shaking.

"Are you . . .?" He paused. "Are you okay?"

I nodded, all business. "Yeah. I just have to grab something."

I heard him shift his weight, taking a step, although toward me or away, I wasn't sure, and not knowing this was enough to make me turn around. He was standing in the doorway to the kitchen, the front door open behind him, turning his head slowly, taking it all in. I felt a surge of shame; I'd been so stupid to bring him here. Like I, of all people, didn't know better than to lead a total stranger to the point where they could hurt me most, knowing how easily they'd be able to find their way back to it.

lock and key

Sarah Dessen

speak

An Imprint of Penguin Group (USA) Inc.

SPEAK
Published by the Penguin Group
Penguin Group (USA) Inc., 345 Hudson Street, New York, New York 10014, U.S.A.
Penguin Group (Canada), 90 Eglinton Avenue East, Suite 700,
Toronto, Ontario, Canada M4P 2Y3 (a division of Pearson Penguin Canada Inc.)
Penguin Books Ltd, 80 Strand, London WC2R 0RL, England
Penguin Ireland, 25 St Stephen's Green, Dublin 2, Ireland (a division of Penguin Books Ltd)
Penguin Group (Australia), 250 Camberwell Road, Camberwell, Victoria 3124, Australia
(a division of Pearson Australia Group Pty Ltd)
Penguin Books India Pvt Ltd, 11 Community Centre,
Panchsheel Park, New Delhi - 110 017, India
Penguin Group (NZ), 67 Apollo Drive, Rosedale, North Shore 0632, New Zealand
(a division of Pearson New Zealand Ltd)
Penguin Books (South Africa) (Pty) Ltd, 24 Sturdee Avenue,
Rosebank, Johannesburg 2196, South Africa

Registered Offices: Penguin Books Ltd, 80 Strand, London WC2R 0RL, England

First published in the United States of America by Viking,
a division of Penguin Young Readers Group, 2008
Published by Speak, an imprint of Penguin Group (USA) Inc., 2009

1 3 5 7 9 10 8 6 4 2

ANGELS FROM MONTGOMERY
Words and music by John Prine
© 1971 (Renewed) Walden Music, Inc. & Sour Grapes Music
All rights administered by WB Music Corp.
All Rights Reserved. Used by Permission of Alfred Publishing Co., Inc.

THE LIBRARY OF CONGRESS HAS CATALOGED THE VIKING EDITION AS FOLLOWS:
Dessen, Sarah.
Lock and key / by Sarah Dessen.
p. cm.
Summary: When she is abandoned by her alcoholic mother, high school senior Ruby
winds up living with her sister Cora, whom she has not seen for ten years, where she learns
about Cora's new life, what makes a family, how to allow people to help her
when she needs it, and that she has something to offer to others as well.
ISBN 978-0-670-01088-2 (hardcover)
[1. Abandoned children—Fiction. 2. Self-actualization (Psychology)—Fiction.
3. Family—Fiction. 4. Child abuse—Fiction. 5. Emotional problems—Fiction.
6. Interpersonal relationships—Fiction.] I. Title.
Pz7.D455Lo 2008 [Fic]—dc22 2007025370

SPEAK ISBN 978-0-14-241472-9

To Leigh Feldman, for seeing me through
this time, every time

and to Jay,
always waiting on the other side

lock and key

Chapter One

"And finally," Jamie said as he pushed the door open, "we come to the main event. Your room."

I was braced for pink. Ruffles or quilting, or maybe even appliqué. Which was probably kind of unfair, but then again, I didn't know my sister anymore, much less her decorating style. With total strangers, it had always been my policy to expect the worst. Usually they—and those that you knew best, for that matter—did not disappoint.

Instead, the first thing I saw was green. A large, high window, on the other side of which were tall trees separating the huge backyard from that of the house that backed up to it. Everything was big about where my sister and her husband, Jamie, lived—from the homes to the cars to the stone fence you saw first thing when you pulled into the neighborhood itself, made up of boulders that looked too enormous to ever be moved. It was like Stonehenge, but suburban. So weird.

It was only as I thought this that I realized we were all still standing there in the hallway, backed up like a traffic jam. At some point Jamie, who had been leading this little tour, had stepped aside, leaving me in the doorway. Clearly, they wanted me to step in first. So I did.

The room was, yes, big, with cream-colored walls. There

were three other windows beneath the big one I'd first seen, although they each were covered with thin venetian blinds. To the right, I saw a double bed with a yellow comforter and matching pillows, a white blanket folded over the foot. There was a small desk, too, a chair tucked under it. The ceiling slanted on either side, meeting in a flat strip in the middle, where there was a square skylight, also covered with a venetian blind—a little square one, clearly custom made to fit. It was so matchy-matchy and odd that for a moment, I found myself just staring up at it, as if this was actually the weirdest thing about that day.

"So, you've got your own bathroom," Jamie said, stepping around me, his feet making soft thuds on the carpet, which was of course spotless. In fact, the whole room smelled like paint and new carpet, just like the rest of the house. I wondered how long ago they had moved in—a month, six months? "Right through this door. And the closet is in here, too. Weird, right? Ours is the same way. When we were building, Cora claimed it meant she would get ready faster. A theory that has yet to be proved out, I might add."

Then he smiled at me, and again I tried to force a smile back. Who was this odd creature, my brother-in-law—a term that seemed oddly fitting, considering the circumstances—in his mountain-bike T-shirt, jeans, and funky expensive sneakers, cracking jokes in an obvious effort to ease the tension of an incredibly awkward situation? I had no idea, other than he had to be the very last person I would have expected to end up with my sister, who was so uptight she wasn't even pretending to smile at his attempts. At least I was trying.

Not Cora. She was just standing in the doorway, barely over the threshold, arms crossed over her chest. She had on a sleeveless sweater—even though it was mid-October, the house was beyond cozy, almost hot—and I could see the definition of her biceps and triceps, every muscle seemingly tensed, the same way they had been when she'd walked into the meeting room at Poplar House two hours earlier. Then, too, it seemed like Jamie had done all the talking, both to Shayna, the head counselor, and to me while Cora remained quiet. Still, every now and again, I could feel her eyes on me, steady, as if she was studying my features, committing me to memory, or maybe just trying to figure out if there was any part of me she recognized at all.

So Cora had a husband, I'd thought, staring at them as we'd sat across from each other, Shayna shuffling papers between us. I wondered if they'd had a fancy wedding, with her in a big white dress, or if they'd just eloped after she'd told him she had no family to speak of. Left to her own devices, this was the story I was sure she preferred—that she'd just sprouted, all on her own, neither connected nor indebted to anyone else at all.

"Thermostat's out in the hallway if you need to adjust it," Jamie was saying now. "Personally, I like a bit of a chill to the air, but your sister prefers it to be sweltering. So even if you turn it down, she'll most likely jack it back up within moments."

Again he smiled, and I did the same. God, this was exhausting. I felt Cora shift in the doorway, but again she didn't say anything.

"Oh!" Jamie said, clapping his hands. "Almost forgot.

The best part." He walked over to the window in the center of the wall, reaching down beneath the blind. It wasn't until he was stepping back and it was opening that I realized it was, in fact, a door. Within moments, I smelled cold air. "Come check this out."

I fought the urge to look back at Cora again as I took a step, then one more, feeling my feet sink into the carpet, following him over the threshold onto a small balcony. He was standing by the railing, and I joined him, both of us looking down at the backyard. When I'd first seen it from the kitchen, I'd noticed just the basics: grass, a shed, the big patio with a grill at one end. Now, though, I could see there were rocks laid out in the grass in an oval shape, obviously deliberately, and again, I thought of Stonehenge. What was it with these rich people, a druid fixation?

"It's gonna be a pond," Jamie told me as if I'd said this out loud.

"A pond?" I said.

"Total ecosystem," he said. "Thirty-by-twenty and lined, all natural, with a waterfall. And fish. Cool, huh?"

Again, I felt him look at me, expectant. "Yeah," I said, because I was a guest here. "Sounds great."

He laughed. "Hear that, Cor? *She* doesn't think I'm crazy."

I looked down at the circle again, then back at my sister. She'd come into the room, although not that far, and still had her arms crossed over her chest as she stood there, watching us. For a moment, our eyes met, and I wondered how on earth I'd ended up here, the last place I knew either one of us wanted me to be. Then she opened her mouth to speak for the first time since we'd pulled up in the driveway and all this, whatever it was, began.

"It's cold," she said. "You should come inside."

* * *

Before one o'clock that afternoon, when she showed up to claim me, I hadn't seen my sister in ten years. I didn't know where she lived, what she was doing, or even who she was. I didn't care, either. There had been a time when Cora was part of my life, but that time was over, simple as that. Or so I'd thought, until the Honeycutts showed up one random Tuesday and everything changed.

The Honeycutts owned the little yellow farmhouse where my mom and I had been living for about a year. Before that, we'd had an apartment at the Lakeview Chalets, the run-down complex just behind the mall. There, we'd shared a one-bedroom, our only window looking out over the back entrance to the J&K Cafeteria, where there was always at least one employee in a hairnet sitting outside smoking, perched on an overturned milk crate. Running alongside the complex was a stream that you didn't even notice until there was a big rain and it rose, overflowing its nonexistent banks and flooding everything, which happened at least two or three times a year. Since we were on the top floor, we were spared the water itself, but the smell of the mildew from the lower apartments permeated everything, and God only knew what kind of mold was in the walls. Suffice to say I had a cold for two years straight. That was the first thing I noticed about the yellow house: I could breathe there.

It was different in other ways, too. Like the fact that

it was a *house*, and not an apartment in a complex or over someone's garage. I'd grown used to the sound of neighbors on the other side of a wall, but the yellow house sat in the center of a big field, framed by two oak trees. There was another house off to the left, but it was visible only by flashes of roof you glimpsed through the trees—for all intents and purposes, we were alone. Which was just the way we liked it.

My mom wasn't much of a people person. In certain situations—say, if you were buying, for instance—she could be very friendly. And if you put her within five hundred feet of a man who would treat her like shit, she'd find him and be making nice before you could stop her, and I knew, because I had tried. But interacting with the majority of the population (cashiers, school administrators, bosses, ex-boyfriends) was not something she engaged in unless absolutely necessary, and then, with great reluctance.

Which was why it was lucky that she had me. For as long as I could remember, I'd been the buffer system. The go-between, my mother's ambassador to the world. Whenever we pulled up at the store and she needed a Diet Coke but was too hungover to go in herself, or she spied a neighbor coming who wanted to complain about her late-night banging around *again*, or the Jehovah's Witnesses came to the door, it was always the same. "Ruby," she'd say, in her tired voice, pressing either her glass or her hand to her forehead. "Talk to the people, would you?"

And I would. I'd chat with the girl behind the counter as I waited for my change, nod as the neighbor again threatened to call the super, ignored the proffered literature as I firmly shut the door in the Jehovah's faces. I was the first line of defense, always ready with an explanation or a bit of spin. "She's at the bank right now," I'd tell the landlord, even as she snored on the couch on the other side of the half-closed door. "She's just outside, talking to a delivery," I'd assure her boss so he'd release her bags for the day to me, while she smoked a much-needed cigarette in the freight area and tried to calm her shaking hands. And finally, the biggest lie of all: "Of course she's still living here. She's just working a lot," which is what I'd told the sheriff that day when I'd been called out of fourth period and found him waiting for me. That time, though, all the spin in the world didn't work. I talked to the people, just like she'd always asked, but they weren't listening.

That first day, though, when my mom and I pulled up in front of the yellow house, things were okay. Sure, we'd left our apartment with the usual drama—owing back rent, the super lurking around watching us so carefully that we had to pack the car over a series of days, adding a few things each time we went to the store or to work. I'd gotten used to this, though, the same way I'd adjusted to us rarely if ever having a phone, and if we did, having it listed under another name. Ditto with my school paperwork, which my mom often filled out with a fake address, as she was convinced that creditors and old landlords would track us down that way. For a long time, I thought this was the way everyone lived. When I got old enough to realize otherwise, it was already a habit, and anything else would have felt strange.

Inside, the yellow house was sort of odd. The kitchen was the biggest room, and everything was lined up against one wall: cabinets, appliances, shelves. Against another wall was a huge propane heater, which in cold weather worked hard to heat the whole house, whooshing to life with a heavy sigh. The only bathroom was off the kitchen, poking out with no insulated walls—my mom said it must have been added on; there'd probably been an outhouse, initial-ly—which made for some cold mornings until you got the hot water blasting and the steam heated things up. The living room was small, the walls covered with dark fake-wood paneling. Even at high noon, you needed a light on to see your hand in front of your face. My mother, of course, loved the dimness and usually pulled the shades shut, as well. I'd come home to find her on the couch, cigarette dangling from one hand, the glow from the TV flashing across her face in bursts. Outside, the sun might be shining, the entire world bright, but in our house, it could always be late night, my mother's favorite time of day.

In the old one-bedroom apartment, I was accustomed to sometimes being awoken from a dead sleep, her lips close to my ear as she asked me to move out onto the couch, please, honey. As I went, groggy and discombobulated, I'd do my best not to notice whoever slipped back in the door behind her. At the yellow house, though, I got my own room. It was small, with a tiny closet and only one window, as well as orange carpet and those same dark walls, but I had a door to shut, and it was all mine. It made me feel like we'd stay longer than a couple of months, that things would be better here. In the end, though, only one of these things turned out to be true.

I first met the Honeycutts three days after we moved in.

It was early afternoon, and we were getting ready to leave for work when a green pickup truck came up the driveway. A man was driving, a woman in the passenger seat beside him.

"Mom," I called out to my mother, who was in the bedroom getting dressed. "Someone's here."

She sighed, sounding annoyed. My mother was at her worst just before going to work, petulant like a child. "Who is it?"

"I don't know," I said, watching as the couple—he in jeans and a denim work shirt, she wearing slacks and a printed top—started to make their way to the house. "But they're about to knock on the door."

"Oh, Ruby." She sighed again. "Just talk to them, would you?"

The first thing I noticed about the Honeycutts was that they were instantly friendly, the kind of people my mother couldn't *stand*. They were both beaming when I opened the door, and when they saw me, they smiled even wider.

"Well, look at you!" the woman said as if I'd done something precious just by existing. She herself resembled a gnome, with her small features and halo of white curls, like something made to put on a shelf. "Hello there!"

I nodded, my standard response to all door knockers. Unnecessary verbals only encouraged them, or so I'd learned. "Can I help you?"

The man blinked. "Ronnie Honeycutt," he said, extending his hand. "This is my wife, Alice. And you are?"

I glanced in the direction of my mother's room. Although usually she banged around a lot while getting ready—

drawers slamming, grumbling to herself—now, of course, she was dead silent. Looking back at the couple, I decided they probably weren't Jehovah's but were definitely peddling something. "Sorry," I said, beginning my patented firm shut of the door, "but we're not—"

"Oh, honey, it's okay!" Alice said. She looked at her husband. "Stranger danger," she explained. "They teach it in school."

"Stranger what?" Ronnie said.

"We're your landlords," she told me. "We just dropped by to say hello and make sure you got moved in all right."

Landlords, I thought. That was even worse than Witnesses. Instinctively, I eased the door shut a bit more, wedging my foot against it. "We're fine," I told them.

"Is your mom around?" Ronnie asked as Alice shifted her weight, trying to see into the kitchen behind me.

I adjusted myself accordingly, blocking her view, before saying, "Actually, she's—"

"Right here," I heard my mother say, and then she was crossing the living room toward us, pulling her hair back with one hand. She had on jeans, her boots, and a white tank top, and despite the fact that she'd just woken up about twenty minutes earlier, I had to admit she looked pretty good. Once my mother had been a great beauty, and occasionally you could still get a glimpse of the girl she had been—if the light was right, or she'd had a decent night's sleep, or, like me, you were just wistful enough to look for it.

She smiled at me, then eased a hand over my shoulder as she came to the door and offered them her other one. "Ruby

Cooper," she said. "And this is my daughter. Her name's Ruby, as well."

"Well, isn't that something!" Alice Honeycutt said. "And she looks just like you."

"That's what they say," my mom replied, and I felt her hand move down the back of my head, smoothing my red hair, which we did have in common, although hers was now streaked with an early gray. We also shared our pale skin— the redhead curse or gift, depending on how you looked at it—as well as our tall, wiry frames. I'd been told more than once that from a distance, we could almost be identical, and although I knew this was meant as a compliment, I didn't always take it that way.

I knew that my mother's sudden reaching out for me was just an act, making nice for the landlords, in order to buy some bargaining time or leverage later. Still, though, I noticed how easy it was for me to fold into her hip, resting my head against her. Like some part of me I couldn't even control had been waiting for this chance all along and hadn't even known it.

"It's our standard practice to just drop by and check in on folks," Ronnie was saying now, as my mother idly twisted a piece of my hair through her fingers. "I know the rental agency handles the paperwork, but we like to say hello face-to-face."

"Well, that's awfully nice of you," my mom said. She dropped my hair, letting her hand fall onto the doorknob so casually you almost would think she wasn't aware of it, or the inch or so she shut it just after, narrowing even farther the space between us and them. "But as Ruby was saying, I'm actually going to work right now. So . . ."

"Oh, of course!" Alice said. "Well, you all just let us know if there's anything you need. Ronnie, give Ruby our number."

We all watched as he pulled a scrap of paper and a pen out of his shirt pocket, writing down the digits slowly. "Here you go," he said, handing it over. "Don't hesitate to call."

"Oh, I won't," my mom said. "Thanks so much."

After a few more pleasantries, the Honeycutts finally left the porch, Ronnie's arm locked around his wife's shoulders. He deposited her in the truck first, shutting the door securely behind her, before going around to get behind the wheel. Then he backed out of the driveway with the utmost caution, doing what I counted to be at least an eight-point turn to avoid driving on the grass.

By then, though, my mother had long left the door and returned to her room, discarding their number in an ashtray along the way. "'Hello face-to-face' my ass," she said as a drawer banged. "Checking up is more like it. Busybodies."

She was right, of course. The Honeycutts were always dropping by unexpectedly with some small, seemingly un-necessary domestic project: replacing the garden hose we never used, cutting back the crepe myrtles in the fall, or installing a birdbath in the front yard. They were over so much, I grew to recognize the distinct rattle of their truck muffler as it came up the driveway. As for my mom, her niceties had clearly ended with that first day. Thereafter, if they came to the door, she ignored their knocks, not even flinching when Alice's face appeared in the tiny crack the living-room window shade didn't cover, white and ghostly with the bright light behind it, peering in.

It was because the Honeycutts saw my mother so rarely that it took almost two months for them to realize she was gone. In fact, if the dryer hadn't busted, I believed they might have never found out, and I could have stayed in the yellow house all the way until the end. Sure, I was behind on the rent and the power was close to getting cut off. But I would have handled all that one way or another, just like I had everything else. The fact was, I was doing just fine on my own, or at least as well as I'd ever done with my mom. Which wasn't saying much, I know. Still, in a weird way, I was proud of myself. Like I'd finally proven that I didn't need her, either.

As it was, though, the dryer *did* die, with a pop and a burning smell, late one October night while I was making macaroni and cheese in the microwave. I had no option but to stretch a clothesline across the kitchen in front of the space heater I'd been using since the propane ran out, hang everything up—jeans, shirts, and socks—and hope for the best. The next morning, my stuff was barely dry, so I pulled on the least damp of it and left the rest, figuring I'd deal with it that evening when I got home from work. But then Ronnie and Alice showed up to replace some supposedly broken front-porch slats. When they saw the clothesline, they came inside, and then they found everything else.

It wasn't until the day they took me to Poplar House that I actually saw the report that the person from social services had filed that day. When Shayna, the director, read it out loud, it was clear to me that whoever had written it had embellished, for some reason needing to make it sound worse than it actually was.

Minor child is apparently living without running water or heat in rental home abandoned by parent. Kitchen area was found to be filthy and overrun with vermin. Heat is non-functioning. Evidence of drug and alcohol use was discovered. Minor child appears to have been living alone for some time.

First of all, I had running water. Just not in the kitchen, where the pipes had busted. This was why the dishes tended to pile up, as it was hard to truck in water from the bathroom just to wash a few plates. As for the "vermin," we'd always had roaches; they'd just grown a bit more in number with the lack of sink water, although I'd been spraying them on a regular basis. And I did have a heater; it just wasn't on. The drug and alcohol stuff—which I took to mean the bottles on the coffee table and the roach in one of the ashtrays—I couldn't exactly deny, but it hardly seemed grounds for uprooting a person from their entire life with no notice.

The entire time Shayna was reading the report aloud, her voice flat and toneless, I still thought that I could talk my way out of this. That if I explained myself correctly, with the proper detail and emphasis, they'd just let me go home. After all, I had only seven months before I turned eighteen, when all of this would be a moot point anyway. But the minute I opened my mouth to start in about topic one, the water thing, she stopped me.

"Ruby," she said, "where is your mother?"

It was only then that I began to realize what would later seem obvious. That it didn't matter what I said, how carefully I crafted my arguments, even if I used every tool of evasion and persuasion I'd mastered over the years. There was only one thing that really counted, now and always, and this was it.

"I don't know," I said. "She's just gone."

* * *

After the tour, the pond reveal, and a few more awkward moments, Jamie and Cora finally left me alone to go downstairs and start dinner. It was barely five thirty, but already it was getting dark outside, the last of the light sinking behind the trees. I imagined the phone ringing in the empty yellow house as Richard, my mother's boss at Commercial Courier, realized we were not just late but blowing off our shift. Later, the phone would probably ring again, followed by a car rolling up the drive, pausing by the front window. They'd wait for a few moments for me to come out, maybe even send someone to bang on the door. When I didn't, they'd turn around hastily, spitting out the Honeycutts' neat grass and the mud beneath it from behind their back wheels.

And then what? The night would pass, without me there, the house settling into itself in the dark and quiet. I wondered if the Honeycutts had already been in to clean things up, or if my clothes were still stretched across the kitchen, ghostlike. Sitting there, in this strange place, it was like I could feel the house pulling me back to it, a visceral tug on my heart, the same way that, in the early days of the fall, I'd hoped it would do to my mom. But she hadn't come back, either. And now, if she did, I wouldn't be there.

Thinking this, I felt my stomach clench, a sudden panic

settling over me, and stood up, walking to the balcony door and pushing it open, then stepping outside into the cold air. It was almost fully dark now, lights coming on in the nearby houses as people came home and settled in for the night in the places they called home. But standing there, with Cora's huge house rising up behind me and that vast yard beneath, I felt so small, as if to someone looking up I'd be unrecognizable, already lost.

Back inside, I opened up the duffel that had been delivered to me at Poplar House; Jamie had brought it up from the car. It was a cheap bag, some promo my mom had gotten through work, the last thing I would have used to pack up my worldly possessions, not that this was what was in it anyway. Instead, it was mostly clothes I never wore—the good stuff had all been on the clothesline—as well as a few textbooks, a hairbrush, and two packs of cotton underwear I'd never seen in my life, courtesy of the state. I tried to imagine some person I'd never met before going through my room, picking these things for me. How ballsy it was to just assume you could know, with one glance, the things another person could not live without. As if it was the same for everyone, that simple.

There was only one thing I really needed, and I knew enough to keep it close at all times. I reached up, running my finger down the thin silver chain around my neck until my fingers hit the familiar shape there at its center. All day long I'd been pressing it against my chest as I traced the outline I knew by heart: the rounded top, the smooth edge on one side, the series of jagged bumps on the other. The night before, as I'd stood in the bathroom at Poplar House, it had been all that was familiar, the one thing I focused on as I faced the mirror. I could not look at the dark hollows under my eyes, or the strange surroundings and how strange I felt in them. Instead, like now, I'd just lifted it up gently, reassured to see that the outline of that key remained on my skin, the one that fit the door to everything I'd left behind.

* * *

By the time Jamie called up the stairs that dinner was ready, I'd decided to leave that night. It just made sense—there was no need to contaminate their pristine home any further, or the pretty bed in my room. Once everyone was asleep, I'd just grab my stuff, slip out the back door, and be on a main road within a few minutes. The first pay phone I found, I'd call one of my friends to come get me. I knew I couldn't stay at the yellow house—it would be the obvious place anyone would come looking—but at least if I got there, I could pick through my stuff for the things I needed. I wasn't stupid. I knew things had already changed, irrevocably and totally. But at least I could walk through the rooms and say good-bye, as well as try to leave some message behind, in case anyone came looking for me.

Then it was just a matter of laying low. After a few days of searching and paperwork, Cora and Jamie would write me off as unsaveable, getting their brownie points for try-ing *and* escaping relatively unscathed. That was what most people wanted anyway.

Now, I walked into the bathroom, my hairbrush in hand. I knew I looked rough, the result of two pretty much sleepless nights and then this long day, but the lighting in the bathroom, clearly designed to be flattering, made me look better than I knew I actually did, which was unsettling. Mirrors, if nothing else, were supposed to be honest. I turned off the lights and brushed my hair in the dark.

Just before I left my room, I glanced down at my watch, noting the time: 5:45. If Cora and Jamie were asleep by, say, midnight at the latest, that meant I only had to endure six hours and fifteen minutes more. Knowing this gave me a sense of calm, of control, as well as the fortitude I needed to go downstairs to dinner and whatever else was waiting for me.

Even with this wary attitude, however, I could never have been prepared for what I found at the bottom of the stairs. There, in the dark entryway, just before the arch that led into the kitchen, I stepped in something wet. And, judging by the splash against my ankle, cold.

"Whoa," I said, drawing my foot back and looking around me. Whatever the liquid was had now spread, propelled by my shoe, and I froze, so as not to send it any farther. Barely a half hour in, and already I'd managed to violate Cora's perfect palace. I was looking around me, wondering what I could possibly find to wipe it up with—the tapestry on the nearby wall? something in the umbrella stand?—when the light clicked on over my head.

"Hey," Jamie said, wiping his hands on a dishtowel. "I thought I heard something. Come on in, we're just about—" Suddenly, he stopped talking, having spotted the puddle and my proximity to it. "Oh, shit," he said.

"I'm sorry," I told him.

"Quick," he said, cutting me off and tossing me the dishtowel. "Get it up, would you? Before she—"

I caught the towel and was about to bend over when I realized it was too late. Cora was now standing in the archway behind him, peering around his shoulder. "Jamie," she said, and he jumped, startled. "Is that—?"

"No," he said flatly. "It's not."

My sister, clearly not convinced, stepped around him and walked over for a closer look. "It is," she said, turning back to look at her husband, who had slunk back farther into the kitchen. "It's pee."

"Cor—"

"It's pee, *again*," she said, whirling around to face him. "Isn't this why we put in that dog door?"

Dog? I thought, although I supposed this was a relief, considering I'd been worried I was about to find out something really disturbing about my brother-in-law. "You have a dog?" I asked. Cora sighed in response.

"Mastery of a dog door takes time," Jamie told her, grabbing a roll of paper towels off a nearby counter and walking over to us. Cora stepped aside as he ripped off a few sheets, then squatted down, tossing them over the puddle and adjacent splashes. "You know that expression. You can't teach an old dog new tricks."

Cora shook her head, then walked back into the kitchen without further comment. Jamie, still down on the floor, ripped off a few more paper towels and then dabbed at my shoe, glancing up at me. "Sorry about that," he said. "It's an issue."

I nodded, not sure what to say to this. So I just folded the dishtowel and followed him into the kitchen, where he tossed the paper towels into a stainless-steel trash can. Cora was by the windows that looked out over the deck, setting the wide, white table there. I watched as she folded cloth napkins, setting one by each of three plates, before laying out silverware: fork, knife, spoon. There were also placemats, water glasses, and a big glass pitcher with sliced lemons floating in it. Like the rest of the house, it looked like something out of a magazine, too perfect to even be real.

Just as I thought this, I heard a loud, rattling sound. It was like a noise your grandfather would make, once he passed out in his recliner after dinner, but it was coming from behind me, in the laundry room. When I turned around, I saw the dog.

Actually first, I saw everything else: the large bed, covered in what looked like sheepskin, the pile of toys—plastic rings, fake newspapers, rope bones—and, most noticeable of all, a stuffed orange chicken, sitting upright. Only once I'd processed all these accoutrements did I actually make out the dog itself, which was small, black and white, and lying on its back, eyes closed and feet in the air, snoring. Loudly.

"That's Roscoe," Jamie said to me as he pulled open the fridge. "Normally, he'd be up and greeting you. But our dog walker came for the first time today, and I think it wore him out. In fact, that's probably why he had that accident in the foyer. He's exhausted."

"What would be *out* of the ordinary," Cora said, "is if he actually went outside."

From the laundry room, I heard Roscoe let out another loud snore. It sounded like his nasal passages were exploding.

"Let's just eat," Cora said. Then she pulled out a chair and sat down.

I waited for Jamie to take his place at the head of the table before claiming the other chair. It wasn't until I was seated and got a whiff of the pot of spaghetti sauce to my left that I realized I was starving. Jamie picked up Cora's plate, putting it over his own, then served her some spaghetti, sauce, and salad before passing it back to her. Then he gestured for mine, and did the same before filling his own plate. It was all so formal, and *normal*, that I felt strangely nervous, so much so that I found myself watching my sister, picking up my fork only when she did. Which was so weird, considering how long it had been since I'd taken any cues from Cora. Still, there had been a time when she had taught me everything, so maybe, like so much else, this was just instinct.

"So tomorrow," Jamie said, his voice loud and cheerful, "we're going to get you registered for school. Cora's got a meeting, so I'll be taking you over to my old stomping ground."

I glanced up. "I'm not going to Jackson?"

"Out of district," Cora replied, spearing a cucumber with her fork. "And even if we got an exception, the commute is too long."

"But it's mid-semester," I said. I had a flash of my locker, the bio project I'd just dropped off the week before, all of it, like my stuff in the yellow house, just abandoned. I swallowed, taking a breath. "I can't just leave everything."

"It's okay," Jamie said. "We'll get it all settled tomorrow."

"I don't mind a long bus ride," I said, ashamed at how tight my voice sounded, betraying the lump that had risen in my throat. So ridiculous that after everything that had happened, I was crying about *school*. "I can get up early, I'm used to it."

"Ruby." Cora leveled her eyes at me. "This is for the best. Perkins Day is an excellent school."

"Perkins Day?" I said. "Are you *serious*?"

"What's wrong with the Day?" Jamie asked.

"Everything," I told him. He looked surprised, then hurt. Great. Now I was alienating the one person who I actually had on my side in this house. "It's not a bad school," I told him. "It's just . . . I won't fit in with anyone there."

This was a massive understatement. For the last two years, I'd gone to Jackson High, the biggest high school in the county. Overcrowded, underfunded, and with half your classes in trailers, just surviving a year there was considered a badge of honor, especially if you were like me and did not exactly run with the most academic of crowds. After I'd moved around so much with my mom, Jackson was the first place I'd spent consecutive years in a long time, so even if it was a total shithole, it was still familiar. Unlike Perkins Day, the elite private school known for its lacrosse team, stellar SAT scores, and the fact that the student parking lot featured more luxury automobiles than a European car dealership. The only contact we ever had with Perkins Day kids was when they felt like slumming at parties. Even then, often their girls stayed in the car, engine running and radio on, cigarettes dangling out the window, too good to even come inside.

Just as I thought this, Jamie suddenly pushed his chair

back, jumping to his feet. "Roscoe!" he said. "Hold on! The dog door!"

But it was too late. Roscoe, having at some point roused himself from his bed, was already lifting his leg against the dishwasher. I tried to get a better look at him but only caught a fleeting glimpse before Jamie bolted across the floor, grabbing him in midstream, and then carried him, still dripping, and chucked him out the small flap at the bottom of the French doors facing us. Then he looked at Cora and, seeing her stony expression, stepped outside himself, the door falling shut with a click behind him.

Cora put a hand to her head, closing her eyes, and I wondered if I should say something. Before I could, though, she pushed back her chair and walked over to pick up the roll of paper towels, then disappeared behind the kitchen island, where I could hear her cleaning up what Roscoe had left behind.

I knew I should probably offer to help. But sitting alone at the table, I was still bent out of shape about the idea of me at Perkins Day. Like all it would take was dropping me in a fancy house and a fancy school and somehow I'd just be fixed, the same way Cora had clearly fixed herself when she'd left me and my mom behind all those years ago. But we were not the same, not then and especially not now.

I felt my stomach clench, and I reached up, pressing my fingers over the key around my neck. As I did so, I caught a glimpse of my watch, the overhead light glinting off the face, and felt myself relax. *Five hours, fifteen minutes*, I thought. Then I picked up my fork and finished my dinner.

* * *

Six hours and fifty long minutes later, I was beginning to worry that my brother-in-law—the Nicest Guy in the World and Lover of Incontinent Creatures—was also an insomniac. Figuring they were the early-to-bed types, I'd gone up to my room to "go to sleep" at nine thirty. Sure enough, I heard Cora come up about forty minutes later, padding past my bedroom to her own, which was at the opposite end of the floor. Her light cut off at eleven, at which point I started counting down, waiting for Jamie to join her. He didn't. In fact, if anything, there were more lights on downstairs now than there had been earlier, slanting across the backyard, even as the houses around us went dark, one by one.

Now I'd been sitting there for almost four hours. I didn't want to turn a light on, since I was supposed to be long asleep, so I'd spent the time lying on the bed, my hands clasped on my stomach, staring at the ceiling and wondering what the hell Jamie was doing. Truth be told, it wasn't that different from the nights a few weeks back, when the power had been cut off temporarily at the yellow house. At least there, though, I could smoke a bowl or drink a few beers to keep things interesting. Here, there was nothing but the dark, the heat cutting off and on at what—after timing them—I'd decided were random intervals, and coming up with possible explanations for the weird, shimmering light that was visible at the far end of the backyard. I was just narrowing it down to either aliens or some sort of celestial neo-suburban phenomenon when suddenly, the windows downstairs went dark. Finally, Jamie was coming to bed.

I sat up, brushing my hair back with my fingers, and

listened. Unlike the yellow house, which was so small and thin-walled you could hear someone rolling over in a bed two rooms away, Cora's palace was hard to monitor in terms of activity and movement. I walked over to my door, easing it open slightly. Distantly, I heard footsteps and a door opening and shutting. Perfect. He was in.

Reaching down, I grabbed my bag, then slowly drew the door open, stepping out into the hallway and sticking close to the wall until I got to the stairs. Downstairs in the foyer I got my first lucky break in days: the alarm wasn't set. Thank God.

I reached for the knob, then eased the door open, sliding my hand with the bag through first. I was just about to step over the threshold when I heard the whistling.

It was cheery, and a tune I recognized—some jingle from a commercial. Detergent, maybe. I looked around me, wondering what kind of company I would have on a subdivision street at one thirty in the morning. Soon enough, I got my answer.

"Good boy, Roscoe! Good boy!"

I froze. It was Jamie. Now I could see him, coming up the other side of the street with Roscoe, who had just lifted his leg on a mailbox, walking in front of him on a leash. *Shit*, I thought, wondering whether he was far enough away not to see if I bolted in the opposite direction, dodging the streetlights. After a quick calculation, I decided to go around the house instead.

I could hear him whistling again as I vaulted off the front steps, then ran through the grass, dodging a sprinkler spigot and heading for the backyard. There, I headed for that light I'd been studying earlier, now hoping that it *was* aliens, or some kind of black hole, anything to get me away.

Instead, I found a fence. I tossed my bag over and was wondering what my chances were of following, not to mention what I'd find there, when I heard a thwacking noise from behind me. When I turned around, I saw Roscoe emerging from his dog door.

At first, he was just sniffing the patio, his nose low to the ground, going in circles. But then he suddenly stopped, his nose in the air. *Uh-oh*, I thought. I was already reaching up, grabbing the top of the fence and scrambling to try and pull myself over, when he started yapping and shot like a bullet right toward me.

Say what you will about little dogs, but they can *move*. In mere seconds, he'd covered the huge yard between us and was at my feet, barking up at me as I dangled from the fence, my triceps and biceps already burning. "Shhh," I hissed at him, but of course this only made him bark more. Behind us, in the house, a light came on, and I could see Jamie in the kitchen window, looking out.

I tried to pull myself up farther, working to get more leverage. I managed to get one elbow over, hoisting myself up enough to see that the source of the light I'd been watching was not otherworldly at all, but a swimming pool. It was big and lit up and, I noticed, occupied, a figure cutting through the water doing laps.

Meanwhile, Roscoe was still yapping, and my bag was already in this strange person's yard, meaning I had little choice but to join it or risk being busted by Jamie. Straining,

I pulled myself up so I was hanging over the fence, and tried to throw a leg to the other side. No luck.

"Roscoe?" I heard Jamie call out from the patio. "Whatcha got there, boy?"

I turned my head, looking back at him, wondering if he could see me. I figured I had about five seconds, if Roscoe didn't shut up, before he headed out to see what his dog had treed. Or fenced. Another fifteen while he crossed the yard, then maybe a full minute before he'd put it all together.

"Hello?"

I was so busy doing all these calculations that I hadn't noticed that the person who'd been swimming laps had, at some point, stopped. Not only that, but he was now at the edge of the pool, looking up at me. It was hard to make out his features, but whoever it was was clearly male and sounded awfully friendly, considering the circumstances.

"Hi," I muttered back.

"Roscoe?" Jamie called out again, and this time, without even turning around, I could hear he was moving, coming closer. Unless I had a burst of superhuman strength or a black hole opened up and swallowed me whole, I needed a Plan B, and fast.

"Do you—?" the guy in the pool said, raising his voice to be heard over Roscoe, who was still barking.

"No," I told him as I relaxed my grip. His face disappeared as I slid down my side of the fence, landing on my feet with mere seconds to spare before Jamie ducked under the small row of trees at the edge of the yard and saw me.

"Ruby?" he said. "What are you doing out here?"

He looked so concerned that for a moment, I actually felt a pang of guilt. Like I'd let him down or something. Which was just ridiculous; we didn't even know each other. "Nothing," I said.

"Is everything okay?" He looked up at the fence, then back at me, as Roscoe, who'd finally shut up, sniffed around his feet, making snorting noises.

"Yeah," I said. I was making it a point to speak slowly. Calmly. Tone was everything. "I was just . . ."

Truth was, at that moment, I didn't know what I was planning to say. I was just hoping for some plausible excuse to pop out of my mouth, which, considering my luck so far, was admittedly kind of a long shot. Still, I was going to go for it. But before I could even open my mouth, there was a thunk from the other side of the fence, and a face appeared above us. It was the guy from the pool, who, in this better light, I could now see was about my age. His hair was blond and wet, and there was a towel around his neck.

"Jamie," he said. "Hey. What's up?"

Jamie looked up at him. "Hey," he replied. To me he said, "So . . . you met Nate?"

I shot a glance at the guy. *Oh, well,* I thought. *It's better than what I had planned.* "Yeah." I nodded. "I was just—"

"She came to tell me my music was too loud," the guy— Nate?—told Jamie. Unlike me, he didn't seem to be straining in the least, holding himself over the top of the fence. I wondered if he was standing on something. To me he added, "Sorry about that. I crank it up so I can hear it under the water."

"Right," I said. "I just . . . I couldn't sleep."

At my feet, Roscoe suddenly coughed, hacking up something. We all looked at him, and then Jamie said slowly, "Well . . . it's late. We've got an early day tomorrow, so . . ."

"Yeah. I should get to bed, too," Nate said, reaching down to pull up one edge of his towel and wiping it across his face. He had to be on a deck chair or something, I thought. No one has that kind of upper-body strength. "Nice meeting you, Ruby."

"You, too," I replied.

He waved at Jamie, then dropped out of sight. Jamie looked at me for a moment, as if still trying to decipher what had happened. I tried not to flinch as he continued to study my face, only relaxing once he'd slid his hands in his pockets and started across the lawn, Roscoe tagging along at his heels.

I'd just reached the line of trees, following him, when I heard a *"Pssst!"* from behind me. When I turned around, Nate had pushed open part of the fence and was passing my bag through. "Might need this," he said.

Like I was supposed to be grateful. *Unbelievable*, I thought as I walked over, picking up the bag.

"So what's it to?"

I glanced up at him. He had his hand on the gate and had pulled on a dark-colored T-shirt, and his hair was starting to dry now, sticking up slightly. In the flickering light from the nearby pool I could finally make out his face enough to see that he was kind of cute, but in a rich-boy way, all jocky and smooth edges, not my type at all. "What?" I said.

"The key." He pointed to my neck. "What's it to?"

Jamie was going into the house now, leaving the door open for me behind him. I reached up, twining my fingers around the chain hanging there. "Nothing," I told him.

I shifted my bag behind me, keeping it in my shadow as I headed across the lawn to the back door. *So close,* I thought. *A shorter fence, a fatter dog, and everything would be different.* But wasn't that always the way. It's never something huge that changes everything, but instead the tiniest of details, irrevocably tweaking the balance of the universe while you're busy focusing on the big picture.

When I got to the house, there was no sign of Jamie or Roscoe. Still, I figured it wasn't worth risking bringing my bag inside, and since the balcony was too high to toss it up, I decided to just stow it someplace and come back down for it in a couple of hours when the coast was clear. So I stuck it beside the grill, then slipped inside just as the shimmering lights from Nate's pool cut off, leaving everything dark between his house and ours.

I didn't see Jamie again as I climbed the stairs to my room. If I had, I wasn't sure what I would have said to him. Maybe he had fallen for my flimsy excuse, aided and abetted by a pool boy who happened to be in the right place at what, for me anyway, turned out to be the wrong time. It was possible he was just that gullible. Unlike my sister, who knew from disappearing and could spot a lie, even a good one, a mile off. She also probably would have happily provided the boost I needed up and over that fence, or at least pointed the way to the gate, if only to be rid of me once and for all.

.

I waited a full hour to slip back downstairs. When I eased open my door, though, there was my bag, sitting right there at my feet. It seemed impossible I hadn't heard Jamie leave it there, but he had. For some reason, seeing it made me feel the worst I had all day, ashamed in a way I couldn't even explain as I reached down, pulling it inside with me.

Chapter Two

My mom hated to work. Far from a model employee, she had never had a job, at least in my recollection, that she actually enjoyed. Instead, in our house, work was a four-letter word, the official end of good times, something to be dreaded and bitched about and, whenever possible, avoided.

Things might have been different if she was qualified for a glamorous occupation like travel agent or fashion designer. Instead, due to choices she'd made, as well as a few circumstances beyond her control, she'd always had low-level, minimum-wage, benefits-only-if-you're-really-lucky kinds of jobs: waitress, retail, telemarketer, temp. Which was why, when she got hired on at Commercial Courier, it seemed like such a good thing. Sure, it wasn't glamorous. But at least it was different.

Commercial Courier called itself an "all-purpose delivery service," but their primary business came from lost luggage. They had a small office at the airport where bags that had been routed to the wrong city or put onto the wrong plane would eventually end up, at which point one of their couriers would deliver them to their proper destination, whether it be a hotel or the bag owner's home.

Before Commercial, my mom had been working as a receptionist in an insurance office, a job she hated because it required the two things she hated above all else: getting up early and dealing with people. When her bosses let her go after six months, she'd spent a couple of weeks sleeping in and grumbling before finally hauling out the classifieds, where she spotted the ad for Commercial. DELIVERY DRIVERS NEEDED, it said. WORK INDEPENDENTLY, DAYS OR NIGHTS. She never would have called any job perfect, but just at a glance, it seemed pretty close. So she called and set up an interview. Two days later, she had a job.

Or, *we* did. The truth was, my mom was not a very good navigator. I'd suspected she was slightly dyslexic, as she was always mixing up her right and left, something that definitely would have been a problem for a job that relied almost entirely on following written driving directions. Luckily, though, her shift didn't start until five p.m., which meant that I could ride along with her, an arrangement that I'd assumed at first would only last for the initial few days, until she got the hang of things. Instead, we became co-workers, eight hours a day, five days a week, just her and me in her banged-up Subaru, reuniting people with their possessions.

Our night always started at the airport. Once the bags were stacked and packed in the car, she'd hand over the sheet of addresses and directions, and we'd set off, hitting the nearby hotels first before venturing farther to neighborhoods and individual homes.

People had one of two reactions when we arrived with their lost luggage. Either they were really happy and grateful, or chose to literally blame the messenger, taking out their ire at the entire airline industry on us. The best tactic, we learned, was empathy. "Don't I know it," my mom would say, holding her clipboard for the person's signature as they ranted on about having to buy new toiletries or clothes in a strange city. "It's an outrage." Usually, this was enough, since it was often more than the airlines had offered up, but occasionally someone would go above and beyond, being a total asshole, at which point my mom would just drop the bag at their feet, turn and walk back to the car, ignoring whatever they shouted after her. "It's karma," she'd say to me as we pulled away. "Watch. I bet we're here again before we know it."

Hotels were better, because we only had to deal with the bellmen or front-desk staff. They'd offer us some kind of perk for fitting them in early on our route, and we became regulars at all the hotel bars, grabbing a quick burger between deliveries.

By the end of the shift, the highways had usually cleared, and we were often the only car cresting silent hills in dark subdivisions. That late, people often didn't want to be bothered by us ringing the bell, so they'd leave a note on their front door asking us to drop the bag on the porch, or tell us, when we called to confirm the delivery, to just pop the trunk of their car and leave it in there. These were always the weirdest trips for me, when it was midnight or even later, and we pulled up to a dark house, trying to be quiet. Like a robbery in reverse, creeping around to leave something rather than take it.

Still, there was also was something reassuring about working for Commercial, almost hopeful. Like things that were lost could be found again. As we drove away, I always tried to imagine what it would be like to open your door to find something you had given up on. Maybe it had seen places you never had, been rerouted and passed through so many strange hands, but still somehow found its way back to you, all before the day even began.

* * *

I'd expected to sleep the same way I had at Poplar House—barely and badly—but instead woke with a start the next morning when Jamie knocked on my door, saying we'd be leaving in an hour. I'd been so out of it that at first I wasn't even sure where I was. Once I made out the skylight over my head, though, with its little venetian blind, it all came back to me: Cora's. My near-escape. And now, Perkins Day. Just three days earlier, I'd been managing as best I could at the yellow house, working for Commercial, and going to Jackson. Now, here, everything had changed again. But I was kind of getting used to that now.

When my mom first took off, I didn't think it was for good. I figured she was just out on one of her escapades, which usually lasted only as long as it took her to run out of money or welcome, a few days at most. The first couple of times she'd done this, I'd been so worried, then overwhelmingly relieved when she returned, peppering her with questions about where she'd been, which irritated her no end. "I just needed some space, okay?" she'd tell me, annoyed, before stalking off to her room to sleep—something that, by the looks of it, she hadn't done much of during the time she'd been gone.

It took me another couple of her disappearances—each a few days longer than the last—before I realized that this was exactly how I *shouldn't* react, making a big deal of it. Instead, I adopted a more blasé attitude, like I hadn't even really noticed she'd been gone. My mother had always been about independence—hers, mine, and ours. She was a lot of things, but clingy had never been one of them. By taking off, I decided, she was teaching me about taking care of myself. Only a weak person needed someone else around all the time. With every disappearance, she was proving herself stronger; it was up to me, in how I behaved, to do the same.

After two weeks with no word from her, though, I'd finally forced myself to go into her room and look through her stuff. Sure enough, her emergency stash—three hundred bucks in cash, last I'd checked—was gone, as were her saving-bonds certificates, her makeup, and, most telling, her bathing suit and favorite summer robe. Wherever she was headed, it was warm.

I had no idea when she'd really left, since we hadn't exactly been getting along. We hadn't exactly *not* been, either. But that fall, the hands-off approach we'd both cultivated had spilled over from just a few days here and there to all the time. Also, she'd stopped going to work—sleeping when I left for school in the morning, sleeping when I returned and headed out to Commercial, and usually out once I returned after all the deliveries were done—so it wasn't like we had a lot of chances to talk. Plus, the rare occasions she was home and awake, she wasn't alone.

Most times, when I saw her boyfriend Warner's beat-up old Cadillac in the driveway, I'd park and then walk around to my bedroom window, which I kept unlocked, and let myself in that way. It meant I had to brush my teeth with bottled water, and made washing my face out of the question, but these were small prices to pay to avoid Warner, who filled the house with pipe smoke and always seemed to be sweating out whatever he'd drunk the day before. He'd park himself on the couch, beer in hand, his eyes silently following me whenever I did have to cross in front of him. He'd never done anything I could point to specifically, but I believed this was due not to innocence but to lack of opportunity. I did not intend to provide him with one.

My mother, however, loved Warner, or so she said. They'd met at Halloran's, the small bar just down the street from the yellow house where she went sometimes to drink beer and sing karaoke. Unlike my mother's other boyfriends, Warner wasn't the meaty, rough-around-the-edges type. Instead, in his standard outfit of dark pants, cheap shirt, deck shoes, hat with captain's insignia, he looked like he'd just stepped off a boat, albeit not necessarily a nice one. I wasn't sure whether he had a nautical past and was pining for it, or was hoping for one still ahead. Either way, he liked to drink and seemed to have some money from somewhere, so for my mom he was perfect.

These days, when I thought about my mom, I sometimes pictured her on the water. Maybe she and Warner had gotten that old Cadillac all the way to Florida, like they'd always talked about doing, and were now on the deck of some boat, bobbing on the open sea. This was at least a prettier picture than the one I actually suspected, the little bit of denial I allowed myself. It wasn't like I had a lot of time for fantasies anyway.

When she left, it was mid-August, and I still had nine months before I turned eighteen and could live alone legally. I knew I had a challenge ahead of me. But I was a smart girl, and I thought I could handle it. My plan was to keep the job at Commercial until Robert, the owner, caught on to my mom's absence, at which point I'd have to find something else. As far as the bills went, because our names were identical I could access my mom's account for whatever paychecks—which were direct-deposited—I *was* able to earn. I figured I was good, at least for the time being. As long as I kept out of trouble at school, the one thing that I knew for sure would blow my cover, no one had to know anything was different.

And who knew? It could even have worked out if the dryer hadn't broken. But while my short-term plans might have changed, the long-term goal remained the same as it had been for as long as I could remember: to be free. No longer dependent or a dependent, subject to the whim or whimsy of my mother, the system, or anyone else, the albatross always weighing down someone's neck. It didn't really matter whether I served out the time at the yellow house or in Cora's world. Once I turned eighteen, I could cut myself off from everyone and finally get what I wanted, which was to be on my own, once and for all.

Now I did the best I could with my appearance, considering I was stuck with the same pair of jeans I'd had on for two days and a sweater I hadn't worn in years. Still, I thought, tugging down the hem of the sweater, which was about two sizes too small, it wasn't like I cared about impressing the people at Perkins Day. Even my best stuff would be their worst.

I grabbed my backpack off the bed, then started down the hall. Cora and Jamie's bedroom door was slightly ajar, and as I got closer, I could hear a soft, tinny beeping, too quiet to be an alarm clock but similar in sound and tone. As I passed, I glanced inside and saw my sister lying on her back, a thermometer poking out of her mouth. After a moment, she pulled it out, squinting at it as the beeping stopped.

I wondered if she was sick. Cora had always been like the canary in the coalmine, the first to catch anything. My mother said this was because she worried too much, that anxiety affected the immune system. She herself, she claimed, hadn't "had a cold in fifteen years," although I ventured to think this was because her own system was pickled rather than calm. At any rate, my memories of growing up with Cora were always colored with her various ailments: ear infections, allergies, tonsillitis, unexplained rashes and fevers. If my mother was right and it was stress related, I was sure I could blame myself for this latest malady, whatever it was.

Down in the kitchen, I found Jamie sitting at the island, a laptop open in front of him, a cell phone pressed to his ear. When he saw me, he smiled, then covered it with one hand. "Hey," he said. "I'll be off in a sec. There's cereal and stuff on the table—help yourself."

I glanced over, expecting to see a single box and some milk. Instead, there were several different boxes, most of them unopened, as well as a plate of muffins, a pitcher of orange juice, and a big glass bowl of fruit salad. "Coffee?" I asked, and he nodded, gesturing toward the opposite counter, where I saw a pot, some mugs laid out in front of it.

". . . yeah, but that's just the point," Jamie was saying as he cocked his head to one side, typing something on the keyboard. "If we're serious about considering this offer, we need to at least set some parameters for the negotiations. It's important."

I walked over to the coffeepot, picking up a mug and filling it. On Jamie's laptop, I could see the familiar front page of UMe.com, the networking site that it seemed like everyone from your favorite band to your grandmother had gotten on in the last year or so. I had a page myself, although due to the fact that I didn't have regular access to a computer, I hadn't checked it in a while.

"But that's just the point," Jamie said, clicking onto another page. "They say they want to preserve the integrity and the basic intention, but they've got corporate mindsets. Look, just talk to Glen, see what he says. No, not this morning, I've got something going. I'll be in by noon, though. Okay. Later."

There was a beep, and he put down the phone, picking up a muffin from beside him and taking a bite just as there was a *ping!* on the screen, the familiar sound of a new message in the UMe inbox. "You have a UMe page?" I asked him as I sat down at the table with my coffee. My sweater rode up again, and I gave it another tug.

He looked at me for a second. "Uh . . . yeah. I do." He nodded at my mug. "You're not eating?"

"I don't like breakfast," I told him.

"That's crazy talk." He pushed back his chair, walking over to grab two bowls out of a nearby cabinet, then stopped at the fridge, pulling it open and getting out some milk. "When I was a kid," he said, coming over and plopping everything onto the table beside me, "my mom fixed us eggs or pancakes every morning. With sausage or bacon, and toast. You gotta have it. It's brain food."

I looked at him over my coffee cup as he grabbed one of the cereal boxes, ripping it open and filling a bowl. Then he added milk, filling it practically to the top, and plopped it on a plate before adding a muffin and a heaping serving of fruit salad. I was about to say something about being impressed with his appetite when he pushed the whole thing across to me. "Oh, no," I said. "I can't—"

"You don't have to eat it all," he said, shaking cereal into his own bowl. "Just some. You'll need it, trust me."

I shot him a wary look, then put down my mug, picking up the spoon and taking a bite. Across the table, his own mouth full of muffin, he grinned at me. "Good, right?"

I nodded just as there was another *ping!* from the laptop, followed immediately by one more. Jamie didn't seem to notice, instead spearing a piece of pineapple with his fork. "So," he said, "big day today."

"I guess," I said, taking another bite of cereal. I hated to admit it, but now I was starving and had to work not to shovel the food in nonstop. I couldn't remember the last time I'd had breakfast.

"I know a new school is tough," he told me as there were

three more pings in quick succession. God, he was popular. "My dad was in the military. Eight schools in twelve years. It sucked. I was always the new kid."

"So how long did you go to Perkins Day?" I asked, figuring maybe a short stint would explain him actually liking it.

Ping. Ping. "I started as a junior. Best two years of my life."

"Really."

He raised an eyebrow at me, picking up a glass and helping himself to some orange juice. "You know," he said, "I understand it's not what you're used to. But it's also not as bad you think."

I withheld comment as four more messages hit his page, followed by a thwacking noise behind me. I turned around just in time to see Roscoe wriggling through his dog door.

"Hey, buddy," Jamie said to him as he trotted past us to his water bowl, "how's the outside world?"

Roscoe's only response was a prolonged period of slurping, his tags banging against the bowl. Now that I finally had a real chance to study him, I saw he was kind of cute, if you liked little dogs, which I did not. He had to be under twenty pounds, and was stocky, black with a white belly and feet, his ears poking straight up. Plus he had one of those pug noses, all smooshed up, which I supposed explained the adenoidal sounds I'd already come to see as his trademark. Once he was done drinking, he burped, then headed over toward us, stopping en route to lick up some stray muffin crumbs.

As I watched Roscoe, Jamie's laptop kept pinging: he had to have gotten at least twenty messages in the last five minutes. "Should you . . . check that or something?" I asked.

"Check what?"

"Your page," I said, nodding at the laptop. "You keep getting messages."

"Nah, it can wait." His face suddenly brightened. "Hey, sleepyhead! You're running late."

"Somebody kept hitting the snooze bar," my sister grumbled as she came in, hair wet and dressed in black pants and a white blouse, her feet bare.

"The same somebody," Jamie said, getting to his feet and meeting her at the island, "who was down here a full half hour ahead of you."

Cora rolled her eyes, kissing him on the cheek and pouring herself a cup of coffee. Then she bent down, mug in her hand, to pet Roscoe, who was circling her feet. "You guys should get going soon," she said. "There'll be traffic."

"Back roads," Jamie said confidently as I pushed back my chair, tugging down my sweater again before carrying my now empty bowl and plate to the sink. "I used to be able to get to the Day in ten minutes flat, including any necessary stoplights."

"That was ten years ago," Cora told him. "Times have changed."

"Not that much," he said.

His laptop pinged again, but Cora, like him, didn't seem to notice. Instead, she was watching me as I bent down, sliding my plate into the dishwasher. "Do you . . . ?" she said, then stopped. When I glanced up at her, she said, "Maybe you should borrow something of mine to wear."

"I'm fine," I said.

She bit her lip, looking right at the strip of exposed

stomach between the hem of my sweater and the buckle on my jeans I'd been trying to cover all morning. "Just come on," she said.

We climbed the stairs silently, her leading the way up and into her room, which was enormous, the walls a pale, cool blue. I was not surprised to see that it was neat as a pin, the bed made with pillows arranged so precisely you just knew there was a diagram in a nearby drawer somewhere. Like my room, there were also lots of windows and a skylight, as well as a much bigger balcony that led down to a series of decks below.

Cora crossed the room, taking a sip from the mug in her hands as she headed into the bathroom. We went past the shower, double sinks, and sunken bath into a room beyond, which turned out not to be a room at all but a closet. A *huge* closet, with racks of clothes on two walls and floor-to-ceiling shelves on the other. From what I could tell, Jamie's things—jeans, a couple of suits, and lots of T-shirts and sneakers—took up a fraction of the space. The rest was all Cora's. I watched from the doorway as she walked over to one rack, pushing some stuff aside.

"You probably need a shirt and a sweater, right?" she said, studying a few cardigans. "You have a jacket, I'm assuming."

"Cora."

She pulled out a sweater, examining it. "Yes?"

"Why am I here?"

Maybe it was the confined space, or this extended period without Jamie to buffer us. But whatever the reason, this question had just somehow emerged, as unexpected to me as I knew it was to her. Now that it was out, though, I was surprised how much I wanted to hear the answer.

She dropped her hand from the rack, then turned to face me. "Because you're a minor," she said, "and your mother abandoned you."

"I'm almost eighteen," I told her. "And I was doing just fine on my own."

"Fine," she repeated, her expression flat. Looking at her, I was reminded how really different we were, me a redhead with pale, freckled skin, such a contrast to her black hair and blue eyes. I was taller, with my mother's thin frame, while she was a couple of inches shorter and curvier. "You call that *fine?*"

"You don't know," I said. "You weren't there."

"I know what I read in the report," she replied. "I know what the social worker told me. Are you saying those accounts were inaccurate?"

"Yes," I said.

"So you weren't living without heat or water in a filthy house."

"Nope."

She narrowed her eyes at me. "Where's Mom, Ruby?"

I swallowed, then turned my head as I reached up, pressing the key around my neck into my skin. "I don't care," I said.

"Neither do I," she replied. "But the fact of the matter is, she's gone and you can't be by yourself. Does that answer your question?"

I didn't say anything, and she turned back to the clothes, pushing through them. "I told you, I don't need to borrow anything," I said. My voice sounded high and tight.

"Ruby, come on," she said, sounding tired. She pulled a black sweater off a hanger, tossing it over her shoulder before moving over to another shelf and grabbing a green T-shirt. Then she walked over, pushing them both at me as she passed. "And hurry. It takes at least fifteen minutes to get there."

Then she walked back through the bathroom, leaving me behind. For a moment, I just stood there, taking in the neat rows of clothes, how her shirts were all folded just so, stacked by color. As I looked down at the clothes she'd given me, I told myself I didn't care what the people at Perkins Day thought about me or my stupid sweater. Everything was just temporary anyway. Me being there, or here. Or anywhere, for that matter.

A moment later, though, when Jamie yelled up that it was time to go, I suddenly found myself pulling on Cora's T-shirt, which was clearly expensive and fit me perfectly, and then her sweater, soft and warm, over it. On my way downstairs, in clothes that weren't mine, to go to a school I'd never claim, I stopped and looked at myself in the bathroom mirror. You couldn't see the key around my neck: it hung too low under both collars. But if I leaned in close, I could make it out, buried deep beneath. Out of sight, hard to recognize, but still able to be found, even if I was the only one to ever look for it.

*   *   *

Cora was right. We got stuck in traffic. After hitting every red light between the house and Perkins Day, we finally pulled into the parking lot just as a bell was ringing.

All the visitor spaces were taken, so Jamie swung his car—a sporty little Audi with all-leather interior—into one in the student lot. I looked to my left—sure enough, parked there was a Mercedes sedan that looked brand-new. On our other side was another Audi, this one a bright red convertible.

My stomach, which had for most of the ride been pretty much working on rejecting my breakfast, now turned in on itself with an audible clench. According to the dashboard clock, it was 8:10, which meant that in a run-down classroom about twenty miles away, Mr. Barrett-Hahn, my homeroom teacher, was beginning his slow, flat-toned read of the day's announcements. This would be roundly ignored by my classmates, who five minutes from now would shuffle out, voices rising, to fight their way through a corridor designed for a student body a fraction the size of the current one to first period. I wondered if my English teacher, Ms. Valhalla—she of the high-waisted jeans and endless array of oversized polo shirts—knew what had happened to me, or if she just assumed I'd dropped out, like a fair amount of her students did during the course of a year. We'd been just about to start *Wuthering Heights*, a novel she'd promised would be a vast improvement over *David Copperfield*, which she'd dragged us through like a death march for the last few weeks. I'd been wondering if this was just talk or the truth. Now I'd never know.

"Ready to face the firing squad?"

I jumped, suddenly jerked back to the present and Jamie, who'd pulled his keys from the ignition and was now just sitting there expectantly, hand on the door handle.

"Oops. Bad choice of words," he said. "Sorry."

He pushed his door open and, feeling my stomach twist again, I forced myself to do the same. As soon as I stepped out of the car, I heard another bell sound.

"Office is this way," Jamie said as we started walking along the line of cars. He pointed to a covered walkway to our right, beyond which was a big green space, more buildings visible on the other side. "That's the quad," he said. "Classrooms are all around it. Auditorium and gym are those two big buildings you see over there. And the caf is here, closest to us. Or at least it used to be. It's been a while since I had a sloppy joe here."

We stepped up on a curb, heading toward a long, flat building with a bunch of windows. I'd just followed him, ducking under an overhang, when I heard a familiar *rat-a-tat-tat* sound. At first, I couldn't place it, but then I turned and saw an old model Toyota bumping into the parking lot, engine backfiring. My mom's car did the same thing, usually at stoplights or when I was trying to quietly drop a bag off at someone's house late at night.

The Toyota, which was white with a sagging bumper, zoomed past us, brake lights flashing as it entered the student parking lot and whipped into a space. I heard a door slam and then footsteps slapping across the pavement. A moment later, a black girl with long braids emerged, running, a backpack over one shoulder. She had a cell phone pressed to one ear and seemed to be carrying on a spirited conversation, even as she jumped the curb, went under the covered walkway, and began to sprint across the green.

"Ah, tardiness. Brings back memories," Jamie said.

"I thought you could get here in ten minutes."

"I could. But there were usually only five until the bell."

As we reached the front entrance and he pulled the glass door open for me, I was aware not of the stale mix of mildew and disinfectant Jackson was famous for but a clean, fresh-paint smell. It was actually very similar to Cora's house, which was a little unsettling.

"Mr. Hunter!" A man in a suit was standing just inside. As soon as he saw us, he strode right over, extending his hand. "The prodigal student returns home. How's life in the big leagues?"

"Big," Jamie said, smiling. They shook hands. "Mr. Thackray, this is my sister-in-law, Ruby Cooper. Ruby, this is Principal Thackray."

"Nice to meet you," Mr. Thackray said. His hand was large and cool, totally enveloping mine. "Welcome to Perkins Day."

I nodded, noting that my mouth had gone bone-dry. My experience with principals—and teachers and landlords and policemen—being as it was, this wasn't surprising. Even without a transgression, that same fight-or-flight instinct set in.

"Let's go ahead and get you settled in, shall we?" Mr. Thackray said, leading the way down the hallway and around the corner to a large office. Inside, he took a seat behind a big wooden desk, while Jamie and I sat in the two chairs opposite. Through the window behind him, I could see a huge expanse of soccer fields lined with bleachers. There was a guy on a riding mower driving slowly down one side, his breath visible in the cold air.

Mr. Thackray turned around, looking out the window, as well. "Looks good, doesn't it? All we're missing is a plaque honoring our generous benefactor."

"No need for that," Jamie said, running a hand through his hair. He sat back, crossing one leg over the other. In his sneakers, jeans, and zip-up hoodie, he didn't look ten years out of high school. Two or three, sure. But not ten.

"Can you believe this guy?" Mr. Thackray said to me, shaking his head. "Donates an entirely new soccer complex and won't even let us give him credit."

I looked at Jamie. "You did that?"

"It's not that big a deal," he said, looking embarrassed.

"Yes, it is," Mr. Thackray said. "Which is why I wish you'd reconsider and let us make your involvement public. Plus, it's a great story. Our students waste more time on UMe.com than any other site, and its owner donates some of the proceeds from that procrastination back into education. It's priceless!"

"Soccer," Jamie said, "isn't exactly education."

"Sports are crucial to student development," Mr. Thackray said. "It counts."

I turned my head, looking at my brother-in-law, suddenly remembering all those pings in his UMe inbox. *You could say that*, he'd said, when I'd asked if he had a page. Clearly, this was an understatement.

". . . grab a few forms, and we'll get a schedule set up for you," Mr. Thackray was saying. "Sound good?"

I realized, a beat too late, he'd been talking to me. "Yeah," I said. Then I swallowed. "I mean, yes."

He nodded, pushing back his chair and getting to his

feet. As he left the room, Jamie sat back, examining the tread of one sneaker. Outside, the guy on the mower had finished one side of the field and was now moving slowly up the other.

"Do you . . . ?" I said to Jamie. He glanced up at me. "You own UMe?"

He let his foot drop. "Well . . . not exactly. It's me and a few other guys."

"But he said you were the owner," I pointed out.

Jamie sighed. "I started it up originally," he said. "When I was just out of college. But now I'm in more of an overseeing position."

I just looked at him.

"CEO," he admitted. "Which is really just a big word, or a really small acronym, actually, for overseer."

"I can't believe Cora didn't tell me," I said.

"Ah, you know Cora." He smiled. "Unless you work eighty hours a week saving the world like she does, she's tough to impress."

I looked out at the guy on the mower again, watching as he puttered past. "Cora saves the world?"

"She tries to," he said. "Hasn't she told you about her work? Down at the public defender's office?"

I shook my head. In fact, I hadn't even known Cora had gone to law school until the day before, when the social worker at Poplar House had asked her what she did for a living. The last I knew, she'd been about to graduate from college, and that was five years ago. And we only knew that because, somehow, an announcement of the ceremony had made its way to us. It was on thick paper, a card with her name on it tucked inside. I remembered studying the envelope, wondering why it had turned up after all this time with no contact. When I'd asked my mom, she'd just shrugged, saying the school sent them out automatically. Which made sense, since by then, Cora had made it clear she wanted no part of us in her new life, and we'd been more than happy to oblige.

"Well," Jamie said as a palpable awkwardness settled over us, and I wondered what exactly he knew about our family, if perhaps my very existence had come as a surprise. Talk about baggage. "I guess you two have a lot of catching up to do, huh?"

I looked down at my hands, not saying anything. A moment later, Mr. Thackray walked back in, a sheaf of papers in his hand, and started talking about transcripts and credit hours, and this exchange was quickly forgotten. Later, though, I wished I had spoken up, or at least tried to explain that once I knew Cora better than anyone. But that was a long time ago, back when she wasn't trying to save the whole world. Only me.

*　　*　　*

When I was a kid, my mom used to sing to me. It was always at bedtime, when she'd come in to say good night. She'd sit on the edge of my bed, brushing my hair back with her fingers, her breath sweet smelling (a "civilized glass" or two of wine was her norm then) as she kissed my forehead and told me she'd see me in the morning. When she tried to leave, I'd protest, and beg for a song. Usually, if she wasn't in too bad a mood, she'd oblige.

Back then, I'd thought my mother made up all the songs

she sang to me, which was why it was so weird the first time I heard one of them on the radio. It was like discovering that some part of you wasn't yours at all, and it made me wonder what else I couldn't claim. But that was later. At the time, there were only the songs, and they were still all ours, no one else's.

My mother's songs fell into three categories: love songs, sad songs, or sad love songs. Not for her the uplifting ending. Instead, I fell asleep to "Frankie and Johnny" and a love affair gone very wrong, "Don't Think Twice It's All Right" and a bad breakup, and "Wasted Time" and someone looking back, full of regret. But it was "Angel from Montgomery," the Bonnie Raitt version, that made me think of her most, then and now.

It had everything my mother liked in a song—heartbreak, disillusionment, and death—all told in the voice of an old woman, now alone, looking back over all the things she'd had and lost. Not that I knew this; to me they were just words set to a pretty melody and sung by a voice I loved. It was only later, when I'd lie in a different bed, hearing her sing late into the night through the wall, that they kept me awake worrying. Funny how a beautiful song could tell such an ugly story. It seemed unfair, like a trick.

If you asked her, my mother would say that nothing in her life turned out the way she planned it. She was *supposed* to go to college and then marry her high-school sweetheart, Ronald Brown, the tailback for the football team, but his parents decided they were getting too serious and made him break up with her, right before Christmas of her junior year. Heartbroken, she'd allowed her friends to drag her to a party where she knew absolutely no one and ended up stuck talking to a guy who was in his freshman year at Middletown Tech, studying to be an engineer. In a kitchen cluttered with beer bottles, he'd talked to her about sus-pension bridges and skyscrapers, "the miracle of buildings," all of which bored her to tears. Which never explained, at least to me, why she ended up agreeing to go out with him, then sleeping with him, thereby producing my sister, who was born nine months later.

So at eighteen, while her classmates graduated, my mom was at home with an infant daughter and a new husband. Still, if the photo albums are any indication, those early years weren't so bad. There are tons of pictures of Cora: in a sunsuit, holding a shovel, riding a tricycle up a front walk. My parents appear as well, although not as often, and rarely together. Every once in a while, though, there's a shot of them—my mom looking young and gorgeous with her long red hair and pale skin, my dad, dark-haired with those bright blue eyes, his arm thrown over her shoulder or around her waist.

Because there was a ten-year gap between Cora and me, I'd always wondered if I was a mistake, or maybe a last-gasp attempt to save a marriage that was already going downhill. Whatever the reason, my dad left when I was five and my sister fifteen. We were living in an actual house in an actual neighborhood then, and we came home from the pool one afternoon to find my mom sitting on the couch, glass in hand. By themselves, neither of these things were noteworthy. Back then, she didn't work, and while she usu-ally waited until my dad got home to pour herself a drink, occasionally she started without him. The thing that we did notice, though, right off, was that there was music playing, and my mom was singing along. For the first time, it wasn't soothing or pretty to me. Instead, I felt nervous, unsettled, as if the cumulative weight of all those sad songs was hitting me at once. From then on, her singing was always a bad sign.

I had vague memories of seeing my dad after the divorce. He'd take us for breakfast on the weekends or a dinner during the week. He never came inside or up to the door to get us, instead just pulling up to the mailbox and sitting there behind the wheel, looking straight ahead. As if he was waiting not for us but for anyone, like a stranger could have slid in beside him and it would have been fine. Maybe it was because of this distance that whenever I tried to remember him now, it was hard to picture him. There were a couple of memories, like of him reading to me, and watching him grilling steaks on the patio. But even with these few things, it was as if even when he was around, he was already distant, a kind of ghost.

I don't remember how or why the visits ceased. I couldn't recall an argument or incident. It was like they happened, and then they didn't. In sixth grade, due to a family-tree project, I went through a period where the mystery of his disappearance was all I could think about, and eventually I did manage to get out of my mom that he'd moved out of state, to Illinois. He'd kept in touch for a little while, but after remarrying and a couple of changes of address he'd vanished, leaving no way for her to collect child support, or any support. Beyond that, whenever I bugged her about it, she made it clear it was not a subject she wanted to discuss. With my mom, when someone was gone, they were gone. She didn't waste another minute thinking about them, and neither should you.

When my dad left, my mom slowly began to withdraw from my daily routine—waking me up in the morning, getting me ready for school, walking me to the bus stop, telling me to brush my teeth—and Cora stepped in to take her place. This, too, was never decided officially or announced. It just happened, the same way my mom just happened to start sleeping more and smiling less and singing late at night, her voice wavering and haunting and always finding a way to reach my ears, even when I rolled myself against the wall tight and tried to think of something, anything else.

Cora became my one constant, the single thing I could depend on to be there and to remain relatively unchanged, day in and day out. At night in our shared room, I'd often have to lie awake listening to her breathing for a long time before I could fall asleep myself.

"Shhh," I remembered her saying as we stood in our nightgowns in our bedroom. She'd press her ear against the door, and I'd watch her face, cautious, as she listened to my mom moving around downstairs. From what she heard—a lighter clicking open, then shut, cubes rattling in a glass, the phone being picked up or put down—she always gauged whether it was safe for us to venture out to brush our teeth or eat something when my mom had forgotten about dinner. If my mom was sleeping, Cora would hold my hand as we tiptoed past her to the kitchen. There I'd hold an old acrylic tray while she quickly piled it with cereal and milk—or, my favorite, English-muffin pizzas she made in the toaster oven, moving stealthily around the kitchen as my mother's breath rose and fell in the next room. When things went well, we'd get back upstairs without her stirring. When they didn't, she'd jerk awake, sitting up with creases on her face, her voice thick as she said, "What are you two doing?"

"It's okay," Cora would say. "We're just getting something to eat."

Sometimes, if she'd been out deeply enough, this was enough. More often, though, I'd hear the couch springs squeak, her feet hitting the hardwood floor, and it was then that Cora always stopped whatever she was in the midst of—sandwich making, picking through my mom's purse for lunch money, pushing the wine bottle, open and sweaty, farther back on the counter—and do the one thing I associated with her more than anything else. As my mother approached, annoyed and usually spoiling for a fight, my sister would always step in front of me. Back then, she was at least a head taller, and I remembered this so well, the sudden shift in my perspective, the view going from something scary to something not. Of course, I knew my mother was still coming toward me, but it was always Cora I kept my eyes on: her dark hair, the sharp angles of her shoulder blades, the way, when things were really bad, she'd reach her hand back to find mine, closing her fingers around it. Then she'd just stand there, as my mother appeared, ready to take the brunt of whatever came next, like the bow of a boat crashing right into a huge wave and breaking it into nothing but water.

Because of this, it was Cora who got the bulk of the stinging slaps, the two-hand pushes that sent her stumbling backward, the sudden, rough tugs on the arm that left red twisty welts and, later, bruises in the shape of fingertips. The transgressions were always hard to understand, and therefore even more difficult to avoid: we were up when we shouldn't have been, we were making too much noise, we provided the wrong answers to questions that seemed to have no right ones. When it was over, my mother would shake her head and leave us, returning to the couch or her bedroom, and I'd always look at Cora, waiting for her to decide what we should do next. More often than not, she'd just leave the room herself, wiping her eyes, and I'd fall in behind her, not talking but sticking very close, feeling safer if she was not just between me and my mom, but between me and the world in general.

Later, I'd develop my own system for dealing with my mom, learning to gauge her mood by the number of glasses or bottles already on the table when I came home, or the inflection in her tone when she said the two syllables that made up my name. I took a few knocks as well, although this became more rare when I hit middle school. But it was always the singing that was the greatest indicator, the one thing that made me hesitate outside a door frame, hanging back from the light. As beautiful as her voice sounded, working its way along the melodies I knew by heart, I knew there was a potential ugliness underneath.

By then, Cora was gone. A great student, she'd spent high school working shifts at Exclamation Taco! for college money and studying nonstop, to better her chances of receiving any one of the several scholarships she'd applied for. My sister was nothing if not driven and had always balanced the chaos that was our lives with a strict personal focus on order and organization. While the rest of the house was constantly dusty and in disarray, Cora's side of our shared room was neat as a pin, everything folded and in its place. Her books were alphabetized, her shoes lined up in a row, her bed always made, the pillow at a perfect right angle to the wall. Sometimes, sitting on my own bed, I'd look across and be amazed at the contrast: it was like a before-and-after shot, or a reverse mirror image, the best becoming the worst, and back again.

In the end, she received a partial scholarship to the U, the state university one town over, and applied for student loans to cover the rest. During the spring and summer of senior year, after she'd gotten her acceptance, there was a weird shift in the house. I could feel it. My sister, who'd spent most of the last year avoiding my mother entirely— going from school to work to bed and back again—suddenly seemed to loosen up, grow lighter. People came to pick her up on weekend nights, their voices rising up to our open windows as she got into their cars and sped away. Girls with easy, friendly voices called asking for Cora, who'd then take the phone into the bathroom where, even through the door, I could hear her voice sounded different speaking back to them.

Meanwhile my mother grew quieter, not saying anything as Cora brought home boxes to pack for school or cleaned out her side of the room. Instead, she just sat on the side porch during those long summer twilights, smoking cigarettes and staring off into the side yard. We never talked about Cora leaving, but as the day grew closer, that shift in the air was more and more palpable, until it was as if I could see my sister extracting herself from us, twisting loose and breaking free, minute by minute. Sometimes at night, I'd wake up with a start, looking over at her sleeping form across the room and feel reassured only fleetingly, knowing that the day would come soon when there would be nothing there at all.

The day she moved out, I woke up with a sore throat. It was a Saturday morning, and I helped her carry her boxes and a couple of suitcases downstairs. My mother stayed in the kitchen, chain-smoking and silent, not watching as we carted out my sister's few possessions, loading them into the trunk of a Jetta that belonged to a girl named Leslie whom I'd never met before that day and never saw again.

"Well," Cora had said, when she pushed the hatchback shut, "I guess that's everything."

I looked up at the house, where I could see my mom through the front window, moving through the kitchen to the den, then back again. And even with everything that had happened, I remember thinking that of course she wouldn't let Cora just go with no good-bye. But as the time passed, she got no closer to the door or to us, and after a while, even when I looked hard, I couldn't see her at all.

Cora, for her part, was just standing there, staring up at the house, her hands in her pockets, and I wondered if she was waiting, too. But then she dropped her hands, letting out a breath. "I'll be back in a sec," she said, and Leslie nodded. Then we both watched her slowly go up the walk and into the house.

She didn't stay long—maybe a minute, or even two. And when she came out, her face looked no different. "I'll call you tonight," she said to me. Then she stepped forward, pulling me into a tight hug. I remembered thinking, as she drove away, that my throat was so sore I'd surely be totally sick within hours. But I wasn't. By the next morning it was gone.

Cora called that first night, as promised, and the following weekend, checking in and asking how I was doing. Both times I could hear chatter in the background, voices and music, as she reported that she liked her roommate and her classes, that everything was going well. When she asked how I was, I wanted to tell her how much I missed her, and that my mom had been drinking a lot since she'd left. Since we'd hardly discussed this aloud face-to-face, though, bringing it up over the phone seemed impossible.

She never asked to speak to my mother, and my mom never once picked up when she called. It was as if their relationship had been a business arrangement, bound by contract, and now that contract had expired. At least that was the way I looked at it, until we moved a few weeks later and my sister stopped calling altogether. Then I realized that deep down in the fine print, my name had been on it as well.

For a long time, I blamed myself for Cora cutting ties with us. Maybe because I hadn't told her I wanted to keep in touch, she didn't know or something. Then I thought that maybe she couldn't find our new number. But whenever I asked my mom about this, she just sighed, shaking her head. "She's got her own life now, she doesn't need us anymore," she explained, reaching out to ruffle my hair. "It's just you and me now, baby. Just you and me."

Looking back, it seemed like it should have been harder to lose someone, or have them lose you, especially when they were in the same state, only a few towns over. It would have been so easy to drive to the U and find her dorm, walk up to her door, and announce ourselves. Instead, as the time passed and it became clear Cora wanted nothing to do with me and my mother, it made sense to wipe our hands of her, as well. This, like the alliance between me and my sister all those years ago, was never officially decided. It just happened.

It wasn't like it was so shocking, anyway. My sister had made a break for it, gotten over the wall and escaped. It was what we both wanted. Which was why I understood, even appreciated, why she didn't want to return for a day or even an hour. It wasn't worth the risk.

There were so many times during those years, though, as we moved from one house to another, that I would find myself thinking about my sister. Usually it was late at night, when I couldn't sleep, and I'd try to picture her in her dorm room forty-odd miles and a world away. I wondered if she was happy, what it was like out there. And if maybe, just maybe, she ever thought of me.

Chapter Three

"Ruby, welcome. Come join us, there's a free seat right over here."

I could feel everyone in the room watching me as I followed the outstretched finger of the teacher, a slight, blonde woman who looked barely out of college, to the end of a long table where there was an empty chair.

According to my new schedule, this was Literature in Practice with an M. Conyers. Back at Jackson, the classes all had basic names: English, Geometry, World History. If you weren't one of the few golden children, anointed early for the AP–Ivy League fast track, you made your choices with the minimal and usually disinterested help of one of the three guidance counselors allotted for the entire class. Here, though, Mr. Thackray had spent a full hour consulting my transcript, reading descriptions aloud from the thick course catalog, and conferring with me about my interests and goals. Maybe it was for Jamie's benefit—he was super donor, after all—but somehow, I doubted it. Clearly, they did things differently here.

Once I sat down, I read over my list of classes, separated into neat blocks—Intro to Calculus, Global Cultures and Practices, Drawing: Life and Form—twice, figuring that would give people adequate time to stare at me before moving on to something else. Sure enough, by the time I lifted my head a couple of minutes later to turn my attention to the teacher, a cursory check revealed everyone else was pretty much doing the same.

"As you know," she was saying, walking over to a table in front of a large dry-erase board and hopping up onto it, "we'll be doing several assignments over the course of the rest of the year. You'll have your research project on the novel of your choosing, and we'll also be reading a series of memoirs and oral histories."

I took a minute, now that I felt a bit more comfortable, to look around the room. It was large, with three big windows on one side that looked out onto the common green, some new-looking computers in the back of the room, and instead of desks, a series of tables, arranged in three rows. The class itself was small—twelve or fourteen people, tops. To my left, there was a girl with long, strawberry-blonde hair, twisted into one of those effortlessly perfect knots, a pencil sticking through it. She was pretty, in that cheerleader/student-council president/future nuclear physicist kind of way, and sitting with her posture ramrod straight, a Jump Java cup centered on the table in front of her. To my right, there was a huge backpack—about fourteen key chains hanging off of it—that was blocking my view of whoever was on the other side.

Ms. Conyers hopped off her desk and walked around it, pulling out a drawer. With her jeans, simple oxford shirt, and red clogs, she looked about twelve, which I figured had to make it difficult to keep control in her classroom. Then again, this didn't seem like an especially challenging group.

Even the row of guys at the back table—pumped-up jock types, slumped over or leaning back in their chairs—looked more sleepy than rowdy.

"So today," she said, shutting the desk drawer, "you're going to begin your own oral history project. Although it isn't exactly a history, as much as a compilation."

She started walking down the aisle between the tables, and I saw now she had a small plastic bowl in her hand, which she offered to a heavyset girl with a ponytail. The girl reached in, pulling out a slip of paper, and Ms. Conyers told her to read what was on it out loud. The girl squinted at it. "Advice," she said.

"Advice," Ms. Conyers repeated, moving on to the next person, a guy in glasses, holding out the bowl to him. "What is advice?"

No one said anything for a moment, during which time she kept distributing slips of paper, one person at a time. Finally the blonde to my left said, "Wisdom. Given by others."

"Good, Heather," Ms. Conyers said to her, holding the bowl out to a skinny girl in a turtleneck. "What's another definition?"

Silence. More people had their slips now, and a slight murmur became audible as they began to discuss them. Finally a guy in the back said in a flat voice, "The last thing you want to get from some people."

"Nice," Ms. Conyers said. By now, she'd gotten to me, and smiled as I reached into the bowl, grabbing the first slip I touched. I pulled it back, not opening it as she moved past the huge backpack to whoever was on the other side. "What else?"

"Sometimes," the girl who'd picked the word said, "you go looking for it when you can't make a decision on your own."

"Exactly," Ms. Conyers said, moving down the row of boys in the back. As she passed one—a guy with shaggy hair who was slumped over his books, his eyes closed—she nudged him, and he jerked to attention, looking around until she pointed at the bowl and he reached in for a slip. "So for instance, if I was going to give Jake here some advice, it would be what?"

"Get a haircut," someone said, and everyone laughed.

"Or," Ms. Conyers said, "get a good night's sleep, because napping in class is *not* cool."

"Sorry," Jake mumbled, and his buddy, sitting beside him in a Butter Biscuit baseball hat, punched him in the arm.

"The point," Ms. Conyers continued, "is that no word has one specific definition. Maybe in the dictionary, but not in real life. So the purpose of this exercise will be to take your word and figure out what it means. Not just to you but to the people around you: your friends, your family, coworkers, teammates. In the end, by compiling their responses, you'll have your own understanding of the term, in all its myriad meanings."

Everyone was talking now, so I looked down at my slip, slowly unfolding it. FAMILY, it said, in simple block print. *Great*, I thought. *The last thing I have, or care about. This must be—*

"Some kind of *joke*," I heard someone say. I glanced over, just as the backpack suddenly slid to one side. "What'd you get?"

I blinked, surprised to see the girl with the braids from

the parking lot who'd been running and talking on her cell phone. Up close, I could see she had deep green eyes, and her nose was pierced, a single diamond stud. She pushed the backpack onto the floor, where it landed with a loud *thunk*, then turned her attention back to me. "Hello?" she said. "Do you speak?"

"Family," I told her, then pushed the slip toward her, as if she might need visual confirmation. She glanced at it and sighed. "What about you?"

"Money," she said, her voice flat. She rolled her eyes. "Of course the one person in this whole place who doesn't have it has to write about it. It would just be too *easy* for everyone else."

She said this loudly enough that Ms. Conyers, who was making her way back to her desk, looked over. "What's the matter, Olivia? Don't like your term?"

"Oh, I like the term," the girl said. "Just not the assignment."

Ms. Conyers smiled, hardly bothered, and moved on, while Olivia crumpled up her slip, stuffing it in her pocket. "You want to trade?" I asked her.

She looked over at my FAMILY again. "Nah," she said, sounding tired. "That I know too much about."

Lucky you, I thought as Ms. Conyers reassumed her position on her desk, a slim book in her hands. "Moving on," she said, "to our reading selection for today. Who wants to start us off on last night's reading of *David Copperfield?*"

Thirty minutes later, after what felt like some major literary déjà-vu, the bell finally rang, everyone suddenly pushing back chairs, gathering up their stuff, and talking at once. As I reached down, grabbing my own backpack off the floor, I couldn't help but notice that, like me, it looked out of place here—all ratty and old, still stuffed with notebooks full of what was now, in this setting, mostly useless information. I'd known that morning I should probably toss everything out, but instead I'd just brought it all with me, even though it meant flipping past endless pages of notes on *David Copperfield* to take even more of the same. Now, I slid the FAMILY slip inside my notebook, then let the cover fall shut.

"You went to Jackson?"

I looked up at Olivia, who was now standing beside the table, cell phone in hand, having just hoisted her own huge backpack over one shoulder. At first, I was confused, wondering if my cheap bag made my past that obvious, but then I remembered the JACKSON SPIRIT! sticker on my notebook, which had been slapped there by some overexcited member of the pep club during study hall. "Uh, yeah," I told her. "I do. I mean . . . I did."

"Until when?"

"A couple of days ago."

She cocked her head to the side, studying my face while processing this information. In the meantime, distantly through the receiver end of her phone, I heard another phone ringing, a call she'd clearly made but had not yet completed. "Me, too," she said, pointing at the coat she had on, which now that I looked more closely, was a Jackson letter jacket.

"Really," I said.

She nodded. "Up until last year. You don't look familiar,

though." Distantly, I heard a click. "*Hello?*" someone said, and she put her phone to her ear.

"It's a big place."

"No kidding." She looked at me for a minute longer, even as whoever was on the other end of the line kept saying hello. "It's a lot different from here."

"Seems like it." I shoved my notebook into my bag.

"Oh, you have *no* idea. You want some advice?"

As it turned out, this was a rhetorical question.

"Don't trust the natives," Olivia said. Then she smiled, like this was a joke, or maybe not, before putting her phone to her ear, our conversation clearly over as she began another one and turned toward the door. "Laney. Hey. What's up? Just between classes. . . . Yeah, no kidding. Well, obviously can't sit around waiting for you to call *me*. . . ."

I pulled my bag over my shoulder, following her out to the hallway, which was now bustling and busy, although at the same time hardly crowded, at least in terms of what I was used to. No one was bumping me, either by accident or on purpose, and if anyone did grab my ass, it would be pretty easy to figure out who it was. According to my schedule, I had Spanish in Conversation next, which was in building C. I figured that since this was my one day I could claim ignorance on all counts, there was no point in rushing, so I took my time as I walked along, following the crowd outside.

Just past the door, on the edge of the quad, there was a huge U-shaped sculpture made of some kind of chrome that caught the sunlight winking off it in little sparks and making everything seem really bright. Because of this effect, it was kind of hard at first to make out the people grouped around it, some sitting, some standing, which was why, when I first heard my name, I had no idea where it was coming from.

"Ruby!"

I stopped, turning around. As my eyes adjusted, I could see the people at the sculpture and immediately identified them as the same kind of crowd that, at Jackson, hung out on the low wall just outside the main office: the see-and-be-seens, the top of the food chain, the group that you didn't join without an express invitation. Not my kind of people. And while it was kind of unfortunate that the one person I knew outside of Perkins Day was one of them, it wasn't all that surprising, either.

Nate was standing on the edge of the green; when he saw me spot him, he lifted a hand, smiling. "So," he said as a short guy wearing a baseball hat skittered between us. "Attempted any great escapes lately?"

I glanced at him, then at his friends—which included the blonde Jump Java girl from my English class, I now no-ticed—who were talking amongst themselves a few feet behind him. *Ha-ha*, I thought. Moments ago, I'd been invis-ible, or as invisible as you can be when you're the lone new person at a school where everyone has probably known each other since birth. Now, though, I was suddenly aware that people were staring at me—and not just Nate's assembled friends, either. Even the people passing us were glancing over, and I wondered how many people had already heard this story, or would before day's end. "Funny," I said, and turned away from him.

"I'm only kidding around," he called out. I ignored this,

continuing on. A moment later he jogged up beside me, planting himself in my path. "Hey," he said. "Sorry. I was just . . . it was just a joke."

I just looked at him. In broad daylight, he looked even more like a jock than the night before—in jeans, a T-shirt with collared shirt over it, rope necklace around his neck, and thick flip-flops on his feet, even though it was way past beach season. His hair, as I'd noticed last night, was that white kind of blond, like he'd spent the summer in the sun, his eyes a bright blue. *Too perfect*, I thought. The truth was, if this was the first time I'd laid eyes on him, I might have felt a little bad about discounting him as a thick jock with a narrow mind-set and an even tinier IQ. As this was our second meeting, though, it was a little easier.

"Let me make it up to you," he said, nodding at my schedule, which I still had in my hand. "You need directions?"

"Nope," I said, pulling my bag higher up on my shoulder.

I expected him to look surprised—I couldn't imagine he got turned down much for anything—but instead he just shrugged. "All right," he said. "I guess I'll just see you around. Or tomorrow morning, anyway."

There was a burst of laughter from beside me as two girls sharing a pair of earphones attached to an iPod brushed past. "What's happening tomorrow morning?"

Nate raised his eyebrows. "The carpool," he said, like I was supposed to have any idea what he was talking about. "Jamie said you needed a ride to school."

"With you?"

He stepped back, putting a hand over his chest. "Careful,"

he said, all serious. "You're going to hurt my feelings."

I just looked at him. "I don't need a ride."

"Jamie seems to think you do."

"I don't."

"Suit yourself," he said, shrugging again. Mr. Easygoing. "I'll come by around seven thirty. If you don't come out, I'll move on. No biggie."

No biggie, I thought. *Who talks like that?* He flashed me another million-dollar smile and turned to leave, sliding his hands into his pockets as he loped back, casual as ever, to his crop of well-manicured friends.

The first warning bell rang just as started toward what I hoped—but was in no way sure—was Building C. *Don't trust the natives*, Olivia had told me, but I was already a step ahead of her: I didn't trust anyone. Not for directions, not for rides, and not for advice, either. Sure, it sucked to be lost, but I'd long ago realized I preferred it to depending on anyone else to get me where I needed to go. That was the thing about being alone, in theory or in principle. Whatever happened—good, bad, or anywhere in between—it was always, if nothing else, all your own.

* * *

After school, I was supposed to take a bus home. Instead, I walked out of Perkins Day's stone gates and a half mile down the road to the Quik Zip, where I bought myself a Zip Coke, then settled inside the phone booth. I held the sticky receiver away from my ear as I dropped in a few coins, then dialed a number I knew by heart.

"Hello?"

"Hey, it's me," I said. Then, too late, I added, "Ruby."

I listened as Marshall took in a breath, then let it out. "Ah," he said finally. "Mystery solved."

"I was a mystery?" I asked.

"You were something," he replied. "You okay?"

This was unexpected, as was the lump that rose up in my throat as I heard it. I swallowed, then said, "Yeah. I'm fine."

Marshall was eighteen and had graduated from Jackson the year before, although we hadn't known each other until he moved in with Rogerson, the guy who sold all my friends their pot. At first, Marshall didn't make much of an impression—just a tall, skinny guy who was always passing through or in the kitchen when we went over there to get bags. I'd never even talked to him until one day I went over by myself and Rogerson wasn't around, so it was just the two of us.

Rogerson was all business and little conversation. You knocked, you came in, got what you needed, and got out. I was expecting pretty much the same with Marshall, and at first he didn't disappoint, barely speaking as I followed him to the living room and watched him measure out the bag. I paid him and was just about to get to my feet when he reached over to a nearby cabinet, pulling open a drawer and taking out a small ceramic bowl. "You want some?" he asked.

"Sure," I replied, and then he handed it over, along with a lighter. I could feel him watching me, his dark eyes narrowed, as I lit it, took some in, and passed it back.

The pot was good, better than the stuff we bought, and I felt it almost instantly, the room and my brain slowly taking on a heavy, rolling haze. Suddenly, everything seemed that much more fascinating, from the pattern on the couch beneath me to Marshall himself, sitting back in his chair, his hands folded behind his head. After a few minutes, I realized we'd stopped passing the bowl back and forth and were just sitting there in silence, for how long I had no idea.

"You know what we need," he said suddenly, his voice low and flat.

"What's that?" My own tongue felt thick, my entire mouth dry.

"Slurpees," he said. "Come on."

I'd been afraid he would ask me to drive, which was completely out of the question, but instead, once outside, he led the way down a path that cut across a nearby field dotted with power lines, emerging a block down from a convenience store. We didn't talk the entire way there, or when we were in the store itself. It was not until we were leaving, in fact, each of us sucking away at our Slurpees—which were cold and sweet and perfect—that he finally spoke.

"Good stuff," he said, glancing over at me.

I nodded. "It's *fantastic.*"

Hearing this, he smiled, which was unnerving simply because it was something I'd never seen before. Even stranger, as we started back across the path, he reached behind him, grabbing my hand, and then held it, walking a little bit ahead, the whole way home. I will never forget that, my Slurpee cold on my teeth and Marshall's palm warm against mine as we walked in the late-afternoon sunshine, those power lines rising up and casting long shadows all around us.

When he stopped walking and kissed me a few minutes later, it was like time had stopped, with the air, my heart, and the world all so still. And it was this I remembered every other time I was with Marshall. Maybe it was the setting, us alone in that field, or because it was the first time. I didn't know yet that this was all either of us was capable of: moments together that were great but also fleeting.

Marshall was not my boyfriend. On the other hand, he wasn't just a friend either. Instead, our relationship was elastic, stretching between those two extremes depending on who else was around, how much either of us had had to drink, and other varying factors. This was exactly what I wanted, as commitments had never really been my thing. And it wasn't like it was hard, either. The only trick was never giving more than you were willing to lose. With Marshall and me, it was like a game called I Could Care Less. I talked to a guy at a party; he disappeared with some girl at the next one. He didn't return my calls; I'd stay away for a while, making him wonder what I was up to. And so on.

We'd been doing this for so long that really, it came naturally. But now, I was so surprised by how nice it was to hear his voice, something familiar in all this newness, that I found myself breaking my own rule, offering up more than I'd planned.

"Yeah, so, I've just been, you know, dealing with some family stuff," I said, easing back against the booth wall behind me. "I moved in with my sister, and—"

"Hang on a sec, okay?" he said, and then I heard his hand cover the receiver, muffling it. Then he was saying something, his words impossible to make out before I heard him come back on. "Sorry," he said, then coughed. "What were you saying?"

And just like that, it was over. Even missing him was fleeting, like everything else.

"Nothing," I told him. "I should go. I'll catch up with you later, okay?"

"Yeah. See you around."

I hung up, leaving my hand on the receiver as I reached into my pocket, pulling out some more change. Then I took a breath and put it back to my ear, dropped in a few coins, and called someone I knew would be more than happy to talk.

"Ruby?" Peyton said as soon as she heard my voice. "Oh my God. What *happened* to you?"

"Well," I said.

But she was already continuing, her voice coming out in a gush. "I mean, I was waiting for you in the courtyard, just like always, and you never showed up! So I'm like, she must be mad at me or something, but then Aaron said the cops had pulled you out of class, and nobody knew why. And then I went by your house, and it was all dark, and—"

"Everything's fine," I said, cutting her off more out of a time concern than rudeness. Peyton was always summarizing, even when you knew the story as well as she did. "It's just a family thing. I'm staying with my sister for a while."

"Well," she said, "it's all *anyone* is talking about, just so you know. You should hear the rumors."

"Yeah?"

"It's terrible!" she said, sounding truly aghast. "They have you doing everything from committing murder to teen prostitution."

"I've been gone for two days," I said.

"Of course, I've been sticking up for you," she added quickly. "I told them there was no way you'd ever sleep with guys for money. I mean, come on."

This was typical Peyton. Defending my honor vigorously, while not realizing that she was implying that I might be capable of murder. "Well," I said, "I appreciate it."

"No problem." I could hear voices behind her; from the sound of it, she was at the clearing a ways down from school, where we always hung out after final bell. "So, like, what's the real story, though? Is it your mom?"

"Something like that," I told her. "Like I said, it's not a big deal."

Peyton was my closest friend at Jackson, but like everyone else, she had no idea my mom had taken off. She'd actually never even met her, which was no accident; as a rule, I preferred to keep my private life just that, private. This was especially important with someone like Peyton, whose family was pretty much perfect. Rich and functional, they lived in a big house in the Arbors, where up until the year before, she'd been the ideal daughter, pulling straight As and lettering in field hockey. During the summer, though, she'd started dating my friend Aaron, who was a harmless but dedicated pothead. In the fall, she'd gotten busted with a joint at school and was asked to leave St. Micheline's, the Catholic school she'd been attending. Her parents, of course, were none too pleased, and hoped Peyton's newfound rebellion was a just a phase that would end when she and Aaron broke up. After a few weeks, they did, but by that point, she and I were already friends.

Peyton was, in a word, cute. Short and curvy, she was

also incredibly naive, which was alternately annoying and endearing. Sometimes I felt more like a big sister to her than a friend—I was always having to rescue her from weird guys at parties, or hold her head when she puked, or explain again how to work the various expensive electronics her parents were always buying her—but she was fun to hang out with, had a car, and never complained about having to come all the way out to pick me up, even though it was on the way to nowhere. Or back.

"So the thing is," I said to her now, "I need a favor."

"Name it," she replied.

"I'm over here by Perkins Day, and I need a ride," I told her. "Can you come get me?"

"At Perkins Day?"

"Near there. Just down the street."

There was a pause, during which time I heard laughter behind her. "God, Ruby . . . I wish I could. But I'm supposed to be home in an hour."

"It's not that far," I said.

"I know. But you know how my mom's been lately." Since the last time Peyton had come home smelling like beer, her parents had instituted a strict accountability program involving constant tracking, elaborate sniff tests, and surprise room searches. "Hey, did you try Marshall? I bet he can—"

"No," I said, shaking my head. Peyton had never quite gotten Marshall's and my arrangement; an incurable romantic, to her, every story was a love story. "It's fine, don't worry about it."

There was another pause, and again, I could hear what

was happening around her: laughter, someone's radio playing, a car engine starting up. It was true what I'd said: it
wasn't that far from there to here, only fifteen miles or so.
But at that moment, it suddenly seemed like a long way.

"You sure?" she asked. "Because I could ask someone
here."

I swallowed, leaning back against the side of the booth.
On the opposite side, above the phone, someone had written WHERE DO YOU SLEEP? in thick black marker. Scratched
underneath, less legibly, was a reply: WITH YOUR MAMA. I
reached up, rubbing my face with my hand. It wasn't like I'd
expected anyone to come rescue me, anyway. "Nah," I said.
"That's all right. I'll figure out something."

"All right," she said. A car horn beeped in the background. "Give me your sister's number, though. I'll call you
tonight, we can catch up."

"I'm still getting settled," I told her. "I'll give you a call
in a few days."

"Okay," she said easily. "And hey, Ruby."

"What?"

"I'm glad you're not a hooker or a murderer."

"Yeah," I said. "Me, too."

I hung up the phone, then stepped out of the booth to
finish off my Coke and contemplate my next move. The
parking lot, which had been mostly empty when I first got
there, had filled up with Perkins Day students. Clearly, this
was some sort of off-site hangout, with people sitting on the
hoods and bumpers of their expensive cars, slumming at
the Quick Zip. Scanning the crowd, I spotted Nate off to the
right, arms crossed over his chest, leaning against the driver's-

side door of a black SUV. A dark-haired girl in a ponytail and a cropped blue jacket was with him, telling some story and gesturing wildly, the Zip Coke in her hand waving back and forth as she spoke. Nate, of course, was smiling as he listened, the epitome of the Nicest Guy in the World.

Then something occurred to me. I glanced at my watch. It was just before four, which meant I had a little over an hour before I'd be late enough for anyone to notice. It was enough time to do what I had to do, if I got going soon. All I needed was a little help, and if I worked things right, maybe I wouldn't even have to ask for it.

As I hitched my backpack over my shoulder and started toward the road, I made it a point not to look at the Perkins Day contingent, even as I passed right in front of them. Instead, I just kept my focus forward, on the big intersection that lay ahead. It was a long walk home, and even farther to where I really needed to be, making this a serious gamble, especially considering how I'd acted earlier. But part of being nice was forgiveness—or so I'd heard—so I rolled the dice anyway.

Two blocks down the road, I heard a car horn, then an engine slowing behind me. I waited until the second beep before arranging my face to look surprised, and turned around. Sure enough, there was Nate.

"Let me guess," he said. He was leaning across the passenger seat, one hand on the wheel, looking up at me. "You don't need a ride."

"Nope," I told him. "Thanks, though."

"This is a major road," he pointed out. "There's not even a sidewalk."

"Who are you, the safety monitor?"

He made a face at me. "So you'd prefer to just walk the six miles home."

"It's not six miles," I said.

"You're right. It's six point two," he replied as a red Ford beeped angrily behind him, then zoomed past. "I run it every Friday. So I know."

"Why are you so hell-bent on driving me somewhere?" I asked.

"I'm chivalrous," he said.

Yeah, right, I thought. *That's one word for it.* "Chivalry's dead."

"And you will be, too, if you keep walking along here." He sighed. "Get in."

And it was just that easy.

* * *

Inside, Nate's car was dark, the interior immaculate, and still smelled new. Even so, there was an air freshener hanging from the rearview. The logo on it said REST ASSURED EXECUTIVE SERVICES: WE WORRY SO YOU DON'T HAVE TO.

"It's my dad's company," he explained when he saw me looking at it. "We work to make life simpler in these complicated times."

I raised my eyebrows. "That sounds like something right off a brochure."

"Because it is," he said. "But I have to say it if anybody asks what we do."

"And what if they want an actual answer?"

"Then," he said, glancing behind him as he switched lanes, "I tell them we do everything from picking up mail to

walking dogs to getting your dry-cleaning to frosting cupcakes for your kid's school party."

I considered this. "Doesn't sound as good."

"I know. Hence the rule."

I sat back in my seat, looking out the window at the
buildings and cars blurring past. Okay, fine. So he wasn't
terrible company. Still, I wasn't here to make friends.

"So look," he said, "about earlier, and that joke I made."

"It's fine," I told him. "Don't worry about it."

He glanced over at me. "What were you doing, though?
I mean, on the fence. If you don't mind my asking."

I did mind. I was also pretty much at his mercy at this
point, so I said, "Wasn't it obvious?"

"Yeah, I suppose it was," he said. "I think I was just, you
know, surprised."

"At what?"

"I don't know." He shrugged. "Just seems like most people would be trying to break *into* that house, not escape it.
Considering how cool Cora and Jamie are, I mean."

"Well," I said. "I guess I'm not most people."

I felt him look at me as I turned my head, looking out
the window again. My knowledge of this part of town was
fairly limited, but from what I could tell, we were getting
close to Wildflower Ridge, Jamie and Cora's neighborhood,
which meant it was time to change the subject. "So anyway," I said, shooting for casual, "I do appreciate the ride."

"No problem," he said. "It's not like we aren't going to
the same place."

"Actually . . ." I paused, then waited for him to look over

at me. When he did, I said, "If you could just drop me off by a bus stop, that'd be great."

"Bus stop?" he said. "Where are you going?"

"Oh, just to a friend's house. I have to pick something up."

We were coming up to a big intersection now. Nate slowed, easing up behind a VW bug with a flower appliqué on the back bumper. "Well," he said, "where is it?"

"Oh, it's kind of far," I said quickly. "Believe me, you don't want to have to go there."

The light changed, and traffic started moving forward. *This is it*, I thought. *Either he takes the bait, or he doesn't.* It was four fifteen.

"Yeah, but the bus will take you ages," he said after a moment.

"Look, I'll be fine," I said, shaking my head. "Just drop me off up here, by the mall."

The thing about negotiations, not to mention manipulation, is you can't go too far in any direction. Refusing once is good, twice usually okay, but a third is risky. You never know when the other person will just stop playing and you end up with nothing.

I felt him glance over at me again, and I made a point of acting like I didn't notice, couldn't see him wavering. *Come on*, I thought. *Come on.*

"Really, it's cool," he said finally, as the entrance to the highway appeared over the next hill. "Just tell me where to go."

* * *

"Man," Nate said as he bumped up the driveway to the yellow house, avoiding holes and a sizable stack of water-logged newspapers. Up ahead, I could already see my mom's Subaru, parked just where I'd left it, gas needle on empty, that last day Peyton had picked me up for school. "Who lives here again?"

"Just this girl I know," I said.

As far as I was concerned, this entire endeavor would be quick and painless. Get in, get what I needed, and get out, hopefully with as little explanation as necessary. Then Nate would take me back to Cora's, and this would all be over. Simple as that.

But then, just as we passed the bedroom window, I saw the curtain move.

It was very quick, so quick I wondered if I'd seen anything at all—just a shift of the fabric an inch to the left, then back again. The exact way it would have to for someone to peer out and yet still not be seen.

I wasn't sure what I'd been expecting to find here. Maybe the Honeycutts, in the midst of some project. Or the house empty, cleaned out as if we'd never been here at all. This possibility, though, had never crossed my mind.

Which was why Nate hadn't even finished parking when I pushed open my door and got out. "Hey. Do you want—?" I heard him call after me, but I ignored him, instead taking the steps two at time and arriving at the front door breathless, my fingers already fumbling for the key around my neck. Once I put it in the lock, the knob, familiar in my hand, turned with a soft click. And then I was in.

"Mom?" I called out, my voice bouncing off all the hard surfaces back at me. I walked into the kitchen, where I could see the clothesline was still strung from one wall to the other, my jeans and shirts now stiff and mildewy as I pushed past them. "Hello?"

In the living room, there was a row of beer bottles on the coffee table, and the blanket we usually kept folded over one arm of the sofa was instead balled into one corner. I felt my heart jump. I would have folded it back. Wouldn't I?

I kept moving, pushing open my bedroom door and flicking on the single bulb overhead. This did look just like I'd left it, save for my closet door being left open, I assumed by whoever packed up the clothes that had been brought to me at Poplar House. I turned, crossing back into the living room and walking over to the other bedroom door, which was shut. Then I put my hand on the knob and closed my eyes.

It wasn't like making a wish or trying to dream something into being real. But in that moment, I tried to remember all the times I'd come home and walked to this same door, easing it open to see my mom curled up in her bed, hair spilling over the pillowcase, already reaching a hand to shield her eyes from the light behind me. This image was so clear in my mind that when I first pushed open the door, I was almost sure I did see a glimpse of red, some bit of movement, and my heart jumped into my throat, betraying in one instant all the emotions I'd denied to myself and everyone else in the last week. Then, though, just as quickly, something shifted. The objects and room itself fell into place: bed, dark walls . . . and that window, where I now remembered the bit of broken pane, half–taped up, where a breeze still could inch in, ruffling the curtain. I'd been mistaken. But even so, I stayed where I was, as if by doing so the room would, in the next moment, suddenly be anything but empty.

"Ruby?"

Nate's voice was low, tentative. I swallowed, thinking how stupid I was, thinking that my mom might have actually come back, when I knew full well that everything she needed she'd taken with her. "I'll be done in a sec," I said to him, hating how my voice was shaking.

"Are you . . . ?" He paused. "Are you okay?"

I nodded, all business. "Yeah. I just have to grab something."

I heard him shift his weight, taking a step, although toward me or away, I wasn't sure, and not knowing this was enough to make me turn around. He was standing in the doorway to the kitchen, the front door open behind him, turning his head slowly, taking it all in. I felt a surge of shame; I'd been so stupid to bring him here. Like I, of all people, didn't know better than to lead a total stranger directly to the point where they could hurt me most, knowing how easily they'd be able to find their way back to it.

"This place," Nate said, looking at the bottles on the table, a lone cobweb stretching across the room between us, "it's, like—"

Suddenly there was a gust of wind outside, and a few leaves blew in the open door, skittering in across the kitchen floor. I felt so shaken, unsettled, that my voice was sharp as I said, "Just wait in the car. All right?"

He looked at me for a second. "Yeah," he said. "Sure thing." Then he stepped outside, pulling the door shut behind him.

Stop it, I told myself, feeling tears pricking my eyes, so stupid. I looked around the room, trying to clear my head and concentrate on what I should take with me, but everything was blurring, and I felt a sob work its way up my throat. I put my hand over my mouth, my shoulders shaking, and forced my feet to move.

Think, think, I kept saying in my head as I walked back to the kitchen and began pulling stuff off the clothesline. Everything was stiff and smelly, and the more I took down the more I could see of the rest of the kitchen: the pots and pans piled in the sink, the buckets I'd used to collect water from the bathroom, the clothesline, now sagging over my head. *I was doing just fine*, I'd told Cora, and at the time, I'd believed it. But now, standing there with my stiff clothes in my arms, the smell of rotting food filling my nostrils, I wasn't so sure anymore.

I reached up, wiping my eyes, and looked back out at Nate, who was sitting behind the wheel of his car, a cell phone to his ear. God only knew what he was thinking. I looked down at my clothes, knowing I couldn't bring them with me, even though they, the few things in the next room, and that beat-up, broken-down Subaru were all I really had. As I dropped them onto the table, I told myself I'd come back for them and everything else, just as soon as I got settled. It was such an easy promise to make. So easy that I could almost imagine another person saying the same thing to themselves as they walked out that door, believing it, too. Almost.

*   *   *

I was not looking forward to the ride home, as God only knew what Nate would say to me, or how I would dodge the questions he would inevitably ask. So I decided, as I locked the door behind me, to go with a route I knew well: complete and total denial. I'd act like nothing out of the ordinary had happened, as if this trip was exactly what I had expected it to be. If I was convincing enough, he'd have no choice but to see it the same way.

I was all casual as I walked back to the car, playing my part. When I got in, though, I realized it wasn't even necessary. He still had the phone clamped to his ear and didn't even glance at me as he shifted into reverse, backing away from the house.

While he was distracted, I took one last look at that window into my mom's room. Talk about denial; even from a distance and in motion, I could tell there was no one inside. There's something just obvious about emptiness, even when you try to convince yourself otherwise.

"It's not a problem," Nate said suddenly, and I glanced over at him. He had his eyes on the road, his mouth a thin line as he listened to whoever was speaking. "Look, I can be there in ten minutes. Maybe even less than that. Then I'll just grab it from her, and—"

Whoever it was cut him off, their voice rising enough that I could hear it, though not make out specific words. Nate reached up, rubbing a hand over his face. "I'll be there in ten minutes," he said, hitting the gas as we turned back onto the main road. "No . . ." He trailed off. "I just had to run this errand for school. Yeah. Yes. Okay."

He flipped the phone shut, dropping it with a clank into the console between our seats. "Problem?" I said.

"Nah," he said. "Just my dad. He's a little . . . controlling about the business."

"You forgot to frost some cupcakes?"

He glanced over at me, as if surprised I was capable of humor. "Something like that," he said. "I have to make a stop on the way home. If you don't mind."

"It's your car," I said with a shrug.

As we merged onto the highway, the phone rang again. Nate grabbed it, glancing at the display, then flipped it open. "Hello? Yes. I'm on the way. On the highway. Ten minutes. Sure. Okay. Bye."

This time, he didn't put the phone down, instead just keeping it in his hand. After a moment, he said, "It's just the two of us, you know. Living together, working together. It can get . . . kind of intense."

"I know," I said.

Maybe it was because my mother was on my mind, but this came out before I even realized it, an unconscious, immediate reaction. It was also the last thing I wanted to be talking about, especially with Nate, but of course then he said, "Yeah?"

I shrugged. "I used to work with my mom. I mean, for a while anyway."

"Really?" I nodded. "What'd you do?"

"Delivered lost luggage for the airlines."

He raised his eyebrows, either surprised or impressed. "People really do that?"

"What, you think they just get teleported to you or something?"

"No," he said slowly, shooting me a look. "I just mean . . . it's one of those things you know gets done. You just don't actually think of someone doing it."

"Well," I said, "I am that someone. Or was, anyway."

We were taking an exit now, circling around to a stoplight. As we pulled up to it, Nate said, "So what happened?"

"With what?"

"The luggage delivery. Why did you quit?"

This time, I knew enough not to answer, only evade. "Just moved on," I said. "That's all."

Thankfully, he did not pursue this further, instead just putting on his blinker and turning into the front entrance of the Vista Mall, a sprawling complex of stores and restaurants. The parking lot was packed as we zipped down a row of cars, then another before pulling up behind an old green Chevy Tahoe. The back door was open, revealing an extremely cluttered backseat piled with boxes and milk crates, which were in turn filled with various envelopes and packing materials. A woman with red hair coiled into a messy bun wearing a fuzzy pink sweater and holding a to-go coffee cup in one hand was bent over them, her back to us.

Nate rolled down his window. "Harriet," he called out.

She didn't hear him as she picked up a crate, shoving it farther back. An empty coffee cup popped out and started to roll away, but she grabbed it, stuffing it in another box.

"Harriet," Nate repeated. Again, no answer as she bent deeper over a crate.

"You're going to have to be louder," I told him as he was barely speaking above a normal tone of voice.

"I know," he said. Then he took a breath, wincing slightly, and put his hand on the horn.

He only did it once, and it was quick: *beep!* Still, the woman literally jumped in the air. Completely vertical, feet off the ground, coffee spilling out of the cup backward, splattering the pavement. Then she whirled around, her free hand to her chest, and goggled at us.

"Sorry," Nate called out. "But you weren't—"

"What are you doing?" she asked him. "Are you *trying* to give me a nervous attack?"

"No." He pushed open his door, quickly climbing out and walking over to her. "Here, let me get that. It's these three? Or the crates, too?"

"All of them," the woman—Harriet?—said, clearly still flustered as she leaned against the Tahoe's bumper, flapping a hand in front of her face. As Nate began to load the boxes into the back of his car, I noticed she was rather pretty, and had on a chunky silver necklace with matching earrings, as well as several rings. "He knows I'm a nervous person," she said to me, gesturing at Nate with her cup. "And yet he beeps. He *beeps*!"

"It was an accident," Nate told her, returning for the last box. "I'm sorry."

Harriet sighed, leaning back against the bumper again and closing her eyes. "No," she said, "it's me. I'm just under this massive deadline, and I'm way behind, and I just knew I wasn't going to get to the shipping place before they closed—"

"—which is why you have us," Nate finished for her, shutting his own back door with a bang. "I'm taking them over right now. No worries."

"They all need to go Ground, not Next Day," she told him. "I can't afford Next Day."

"I know."

"And be sure you get the tracking information, because they're promised by the end of the week, and there's been bad weather out West. . . ."

"Done," Nate told her, pulling his door open.

Harriet considered this as she stood there clutching her coffee cup. "Did you drop off that stuff at the cleaners yesterday?"

"Ready on Thursday," Nate told her.

"What about the bank deposit?" she asked.

"Dad did it this morning. Receipt is in the envelope in your mailbox."

"Did he remember to—"

"—lock it back? Yes. The key is where you said to leave it. Anything else?"

Harriet drew in a breath, as if about to ask another question, then slowly let it out. "No," she said slowly. "At least not right at this moment."

Nate slid behind the wheel. "I'll e-mail you all the tracking info as soon as I get home. Okay?"

"All right," she said, although she sounded uncertain as he cranked the engine. "Thanks."

"No problem. Call if you need us."

She nodded but was still standing by her bumper, gripping her cup and looking uncertain, as we pulled away. I waited until we'd turned onto the main road again before saying, "That's resting assured?"

"No," Nate said, his voice tired. "That's Harriet."

By the time we pulled up to Cora's, it was five thirty. Only a little over an hour had passed since he'd picked me up, and yet it felt like so much longer. As I gathered up my stuff, pushing the door open, his phone rang again; he glanced at the display, then back at me. "Dad's getting nervous," he said. "I better go. I'll see you tomorrow morning?"

I looked over at him, again taking in his solid good looks and friendly expression. Fine, so he was a nice guy, and maybe not entirely the dim jock that I'd pegged him as at first glance. Plus, he had helped me out, not once but twice, and maybe to him this meant my previous feelings about a carpool would no longer be an issue. But I could not so easily forget Peyton earlier on the other end of that pay-phone line, how quickly she had turned me down at the one moment I'd really needed her.

"Thanks for the ride," I said.

Nate nodded, flipping his phone open, and I shut the door between us. I wasn't sure whether he had noticed I hadn't answered his question, or if he'd even care. Either way, by the time I was halfway down the walk, he was gone.

*   *   *

Earlier that morning, after we'd set up my schedule, Jamie headed off to work and Mr. Thackray started to walk me off to my English class. We were about halfway there when I suddenly heard Jamie calling after us.

"Hold up!"

I turned around, looking down the hallway, which was rapidly filling with people streaming out of their first class, and spotted him bobbing through the crowd. When he reached us, slightly out of breath, he smiled and held his hand out to me, gesturing for me to do the same.

My first instinct was to hesitate, wondering what else he could possibly offer me. But when I opened up my hand, palm flat, and he dropped a key into it, it seemed ridiculous to have expected anything else.

"In case you beat us home," he said. "Have a good day!"

At the time, I'd nodded, closing my hand around the key and slipping it into my pocket, where I'd totally forgotten about it until now, as I walked up to the front door of the house and pulled it out. It was small and on a single silver fob, with the words WILDFLOWER RIDGE engraved on the other side. Weird how it had been there all day, and I hadn't even felt it or noticed. The one around my neck I was always aware of, both its weight and presence, but maybe that was because it was closer to me, where it couldn't be missed.

Cora's door swung open almost soundlessly, revealing the big, airy foyer. Like at the yellow house, everything was still and quiet, but in a different way. Not untouched or forgotten, but more expectant. As if even a house knew the difference between someone simply stepping out for while and being gone for good.

I shut the door behind me. From the foyer, I could see

into the living room, where the sun was already beginning to sink in the sky, disappearing behind the trees, casting that special kind of warm light you only get right before sunset.

I was still just standing there watching this, when I heard a tippity-tapping noise coming from my left. I glanced over; it was Roscoe, making his way through the kitchen. When he saw me, his ears perked up straight on his head. Then he sat down and just stared at me.

I stayed where I was, wondering if he was going to start barking at me again, which after starting a new school and breaking into my old house was going to be the last thing I could take today. Thankfully, he didn't. Instead, he just began to lick himself, loudly. I figured this signaled it was safe to continue on to the kitchen, which I did, giving him a wide berth as I passed.

On the island, there was a sticky note, and even though it had been years since I'd seen it, I immediately recognized my sister's super neat handwriting, each letter so perfect you had to wonder if she'd done a rough draft first. *J*, it said, *Lasagna is in the fridge, put it in (350) as soon as you get home. See you by seven at the latest. Love, me.*

I picked the note up off the counter, reading it again. If nothing else, this made it clear to me that my sister had, in fact, finally gotten everything she wanted. Not just the things that made up the life she'd no doubt dreamed of—the house, the job, the security—all those nights in our shared room, but someone to share it with. To come home to and have dinner with, to leave a note for. Such simple, stupid things, and yet in the end, they were the true proof of a real life.

Which was why, after she'd worked so hard to get here, it had to really suck to suddenly have me drop back in at the very moment she'd started to think she'd left the old life behind for good. *Oh, well*, I thought. The least I could do was put in the lasagna.

I walked over to the oven and preheated it, then found the pan in the fridge and put it on the counter. I was pulling off the Saran wrap when I felt something against my leg. Looking down, I saw Roscoe had at some point crossed the room and was now sitting between my feet, looking up at me.

My first thought was that he had peed on the floor and was waiting for me to yell at him. But then I realized he was shaking, bouncing back and forth slightly from one of my ankles to the other. "What?" I asked him, and in response he burrowed down farther, pressing himself more tightly against me. All the while, he kept his big bug eyes on me, as if pleading, but for what, I had no idea.

Great, I thought. Just what I needed: the dog dies on my watch, thereby officially cementing my status as a complete blight on the household. I sighed, then stepped carefully around Roscoe to the phone, picking it up and dialing Jamie's cell-phone number, which was at the top of a list posted nearby. Before I was even done, Roscoe had shuffled across the floor, resituating himself at my feet, the shaking now going at full force. I kept my eyes on him as the phone rang twice, and then, thankfully, Jamie picked up.

"Something's wrong with the dog," I reported.

"Ruby?" he said. "Is that you?"

"Yes." I swallowed, looking down at Roscoe again, who in turn scooted closer, pressing his face into my calf. "I'm sorry to bother you, but he's just acting really . . . sick. Or something. I didn't know what to do."

"Sick? Is he throwing up?"

"No."

"Does he have the runs?"

I made a face. "No," I said. "At least, I don't think so. I just came home and Cora had left this note about the lasagna, so I put it in and—"

"Oh," he said slowly. "Okay. It's all right, you can relax. He's not sick."

"He's not?"

"Nope. He's just scared."

"Of lasagna?"

"Of the oven." He sighed. "We don't really understand it. I think it may have something to do with this incident involving some Tater Tots and the smoke detector."

I looked down at Roscoe, who was still in full-on tremulous mode. You had to wonder how such a thing affected a little dog like that—it couldn't be good for his nervous system. "So," I said as he stared up at me, clearly terrified, "how do you make it stop?"

"You can't," he said. "He'll do it the entire time the oven's on. Sometimes he goes and hides under a bed or the sofa. The best thing is to just act normal. If he drives you too crazy, just shut him in the laundry room."

"Oh," I said as the dog rearranged himself, wedging himself between my shoe and the cabinet behind me. "Okay."

"Look, I'm breaking up," he said, "but I'll be home soon. Just—"

There was a buzz, and then he was gone, dropping off

altogether. I hung up, replacing the phone carefully on its base. I wasn't sure what "soon" meant, but I hoped it meant he was only a few blocks away, as I was not much of an animal person. Still, looking down at Roscoe trembling against my leg, it seemed kind of mean to just shut him up in a small space, considering the state he was in.

"Just relax, okay?" I said, untangling myself from around him and walking to the foyer to my bag. For a moment he stayed where he was, but then he started to follow me. The last thing I wanted was any kind of company, so I started up the stairs at a quick clip, hoping he'd get the message and stay behind. Surprisingly, it worked; when I got to the top of the stairs and looked down, he was still in the foyer. Staring up at me looking pitiful, but still there.

Up in my room, I washed my face, then slid Cora's sweater off and lay back across the bed. I don't know how long I was there, staring out the windows at the last of the sunset, before Roscoe came into the room. He was moving slowly, almost sideways, like a crab. When he saw that I'd noticed him, his ears went flat on his head, as if he was expecting to be ejected but couldn't help taking a shot anyway.

For a moment, we just looked at each other. Then, tentatively, he came closer, then a bit closer still, until finally he was wedged between my feet, with the bed behind him. When he started shaking again, his tags jingling softly, I rolled my eyes. I wanted to tell him to cut it out, that we all had our problems, that I was the last person he should come looking to for solace. But instead, I surprised myself by saying none of this as I sat up, reaching a hand down to his head. The moment I touched him, he was still.

Chapter Four

At first, it just a rumbling, punctuated by the occasional shout: the kind of thing that you're aware of, distantly, and yet can still manage to ignore. Right as my clock flipped over to 8:00, though, the real noise began.

I sat up in bed, startled, as the room suddenly filled with the clanking of metal hitting rock. It wasn't until I got up and went out on my balcony and saw the backhoe that it all started to make sense.

"Jamie!"

I glanced to my right, where I could see my sister, in her pajamas, standing on her own balcony. She was clutching the railing, looking down at her husband, who was on the back lawn looking entirely too awake, a mug of coffee in his hands and Roscoe at his feet. When he looked up and saw her, he grinned. "Great, right?" he said. "You can really visualize it now!"

Most of Cora's response to this was lost in the ensuing din as the backhoe dug once more into the lawn, scooping up more earth from within Jamie's circle of rocks and swinging to the side to dump it on the already sizable pile there. As it moved back, gears grinding, to go in again, I just caught the end, when she was saying, ". . . Saturday morning, when some people might want to *sleep*."

"Honey, it's the pond, though," Jamie replied, as if he had heard every word. "We talked about this. Remember?"

Cora just looked at him, running a hand through her hair, which was sticking up on one side. Then, without further comment, she went inside. Jamie watched her go, his face quizzical. "Hey!" he shouted when he saw me. The backhoe dug down again, with an even louder clank. "Pretty cool, don't you think? If we're lucky, we'll have it lined by tonight."

I nodded, watching as the machine dumped another load of dirt onto the pile. Jamie was right, you could really picture it now: there was a big difference between a theoretical pond and a huge hole in the ground. Still, it was hard to imagine what he wanted—a total ecosystem, a real body of water, with fish and everything—seeming at home in the middle of such a flat, square yard. Even with the best landscaping, it would still look as if it had fallen from the sky.

Back inside, I flopped back into bed, although sleeping was clearly no longer an option. Hard to believe that the previous Saturday, I'd been at the yellow house, waking up on the couch with our old moldy afghan curled around me. Fast-forward a week, and here I was at Cora's. My basic needs were certainly being met—running water, heat, food—but it was still strange to be here. Everything felt so temporary, including me, that I hadn't even unpacked yet—my bag was still right by the bed, where I was living out of it like I was on a vacation, about to check out at any moment. Sure, it meant the little bit of stuff I had was that much more wrinkled, but rolling over every morning and seeing all my worldly possessions right there beside me made me feel somewhat in control of my situation. Which I needed, considering that everything else seemed completely out of my hands.

* * *

"The bus?" Jamie said that first night, when he mentioned Nate picking me up and I told him I'd prefer alternate transportation. "Are you serious?"

"There isn't a Perkins Day bus in the morning," Cora said from across the table. "They only run in the afternoon, to accommodate after-school activities."

"Then I'll take the city bus," I said.

"And go to all that trouble?" Jamie asked. "Nate's going to Perkins anyway. And he offered."

"He was just being nice," I said. "He doesn't really want to drive me."

"Of course he does," Jamie said, grabbing another roll from the basket between us. "He's a prince. And we're chipping in for gas. It's all taken care of."

"The bus is fine," I said again.

Cora, across the table, narrowed her eyes at me. "What's really going on here?" she asked. "You don't like Nate or something?"

I picked up my fork, spearing a piece of asparagus. "Look," I said, trying to keep my voice cool, collected, "it just seems like a big hassle. If I ride the bus, I can leave when I want, and not be at the mercy of someone else."

"No, you'll be at the mercy of the bus schedule, which is *much* worse," Jamie said. He thought for a second. "Maybe we should just get you a car. Then you can drive yourself."

"We're not buying another car," Cora said flatly.

"She's seventeen," Jamie pointed out. "She'll need to go places."

"Then she'll ride the bus. Or ride with Nate. Or borrow yours."

"Mine?"

Cora just looked at him, then turned her attention to me. "If you want to do the bus, fine. But if it makes you late, you have to do the carpool. All right?"

I nodded. Then, after dinner, I went online and printed out four different bus schedules, circling the ones I could catch from the closest stop and still make first bell. Sure, it meant getting up earlier and walking a few blocks. But it would be worth it.

Or so I thought, until I accidentally hit the snooze bar a few extra times the next morning and didn't get downstairs until 7:20. I was planning to grab a muffin and hit the road, running if necessary, but of course Cora was waiting for me.

"First bell in thirty minutes," she said, not looking up from the paper, which she had spread out in front of her. She licked a finger, turning a page. "There's no way."

So ten minutes later, I was out by the mailbox cursing myself, muffin in hand, when Nate pulled up. "Hey," he said, reaching across to push the door open. "You changed your mind."

That was just the thing, though. I hadn't. If anything, I was more determined than ever to not make friends, and this just made it harder. Still, it wasn't like I had a choice, so I got in, easing the door shut behind me and putting my muffin in my lap.

"No eating in the car."

The voice was flat, toneless, and came from behind me. As I slowly turned my head, I saw the source: a short kid wearing a peacoat and some serious orthodontia, sitting in the backseat with a book open in his lap.

"What?" I said.

He leaned forward, his braces—and attached headgear— catching the sunlight coming through the windshield. His hair was sticking up. "No eating in the car," he repeated, robotlike. Then he pointed at my muffin. "It's a rule."

I looked at Nate, then back at the kid. "Who are you?"

"Who are *you*?"

"This is Ruby," Nate said.

"Is she your new girlfriend?" the kid asked.

"No," Nate and I said in unison. I felt my face flush.

The kid sat back. "Then no eating. Girlfriends are the only exception to carpool rules."

"Gervais, pipe down," Nate said.

Gervais picked up his book, flipping a page. I looked at Nate, who was now pulling out onto the main road, and said, "So . . . where do you take him? The middle school?"

"Wrong," Gervais said. His voice was very nasal and an- noying, like a goose honking.

"He's a senior," Nate told me.

"A senior?"

"What are you, deaf?" Gervais asked.

Nate shot him a look in the rearview. "Gervais is accel- erated," he said, changing lanes. "He goes to Perkins in the morning, and afternoons he takes classes at the U."

"Oh," I said. I glanced back at Gervais again, but he ignored me, now immersed in his book, which was big and thick, clearly a text of some kind. "So . . . do you pick up anyone else?"

"We used to pick up Heather," Gervais said, his eyes still on his book, "when she and Nate were together. She got to eat in the car. Pop-Tarts, usually. Blueberry flavor."

Beside me, Nate cleared his throat, glancing out the window.

"But then, a couple of weeks ago," Gervais continued in the same flat monotone, turning a page, "she dumped Nate. It was big news. He didn't even see it coming."

I looked at Nate, who exhaled loudly. We drove on for another block, and then he said, "No. We don't pick up anyone else."

Thankfully, this was it for conversation. When we pulled into the parking lot five minutes later, Gervais scrambled out first, hoisting his huge backpack over his skinny shoulders and taking off toward the green without a word to either of us.

I'd planned to follow him, also going my own way, but before I could, Nate fell into step beside me. It was clear this just came so easily to him, our continuing companionship assumed without question. I had no idea what that must be like.

"So look," he said, "about Gervais."

"He's charming," I told him.

"That's one word for it. Really, though, he's not—"

He trailed off suddenly, as a green BMW whizzed past us, going down a couple of rows and whipping into a space. A moment later, the driver's-side door opened, and the blonde from my English class—in a white cable sweater, sunglasses parked on her head—emerged, pulling an over-stuffed tote bag behind her. She bumped the door shut with her hip, then started toward the main building, fluffing her hair with her fingers as she walked. Nate watched her for a moment, then coughed, stuffing his hands in his pockets.

"Really what?" I said.

"What's that?" he asked.

Ahead of us, the blonde—who I had now figured out was the infamous, blueberry Pop-Tart–eating Heather—was crossing to a locker, dropping her bag at her feet. "Nothing," I said. "See you around."

"Yeah," he replied, nodding, clearly distracted as I quick-ened my pace, finally able to put some space between us. "See you."

He was still watching her as I walked away. Which was kind of pathetic but also not my problem, especially since from now on I'd be sticking to my original plan and catch-ing the bus, and everything would be fine.

Or so I thought until the next day, when I again over-slept, missing my bus window entirely. At first, I was com-pletely annoyed with myself, but then, in the shower, I decided that maybe it wasn't so bad. After all, the ride was a short one. At least distance-wise.

"What kind of shampoo is that?" Gervais demanded from the backseat as soon as I got in the car, my hair still damp.

I turned back and looked at him. "I don't know," I said. "Why?"

"It stinks," he told me. "You smell like trees."

"Trees?"

"Gervais," Nate said. "Watch it."

"I'm just saying," Gervais grumbled, flopping back against the seat. I turned around, fixing my gaze on him. For a moment, he stared back, insolent, his eyes seemingly huge behind his glasses. But as I kept on, steady, unwavering, he finally caved and turned to stare out the window. *Twelve-year-olds*, I thought. *So easy to break.*

When I turned back to face forward, Nate was watching me. "What?" I said.

"Nothing," he replied. "Just admiring your technique."

At school, Gervais did his normal scramble-and-disappearing act, and again Nate walked with me across the parking lot. This time, I was not only aware of him beside me—which was still just so odd, frankly—but also the ensuing reactions from the people gathered around their cars, or ahead of us at the lockers: stares, raised eyebrows, entirely too much attention. It was unsettling, not to mention distracting.

When I'd started at Perkins, I'd instinctively gone into New School Mode, a system I'd perfected over the years when my mom and I were always moving. Simply put, it was this: come in quietly, fly under the radar, get in and out each day with as little interaction as possible. Because Perkins Day was so small, though, I was realizing it was inevitable that I'd attract some attention, just because I was new. Add in the fact that someone had figured out my connection to Jamie—"Hey, UMe!" someone had yelled as I walked in the hall a couple of days earlier—and staying anonymous was that much more difficult.

Nate deciding we were friends, though, made it almost

impossible. Even by my second day, I'd figured out he was one of the most popular guys at Perkins, which made me interesting (at least to these people, anyway) simply by standing next to him. Maybe some girls would have liked this, but I was not one of them.

Now, I looked over at him, annoyed, as a group of cheerleaders standing in a huddle by a shiny VW tittered in our wake. He didn't notice, too busy watching that same green BMW, which was parked a couple of rows over. I could see Heather behind the wheel, her Jump Java cup in one hand. Jake Bristol, the sleeper from my English class, was leaning in to talk to her, his arms resting on her open window.

This was not my problem. And yet, as with Gervais, when I saw bad behavior, I just couldn't help myself. Plus, if he was going to insist on walking with me, he almost deserved it.

"You know," I said to him. "Pining isn't attractive. On anyone."

He glanced over at me. "What?"

I nodded at Heather and Jake, who were still talking. "The worst thing you can do if you miss or need someone," I said, "is let them know it."

"I don't miss her," he said.

Yeah, right. "Okay," I replied, shrugging. "All I'm saying is that even if you do want her back, you should act like you don't. No one likes someone who's all weak and pitiful and needy. It's basic relationship 101."

"Relationship 101," he repeated, skeptical. "And this is a course you teach?"

"It's only advice," I told him. "Ignore it if you want."

Really, I assumed he'd do just that. The next morning, though, as he again fell into step beside me—clearly, this was a habit now—and we began crossing the parking lot, Heather's car once again came into view. Even I noticed it, and her, by now. But Nate, I saw, did not. Or at least didn't act like it. Instead, he glanced over at me and then just kept walking.

As the week went on—and my losses to the snooze bar continued—I found myself succumbing to the carpool and, subsequently, our walk together into school itself, audience and all. Resistance was futile, and Nate and I were becoming friends, or something like it. At least as far as he was concerned.

Which was just crazy, because we had absolutely nothing in common. Here I was, a loner to the core, burnout personified, with a train wreck of a home life. And in the other corner? Nate, the good son, popular guy, and all around nice, wholesome boy. Not to mention—as I found out over the next week—student body vice president, homecoming king, community liaison, champion volunteerer. His name just kept coming up, in event after event listed in the flat monotone of the guy who delivered the announcements each morning over the intercom. Going to the senior class trip fund-raiser? Contact Nate Cross. Pitching in to help with the annual campus cleanup? Talk to Nate. Need a study buddy for upcoming midterms? Nate Cross is your man.

He was not my man, however, although as the week— not to mention the staring I'd first noticed in the parking lot—continued, it was clear some people wanted to think otherwise. It was obvious Heather and Nate's breakup had been huge news, at least judging by the fact that weeks later, I was still hearing about their relationship: how they'd dated since he'd moved from Arizona freshman year, been junior prom king and queen, had plans to go off to the U for college in the fall together. For all these facts, though, the cause of their breakup remained unclear. Without even trying, I'd heard so many different theories—He cheated with some girl at the beach! She wanted to date other guys!—that it was obvious no one really knew the truth.

Still, it did explain why they were all so interested in me. The hot popular guy starts showing up with new girl at school, right on the heels of breakup with longtime love. It's the next chapter, or so it seems, so of course people would make their assumptions. And in another school, or another town, this was probably the case. But not here.

As for Perkins Day itself, it *was* a total culture shift, with everything from the teachers (who actually seemed happy to be there) to the library (big, with all working, state-of-the-art computers) to the cafeteria (with salad bar and smoothie station) completely different from what I'd been used to. Also, the small class size made slacking off pretty much a non-option, and as a result, I was getting my ass kicked academically. I'd never been the perfect student by a long shot, but at Jackson I'd still managed to pull solid Bs, even with working nights and my quasi-extracurricular activities. Now, without transportation or friends to distract me, I had all the time in the world to study, and yet I was still struggling, big-time. I kept telling myself it didn't matter, that I'd probably only be there until I could raise the money to take off, so there wasn't any real point in killing myself to keep up. But then, I'd find myself sitting in my room with nothing to do, and pull out the books and get to work, if only for the distraction.

The mentality at Perkins was different, as well. For instance, at Jackson at lunch, due to the cramped cafeteria, lack of coveted picnic tables, and general angst, there was always some kind of drama going on. Fistfights, yelling, little scuffles breaking out and settling down just as quickly, lasting hardly long enough for you to turn your head and notice them. At Perkins, everyone coexisted peacefully in the caf and on the green, and the most heated anything ever got was when someone at the HELP table got a little too fired up about some issue and it burst into a full-fledged debate, but even those were usually civil.

The HELP table itself was another thing I just didn't get. Every day at lunch, just as the period began, some group would set up shop at one of the tables right by the caf entrance, hanging up a sign and laying out brochures to rally support for whatever cause they were promoting. So far, in the time I'd been there, I'd seen everything from people collecting signatures for famine relief to asking for spare change to buy a new flat-screen TV for the local children's hospital. Every day there was something new, some other cause that needed our help and attention RIGHT NOW SO PLEASE SIGN UP or GIVE or LEND A HAND—IT'S THE LEAST YOU CAN DO!

It wasn't like I was a cruel or heartless person. I believed in charity as much as anyone else. But after everything I'd been through the last few months, I just couldn't wrap my mind around reaching out to others. My mother had taught me too well to look out for number one, and right now, in this strange world, this seemed smarter than ever. Still, every time I passed the HELP table, taking in that day's cause—Upcoming AIDS walk! Buy a cookie, it benefits early literacy! Save the Animals!—I felt strangely unsettled by all this want, not to mention the assumed and steady outpouring of help in return, which seemed to come as instinctively to the people here as keeping to myself did to me.

One person who clearly was a giver was Heather Wainwright, who always seemed to be at the HELP table, regardless of the cause. I'd seen her lecturing a group of girls with smoothies on the plight of the Tibetans, selling cupcakes for cancer research, and signing up volunteers to help clean up the stretch of highway Perkins Day sponsored, and she seemed equally passionate about all of them. This was yet another reason, at least in my mind, that whatever rumors were circulating about Nate and me couldn't have been more off the mark. Clearly, I wasn't his type, by a long shot.

Of course, if I had wanted to make friends with people more like me, I could have. The burnout contingent at Perkins Day was less scruffy than their Jackson counterparts but still easily recognizable, hanging out by the far end of the quad near the art building in a spot everyone called the Smokestack. At Jackson, the stoners and the art freaks were two distinct groups, but at Perkins, they had comingled, either because of the reduced population or the fact that there was safety in numbers. So alongside the guys in the rumpled Phish T-shirts, Hackey-sacking in their flip-flops,

you also had girls in dresses from the vintage shop and combat boots, sporting multicolored hair and tattoos. The population of the Smokestack usually showed up about halfway
through lunch, trickling in from the path that led to the
lower soccer fields, which were farthest away from the rest
of the school. Once they arrived, they could be seen fur-
tively trading Visine bottles and scarfing down food from
the vending machine, stoner behavior so classic and obvious
I was continually surprised the administration didn't swoop
in and bust them en masse.

It would have been so easy to walk over and join them,
but even after a few lunches spent with only my sandwich,
I still hadn't done so. Maybe because I wouldn't be there
long, anyway—it wasn't like there was much point in making friends. Or maybe it was something else. Like the fact
that I had a second chance now, an opportunity, whether I'd
first welcomed it or not, to do things differently. It seemed
stupid to not at least try to take it. It wasn't like the old way
had been working for me so well, anyway.

Still, there was one person at Perkins Day that, if pressed,
I could imagine hanging out with. Maybe because she was
the only one less interested in making friends than I was.

By now, I'd figured out a few things about Olivia Davis,
my seatmate and fellow Jackson survivor. Number one: she
was *always* on the phone. The minute the bell rang, she had
it out and open, quick as a gunslinger, one finger already
dialing. She kept it clamped to her ear as she walked between classes and all through lunch, which she also spent
alone, eating a sandwich she brought from home and talk-

ing the entire time. From the few snippets I overheard before our class started and just after it ended, she was mostly talking to friends, although occasionally she'd affect an annoyed, flat tone that screamed parental conversation. Usually, though, she was all noisy chatter, discussing the same things, in fact, that I heard from everyone else in the hallways or around me in my classrooms—school, parties, stress—except that her conversations were one-sided, her voice the only one I could hear.

It was also clear that Olivia was at Perkins Day under protest, and a vocal one at that. I had strong opinions about our classmates and their lifestyles but kept these thoughts to myself. Olivia practiced no such discretion.

"Yeah, right," she'd say under her breath as Heather Wainwright began a long analysis of the symbolism of poverty in *David Copperfield*. "Like *you* know from poverty. In your BMW and million-dollar mansion."

"Ah, yes," she'd murmur as one of the back-row jocks, prodded by Ms. Conyers to contribute, equated his experience not making starter with a character's struggle, "tell us about your pain. We're *riveted*."

Sometimes she didn't say anything but still made her point by sighing loudly, shaking her head, and throwing why-me-Lord? looks up at the ceiling. At first, her tortuous endurance of second period was funny to me, but after a while, it got kind of annoying, not to mention distracting. Finally, on Friday, after she'd literally tossed her hands up as one of our classmates struggled to define "blue collar," I couldn't help myself.

"If you hate this place so much," I said, "why are you here?"

She turned her head slowly, as if seeing me for the first time. "Excuse me?" she said.

I shrugged. "It's not like it's cheap. Seems like a waste of money is all I'm saying."

Olivia adjusted herself in her seat, as if perhaps a change of position might help her to understand why the hell I was talking to her. "I'm sorry," she said, "but do we know each other?"

"It's just a question," I said.

Ms. Conyers, up at the front of the room, was saying something about the status quo. I flipped a few pages in my notebook, feeling Olivia watching me. After a moment, I looked up and met her gaze, letting her know she didn't intimidate me.

"Why are *you* here?" she asked.

"No choice in the matter," I told her.

"Me neither," she replied. I nodded. This was enough, as far as I was concerned. But then she continued. "I was doing just fine at Jackson. It was my dad that wanted me here and made me apply for a scholarship. Better education, better teachers. Better class of friends, all that. You happy now?"

"Never said I wasn't," I told her. "You're the one moaning and groaning over there."

Olivia raised her eyebrows. Clearly, I'd surprised her, and I had a feeling this wasn't so easy to do. "What's your name again?"

"Ruby," I told her. "Ruby Cooper."

"Huh," she said, like this answered some other question, as well. The next time I saw her, though, in the quad between classes, she didn't just brush by, ignoring me in favor of whoever was talking in her ear. She didn't speak to me, either. But I did get a moment of eye contact, some acknowledgment, although of what I wasn't sure, and still couldn't say.

*   *   *

Now, lying on my bed Saturday morning, I heard a crash from outside, followed by more beeping. I got up and walked to the window, looking down at the yard. The hole was even bigger now, the red clay and exposed rock a marked contrast to the even green grass on either side of it. Jamie was still on the patio with the dog, although now he had his hands in his pockets and was rocking back on his heels as he watched the machine dig down again. It was hard to remember what the yard had looked like even twelve hours before, undisturbed and pristine. Like it takes so little not only to change something, but to make you forget the way it once was, as well.

Downstairs in the kitchen, the noise was even louder, vibrations rattling the glass in the French doors. I could see that Cora, now dressed, her hair damp from the shower, had joined Jamie outside. He was explaining something to her, gesturing expansively as she nodded, looking less than enthusiastic.

I got myself some cereal, figuring if I didn't, someone would give me another breakfast lecture, then picked up a section of the newspaper from the island. I was on my way to sit down when there was a bang behind me and Roscoe popped through the dog door.

When he saw me, his ears perked up and he pattered over, sniffing around my feet. I stepped over him, walking to the table, but of course he followed me, the way he'd taken to doing ever since the night of the lasagna trauma. Despite my best efforts to dissuade him, the dog liked me.

"You know," Jamie had said the day before, watching as Roscoe stared up at me with his big bug eyes during dinner, "it's pretty amazing, actually. He doesn't bond with just anyone."

"I'm not really a dog person," I said.

"Well, he's not just a dog," Jamie replied. "He's Roscoe."

This, however, was little comfort at times like this, when I just wanted to read my horoscope in peace and instead had to deal with Roscoe attending to his daily toilette—heavy on the slurping—at my feet. "Hey," I said, nudging him with the toe of my shoe. "Cut it out."

He looked up at me. One of his big eyes was running, which seemed to be a constant condition. After a moment, he went back to what he was doing.

"You're up," I heard Cora say from behind me as she came in the patio door. "Let me guess. Couldn't sleep."

"Something like that," I said.

She poured herself a cup of coffee, then walked over to the table. "Me," she said with a sigh as she sat down, dropping a hand to pat Roscoe's head, "I wanted a pool. Something we could swim in."

I glanced up at her, then out at the backhoe, which was swinging down into the hole. "Ponds are nice, though," I said. "You'll have fish."

She sighed. "So typical. He's already won you over."

I shrugged, turning a page. "I don't take sides."

I felt her look at me as I said this, her eyes staying on

me as I scanned the movie listings. Then she picked up her mug, taking another big sip, before saying, "So. I think we need to talk about a few things."

Just as she said this, the backhoe rattled to a stop, making everything suddenly seem very quiet. I folded the paper, pushing it aside. "Okay," I said. "Go ahead."

Cora looked down at her hands, twining her fingers through the handle of her cup. Then she raised her gaze, making a point of looking me straight in the eye as she said, "I think it's safe to say that this . . . situation was unexpected for both of us. It's going to take a bit of adjustment."

I took another bite of cereal, then looked at Roscoe, who was lying at Cora's feet now, his head propped up on his paws, legs spread out flat behind him like a frog. "Clearly," I said.

"The most important things," she continued, sitting back, "at least to Jamie and me, are to get you settled in here and at school. Routine is the first step to normalcy."

"I'm not a toddler," I told her. "I don't need a schedule."

"I'm just saying we should deal with one thing at a time," she said. "Obviously, it won't all run smoothly. But it's important to acknowledge that while we may make mistakes, in the long run, we may also learn from them."

I raised my eyebrows. Maybe I was still in survival mode, but this sounded awfully touchy-feely to me, like a direct quote from some book like *Handling Your Troubled Teen*. Turned out, I wasn't so far off.

"I also think," Cora continued, "that we should set you up to see a therapist. You're in a period of transition, and talking to someone can really—"

"No," I said.

She looked up at me. "No?"

"I don't need to talk to anyone," I told her. "I'm fine."

"Ruby," she said. "This isn't just me. Shayna at Poplar House really felt you would benefit from some discussion about your adjustment."

"Shayna at Poplar House knew me for thirty-six hours," I said. "She's hardly an expert. And sitting around talking about the past isn't going to change anything. There's no point to it."

Cora picked up her coffee cup, taking a sip. "Actually," she said, her voice stiff, "some people find therapy to be very helpful."

Some people, I thought, watching her as she took another slow sip. *Right*.

"All I'm saying," I said, "is that you don't need to go to a lot of trouble. Especially since this is temporary, and all."

"Temporary?" she asked. "How do you mean?"

I shrugged. "I'm eighteen in a few months."

"Meaning what?"

"Meaning I'm a legal adult," I told her. "I can live on my own."

She sat back. "Ah, yes," she said. "Because that was working out *so* well for you before."

"Look," I said as the backhoe started up again outside, startling Roscoe, who had nodded off, "you should be happy. You'll only be stuck with me for a little while and then I'll be out of your hair."

For a moment, she just blinked at me. Then she said, "To go where? Back to that house? Or will you get your own apartment, Ruby, with all the money at your disposal?"

I felt my face flush. "You don't—"

"Or maybe," she continued, loudly and dramatically, as if there was an audience there to appreciate it, "you'll just go and move back in with Mom, wherever she is. Because she probably has a great place with a cute guest room all set up and waiting for you. Is that your plan?"

The backhoe was rumbling again, scooping, digging deeper.

"You don't know anything about me," I said to her. "Not a thing."

"And whose fault is that?" she asked.

I opened my mouth, ready to answer this; it was a no-brainer, after all. Who had left and never returned? Stopped calling, stopped caring? Managed to forget, once she was free and past it, the life that she'd left behind, the one I'd still been living? But even as the words formed on my lips, I found myself staring at my sister, who was looking at me so defiantly that I found myself hesitating. Here, in the face of the one truth I knew by heart.

"Look," I said, taking another bite, "all I'm saying is that you shouldn't have to turn your whole life upside down. Or Jamie's, either. Go on as you were. It's not like I'm a baby you suddenly have to raise or something."

Her expression changed, the flat, angry look giving way to something else, something not exactly softer, but more distant. Like she was backing away, even while staying in the same place. She looked down at her coffee cup, then cleared her throat. "Right," she said curtly. "Of course not."

She pushed her chair up, getting to her feet, and I

watched her walk to the coffeemaker and pour herself another cup. A moment later, with her back still to me, she
said, "You will need some new clothes, though. At least a
few things."

"Oh," I said, looking down at my jeans, which I'd washed
twice in three days, and the faded T-shirt I'd worn my last
day at Jackson. "I'm okay."

Cora picked up her purse. "I've got an appointment this
morning, and Jamie has to be here," she said, taking out a
few bills and bringing them over to me. "But you can walk
to the new mall. There's a greenway path. He can show you
where it is."

"You don't have to—"

"Ruby. Please." Her voice was tired. "Just take it."

I looked at the money, then at her. "Okay," I said.
"Thanks."

She nodded but didn't say anything, instead just turning
around and walking out of the room, her purse under her
arm. Roscoe lifted his head, watching her go, then turned
his attention to me, watching as I unfolded the money. It
was two hundred bucks. *Not bad*, I thought. Still, I waited
another moment, until I was sure she'd gone upstairs, before pocketing it.

The door rattled beside me as Jamie came in, empty
coffee mug dangling from one finger. "Morning!" he said,
clearly on a pond high as he walked to the island, grabbing
a muffin out of the box on the table on his way. Roscoe
jumped up, following him. "So, did you guys get your shopping day all planned out? And FYI, there's no just browsing
with her. She *insists* on a plan of attack."

"We're not going shopping," I said.

"You aren't?" He turned around. "I thought that was the plan. Girls' day out, lunch and all that."

I shrugged. "She said she has an appointment."

"Oh." He looked at me for a moment. "So . . . where'd she go?"

"Upstairs, I think."

He nodded, then glanced back out at the backhoe, which was backing up—*beep beep*. Then he looked at me again before starting out of the room, and a moment later, I heard the steady thump of him climbing the stairs. Roscoe, who had followed him as far as the doorway, stopped, looking back at me.

"Go ahead," I told him. "Nothing to see here."

Of course, he didn't agree with this. Instead, as Cora's and Jamie's voices drifted down from upstairs—discussing me, I was sure—he came closer, tags jingling, and plopped down at my feet again. Funny how in a place this big, it was so hard to just be alone.

*　　*　　*

An hour and a half later, dressed and ready with Cora's money in my pocket, I headed outside to ask Jamie for directions to the shortcut to the mall. I found him at the far end of the yard, beyond the now sizable and deep hole, talking to a man by Nate's fence.

At first, I assumed it was one of the guys from the digging company, several of whom had been milling around ever since the backhoe had arrived. Once I got closer, though, it became apparent that whoever this guy was, he didn't drive machinery for a living.

He was tall, with salt-and-pepper gray hair and tanned skin, and had on faded jeans, leather loafers, and what I was pretty sure was a cashmere sweater, a pair of expensive-looking sunglasses tucked into his collar. As he and Jamie talked, he was spinning his car keys around one finger, then folding them into his palm, again and again. *Spin, clank, spin, clank*.

". . . figured you were digging to China," the man was saying as I came into earshot. "Or for oil, maybe."

"Nope, just putting in a pond," Jamie said.

"A pond?"

"Yeah." Jamie slid his hands into his pockets, glancing over at the hole again. "Organic to the landscaping and the neighborhood. No chemicals, all natural."

"Sounds expensive," the man said.

"Not really. I mean, the initial setup isn't cheap, but it's an investment. Over time, it'll really add to the yard."

"Well," the man said, flicking his keys again, "if you're looking for an investment, we should sit down and talk. I've got some things cooking that might interest you, really up-and-coming ideas. In fact—"

"Ruby, hey," Jamie said, cutting him off as he spotted me. He slid an arm over my shoulder, saying, "Blake, this is Ruby, Cora's sister. She's staying with us for a while. Ruby, this is Blake Cross. Nate's dad."

"Nice to meet you," Mr. Cross said, extending his hand. He had a firm handshake, the kind I imagined they must teach in business school: two pumps, with solid eye contact the entire time. "I was just trying to convince your brother-in-law it's a better thing to put money in a good idea than the ground. Don't you agree?"

"Um," I said as Jamie shot me a sympathetic smile. "I don't know."

"Of course you do! It's basic logic," Mr. Cross said. Then he laughed, flicking his keys again, and looked at Jamie, who was watching the backhoe again.

"So," I said to Jamie, "Cora said you could tell me how to get to the mall?"

"The mall?" Jamie asked. "Oh, the greenway. Sure. It's just down the street, to the right. Stones by the entrance."

"Can't miss it," Mr. Cross said. "Just look for all the people not from this neighborhood traipsing through."

"Blake," Jamie said, "it's a community greenway. It's open to everyone."

"Then why put it in a private, gated neighborhood?" Mr. Cross asked. "Look, I'm as community oriented as the next person. But there's a reason we chose to live here, right? Because it's exclusive. Open up a part of it to just anyone and you lose that."

"Not necessarily," Jamie said.

"Come on," Mr. Cross said. "I mean, what'd you spend on your place here?"

"You know," Jamie said, obviously uncomfortable, "that's not really—"

"A million—or close to it, right?" Mr. Cross continued, over him. Jamie sighed, looking over at the backhoe again. "And for that price, you should get what you want, whether it be a sense of security, like-minded neighbors, exclusivity—"

"Or a pond," I said, just as the backhoe banged down again, then began to back up with a series of beeps.

"What's that?" Mr. Cross asked, cupping a hand over his ear.

"Nothing," I said. Jamie looked over at me, smiling. "It was nice to meet you."

He nodded, then turned his attention back to Jamie as I said my good-byes and started across the yard. On my way, I stopped at the edge of the hole, looking down into it. It was deep, and wide across, much more substantial than what I'd pictured based on Jamie's description. A lot can change between planning something and actually doing it. But maybe all that really matters is that anything is different at all.

Chapter Five

Maybe it was my talk with Cora, or just the crazy week I'd had. Whatever the reason, once I got to the mall, I found myself heading to the bus stop. Two transfers and forty minutes later, I was at Marshall's.

He lived in Sandpiper Arms, an apartment complex just through the woods from Jackson that was best known for its cheap rent and the fact that its units were pre-furnished. They were also painted an array of pastel colors, candy pinks and sky blues, bright, shiny yellows. Marshall's was lime green, which wasn't so bad, except for some reason going there always made me want a Sprite.

When I first knocked on the door, nobody answered. After two more knocks, I was about to pull out my bus schedule and start plotting my ride home, but then the door swung open, and Rogerson peered out at me.

"Hey," I said. He blinked, then ran a hand through his thick dreadlock-like hair, squinting in the sun. "Is Marshall here?"

"Bedroom," he replied, dropping his hand from the door and shuffling back to his own room. I didn't know much about Rogerson, other than the pot thing and that he and Marshall worked together in the kitchen at Sopas, a Mexican joint in town. I'd heard rumors about him spending some time in jail—something about assault—but he wasn't the most talkative person and pretty much kept to himself, so who knew what was really true.

I stepped inside, shutting the door behind me. It took a minute for my eyes to adjust: Marshall and Rogerson, like my mother, preferred things dim. Maybe it was a late-shift thing, this aversion to daylight in general, and morning specifically. The room smelled like stale smoke as I moved forward, down the narrow hallway, passing the small kitchen, where pizza boxes and abandoned soda bottles crowded the island. In the living room, some guy was stretched out across the sofa, a pillow resting on his face: I could see a swath of belly, pale and ghostly, sticking out from under his T-shirt, which had ridden up slightly. Across the room, the TV was on, showing bass fishing on mute.

Marshall's door was closed, but not all the way. "Yeah?" he said, after I knocked.

"It's me," I replied. Then he coughed, which I took as permission to enter and pushed it open.

He was sitting at the pre-fab desk, shirtless, the window cracked open beside him, rolling a cigarette. His skin, freckled and pale, seemed to almost glow in the bit of light the window allowed, and, this being Marshall, you could clearly make out his collarbones and ribs. The boy was skinny, but unfortunately for me, I liked skinny boys.

"There she is," he said, turning to face me. "Long time no see."

I smiled, then cleared a space for myself across from him on the unmade bed and sat down. The room itself was a mess of clothes, shoes, and magazines, things strewn all over the place. One thing that stuck out was a box of candy, one of those samplers, on the bureau top, still wrapped in plastic. "What's that?" I asked. "You somebody's Valentine?"

He picked up the cigarette, sticking it into his mouth, and I instantly regretted asking this. It wasn't like I cared who else he saw, if anybody. "It's October."

"Could be belated," I said with a shrug.

"My mom sent it. You want to open it?" I shook my head, then watched as he sat back, exhaling smoke up into the air. "So what's going on?"

I shrugged. "Not much. I'm actually looking for Peyton. You seen her?"

"Not lately." A phone rang in the other room, then abruptly stopped. "But I've been working a lot, haven't been around much. I'm about to take off—have to work lunch today."

"Right," I said, nodding. I sat back, looking around me, as a silence fell over us. Suddenly I felt stupid for coming here, even with my lame excuse. "Well, I should go, too. I've got a ton of stuff to do."

"Yeah?" he said slowly, leaning forward, elbows on his knees, closer to me. "Like what?"

I shrugged, starting to push myself to my feet. "Nothing that would interest you."

"No?" he asked, stopping me by moving a little closer, his knees bumping mine. "Try me."

"Shopping," I said.

He raised his eyebrows. "No kidding," he said. "One week at Perkins Day and you're already fashion-conscious."

"How'd you know I was at Perkins Day?" I asked.

Marshall shrugged, pulling back a bit. "Someone was talking about it," he said.

"Really."

"Yeah." He looked at me for a moment, then slid his hands out, moving them up my thighs to my waist. Then he ducked his head down, resting it in my lap, and I smoothed my hands over his hair, running it through my fingers. As I felt him relax into me, another silence fell, but this one I was grateful for. After all, with me and Marshall, it had never been about words or conversation, where there was too much to be risked or lost. Here, though, in the quiet, pressed against each other, this felt familiar to me. And it was nice to let someone get close again, even if it was just for a little while.

It was only later, when I was curled up under his blankets, half asleep, that I was reminded of everything that had happened since the last time I'd been there. Marshall was getting ready for work, digging around for his belt, when he laid something cool on my shoulder. Reaching up, I found the key to Cora's house, still on its silver fob, which must have slipped out of my pocket at some point. "Better hang on to that," he said, his back to me as he bent over his shoes. "If you want to get home."

As I sat up, closing it in my hand, I wanted to tell him that Cora's house wasn't home, that I wasn't even sure what that word meant anymore. But I knew he didn't really care, and anyway he was already pulling on a Sopas T-shirt, getting ready to leave. So instead, I began collecting my own clothes, all business, just like him. I didn't necessarily have to get out first, but I wasn't about to be left behind.

* * *

I'd never been much of a shopper, mostly because, like sky-diving or playing polo, it wasn't really within my realm of possibility. Before my mom needed me for Commercial, I'd had a couple of jobs of my own—working at greasy fast-food joints, ringing up shampoo and paper towels at discount drugstores—but all that money I'd tried to put away. Even then I'd had a feeling that someday I would need it for something more than sweaters and lipsticks. Sure enough, once my mom had taken off, I'd pretty much cleared out my savings, and now I was back at zero, just when I needed money most.

Which was why it felt so stupid to even be buying clothes, especially with two hundred bucks I'd scored by doing absolutely nothing. On the flip side, though, I couldn't keep wearing the same four things forever. Plus, Cora was already pissed at me; making her think I'd just pocketed her money would only make things worse. So I forced myself through the narrow aisles of store after store, loud music blasting overhead as I scoured clearance racks for bargains.

It wasn't like I could have fit in at Perkins on my budget, even if I wanted to. Which, of course, I didn't. Still, in the time I'd been there, I'd noticed the irony in what all the girls were wearing, which was basically expensive clothes made to look cheap. Two-hundred-dollar jeans with rips and patches, Lanoler cashmere sweaters tied sloppily around their waists, high-end T-shirts specifically weathered and faded to look old and worn. My old stuff at the yellow house, mildew aside, would have been perfect; as it was, I was forced to buy not only new stuff but cheap new stuff, and the difference was obvious. Clearly, you had to spend a lot of money to properly look like you were slumming.

Still, after an hour and a half, I'd vastly increased my working wardrobe, buying two new pairs of jeans, a sweater, a hoodie, and some actual cheap T-shirts that, mercifully, were five for twenty bucks. Still, seeing my cash dwindle made me very nervous. In fact, I felt slightly sick as I started down the airy center of the mall toward the exit, which was probably why I noticed the HELP WANTED sign ahead right away. Stuck to the side of one of the many merchandise carts arranged to be unavoidable, it was like a beacon, pulling me toward it, step-by-step.

As I got closer, I saw it was on a jewelry stall, which appeared to be unmanned, although there were signs of someone having just left: a Jumbo Smoothie cup sweating with condensation was sitting on the register, and there was a stick of incense burning, the smoke wafting in long curlicues up toward the high, bright glass atrium-like ceiling above. The jewelry itself was basic but pretty, with rows and rows of silver-and-turquoise earrings, a large display of beaded necklaces, and several square boxes filled with rings of all sizes. I reached forward, drawing out a thick one with a red stone, holding it up in front of me and turning it in the light.

"Oh! Wait! Hello!"

I jumped, startled, then immediately put the ring back just as the redheaded woman from whom Nate had been picking up the boxes that day—Harriet—came bustling up, a Jump Java cup in one hand, out of breath but talking anyway.

"Sorry!" she gasped, planting it beside the smoothie cup on the register. "I've been trying to kick my caffeine habit—" here she paused, sucking in a big, and much needed, by the sound of it, breath—"by switching to smoothies. Healthy, right? But then the headache hit and I could feel myself crashing and I just had to run down for a fix." She took another big breath, now fanning her flushed face with one hand. "But I'm here now. Finally."

I just looked at her, not exactly sure what to say, especially considering she was still kind of wheezing. Now that I was seeing her up close, I figured she was in her mid-thirties, maybe a little older, although her freckles, hair, and outfit—low-slung jeans, suede clogs, and Namaste T-shirt—made it hard to pinpoint exactly.

"Wait," she said, putting her coffee on the register and pointing at me, a bunch of bangles sliding down her hand. "Do I know you? Have you bought stuff here before?"

I shook my head. "I was with Nate the other day," I said. "When he came to pick up those things from you."

She snapped her fingers, the bangles clanging again. "Right. With the beeping. God! I'm still recovering from that."

I smiled, then looked down at the display again. "Do you make all this yourself?"

"Yep, I'm a one-woman operation. To my detriment, at times." She hopped up on a stool by the register, picking up her coffee again. "I just made those ones with the red stones, on the second row. People think redheads can't wear red, but they're wrong. One of the first fallacies of my life. And I believed it for *years*. Sad, right?"

I glanced over at her, wondering if she'd been able to tell from a distance that this, in fact, was the one I'd been looking at. I nodded, peering down at it again.

"I love *your* necklace," she said suddenly. When I glanced over to see her leaning forward slightly, studying it, instinctively my hand rose to touch it.

"It's just a key," I said.

"Maybe." She took another sip of her coffee. "But it's the contrast that's interesting. Hard copper key, paired with such a delicate chain. You'd think it would be awkward or bulky. But it's not. It works."

I looked down at my necklace, remembering the day that—fed up with always losing my house key in a pocket or my backpack—I'd gone looking for a chain thin enough to thread through the top hole but still strong enough to hold it. At the time, I hadn't been thinking about anything but managing to keep it close to me, although now, looking in one of the mirrors opposite, I could see what she was talking about. It was kind of pretty and unusual, after all.

"Excuse me," a guy with a beard and sandals standing behind a nearby vitamin kiosk called out to her. "But is that a coffee you're drinking?"

Harriet widened her eyes at me. "No," she called out over her shoulder cheerily. "It's herbal tea."

"Are you lying?"

"Would I lie to you?"

"Yes," he said.

She sighed. "Fine, fine. It's coffee. But organic free-trade coffee."

"The bet," he said, "was to give up all caffeine. You owe me ten bucks."

"Fine. Add it to my tab," she replied. To me she added, "God, I *always* lose. You'd think I'd learn to stop betting."

I wasn't sure what to say to this, so I looked over the necklaces for another moment before saying, "So . . . are you still hiring?"

"No," she replied. "Sorry."

I glanced at the sign. "But—"

"Okay, *maybe* I am," she said. Behind her, the vitamin guy coughed loudly. She looked at him, then said reluctantly, "Yes. I'm hiring."

"All right," I said slowly.

"But the thing is," she said, picking up a nearby feather duster and busily running it across a display of bracelets, "I hardly have any hours to offer. And what I *can* give you is erratic, because you'd have to work around my schedule, which varies wildly. Some times I might need you a lot, others hardly at all."

"That's fine," I said.

She put the duster down, narrowing her eyes at me. "This is boring work," she warned me. "Lots of sitting in one place while everyone passes you by. It's like solitary confinement."

"It is not," Vitamin Guy said. "For God's sake."

"I can handle it," I told her as she shot him a look.

"It's like I said, I'm a one-woman operation," she added. "I just put up that sign. . . . I don't know why I put it up. I mean, I'm doing okay on my own."

There was pointed cough from the vitamin kiosk. She turned, looking at the guy there. "Do you need some water or something?"

"Nope," he replied. "*I'm* fine."

For a moment they just stared at each other, with me between them. Clearly, something was going on here, and my life was complicated enough. "You know, forget it," I said. "Thanks anyway."

I stepped back from the kiosk, hoisting my bags farther up my wrist. Just as I began to walk away, though, I heard another cough, followed by the loudest sigh yet.

"You have retail experience?" she called out.

I turned back. "Counter work," I said. "And I've cashiered."

"What was your last job?"

"I delivered lost luggage for the airlines."

She'd been about to fire off another question, but hearing this, she stopped, eyes widening. "Really."

I nodded, and she looked at me for a moment longer, during which time I wondered if I actually wanted to work for someone who seemed so reluctant to hire me. Before I could begin to consider this, though, she said, "Look, I'll be honest with you. I don't delegate well. So this might not work out."

"Okay," I said.

Still, I could feel her wavering. Like something balanced on the edge, that could go either way.

"Jesus," Vitamin Guy said finally. "Will you tell the girl yes already?"

"Fine," she said, throwing up her hands like she'd lost another bet, a big one. "We'll give it a try. But only a try."

"Sounds good," I told her. Vitamin Guy smiled at me.

She still looked wary, though, as she stuck out her hand. "I'm Harriet."

"Ruby," I said. And with that, I was hired.

* * *

Harriet was not lying. She was a total control freak, something that became more than clear over the next two hours, as she walked me through an in-depth orientation, followed by an intricate register tutorial. Only after I'd endured both of these things—as well as a pop quiz on what I'd learned—and had her shadow me while I waited on four separate customers did she finally decide to leave me alone while she went for another coffee.

"I'll just be right here," she said, pointing to the Jump Java outpost, which was less than five hundred feet away. "If you scream, I'll hear you."

"I won't scream," I assured her.

She hardly looked convinced, however, as she walked away, checking back on me twice before I stopped counting.

Once she was gone, I tried to both relax and remember everything I'd just been taught. I was busy dusting the displays when the vitamin guy walked over.

"So," he said. "Ready to quit yet?"

"She is a little intense," I agreed. "How do her other employees deal with it?"

"They don't," he said. "I mean, she doesn't have any others. Or she hasn't. You're the first."

This, I had to admit, explained a lot. "Really."

He nodded, solemn. "She's needed help forever, so this is a big step for her. Huge, in fact," he said. Then he reached into his pocket, pulling out a handful of small pill packs. "I'm Reggie, by the way. Want some free B-complexes?"

I eyed them, then shook my head. "Ruby. And um, no thanks."

"Suit yourself," he said. "Yo, Nate! How those shark-cartilage supplements treating you? Changed your life yet?"

I turned around. Sure enough, there was Nate, walking toward us, carrying a box in his hands. "Not yet," he said, shifting to slapping hands with Reggie. "But I only just started them."

"You got to keep them up, man," Reggie said. "Every day, twice a day. Those aches and pains will be gone. It's miraculous."

Nate nodded, then looked at me. "Hey," he said.

"Hi."

"She works for Harriet," Reggie said, nudging him.

"No way," Nate said, incredulous. "Harriet actually hired someone?"

"Why is that so surprising?" I said. "She had a HELP WANTED sign up."

"For the last six months," Nate said, putting his box down on the stool behind me.

"And tons of people have applied," Reggie added. "Of course she had a reason for rejecting every one of them. Too perky, bad haircut, possible allergies to the incense . . ."

"She hired you, though," I said to Nate. "Right?"

"Only under duress," he replied, pulling some papers out of the box.

"Which is why," Reggie said, popping a B-complex, "it's so huge that she agreed to take you on."

"No kidding," Nate said. "It is pretty astounding. Maybe it's a redhead thing?"

"Like does speak to like," Reggie agreed. "Or perhaps our Harriet has finally realized how close she is to a stress-related breakdown. I mean, have you seen how much coffee she's been drinking?"

"I thought she switched to smoothies. You guys made a bet, right?"

"Already caved," Reggie said. "She owes me, like, a thousand bucks now."

"What are you guys doing?" Harriet demanded as she walked up, another large coffee in hand. "I finally hire someone and you're already distracting her?"

"I was just offering her some B-complexes," Reggie said. "I figured she'll need them."

"Funny," she grumbled, walking over to take the paper Nate was holding out to her.

"You know," he said to her as she scanned it, "personally, I think it's a great thing you finally admitted you needed help. It's the first step toward healing."

"I'm a small-business owner," she told him. "Working a lot is part of the job. Just ask your dad."

"I would," Nate said. "But I never see him. He's always working."

She just looked at him, then grabbed a pen from the register, signing the bottom of the paper and handing it back to him. "Do you want a check today, or can you bill me?"

"We can send a bill," he said, folding the paper and sliding it into his pocket. "Although you know my dad's pushing his new auto-draft feature these days."

"What's that?"

"We bill you, then take it directly out of your account. Draft it and forget it, no worries," Nate explained. "Want to sign up? I've got the forms in the car. It'll make your life even easier."

"No," Harriet said with a shudder. "I'm already nervous enough just letting you mail stuff."

Nate shot me a told-you-so look. "Well, just keep it in mind," he told her. "You need anything else right now?"

"Nothing you can help me with," Harriet replied, sighing. "I mean, I still have to teach Ruby so much. Like how to organize the displays, the setup and closing schedule, the right way to organize stock alphabetically by size and stone . . ."

"Well," Nate said, "I'm sure that's doable."

"Not to mention," she continued, "the process for the weekly changing of the padlock code on the cash box, alternating the incense so we don't run out of any one kind too quickly, and our emergency-response plan."

"Your what?" Reggie asked.

"Our emergency-response plan," Harriet said.

He just looked at her.

"What, you don't have a system in place as to how to react if there's a terrorist attack on the mall? Or a tornado?

What if you have to vacate the stall quickly and efficiently?"

Reggie, eyes wide, shook his head slowly. "Do you sleep at night?" he asked her.

"No," Harriet said. "Why?"

Nate stepped up beside me, his voice low in my ear. "Good luck," he said. "You're going to need it."

I nodded, and then he was gone, waving at Harriet and Reggie as he went. I turned back to the display, bracing myself for the terrorism-preparedness tutorial, but instead she picked up her coffee, taking another thoughtful sip. "So," she said, "you and Nate are friends?"

"Neighbors," I told her. She raised her eyebrows, and I added, "I mean, we just met this week. We ride to school together."

"Ah." She put the coffee back on the register. "He's a good kid. We joke around a lot, but I really like him."

I knew I was supposed to chime in here, agree with her that he was nice, say I liked him, too. But if anyone could understand why I didn't do this, I figured it had to be Harriet. She didn't delegate well in her professional life; I had the same reluctance, albeit more personal. Left to my own devices, I'd be a one-woman operation, as well. Unfortunately, though, with Nate the damage was already done. If I'd never tried to take off that first night, if I'd gotten a ride from someone else, we'd still really just be neighbors, with no ties to each other whatsoever. But now here I was, too far gone to be a stranger, not ready to be friends, the little acquaintance we had made still managing to be, somehow, too much.

*   *   *

When I got back to Cora's house later that evening, the driveway was packed with cars and the front door was open, bright light spilling out onto the steps and down the walk. As I came closer, I could see people milling around in the kitchen, and there was music coming from the backyard.

I waited until the coast was clear before entering the foyer, easing the door shut behind me. Then, bags in hand, I quickly climbed the stairs, stopping only when I was at the top to look down on the scene below. The kitchen was full of people gathered around the island and table, the French doors thrown open as others milled back and forth from the backyard. There was food laid out on the counters, something that smelled great—my stomach grumbled, reminding me I'd skipped lunch—and several coolers filled with ice and drinks were lined up on the patio. Clearly, this wasn't an impromptu event, something decided at the last minute. Then again, me being here hadn't exactly been a part of Cora and Jamie's plan, either.

Just as I thought this, I heard voices from my right. Looking over, I saw Cora's bedroom door was open. Inside, two women, their backs to me, were gathered around the entrance to her bathroom. One was petite and blonde, wearing jeans and a sweatshirt, her hair in a ponytail. The other was taller, in a black dress and boots, a glass of red wine in one hand.

". . . okay, you know?" the blonde was saying. "You know the minute you stop thinking about it, it'll happen."

"Denise," the brunette said. She shook her head, taking a sip of her wine. "That's not helpful. You're making it sound like it's her fault or something."

"That's not what I meant!" Denise said. "All I'm saying is that you have plenty of time. I mean, it seems like just yesterday when we were all so *relieved* to get our periods when we were late. Remember?"

The brunette shot her a look. "The point is," she said, turning back to whoever they were speaking to, "that you're doing everything right: charting your cycle, taking your temperature, all that. So it's really frustrating when it doesn't happen when you want it to. But you've only just started this whole process, and there are a lot of ways to get pregnant these days. You know?"

I was moving away from the door, having realized this conversation was more than private, even before both women stepped back and I saw my sister walk out of her bathroom, nodding and wiping her eyes. Before she could see me, I flattened myself against the wall by the stairs, holding my breath as I tried to process this information. Cora wanted a *baby*? Clearly, her job and marital status weren't the only things that had changed in the years we'd been apart.

I could hear them still talking, their voices growing louder as they came toward the door. Just before they got to me, I pushed myself back up on the landing, as if I was just coming up the stairs, almost colliding with the blonde in the process.

"Oh!" She gasped, her hand flying up to her chest. "You scared me . . . I didn't see you there."

I glanced past them at Cora, who was watching me

with a guarded expression, as if wondering what, if anything, I'd heard. Closer up, I could see her eyes were red-
rimmed, despite the makeup she'd clearly just reapplied
in an effort to make it seem otherwise. "This is Ruby," she
said. "My sister. Ruby, this is Denise and Charlotte."

"Hi," I said. They were both studying me intently, and
I wondered how much of our story they'd actually been
told.

"It's so nice to meet you!" Denise said, breaking into a
big smile. "I can see the family resemblance, I have to say!"

Charlotte rolled her eyes. "Excuse Denise," she said to
me. "She feels like she always has to say something, even
when it's completely inane."

"How is that inane?" Denise asked.

"Because they don't look a thing alike?" Charlotte replied.

Denise looked at me again. "Maybe not hair color," she
said. "Or complexion. But in the face, around the eyes . . .
you can't see that?"

"No," Charlotte told her, taking another sip of her wine.
After swallowing, she added, "No offense, of course."

"None taken," Cora said, steering them both out of the
doorway and down the stairs. "Now go eat, you guys. Jamie
bought enough barbecue to feed an army, and it's getting
cold."

"You coming?" Charlotte asked her as Denise started
down to the foyer, her ponytail bobbing with each step.

"In a minute."

Cora and I both stood there, watching them as they

made their way downstairs, already bickering about something else as they disappeared into the kitchen. "They were my suitemates in college," she said to me. "The first week I thought they hated each other. Turned out it was the opposite. They've been best friends since they were five."

"Really," I said, peering down into the kitchen, where I could now see Charlotte and Denise working their way through the crowd, saying hello as they went.

"You know what they say. Opposites attract."

I nodded, and for a moment we both just looked down at the party. I could see Jamie now, out in the backyard, standing by a stretch of darkness that I assumed was the pond.

"So," Cora said suddenly, "how was the mall?"

"Good," I said. Then, as it was clear she was waiting for more detail, I added, "I got some good stuff. And a job, actually."

"A job?"

I nodded. "At this jewelry place."

"Ruby, I don't know." She crossed her arms over her chest, leaning back against the rail behind her. "I think you should just be focusing on school for the time being."

"It's only fifteen hours a week, if that," I told her. "And I'm used to working."

"I'm sure you are," she said. "But Perkins Day is more rigorous, academically, than you're used to. I saw your transcripts. If you want to go to college, you really need to make your grades and your applications the number one priority."

College? I thought. "I can do both," I said.

"You don't have to, though. That's just the point." She shook her head. "When I was in high school, I was working thirty-hour weeks—I had no choice. You do."

"This isn't thirty hours," I said.

She narrowed her eyes at me, making it clear I just wasn't getting what she was saying. "Ruby, we want to do this for you, okay? You don't have to make things harder than they have to be just to prove a point."

I opened my mouth, ready to tell her that I'd never asked her to worry about my future, or make it her problem. That I was practically eighteen, as well as being completely capable of making my own decisions about what I could and could not handle. And that being in my life for less than a week didn't make her my mother or guardian, regardless of what it said on any piece of paper.

But just as I drew in a breath to say all this, I looked again at her red eyes and stopped myself. It had been a long day for both of us, and going further into this would only make it longer.

"Fine," I said. "We'll talk about it. Later, though. All right?"

Cora looked surprised. She clearly had not been expecting me to agree, even with provisions. "Fine," she said. She swallowed, then glanced back down at the party. "So, there's food downstairs, if you haven't eaten. Sorry I didn't mention the party before—everything's been kind of crazy."

"It's okay," I said.

She looked at me for another moment. "Right," she said slowly, finally. "Well, I should get back downstairs. Just . . . come down whenever."

I nodded, and then she stepped past me and started down the stairs. Halfway down, she looked back up at me, and I knew she was still wondering what exactly had precipitated this sudden acquiescence. I couldn't tell her, of course, what I'd overheard. It wasn't my business, then or now. But as I started to my room, I kept thinking about what Denise had said, and the resemblance she claimed to be able to see. Maybe my sister and I shared more than we thought. We were both waiting and wishing for something we couldn't completely control: I wanted to be alone, and she the total opposite. It was weird, really, to have something so contrary in common. But at least it was something.

*   *   *

". . . all I can say is, acupuncture works. What? No, it doesn't hurt. At all."

". . . so that was it. I decided that night, no more blind dates. I don't care if he *is* a doctor."

". . . only thirty thousand miles and the original warranty. I mean, it's such a steal!"

I'd been walking through the party for a little more than twenty minutes, nodding at people who nodded at me and picking at my second plate of barbecue, coleslaw, and potato salad. Even though Jamie and Cora's friends seemed nice enough, I was more than happy not to have to talk to anyone, until I heard one voice that cut through all the others.

"Roscoe!"

Jamie was standing at the back of the yard, past the far end of the pond, peering into the dark. As I walked over to him, I got my first up-close look at the pond, which I was surprised to see was already filled with water, a hose dangling in from one side. In the dark it seemed even bigger, and I couldn't tell how deep it was: it looked like it went down forever.

"What's going on?" I asked when I reached him.

"Roscoe's vanished," he said. "He tends to do this. He's not fond of crowds. It's not at the level of the smoke detector, but it's still a problem."

I looked into the dark, then slowly turned back to the pond. "He can swim, right?"

Jamie's eyes widened. "Shit," he said. "I didn't even think about that."

"I'm sure he's not in there," I told him, feeling bad for even suggesting it as he walked to the pond's edge, peering down into it, a worried look on his face. "In fact—"

Then we both heard it: a distinct yap, high-pitched and definitely not obscured by water. It was coming from the fence. "Thank God," Jamie said, turning back in that direction. "Roscoe! Here, boy!"

There was another series of barks, but no Roscoe. "Looks like he might have to be brought in by force," Jamie said with a sigh. "Let me just—"

"I'll get him," I said.

"You sure?"

"Yeah. Go back to the party."

He smiled at me. "All right. Thanks."

I nodded, then put my plate down by a nearby tree as he walked away. Behind me, the party was still going strong, but the voices and music diminished as I walked to the end of the yard, toward the little clump of trees that ran alongside the fence. Not even a week earlier, I'd been running across this same expanse, my thoughts only of getting away. Now, here I was, working to bring back the one thing that had stopped me. Stupid dog.

"Roscoe," I called out as I ducked under the first tree, leaves brushing across my head. "Roscoe!"

No reply. I stopped where I was, letting my eyes adjust to the sudden darkness, then turned back to look at the house. The pond, stretching in between, looked even more vast from here, the lights from the patio shimmering slightly in its surface. Nearer now, I heard another bark. This time it sounded more like a yelp, actually.

"Roscoe," I said, hoping he'd reply again, Marco Polo–style. When he didn't, I took a few more steps toward the fence, repeating his name. It wasn't until I reached it that I heard some frantic scratching from the other side. "Roscoe?"

When I heard him yap repeatedly, I quickened my pace, moving down to where I thought the gate was, running my hand down the fence. Finally, I felt a hinge, and a couple of feet later, a gap. Very small, almost tiny. But still big enough for a little dog, if he tried hard enough, to wriggle through.

When I crouched down, the first thing I saw was Mr. Cross, standing with his hands on his hips by the pool. "All right," he said, looking around him. "I know you're here, I saw what you did to the garbage. Get out and show yourself."

Uh-oh, I thought. Sure enough, I spotted Roscoe cowering behind a potted plant. Mr. Cross clearly hadn't yet seen him, though, as he turned, scanning the yard again. "You have to come out sometime," he said, bending down and looking under a nearby chaise lounge. "And when you do, you'll be sorry."

As if in response, Roscoe yelped, and Mr. Cross spun, spotting him instantly. "Hey," he said. "Get over here!"

Roscoe, though, was not as stupid as I thought. Rather than obeying this order, he took off like a shot, right toward the fence and me. Mr. Cross scrambled to grab him as he passed, missing once, then getting him by one back leg and slowly pulling him back.

"Not so fast," he said, his voice low, as Roscoe struggled to free himself, his tags clanking loudly. Mr. Cross yanked him closer, his hand closing tightly over the dog's narrow neck. "You and I, we have some—"

"Roscoe!"

I yelled so loudly, I surprised myself. But not as much as Mr. Cross, who immediately released the dog, then stood up and took a step back. Our eyes met as Roscoe darted toward me, wriggling through the fence and between my legs, and for a moment, we just looked at each other.

"Hi there," he called out, his voice all friendly-neighbor-like, now. "Sounds like quite a party over there."

I didn't say anything, just stepped back from the fence, putting more space between us.

"He gets into our garbage," he called out, shrugging in a what-can-you-do? kind of way. "Jamie and I have discussed it. It's a problem."

I knew I should respond in some way; I was just standing there like a zombie. But all I could see in my mind was his hand over Roscoe's neck, those fingers stretching.

"Just tell Jamie and Cora to try to keep him on that side, all right?" Mr. Cross said. Then he flashed me that same white-toothed smile. "Good fences make good neighbors, and all that."

Now I did nod, then stepped back, pulling the gate shut. The last glimpse I had of Mr. Cross was of him standing by the pool, hands in his pockets, smiling at me, his face rippled with the lights from beneath the water.

I turned to walk back to our yard, trying to process what I'd just seen and why exactly it had creeped me out so much. I still wasn't sure, even as I came up on Roscoe, who was sniffing along the edge of the pond. But I scooped him up under my arm and carried him the rest of the way, anyway.

*   *   *

As we got closer to the house, I heard the music. At first, it was just a guitar, strumming, but then another instrument came in, more melodic. "All right," someone said over the strumming. "Here's an old favorite."

I put Roscoe on the ground, then stepped closer to the assembled crowd. As a guy in a leather jacket standing in front of me shifted to the left, I saw it was Jamie who had spoken. He was sitting on one of the kitchen chairs, playing a guitar, a beer at his feet, a guy with a banjo nodding beside him as they went into an acoustic version of Led Zeppelin's "Misty Mountain Hop." His voice, I realized, was not bad, and his playing was actually pretty impressive. So strange how my brother-in-law kept surprising me: his incredible career, his passion for ponds, and now, this music. All things I might never have known had I found that gate the first night.

"Having fun?"

I turned around to see Denise, Cora's friend, standing beside me. "Yeah," I said. "It's a big party."

"They always are," she said cheerfully, taking a sip of the beer in her hand. "That's what happens when you're overwhelmingly social. You accumulate a lot of people."

"Jamie does seem kind of magnetic that way."

"Oh, I meant Cora," she replied as the song wrapped up, the crowd breaking into spontaneous applause. "But he is, too, you're right."

"Cora?" I asked.

She looked at me, clearly surprised. "Well . . . yeah," she said. "You know how she is. Total den-mother type, always taking someone under her wing. Drop her in a roomful of strangers, and she'll know everyone in ten minutes. Or less."

"Really," I said.

"Oh, yeah," she replied. "She's just really good with people, you know? Empathetic. I personally couldn't have survived my last breakup without her. Or any of my breakups, really."

I considered this as Denise took another sip of her beer, nodding to a guy in a baseball cap as he pushed past us. "I guess I don't really know that side of her," I said. "I mean, we've been out of touch for a while."

"I know," she said. Then she quickly added, "I mean, she talked about you a lot in college."

"She did?"

"Oh, yeah. Like, all the time," she said, emphatic. "She really—"

"Denise!" someone yelled, and she turned, looking over the shoulder of the guy beside us. "I need to get that number from you, remember?"

"Right," she said, then smiled at me apologetically. "One sec. I'll be right back. . . ."

I nodded as she walked away, wondering what she'd been about to say. Thinking this, I scanned the crowd until I spotted Cora standing just outside the kitchen door with Charlotte. She was smiling, looking much happier than the last time I'd seen her. At some point she'd pulled her hair back, making her look even younger, and she had on a soft-looking sweater, a glass of wine in her hand. Here I'd just assumed all these people were here because of Jamie, but of course my sister could have changed in the years we'd been apart. *She has her own life now*, my mom had told me again and again. This was it, and I wondered what that must be like, to actually get to start again, forget the world you knew before and leave everything behind. Maybe it had even been easy.

Easy. I had a flash of myself, just a week earlier, coming home from a long night at Commercial to the darkness of the yellow house. How much had I thought about it—my home or my school or anything from before—in the last few days? Not as much as I should have. All this time, I'd been so angry Cora had forgotten me, just wiped our shared slate clean, but now I was doing the same thing. Where *was* my mother? Was it really this easy, once you escaped, to just not care?

I suddenly felt tired, overwhelmed, everything that had happened in the last week hitting me at once. I stepped back from the crowd, slipping inside. As I climbed the stairs, I was glad for the enclosed space of my room, even if it, too, was temporary like everything else.

I just need to sleep, I told myself, kicking off my shoes and sinking down onto the bed. I closed my eyes, trying to shut out the singing, doing all I could to push myself into the darkness and stay there until morning.

When I woke up, I wasn't sure how long I'd been asleep, hours or just minutes. My mouth was dry, my arm cramped from where I'd been lying on it. As I rolled over, stretching out, my only thought was to go back to the dream I'd been having, which I couldn't remember, other than it had been good, in that distant, hopeful way unreal things can be. I was closing my eyes, trying to will myself back, when I heard some laughter and clapping from outside. The party was still going on.

When I went out onto my balcony, I saw the crowd had dwindled to about twenty people or so. The banjo player was gone, and just Jamie remained, plucking a few notes as people chatted around him.

"It's getting late," Charlotte, who'd put on a sweater over her dress, said. She stifled a yawn with her hand. "Some of us have to be up early tomorrow."

"It's Sunday," Denise, sitting beside her, said. "Who doesn't sleep in on Sunday?"

"One last song," Jamie said. He glanced around, looking behind him to a place I couldn't see from my vantage point. "What do you think?" he said. "One song?"

"Come on," Denise pleaded. "Just one."

Jamie smiled, then began to play. It was cold outside, at least to me, and I turned back to my room, feeling a yawn of my own rising up, ready to go back to bed. But then I realized there was something familiar about what he was playing; it was like it was tugging at some part of me, faint but persistent, a melody I thought was mine alone.

" 'I am an old woman, named after my mother. . . .' "

The voice was strong and clear, and also familiar, but in a distant way. Similar to the one I knew, and yet different—prettier and not as harsh around the edges.

" 'My old man is another child that's grown old. . . .' "

It was Cora. Cora, her voice pure and beautiful as it worked its way along the notes we'd both heard so many times, the song more than any other that made me think of my mother. I thought of how strange I'd felt earlier, thinking we'd both just forgotten everything. But this was scary, too, to be so suddenly connected, prompting a stream of memories—us in our nightgowns, her reaching out for me, listening to her breathing, steady and soothing, from across a dark room—rushing back too fast to stop.

I felt a lump rise in my throat, raw and throbbing, but even as the tears came I wasn't sure who I was crying for. Cora, my mom, or maybe, just me.

Chapter Six

I could not prove it scientifically. But I was pretty sure Gervais Miller was the most annoying person on the planet.

First, there was the voice. Flat and nasal with no inflection, it came from the backseat, offering up pronouncements and observations. "Your hair's matted in the back," he'd tell me, when I hadn't had adequate time with the blowdryer. Or when I pulled a shirt last-minute from the laundry: "You stink like dryer sheets." Attempts to ignore him by pretending to study only resulted in a running commentary on my academic prowess, or lack thereof. "Intro to Calculus? What are you, stupid?" or "Is that a *B* on that paper?" And so on.

I wanted to punch him. Daily. But of course I couldn't, for two reasons. First, he was just a kid. Second, between his braces and his headgear, there was really no way to get at him and really make an impact. (The fact that I'd actually thought about it enough to draw this conclusion probably should have worried me. It did not.)

When it all got to be too much, I'd just turn around and shoot him the evil eye, which usually did the trick. He'd quiet down for the rest of the ride, maybe even the next day, as well. In time, though, his obnoxiousness would return, often even stronger than before.

In my more rational moments, I tried to feel empathy for Gervais. It had to be hard to be a prodigy, supersmart but so much younger than everyone else at school. Whenever I saw him in the halls, he was always alone, backpack over both shoulders, walking in his weird, leaning-forward way, as if powering up to head-butt someone in the chest.

Being a kid, though, Gervais also lacked maturity, which meant that he found things like burps and farts *hysterical*, and even funnier when they were his own. Put him in a small, enclosed space with two people every morning, and there was no end to the potential for hilarity. Suffice it to say, we always knew what he'd had for breakfast, and even though it was nearing winter, I often kept my window open, and Nate did the same.

On the Monday after Cora's party, though, when I got into the car at seven thirty, something just felt different. A moment later, I realized why: the backseat was empty.

"Where's Gervais?" I asked.

"Doctor's appointment," Nate said.

I nodded, then I settled into my seat to enjoy the ride. My relief must have been palpable, because a moment later Nate said, "You know, he's not so bad."

"Are you joking?" I asked him.

"I mean," he said, "I'll admit he's not the easiest person to be around."

"Please." I rolled my eyes. "He's *horrible*."

"Come on."

"He stinks," I said, holding up a finger. Then, adding another, I said, "And he's rude. And his burps could wake the dead. And if he says one more thing about my books or my classes I'm going to—"

It was at about this point that I realized Nate was looking at me like I was crazy. So I shut up, and we just drove in silence.

"You know," he said after a moment, "it's a shame you feel that way. Because I think he likes you."

I just looked at him. "Did you not hear him tell me I was fat the other day?"

"He didn't say you were *fat*," Nate replied. "He said you looked a little rotund."

"How is that different?"

"You know," he said, "I think you're forgetting Gervais is twelve."

"I assure you I am not."

"And," he continued, "boys at twelve aren't exactly slick with the ladies."

"'Slick with the ladies'?" I said. "Are *you* twelve?"

He switched lanes, then slowed for a light. "He teases you," he said slowly, as if I was stupid, "*because* he likes you."

"Gervais does not like me," I said, louder this time.

"Whatever." The light changed. "But he never talked to Heather when she rode with us."

"He didn't?"

"Nope. He just sat back there, passing gas, without comment."

"Nice," I said.

"It really was." Nate downshifted as we slowed for a red light. "All I'm saying is that maybe he just wants to be friends but doesn't exactly know how to do it. So he says you smell like trees or calls you rotund. That's what kids do."

I rolled my eyes, looking out the window. "Why," I said, "would Gervais want to be friends with me?"

"Why wouldn't he?"

"Because I'm not a friendly person?" I said.

"You're not?"

"Are you saying you think I am?"

"I wouldn't say you're unfriendly."

"I would," I said.

"Really."

I nodded.

"Huh. Interesting."

The light changed, and we moved forward.

"Interesting," I said, "meaning what?"

He shrugged, switching lanes. "Just that I don't see you that way. I mean, you're reserved, maybe. Guarded, definitely. But not unfriendly."

"Maybe you just don't know me," I said.

"Maybe," he agreed. "But unfriendly is usually one of those things you pick up on right away. You know, like B.O. There's no hiding it if it's there."

I considered this as we approached another light. "So when we met that first night," I said, "by the fence, you thought I was friendly?"

"I didn't think you weren't," he said.

"I wasn't very nice to you."

"You were jumping a fence. I didn't take it personally."

"I didn't even thank you for covering for me."

"So?"

"So I should have. Or at least not been such a bitch to you the next day."

Nate shrugged, putting on his blinker. "It's not a big deal."

"It is, though," I said. "You don't have to be so nice to everyone, you know."

"Ah," he said, "but that's the thing. I do. I'm compulsively friendly."

Of course he was. And I'd noticed it first thing that night by the fence, because it, too, was something you couldn't hide. Maybe I could have tried to explain myself more to Nate, that there was a reason I was this way, but he was already reaching forward, turning on the radio and flipping to WCOM, the local community station he listened to in the mornings. The DJ, some girl named Annabel, was announcing the time and temperature. Then she put on a song, something peppy with a bouncy beat. Nate turned it up, and we let it play all the way to school.

When we got out of the car, we walked together to the green, and then I peeled off to my locker, just like always, while he headed to the academic building. After I'd stuffed in a few books and taken out a couple of others, I shut the door, hoisting my bag back over my shoulder. Across the green, I could see Nate approaching his first-period class. Jake Bristol and two other guys were standing around outside. As he walked up, Jake reached out a hand for a high five, while the other two stepped back, waving him through. I was late myself, with other things to think about. But I stayed there and watched as Nate laughed and stepped

through the door, and they all fell in, following along behind him, before I turned and walked away.

*   *   *

"All right, people," Ms. Conyers said, clapping her hands.
"Let's get serious. You've got fifteen minutes. Start asking
questions."

The room got noisy, then noisier, as people left their seats
and began to move around the room, notebooks in hand.
After slogging my way through an extensive test on *David
Copperfield* (ten IDs, two essays), all I wanted to do was collapse. Instead, to get us started on our "oral definition" projects, we were supposed to interview our classmates, getting
their opinions on what our terms meant. This was good;
I figured I needed all the help I could get, considering the
way I defined my own family kept changing.

It had been almost two weeks since I'd come to Cora's,
and I was slowly getting adjusted. It wasn't like things were
perfect, but we had fallen into a routine, as well as an understanding. For my part, I'd accepted that leaving, at least
right now, was not in my best interest. So I'd unpacked my
bag, finally unloading my few possessions into the big, empty drawers and closet. I wasn't ready to spread out farther
into the house itself—I took my backpack upstairs with me
as soon as I came home and stood by the dryer as my clothes
finished, then folded them right away. It was a big place.
God only knew how much could get lost there.

It was weird to be living in such sudden largess, especially after the yellow house. Instead of stretching a pack
of pasta over a few days and scraping together change for

groceries, I had access to a fully packed pantry, as well as a freezer stocked with just about every entrée imaginable. And that wasn't even counting the "pocket money" Jamie was always trying to give me: twenty bucks for lunch here, another forty in case I needed school supplies there. Maybe someone else would have accepted all this easily, but I was still so wary, unsure of what would be expected of me in return, that at first I refused it. Over time, though, he wore me down and I gave in, although spending it was another matter entirely. I just felt better with it stashed away. After all, you never knew when something, or everything, might change.

Cora had compromised, as well. After much discussion—and some helpful lobbying from Jamie—it was decided I could work for Harriet through the holidays, at which point we'd "reconvene on the subject" and "evaluate its impact on my grades and school performance." As part of the deal, I also had to agree to attend at least one therapy session, an idea I was not at all crazy about. I needed the money, though, so I'd bitten my tongue and acquiesced. Then we'd reached across the kitchen island, shaking on it, her hand small and cool, her strong grip surprising me more than it probably should have.

I'd been thinking about my mother a lot, even more than when she'd first left, which was weird. Like it took a while to really miss her, or let myself do so. Sometimes at night, I dreamed about her; afterward, I always woke up with the feeling that she'd just passed through the room, convinced I could smell lingering smoke or her perfume in the air. Other times, when I was half asleep, I was sure I

could feel her sitting on the side of my bed, one hand strok-
ing my hair, the way she'd sometimes done late at night or
early in the morning. Back then, I'd always been irritated,
wishing she'd go to sleep herself or leave me alone. Now,
even when my conscious mind told me it was just a dream,
I remained still, wanting it to last.

When I woke up, I always tried to keep this image in
my head, but it never stayed. Instead, there was only how
she'd looked the last time I'd seen her, the day before she'd
left. I'd come home from school to find her both awake
and alone, for once. By then, things hadn't been good for
a while, and I'd expected her to look bleary, the way she
always did after a few beers, or sad or annoyed. But instead,
as she turned her head, her expression had been one of surprise, and I remembered thinking maybe she'd forgotten
about me, or hadn't been expecting me to return. Like it
was me who was leaving, and I just didn't know it yet.

In daylight, I was more factual, wondering if she'd made
it to Florida, or if she was still with Warner. Mostly, though,
I wondered if she had tried to call the yellow house, made
any effort to try and locate me. I wasn't sure I even wanted
to talk to her or see her, nor did I know if I ever would. But
it was important to simply be sought, even if you didn't ever
want to be found.

What is family? I'd written in my notebook that first
day, and as I opened it up now I saw the rest of the page was
blank, except for the definition I'd gotten from the dictionary: *a set of relations, esp. parents and children.* Eight words,
and one was an abbreviation. If only it was really that easy.

Now Ms. Conyers called out for everyone to get to work,

so I turned to Olivia, figuring I'd hit her up first. She hardly looked like she was in the mood for conversation, though, sitting slumped in her chair. Her eyes were red, a tissue clutched in one hand as she pulled the Jackson High letter jacket she always wore more tightly around herself.

"Remember," Ms. Conyers was saying, "you're not just asking what your term means literally, but what it means to the person you're speaking with. Don't be afraid to get personal."

Considering Olivia was hardly open on a *good* day, I decided maybe I should take a different tack. My only other option, though, was Heather Wainwright, on my other side, who was also looking around for someone to talk to, and I wasn't sure I wanted to go there.

"Well? Are we doing this or not?"

I turned back to Olivia. She was still sitting facing forward, as if she hadn't spoken at all. "Oh," I said, then shot a pointed look at the tissue in her hand. In response, she crumpled it up smaller, tucking it down deeper between her fingers. "All right. What does family mean to you?"

She sighed, reaching up to rub her nose. All around us, I could hear people chattering, but she was silent. Finally she said, "Do you know Micah Sullivan?"

"Who?"

"Micah Sullivan," she repeated. "Senior? On the football team? Hangs out with Rob Dufresne?"

It wasn't until I'd heard this last name that I realized she was talking about Jackson. Rob Dufresne had sat across from me in bio sophomore year. "Micah," I said, trying to think. Already, my classmates at Jackson were a big blur, their faces all running together. "Is he really short?"

"No," she snapped. I shrugged, picking up my pen. Then she said, "Okay, so he's not as *tall* as some people."

"Drives a blue truck?"

Now she looked at me. "Yeah," she said slowly. "That's him."

"I know of him."

"Did you ever see him with a girl? At school?"

I thought for another moment, but all I could see was Rob Dufresne going dead pale as we contemplated our frog dissection. "Not that I remember," I said. "But like you said, it's a big place."

She considered this for a moment. Then, turning to face me, she said, "So you never saw him all over some field-hockey player, a blonde with a tattoo on her lower back. Minda or Marcy or something like that?"

I shook my head. She looked at me for a long moment, as if not sure whether to trust me, then faced forward again, pulling her jacket more tightly around her. "Family," she announced. "They're the people in your life you don't get to pick. The ones that are given to you, as opposed to those you get to choose."

Since my mind was still on Micah and the field-hockey player, I had to scramble to write this down. "Okay," I said. "What else?"

"You're bound to them by blood," she continued, her voice flat. "Which, you know, gives you that much more in common. Diseases, genetics, hair, and eye color. It's like, they're part of your blueprint. If something's wrong with you, you can usually trace it back to them."

I nodded and kept writing.

"But," she said, "even though you're stuck with them, at the same time, they're also stuck with you. So that's why they always get the front rows at christenings and funerals. Because they're the ones that are there, you know, from the beginning to the end. Like it or not."

Like it or not, I wrote. Then I looked at these words and all the others I'd scribbled down. It wasn't much. But it was a start. "Okay," I said. "Let's do yours."

Just then, though, the bell rang, triggering the usual cacophony of chairs being banged around, backpacks zipping, and voices rising. Ms. Conyers was saying something about having at least four definitions by the next day, not that I could really hear her over all the noise. Olivia had already grabbed her phone, flipping it open and calling someone on speed dial. As I put my notebook away, I watched her stuff the tissue in her pocket, then run a hand over her braids as she got to her feet.

"It's Melissa," I told her as she turned to walk away.

She stopped, then looked at me, slowly lowering her phone from her ear. "What?"

"The blonde with the back tattoo. Her name is Melissa West," I said, picking up my bag. "She's a sophomore, a total skank. And she plays soccer, not field hockey."

People were moving past us now, en route to the door, but Olivia stayed where she was, not even seeming to notice as Heather Wainwright passed by, glancing at her red eyes before moving on.

"Melissa West," she repeated.

I nodded.

"Thanks."

"You're welcome," I told her. Then she put her phone back to her ear slowly, and walked away.

* * *

When I came out of school that afternoon after final bell, Jamie was waiting for me.

He was leaning against his car, which was parked right outside the main entrance, his arms folded over his chest. As soon as I saw him, I stopped walking, hanging back as people streamed past me on either side, talking and laughing. Maybe I was just being paranoid, but the last time someone had showed up unexpectedly for me at school, it hadn't been to deliver good news.

In fact, it wasn't until after I'd begun to mentally list the various offenses for which I *could* be busted that I realized there really weren't any. All I'd done lately was go to school, go to work, and study. I hadn't even been out on a weekend night. Still, I stayed where I was, hesitant out of force of habit or something else, until the crowd cleared and he spotted me.

"Hey," he called out, raising his hand. I waved back, then pulled my bag more tightly over my shoulder as I started toward him. "You working today?"

I shook my head. "No."

"Good. I need to talk to you about something."

He stepped away from the car, pulling the passenger door open for me. Once in, I forced myself to take a breath as I watched him round the front bumper, then get in and join me. He didn't crank the engine, though, just sat there instead.

Suddenly, it hit me. He was going to tell me I had to leave. Of course. The very minute I allowed myself to relax, they would decide they'd had enough of me. Even worse, as I thought this, I felt my breath catch, suddenly realizing how much I didn't want it to happen.

"The thing is . . ." Jamie said, and now I could hear my heart in my ears. "It's about college."

This last word—*college*—landed in my ears with a clunk. It was like he'd said *Minnesota* or *fried chicken*, that unexpected. "College," I repeated.

"You are a senior," he said as I sat there, still blinking, trying to decide if I should be relieved or more nervous. "And while you haven't exactly had the best semester—not your fault, of course—you did take the SATs last year, and your scores weren't bad. I was just in talking to the guidance office. Even though it's already November, they think that if we really hustle, we can still make the application deadlines."

"You went to the guidance office?" I asked.

"Yeah," he said. I must have looked surprised, because then he added, "I know, I know. This is more Cora's department. But she's in court all week, and besides, we decided that maybe . . ."

I glanced over at him as he trailed off, leaving this unfinished. "You decided maybe what?"

He looked embarrassed. "That it was better for me to bring this up with you. You know, since Cor was kind of tough on you about your job at first, and the therapy thing. She's tired of being the bad guy."

An image of a cartoon character twirling a mustache as

they tied someone to the train tracks immediately popped into my head. "Look," I said, "school isn't really part of my plans."

"Why not?"

I probably should have had an answer to this, but the truth was that I'd never actually been asked it before. Everyone else assumed the same thing that I had from day one: girls like me just didn't go further than high school, if they even got that far. "It's just . . ." I said, stalling. "It's not really been a priority."

Jamie nodded slowly. "It's not too late, though."

"I think it is."

"But if it isn't?" he asked. "Look, Ruby. I get that this is your choice. But the thing is, the spring is a long way away. A lot could change between now and then. Even your mind."

I didn't say anything. The student parking lot was almost empty now, except for a couple of girls with field-hockey sticks and duffel bags sitting on the curb.

"How's this," he said. "Just make a deal with me and agree to apply. That way, you're not ruling anything out. Come spring, you still decide what happens next. You just have more options."

"You're assuming I'll get in somewhere. That's a big assumption."

"I've seen your transcripts. You're not a bad student."

"I'm no brain, either."

"Neither was I," he said. "In fact, in the interest of full disclosure, I'll tell you I wasn't into the idea of higher education, either. After high school, I wanted to take my guitar and move to New York to play in coffeehouses and get a record deal."

"You did?"

"Yup." He smiled, running his hand over the steering wheel. "However, my parents weren't having it. I was going to college, like it or not. So I ended up at the U, planning to leave as soon as I could. The first class I took was coding for computers."

"And the rest is history," I said.

"Nah." He shook his head. "The rest is now."

I eased my grip on my bag, letting it rest on the floorboard between my feet. The truth was, I liked Jamie. So much that I wished I could just be honest with him and say the real reason that even applying scared me: it was one more connection at a time when I wanted to be doing the total opposite. Yes, I'd decided to stay here as long as I had to, but only because really, I'd had no choice. If I went to college—at least this way, with him and Cora backing me— I'd be in debt, both literally and figuratively, at the one time when all I wanted was to be free and clear, owing no one anything at all.

Sitting there, though, I knew I couldn't tell him this. So instead, I said, "So I guess you never have regrets. Wish you'd gone to New York, like you wanted."

Jamie sat back, leaning his head on the seat behind him. "Sometimes I do. Like on a day like today, when I'm dealing with this new advertising campaign, which is making me nuts. Or when everyone in the office is whining and I think my head's going to explode. But it's only in moments. And anyway, if I hadn't gone to the U, I wouldn't have met your sister. So that would have changed everything."

"Right," I said. "How did you guys meet, anyway?"

"Talk about being the bad guy." He chuckled, looking down at the steering wheel, then explained, "She doesn't exactly come across that well in the story."

I had to admit I was intrigued now. "Why not?"

"Because she yelled at me," he said flatly. I raised my eyebrows. "Okay, she'd say she didn't yell, that she was just being assertive. But her voice *was* raised. That's indisputable."

"Why was she yelling at you?"

"Because I was playing guitar outside on the dorm steps one night. Cor's not exactly pleasant when you get between her and her sleep, you know?" I actually didn't but nodded, anyway. "So there I was, first week of classes freshman year, strumming away on a nice late summer night, and suddenly this girl just opens up her window and lets me have it."

"Really."

"Oh, yeah. She just went ballistic. Kept saying it was so inconsiderate, keeping people up with my noise. That's what she called it. Noise. I mean, here I was, thinking I was an artiste, you know?"He laughed again, shaking his head.

I said, "You're awfully good-natured about it, considering."

"Yeah, well," he said. "That was just that first night. I didn't know her yet."

I didn't say anything, instead just looked down at my backpack strap, running it through my fingers.

"My point is," Jamie continued, "not everything's perfect, especially at the beginning. And it's all right to have a little bit of regret every once in a while. It's when you feel it all the time and can't do anything about it . . . that's when you get into trouble."

Over on the curb, the girls with the field-hockey sticks were laughing at something, their voices muffled by my window. "Like," I said, "say, not applying to college, and then wishing you had?"

He smiled. "Okay, fine. So subtlety is not my strong suit. Do we have a deal or what?"

"This isn't a deal," I pointed out. "It's just me agreeing to what you want."

"Not true," he replied. "You get something in return."

"Right," I said. "A chance. An opportunity I wouldn't have otherwise."

"And something else, too."

"What's that?"

"Just wait," he said, reaching forward to crank the engine. "You'll see."

*   *   *

"A fish?" I said. "Are you serious?"

"Totally!" Jamie grinned. "What more could you want?"

I figured it was best not to answer this, and instead turned my attention back to the round tank between us, which was filled with white koi swimming back and forth. In rows all around us were more tanks, also filled with fish I'd never heard of before: comets, shubunkin, mosquito fish, as well as many other colors of koi, some solid, some speckled with black or red.

"I'm going to go find someone to test my water, make sure it's all balanced," he said, pulling a small plastic container out of his jacket pocket. "Take your time, all right? Pick a good one."

A good one, I thought, looking back down at the fish in the tank beneath me. Like you could tell with a glance, somehow judge their temperament or hardiness. I'd never had a fish—or any pet, for that matter—but from what I'd heard they could die at the drop of a hat, even when kept in a safe, clean tank. Who knew what could happen outside, in a pond open to the elements and everything else?

"Do you need help with the fish?"

I turned around, prepared to say no, only to be startled to see Heather Wainwright standing behind me. She had on jeans and a DONOVAN LANDSCAPING T-shirt, a sweater tied around her waist, and seemed equally surprised by the sight of me.

"Hey," she said. "It's Ruby, right?"

"Yeah. I'm, um, just looking."

"That's cool." She stepped up to the tank, next to me, dropping a hand down into the water: as she did so, the fish immediately swam toward her, circling her fingers. She glanced up at me and said, "They get crazy when they think you're going to feed them. They're like begging dogs, practically."

"Really."

"Yep." She pulled her hand out and wiped it on her jeans. I had to admit, I was surprised to see she worked at a place like this. For some reason, I would have pegged her as the retail type, more at home in a mall. No, I realized a beat later. That was me. Weird. "The goldfish aren't quite as aggressive. But the koi are prettier. So it's a tradeoff."

"My brother-in-law just built a pond," I told her as she bent down and adjusted a valve on the side of the tank. "He's obsessed with it."

"They are pretty awesome," she said. "How big did he go?"

"Big." I glanced over at the greenhouses, where Jamie had headed. "He should be back soon. I'm supposed to be picking a fish."

"Just one?"

"It's my personal fish," I told her, and she laughed. Never in a million years would I have imagined myself here, by a fish tank, with Heather Wainwright. Then again, I wasn't supposed to be here with anyone, period. What I'd noticed, though, was that more and more lately, when I tried to picture where I *did* belong, I couldn't. At first, it had been easy to place myself in my former life, sitting at a desk at Jackson, or in my old bedroom. But now it was like I was already losing my old life at the yellow house, without this one feeling real, either. I was just stuck somewhere in the middle, vague and undefined.

"So you're friends with Nate," Heather said after a moment, adjusting the valve again. "Right?"

I glanced over at her. The whole school had noticed, or so it seemed; it only made sense she would have, as well. "We're neighbors," I told her. "My sister lives behind him."

She reached up to tuck a stray piece of hair behind her ear. "I guess you've heard we used to go out," she said.

"Yeah?" I said.

She nodded. "We broke up this fall. It was big news for a while there." She sighed, touching her hand to the water again. "Then Rachel Webster got pregnant. Which I wasn't happy about, of course. But it did make people stop talking about us, at least for a little while."

"Perkins Day is a small school," I said.

"Tell me about it." She sat back, wiping her hand on her jeans, then looked over at me. "So . . . how's he doing these days?"

"Nate?" I asked.

She nodded.

"I don't know," I said. "Fine, I guess. Like I said, we're not that close."

She considered this as we both watched the fish circling, first one way, then another. "Yeah," she said finally. "He's hard to know, I guess."

This hadn't been what I meant, actually, not at all. If anything, in my mind, Nate was too easy to read, all part of that friendly thing. But saying this seemed odd at that moment, so I just stayed quiet.

"Anyway," Heather continued a beat later, "I just . . . I'm glad you and Nate are friends. He's a really good guy."

I had to admit this was not what I was expecting—it wasn't exactly ex-girlfriend behavior. Then again, she was the queen of compassion, if her time logged at the HELP table was any indication. Of course Nate would fall in love with a *nice* girl. What else did I expect?

"Nate has a lot of friends," I told her now. "I doubt one more makes that much of a difference."

Heather studied my face for a moment. "Maybe not," she said finally. "But you never know, right?"

What? I thought, but then I felt a hand clap my shoulder; Jamie was behind me. "So the water's good," he said. "You find the perfect one yet?"

"How do you even pick?" I asked Heather.

"Just go on instinct," she replied. "Whichever one speaks to you."

Jamie nodded sagely. "There you go," he said to me. "Let the fish speak."

"There's also the issue of who runs from the net," Heather added. "That often makes the decision for you."

In the end, it was a mix of both these things—me pointing and Heather swooping in—that got me my fish. I went with a small white koi, which looked panicked as I held it in its plastic bag, circling again and again as Jamie picked out a total of twenty shubunkins and comets. He also got several more koi, although no other white ones, so I could always find mine in the crowd.

"What are you going to name it?" he asked me as Heather shot oxygen from a canister into the bags for the ride home.

"Let's just see if it survives first," I said.

"Of course it will," he replied as if there was no question.

Heather rang us up, then carried the bags out to the car, where she carefully arranged them in a series of cardboard boxes in the backseat.

"You will need to acclimate them slowly," she explained as the fish swam around and around in their bags, their faces popping up, then disappearing. "Put the bags in the water for about fifteen minutes so they can get adjusted to the temperature. Then open the bags and let a little bit of your pond water in to mix with what they're in. Give it another fifteen minutes or so, and then you can let them go."

"So the key is to ease them into it," Jamie said.

"It's a big shock to their systems, leaving the tank," Heather replied, shutting the back door. "But they usually do fine in the end. It's herons and waterbirds you really need to worry about. One swoop, and they can do some serious damage."

"Thanks for all your help," Jamie told her as he slid back behind the wheel.

"No problem," she said. "See you at school, Ruby."

"Yeah," I said. "See you."

As Jamie began backing out, he glanced over at me. "Friend of yours?"

"No," I said. "We just have a class together."

He nodded, not saying anything else as we pulled out into traffic. It was rush hour, and we didn't talk as we hit mostly red lights heading toward home. Because my fish was alone, in a small bag, I was holding it in my lap, and I could feel it darting from one side to the other. *It's a big shock to their systems*, Heather had said. I lifted the bag up to eye level, looking at my fish again. Who knew if it—or anything—would survive the week, or even the night.

Still, when we got back to Cora's, I went with Jamie to the backyard, then crouched by the pond, easing my bag into it and watching it bob there for those fifteen minutes before letting in that little bit of water, just as I was told. When I finally went to release the koi, it was almost totally dark outside. But even so, I could see my fish, white and bright, as it made its way past the opening into the vast body of water that lay beyond. I expected it to hesitate, or even turn back, but it didn't. It just swam, quick enough to blur, before diving down to the bottom, out of sight.

*　　*　　*

When Jamie first called up the stairs to me, I was sure I'd heard wrong.

"Ruby! One of your friends is here to see you!"

Instinctively, I looked at the clock—it was 5:45, on a random Tuesday—then out the window over at Nate's house. His pool lights were on, and I wondered if he'd come over for some reason. But surely, Jamie would've identified him by name.

"Okay," I replied, pushing my chair back and walking out into the hallway. "But who is—?"

By then, though, I'd already looked down into the foyer and gotten the answer as I spotted Peyton, who was standing there patting Roscoe as Jamie looked on. When she glanced up and saw me, her face broke into a wide smile. "Hey!" she said, with her trademark enthusiasm. "I found you!"

I nodded. I knew I should have been happy to see her— as unlike Nate or Heather, she actually *was* my friend—but instead I felt strangely uneasy. After all, I'd never even invited her into the yellow house, always providing excuses about my mom needing her sleep or it being a bad time— keeping the personal, well, personal. But now here she was, already in.

"Hey," I said when I reached the foyer. "What's going on?"

"Are you surprised?" she asked, giggling. "You would

not believe what I went through to track you down. I was like Nancy Drew or something!"

Beside her, Jamie smiled, and I forced myself to do the same, even as I noticed two things: that she reeked of smoke and that her eyes were awfully red, her mascara pooled beneath them. Peyton had always been bad with Visine, and clearly this had not changed. Plus, even though she was dressed as cute as ever—hair pulled back into two low ponytails, wearing jeans and red shirt with an apple on it, a sweater tied loosely around her waist—she had always been the kind of person who, when high, looked it, despite her best efforts. "How did you find me?" I asked her.

"Well," she said, holding her hands, palms facing out and up to set the scene, "it was like this. You'd told me you were living in Wildflower Ridge, so—"

"I did?" I asked, trying to think back.

"Sure. On the phone that day, remember?" she said. "So I figure, it can't be that big of a neighborhood, right? But then, of course, I get over here and it's freaking *huge*."

I glanced at Jamie, who was following this story, a mild smile on his face. Clueless, or so I hoped.

"Anyway," Peyton continued, "I'm driving around, getting myself totally lost, and then I finally just pull over on the side of the road, giving up. And right then, then I see this, like, totally hot guy walking a dog down the sidewalk. So I rolled down my window and asked him if he knew you."

Even before she continued, I had a feeling what was coming next.

"And he did!" she said, clapping her hands. "So he pointed me this way. Very nice guy, by the way. His name was—"

"Nate," I finished for her.

"Yeah!" She laughed again, too loudly, and I got another whiff of smoke, even stronger this time. Like I hadn't spent ages teaching her about the masking ability of breath mints. "And here I am. It all worked out in the end."

"Clearly," I said, just as I heard the door that led from the garage to the kitchen open then shut.

"Hello?" Cora called out. Roscoe, ears perked, trotted toward the sound of her voice. "Where is everybody?"

"We're in here," Jamie replied. A moment later, she appeared in the entrance to the foyer in her work clothes, the mail in one hand. "This is Ruby's friend Peyton. This is Cora."

"You're Ruby's sister?" Peyton asked. "That's so cool!"

Cora gave her the once-over—subtly, I noticed—then extended her hand. "Nice to meet you."

"You, too," Peyton replied, pumping it eagerly. "Really nice."

My sister was smiling politely. Her expression barely changed, only enough to make it more than clear to me that she had seen—and probably smelled—what Jamie had not. Like Peyton's mom, she didn't miss much. "Well," she said. "I guess we should think about dinner?"

"Right," Jamie said. "Peyton, can you stay?"

"Oh," Peyton said, "actually—"

"She can't," I finished for her. "So, um, I'm going to go ahead and give her the tour, if that's all right."

"Sure, sure," Jamie said. Beside him, Cora was studying Peyton, her eyes narrowed, as I nodded for her to follow me into the kitchen. "Be sure to show her the pond!"

"Pond?" Peyton said, but by then I was already tugging her onto the deck, the door swinging shut behind us. I waited until we were a few feet away from the house before stopping and turning to face her.

"What are you *doing*?" I asked.

She raised her eyebrows. "What do you mean?"

"Peyton, you're blinded. And my sister could totally tell."

"Oh, she could not," she said easily, waving her hand. "I used Visine."

I rolled my eyes, not even bothering to address this. "You shouldn't have come here."

For a moment, she looked hurt, then pouty. "And you should have called me," she replied. "You said you were going to. Remember?"

Cora and Jamie were by the island in the kitchen now, looking out at us. "I'm still getting settled in," I told her, but she turned, ignoring this as she walked over to the pond. In her ponytails and in profile, she looked like a little kid. "Look, this is complicated, okay?"

"For me, too," she said, peering down into the water. As I stepped up beside her I saw it was too dark to see anything, but you could hear the pump going, the distant waterfall. "I mean, a lot's happened since you left, Ruby."

I glanced back inside. Jamie was gone, but Cora remained, and she was looking right at me. "Like what?"

Peyton glanced over at me, then shrugged. "I just . . ."

she said softly. "I wanted to talk to you. That's all."

"About what?"

She took in a breath, then let it out just as Roscoe popped through the dog door and began to trot toward us. "Nothing," she said, turning back to the water. "I mean, I miss you. We used to hang out every day, and then you just disappear. It's weird."

"I know," I said. "And believe me, I'd go back to the way things were in a minute if I could. But it's just not an option. This is my life now. At least for a little while."

She considered this as she looked at the pond, then turned slightly, taking in the house rising up behind us. "It is different," she said.

"Yeah," I agreed. "It is."

In the end, Peyton stayed for less than an hour, just long enough to get a tour, catch me up on the latest Jackson gossip, and turn down two more invitations to stay for dinner from Jamie, who seemed beside himself with the fact that I actually had a real, live friend. Cora, however, had a different take, or so I found out later, when I was folding clothes and looked up to see her standing in my bedroom doorway.

"So," she said, "tell me about Peyton."

I focused on pairing up socks as I said, "Not much to tell."

"Have you two been friends a long time?"

I shrugged. "A year or so. Why?"

"No reason." She leaned against the doorjamb, watching as I moved on to jeans. "She just seemed . . . sort of scattered, I guess. Not exactly your type."

It was tempting to point out that Cora herself wasn't exactly in a position to claim to know me that well. But I held my tongue, still folding.

"Anyway," she continued, "in the future, though, if you could let us know when you were having people over, I'd appreciate it."

Like I'd had so many people showing up—all one of them!—that this was suddenly a problem. "I didn't know she was coming," I told her. "I forgot she even knew where I was staying."

She nodded. "Well, just keep it in mind. For next time."

Next time, I thought. *Whatever.* "Sure," I said aloud.

I kept folding, waiting for her to say something else. To go further, insinuating more, pulling me into an argument I didn't deserve, much less want to have. But instead, she just stepped back out of the doorway and started down the hall to her own room. A moment later, she called out for me to sleep well, and I responded in kind, these nicer last words delivered like an afterthought to find themselves, somewhere, in the space between us.

Chapter Seven

Usually I worked for Harriet from three thirty till seven, during which time she was supposed to take off to eat a late lunch and run errands. Invariably, however, she ended up sticking around for most of my shift, her purse in hand as she fretted and puttered, unable to actually leave.

"I'm sorry," she'd say, reaching past me to adjust a necklace display I'd already straightened twice. "It's just . . . I like things a certain way, you know?"

I knew. Harriet had built her business from the ground up, starting straight out of art school, and the process had been difficult, involving struggle, the occasional compromise of artistic integrity, and a near brush with bankruptcy. Still, she'd soldiered on, just her against the world. Which was why, I figured, it was so hard for her to adjust to the fact that now there were two of us.

Still, sometimes her neurosis was so annoying—following along behind me, checking and redoing each thing I did, taking over every task so I sometimes spent entire shifts doing nothing at all—that I wondered why she'd bothered to hire me. One day, when she had literally let me do nothing but dust for hours, I finally asked her.

"Truth?" she said. I nodded. "I'm overwhelmed. My orders are backed up, I'm constantly behind in my books, and

I'm completely exhausted. If it wasn't for caffeine, I'd be dead right now."

"Then let me help you."

"I'm *trying*." She took a sip from her ever-present coffee cup. "But it's hard. Like I said, I've always been a one-woman operation. That way, I'm responsible for everything, good and bad. And I'm afraid if I relinquish any control . . ."

I waited for her to finish. When she didn't, I said, "You'll lose everything."

Her eyes widened. "Yes!" she said. "How did you know?"

Like I was going to go there. "Lucky guess," I said instead.

"This business is the only thing I've ever had that was all mine," she said. "I'm scared to death something will happen to it."

"Yeah," I said as she took another gulp of coffee, "but accepting help doesn't have to mean giving up control."

It occurred to me, saying this, that I should take my own advice. Thinking back over the last few weeks, however—staying at Cora's, my college deal with Jamie—I realized maybe I already had.

Harriet was so obsessed with her business that, from what I could tell, she had no personal life whatsoever. During the day, she worked at the kiosk; at night, she went straight home, where she stayed up into the early hours making more pieces. Maybe this was how she wanted it. But there were clearly others who would welcome a change.

Like Reggie from Vitamin Me, for example. When he was going for food, he always stopped to see if she needed anything. If things were slow, he'd drift over to the open space between our two stalls to shoot the breeze. When

Harriet said she was tired, he instantly offered up B-complexes; if she sneezed, he was like a quick draw with the echinacea. One day after he'd brought her an herbal tea and some ginkgo biloba—she'd been complaining she couldn't remember anything anymore—she said, "He's just so nice. I don't know why he goes to so much trouble."

"Because he likes you," I said.

She jerked her head, surprised, and looked at me. "What?"

"He likes you," I repeated. To me, this was a no-brainer, as obvious as daylight. "You know that."

"Reggie?" she'd said, her surprised tone making it clear she did not. "No, no. We're just friends."

"The man gave you ginkgo," I pointed out. "Friends don't do that."

"Of course they do."

"Harriet, come on."

"I don't even know what you're talking about. I mean, we're friends, but the idea of something more is just . . ." she said, continuing to thumb through the receipts. Then, suddenly, she looked up at me, then over at Reggie, who was helping some woman with some protein powder. "Oh my God. Do you really think?"

"Yes," I said flatly, eyeing the ginkgo, which he'd piled neatly on the register with a note. Signed with a smiley face. "I do."

"Well, that's just ridiculous," she said, her face flushing.

"Why? Reggie's nice."

"I don't have time for a relationship," she said, picking up her coffee and taking a gulp. The ginkgo she now eyed warily, like it was a time bomb, not a supplement. "It's al-most Christmas. That's my busiest time of the year."

"It doesn't have to be one or the other."

"There's just no way," she said flatly, shaking her head.

"Why not?"

"Because it won't work." She banged open the register drawer, sliding in the receipts. "Right now, I can only focus on myself and this business. Everything else is a distraction."

I was about to tell her this didn't have to be true, neces-sarily. That she and Reggie already had a relationship: they were friends, and she could just see how it went from there. But really, I had to respect where she was coming from, even if in this case I didn't agree with it. After all, I'd been determined to be a one-woman operation, as well, although lately this had been harder than you'd think. I'd found this out firsthand a few days earlier, when I was in the kitchen with Cora, minding my own business, and suddenly found myself swept up in Jamie's holiday plans.

"Wait," Cora said, looking down at the shirt on the table in front of her. "What is this for again?"

"Our Christmas card!" Jamie said, reaching into the bag he was holding to pull out another shirt—also a denim but-ton-up, identical to hers—and handing it to me. "Remem-ber how I said I wanted to do a photo this year?"

"You want us to wear matching shirts?" Cora asked as he took out yet one more, holding it up against his chest. "Seriously?"

"Yeah," Jamie said. "It's gonna be great. Oh, and wait. I forgot the best part!"

He turned, jogging out of the room into the foyer.

Cora and I just stared at each other across the table.

"Matching shirts?" I said.

"Don't panic," she said, although her own expression was hardly calm. She looked down at her shirt again. "At least, not yet."

"Check it out," Jamie said, coming back into the room. He had something behind his back, which he now presented to us, with a flourish. "For Roscoe!"

It was—yes—a denim shirt. Dog sized. With a red bow tie sewn on. Maybe I should have been grateful mine didn't have one of these, but frankly, at that moment, I was too horrified.

"Jamie," Cora said as he bent down beneath the table. I could hear banging around, along with some snuffling, as I assumed he attempted to wrangle Roscoe, who'd been dead asleep, into his outfit. "I'm all for a Christmas card. But do you really think we need to match?"

"In my family, we *always* wore matching outfits," he said, his voice muffled from the underside of the table. "My mom used to make sweaters for all of us in the same colors. Then we'd pose, you know, by the stairs or the fireplace or whatever, for our card. So this is a continuation of the tradition."

I looked at Cora. *"Do something,"* I mouthed, and she nodded, holding up her hand.

"You know," she said as Jamie finally emerged from the table holding Roscoe, who looked none too happy and was already gnawing at the bow tie, "I just wonder if maybe a regular shot would work. Or maybe just one of Roscoe?"

Jamie's face fell. "You don't want to do a card with all of us?"

"Well," she said, glancing at me, "I just . . . I guess it's just not something we're used to. Me and Ruby, I mean. Things were different at our house. You know."

This, of course, was the understatement of the century. I had a few memories of Christmas when my parents were still together, but when my dad left, he pretty much took my mom's yuletide spirit with him. After that, I'd learned to dread the holidays. There was always too much drinking, not enough money, and with school out I was stuck with my mom, and only my mom, for weeks on end. No one was happier to see the New Year come than I was.

"But," Jamie said now, looking down at Roscoe, who had completely spit-soaked the bow tie and had now moved on to chewing the shirt's sleeve, "that's one reason I really wanted to do this."

"What is?"

"You," he said. "For you. I mean, and Ruby, too, of course. Because, you know, you missed out all those years."

I turned to Cora again, waiting for her to go to bat for us once more. Instead, she was just looking at her husband, and I could have sworn she was tearing up. Shit.

"You know what?" she said as Roscoe coughed up some bow tie. "You're absolutely right."

"What?" I said.

"It'll be fun," she told me. "And you look good in blue."

This was little comfort, though, a week later, when I found myself posing by the pond, Roscoe perched in my lap, as Jamie fiddled with his tripod and self-timer. Cora, beside me in her shirt, kept shooting me apologetic looks, which I was studiously ignoring. "You have to understand," she said under her breath as Roscoe tried to lick my face. "He's just like this. The house, and the security, this whole life. . . . He's always wanted to give me what I didn't have. It's really sweet, actually."

"Here we go!" Jamie said, running over to take his place on Cora's other side. "Get ready. One, two . . ."

At three, the camera clicked, then clicked again. Never in a million years I thought, when I saw the pictures later, stacked up next to their blank envelopes on the island. HAPPY HOLIDAYS FROM THE HUNTERS! it said, and looking at the shot, you could almost think I was one of them. Blue shirt and all.

I wasn't the only one being forced out of my comfort zone. About a week later, I was at my locker before first bell when I felt someone step up beside me. I turned, assuming it was Nate—the only person I ever really talked to at school on a regular basis—but was surprised to see Olivia Davis standing there instead.

"You were right," she said. No hello or how are you. Then again, she didn't have her phone to her ear, either, so maybe this was progress.

"About what?"

She bit her lip, looking off to the side for a moment as a couple of soccer players blew past, talking loudly. "Her name is Melissa. The girl my boyfriend was cheating with."

"Oh," I said. I shut my locker door slowly. "Right."

"It's been going on for weeks, and nobody told me," she

continued, sounding disgusted. "All the friends I have there, and everyone I talk to regularly . . . yet somehow, it just doesn't come up. I mean, come on."

I wasn't sure what to say to this. "I'm sorry," I told her. "That sucks."

Olivia shrugged, still looking across the hallway. "It's fine. Better I know than not, right?"

"Definitely," I agreed.

"Anyway," she said, her tone suddenly brisk, all business, "I just wanted to say, you know, thanks. For the tip."

"No problem."

Her phone rang, the sound already familiar to me, trilling from her pocket. She pulled it out, glancing at it, but didn't open it. "I don't like owing people things," she told me. "So you just let me know how we get even here, all right?"

"You don't owe me anything," I said as her phone rang again. "I just gave you a name."

"Still. It counts." Her phone rang once more, and now she did flip it open, putting it to her ear. "One sec," she said, then covered the receiver. "Anyway, keep it in mind."

I nodded, and then she was turning, walking away, already into her next conversation. So Olivia didn't like owing people. Neither did I. In fact, I didn't like people period, unless they gave me a reason to think otherwise. Or at least, that was the way I had been, not so long ago. But lately, I was beginning to think it was not just my setting that had changed.

Later that week, Nate and I were getting out of the car before school, Gervais having already taken off at his usual breakneck pace. By this point, we weren't attracting as much attention—there was another Rachel Webster, I supposed, providing grist for the gossip mill—although we still got a few looks. "So anyway," he was telling me, "then I said that I thought maybe, just maybe, she could hire me and my dad to get her house in order. I mean, you should see it. There's stuff piled up all over the place—mail and newspapers and laundry. God. *Piles* of laundry."

"Harriet?" I said. "Really? She's so organized at work."

"That's work, though," he replied. "I mean—"

"Nate!"

He stopped walking and turned to look over at a nearby red truck, a guy in a leather jacket and sunglasses standing next to it. "Robbie," he said. "What's up?"

"You tell me," the guy called back. "Coach said you've quit the team for good now. And you had that U scholarship in the bag, man. What gives?"

Nate glanced at me, then pulled his bag farther up his shoulder. "I'm just too busy," he said as the guy came closer. "You know how it is."

"Yeah, but come on," the guy replied. "We need you! Where's your senior loyalty?"

I heard Nate say something but couldn't make it out as I kept walking. This clearly had nothing to do with me. I was about halfway to the green when I glanced behind me. Already, Nate was backing away from the guy in the leather jacket, their conversation wrapping up.

I only had a short walk left to the green. The same one I would have been taking alone, all this time, if left to my own devices. But as I stepped up onto the curb, I had a flash of Olivia, her reluctant expression as she stood by my locker, wanting to be square, not owing me or anyone anything. It was a weird feeling, knowing you were indebted, if not connected. Even stranger, though, was being aware of this, not liking it, and yet still finding yourself digging in deeper, anyway. Like, for instance, consciously slowing your steps so it still looked accidental for someone to catch up from behind, a little out of breath, and walk with you the rest of the way.

*   *   *

The picture was of a group of people standing on a wide front porch. By their appearance—sideburns and loud prints on the men, printed flowy dresses and long hair on the women—I guessed it was taken sometime in the seventies. In the back, people were standing in haphazard rows; in the front, children were plopped down, sitting cross-legged. One boy had his tongue sticking out, while two little girls in front wore flowers in their hair. In the center, there was a girl in a white dress sitting in a chair, two elderly women on each side of her.

There had to be fifty people in all, some resembling each other, others looking like no one else around them. While a few were staring right into the camera with fixed smiles on their faces, others were laughing, looking off to one side or the other or at each other, as if not even aware a picture was being taken. It was easy to imagine the photographer giving up on trying to get the shot and instead just snapping the shutter, hoping for the best.

I'd found the photo on the island when I came downstairs, and I picked it up, carrying it over to the table to look at while I ate my breakfast. By the time Jamie came down twenty minutes later, I should have long moved on to the paper and my horoscope, but I was still studying it.

"Ah," he said, heading straight to the coffeemaker. "You found the ad. What do you think?"

"This is an ad?" I asked. "For what?"

He walked over to the island. "Actually," he said, digging around under some papers, "that's not the ad. This is."

He slid another piece of paper in front of me. At the top was the picture I'd been looking at, with the words IT'S ABOUT FAMILY in thick typewriter-style block print beneath it. Below that was another picture, taken in the present day, of a bunch of twenty-somethings gathered on what looked like the end zone of a football field. They were in T-shirts and jeans, some with arms around each other, others with hands lifted in the air, clearly celebrating something. IT'S ABOUT FRIENDS, it said underneath. Finally, a third picture, which was of a computer screen, filled with tiny square shots of smiling faces. Looking more closely, I could see they were same ones as in the other pictures, cut out and cropped down, then lined up end to end. Underneath, it said, IT'S ABOUT CONNECTING: UME.COM.

"The idea," Jamie explained over my shoulder, "is that while life is getting so individualistic—we all have our own phones, our own e-mail accounts, our own everything—we continue to use those things to reach out to each other. Friends, family . . . they're all part of communities we make and depend on. And UMe helps you do that."

"Wow," I said.

"Thousands spent on an advertising agency," he said,

reaching for the cereal box between us, "hours wasted in endless meetings, and a major print run about to drop any minute. And all you can say is 'wow'?"

"It's better than 'it sucks,'" Cora said, entering the kitchen with Roscoe at her heels. "Right?"

"Your sister," Jamie told me in a low voice, "does not like the campaign."

"I never said that," Cora told him, pulling the fridge open and taking out a container of waffles as Roscoe headed my way, sniffing the floor. "I only said that I thought your family might not like being featured, circa nineteen seventy-six, in magazines and bus shelters nationwide."

I looked back at the top picture, then at Jamie. "This is your family?"

"Yep," he said.

"And that's not even all of them," Cora added, sticking some waffles into the toaster oven. "Can you even believe that? They're not a family. They're a tribe."

"My grandmother was one of six children," Jamie explained.

"Ah," I said.

"You should have seen it when we got married," Cora said. "I felt like I'd crashed my own wedding. I didn't know *anybody*."

It took a beat for the awkwardness following this statement to hit, but when it did, we all felt it. Jamie glanced up at me, but I focused on finishing the bite of cereal I'd just taken, chewing carefully as Cora flushed and turned her attention to the toaster oven. Maybe it would have been easier to actually *acknowledge* the weirdness that was our estrangement and the fact that my mom and I hadn't even known Cora had gotten married, much less been invited to the wedding. But of course, we didn't. Instead we just sat there, until suddenly the smoke detector went off, breaking the silence.

"Shit," Jamie said, jumping up as ear-piercing beeping filled the room. Immediately I looked at Roscoe, whose ears had gone flat on his head. "What's burning?"

"It's this stupid toaster oven," Cora said, pulling it open and waving her hand back and forth in front of it. "It always does this. Roscoe, honey, it's okay—"

But it was too late. The dog was already bolting out of the room, in full flight mode, the way he'd taken to doing the last week or so. For some reason, Roscoe's appliance anxiety had been increasing, spurred on not only by the oven but anything in the kitchen that beeped or had the potential to do so. The smoke detector, though, remained his biggest fear. Which, I figured, meant that right about now he was probably up in my bathroom closet, his favorite hiding place of late, shaking among my shoes and waiting for the danger to pass.

Jamie grabbed the broom, reaching it up to hit the detector's reset button, and finally the beeping stopped. As he got down and came back to the table, Cora followed him, sliding into a chair with her waffle, which she then nibbled at halfheartedly.

"It may be time to call a professional," she said after a moment.

"I'm not putting the dog on antidepressants," Jamie told her, picking up the paper and scanning the front page. "I don't care how relaxed Denise's dachshund is now."

"Lola is a Maltese," Cora said, "and it wouldn't necessarily mean that. Maybe there's some training we can do, something that will help him."

"We can't keep coddling him, though," Jamie said. "You know what the books say. Every time you pick him up or soothe him when he's freaking out like that, you're reinforcing the behavior."

"So you'd prefer we just stand by and let him be traumatized?"

"Of course not," Jamie said.

Cora put down her waffle, wiping her mouth with a napkin. "Then I just think that there's got to be a way to acknowledge his fear and at the same time—"

"Cora." Jamie put down the paper. "He's a dog, not a child. This isn't a self-esteem issue. It's Pavlovian. Okay?"

Cora just looked at him for a moment. Then she pushed back her chair, getting to her feet, and walked to the island, dropping her plate into the sink with a loud clank.

As she left the room, Jamie sighed, running a hand over his face as I pulled the family picture back toward me. Again, I found myself studying it: the varied faces, some smiling, some not, the gentle regalness of the elderly women, who were staring right into the camera. Across the table, Jamie was just sitting there, looking out at the pond.

"I do like the ad, you know," I said to him finally. "It's cool."

"Thanks," he said, distracted.

"Are you in this picture?" I asked him.

He glanced over at it as he pushed his chair out and got

to his feet. "Nah. Before my time. I didn't come along for a few more years. That's my mom, though, in the white dress. It was her wedding day."

As he left the room, I looked down at the picture again, and at the girl in the center, noticing how serene and happy she looked surrounded by all those people. I couldn't imagine what it would be like to be one of so many, to have not just parents and siblings but cousins and aunts and uncles, an entire tribe to claim as your own. Maybe you would feel lost in the crowd. Or sheltered by it. Whatever the case, one thing was for sure: like it or not, you'd never be alone.

* * *

Fifteen minutes later I was standing in the warmth of the foyer, waiting for Nate to pull up at the mailbox, when the phone rang.

"Cora?" the caller said, skipping a hello.

"No," I said. "This is—"

"Oh, Ruby, hi!" The voice was a woman's, entirely perky. "It's Denise, Cora's old roommate—from the party?"

"Right. Hi," I said, turning my head as Cora came down the stairs, briefcase in her hand.

"So how's life?" Denise asked. "School okay? It's gotta be a big adjustment, starting at a new place. But Cora did say it's not the first time you've switched schools. Personally, I lived in the same place my whole entire life, which is really not much better, actually, because—"

"Here's Cora," I said, holding the phone out as she got to the bottom step.

"Hello?" Cora said as she took it from me. "Oh, hey.

Yeah. At nine." She reached up, tucking a piece of hair behind her ear. "I will."

I walked over to the window by the door, looking for Nate. He was usually right on time, and when he wasn't, it was often because Gervais—who had trouble waking up in the morning and was often dragged to the car by his mother—held things up.

"No, I'm all right," Cora was saying. She'd gone down the hallway, but only a few steps. "Things are just kind of tense. I'll call you after, okay? Thanks for remembering. Yeah. Bye."

There was a beep as she hung up. When I glanced back at her, she said, "Look. About earlier, and what I said about the wedding. . . . I didn't mean to make you feel uncomfortable."

"It's fine," I said just as the phone rang again. She looked down at it, then answered.

"Charlotte, hey. Can I call you back? I'm kind of in the middle of—Yeah. Nine a.m. Well, hopefully." She nodded. "I know. Positivity. I'll let you know how it goes. Okay. Bye."

This time, as she hung up, she sighed, then sat down on the bottom step, laying the phone beside her. When she saw me watching her she said, "I have a doctor's appointment this morning."

"Oh," I said. "Is everything—are you all right?"

"I don't know," she replied. Then she quickly added, "I mean, I'm fine, health-wise. I'm not sick or anything."

I nodded, not sure what to say.

"It's just . . ." She smoothed her skirt with both hands.

"We've been trying to get pregnant for a while, and it's just not happening. So we're meeting with a specialist."

"Oh," I said again.

"It's all right," she said quickly. "Lots of people have problems like this. I just thought you should know, in case you ever have to take a message from a doctor's office or something. I didn't want you to worry."

I nodded, turning back to the window. This would be a great time for Nate to show up, I thought. But of course he didn't. Stupid Gervais. And then I heard Cora draw in a breath.

"And like I was saying, about earlier," she said. "About the wedding. I just . . . I didn't want you to feel like I was . . ."

"It's fine," I said again.

". . . still mad about that. Because I'm not."

It took me a moment to process this, like the sentence fell apart between us and I had to string the words back together. "Mad?" I said finally. "About what?"

"You and Mom not coming," she said. She sighed. "Look, we don't have to talk about this. It's ancient history. But this morning, when I said that thing about the wedding, you just looked so uncomfortable, and I knew you probably felt bad. So I thought maybe it would be better to just clear the air. Like I said, I'm not mad anymore."

"You didn't invite us to your wedding," I said.

Now she looked surprised. "Yes," she said slowly. "I did."

"Well, then the invitation must have gotten lost in the mail, because—"

"I brought it to Mom, Ruby," she said.

"No, you didn't." I swallowed, taking a breath. "You . . . you haven't seen Mom in years."

"That's not true," she said simply, as if I'd told her the wrong time, something that innocuous. "I brought the invitation to her personally, at the place she was working at the time. I wanted you there."

Cars were passing by the mailbox, and I knew any moment one of them would be Nate's, and I'd have to leave. But right then, I couldn't even move. I was flattened against the window, as if someone had knocked the wind out of me. "No," I said again. "You disappeared. You went to college, and you were gone. We never heard from you."

She looked down at her skirt. Then, quietly, she said, "That's not true."

"It is. I was there." But even to me, I sounded unsure, at the one time I wanted—needed—to be absolutely positive. "If you'd ever tried to reach us—"

"Of *course* I tried to reach you," she said. "I mean, the time I spent tracking you down alone was—"

Suddenly, she stopped talking. Mid-sentence, mid-breath. In the silence that followed, a red BMW drove past, then a blue minivan. Normal people, off to their normal lives. "Wait," she said after a moment. "You do know about all that, don't you? You have to. There's no way she could have—"

"I have to go," I said, but when I reached down for the doorknob and twisted it, I heard her get to her feet and come up behind me.

"Ruby, look at me," she said, but I stayed where I was,

facing the small crack in the door, feeling cold air coming through. "All I wanted was to find you. The entire time I was in college, and after. . . . I was trying to get you out of there."

Now, of course, Nate did pull up to the curb. Perfect timing. "You left that day, for school," I said, turning to face her. "You never came back. You didn't call or write or show up for holidays—"

"Is that what you really think?" she demanded.

"That's what I know."

"Well, you're wrong," she said. "Think about it. All those moves, all those houses. A different school every time. The jobs she could never hold, the phone that was rarely hooked up, and then never in her real name. Did you ever wonder why she put down fake addresses on all your school stuff? Do you think that was some kind of accident? Do you have any idea how hard she made it for me to find you?"

"You didn't try," I said, and now my voice was cracking, loud and shaky, rising up into the huge space above us.

"I did," Cora said. Distantly, from outside, I heard a beep: Nate, getting impatient. "For years I did. Even when she told me to stop, that you wanted nothing to do with me. Even when you ignored my letters and messages—"

My throat was dry, hard, as I tried to swallow.

"—I still kept coming back, reaching out, all the way up to the wedding. She swore she would give you the invitation, give you the choice to come or not. By that time I had threatened to get the courts involved so I could see you, which was the last thing she wanted, so she promised me. She *promised* me, Ruby. But she couldn't do it. She upped and moved you away again instead. She was so afraid of being alone, of you leaving, too, that she never gave you the chance. Until this year, when she knew that you'd be turning eighteen, and you could, and most likely would. So what did she do?"

"Stop it," I said.

"She left you," she finished. "Left you alone, in that filthy house, before you could do the same to her."

I felt something rising in my throat—a sob, a scream—and bit it back, tears filling my eyes, and I hated myself for crying, showing any weakness here. "You don't know what you're talking about," I said.

"I do, though." And now her voice was soft. Sad. Like she felt sorry for me, which was the most shameful thing of all. "That's the thing. I do."

Nate beeped again, louder and longer this time. "I have to go," I said, yanking the door open.

"Wait," Cora said. "Don't just—"

But I ran outside, pulling the door shut behind me. I didn't want to talk anymore. I didn't want anything, except a moment of peace and quiet to be alone and try to figure what exactly had just happened. All those years there were so many things I couldn't rely on, but this, the story of what had happened to my family, had always been a given, understood. Now, though, I wasn't so sure. What do you do when you only have two people in your life, neither of whom you've ever been able to fully trust, and yet you have to believe one of them?

I heard the door open again. "Ruby," Cora called out. "Just wait a second. We can't leave it like this."

But this, too, wasn't true. Leaving was easy. It was everything else that was so damned hard.

* * *

I'd only just gotten my door shut and seat belt on when it started.

"What's wrong with *you?* You look like crap."

I ignored Gervais, instead keeping my eyes fixed straight ahead. Still, I could feel Nate looking at me, concerned, so I said, "I'm fine. Let's just go." It took him another moment, but then he was finally hitting the gas and we were pulling away.

For the first few blocks, I just tried to breathe. *It's not true,* I kept thinking, and yet in the next beat it was all coming back: those moves and new schools, and the paperwork we always fudged—addresses, phone—because of bad landlords or creditors. The phones that were never hooked up, that graduation announcement my mom had said was just sent out automatically. *Just you and me, baby. Just you and me.*

I swallowed, keeping my eyes on the back of the bus in front of us, which was covered with an ad reading IT'S A FESTIVAL OF SALADS! I narrowed my focus to just these five words, holding them in the center of my vision, even as there was a loud, ripping burp from behind me.

"Gervais." Nate hit his window button. As it went down he said, "What did we just spend a half hour talking about with your mom?"

"I don't know," Gervais replied, giggling.

"Then let me refresh your memory," Nate said. "The burping and farting and rudeness stops right now. Or else."

"Or else what?"

We pulled up to a red light, and Nate turned around, then leaned back between our seats. Suddenly, he was so close to me that even in my distracted state I couldn't help but breathe in the scent of the USWIM sweatshirt he had on: a mix of clean and chlorine, the smell of water. "Or else," he said, his voice sounding very un-Nate-like, stern and serious, "you go back to riding with the McClellans."

"No way!" Gervais said. "The McClellans are *first-graders*. Plus, I'd have to walk from the lower school."

Nate shrugged. "So get up earlier."

"I'm *not* getting up earlier," Gervais squawked. "It's already too early!"

"Then quit being such a pain in the ass," Nate told him, turning back around as the light changed.

A moment later I felt Nate glance at me. I knew he was probably expecting a thank-you, since he'd clearly gone to Mrs. Miller that morning to talk about Gervais because of what I'd said, trying to make things better. But I was so tired, suddenly, of being everyone's charity case. I never asked anyone to help me. If you felt compelled to anyway, that was your problem, not mine.

When we pulled into the lot five minutes later, for the first time I beat Gervais out of the car, pushing my door open before we were even at a full stop. I was already a row of cars away when Nate yelled after me. "Ruby," he said. "Wait up."

But I didn't, not this time. I just kept going, walking faster. By the time I reached the green, the first bell hadn't yet rung, and people were everywhere, pressing on all sides.

When I saw the door to the bathroom, I just headed straight for it.

Inside, there were girls at the sinks checking their make-up and talking on the phone, but the stalls were all empty as I walked past them, sliding into the one by the wall and locking the door. Then I leaned against it, closing my eyes.

All those years I'd given up Cora for lost, hated her for leaving me. What if I had been wrong? What if, somehow, my mother had managed to keep her away, the only other person I'd ever had? And if she had, why?

She left you, Cora had said, and it was these three words, then and now, that I heard most clearly of all, slicing through the roaring in my head like someone speaking right into my ear. I didn't want this to make sense, for her to be right in any way. But even I could not deny the logic of it. My mother had been abandoned by a husband and one daughter; she'd had enough of being left. So she'd done what she had to do to make sure it didn't happen again. And this, above all else, I could understand. It was the same thing I'd been planning to do myself.

The bell rang overhead, and the bathroom slowly cleared out, the door banging open and shut as people headed off to class. Then, finally, it was quiet, the hallways empty, the only sound the flapping of the flag out on the green, which I could hear from the high half-open windows that ran along the nearby wall.

When I was sure I was alone, I left the stall and walked over to the sinks, dropping my bag at my feet. In the mirror overhead, I realized Gervais had been right: I looked ter-rible, my face blotchy and red. I reached down, watching my fingers as they picked up the key at my neck, then closed themselves tightly around it.

"I told you, I had to get a pass and sign out," I heard a voice say suddenly from outside. "Because this place is like a prison, okay? Look, just hold tight. I'll be there as soon as I can."

I looked outside, just in time to see Olivia passing by, phone to her ear, walking down the breezeway to the parking lot. As soon as I saw her take her keys out of her backpack, I grabbed my bag and bolted.

I caught up with her by a row of lockers just as she was folding her phone into her back pocket. "Hey," I called out, my voice bouncing off the empty corridor all around us. "Where are you going?"

When she turned around and saw me, her expression was wary, at best. Then again, with my blotchy face, not to mention being completely out of breath, I couldn't exactly blame her. "I have to go pick up my cousin. Why?"

I came closer, taking a breath. "I need a ride."

"Where?"

"Anywhere."

She raised her eyebrows. "I'm going to Jackson, then home. Nowhere else. I have to be back here by third."

"That's fine," I told her. "Perfect, in fact."

"You have a pass?"

I shook my head.

"So you want me to just take you off campus anyway, risking my ass, even though it's totally against the rules."

"Yes," I said.

She shook her head, no deal.

"But we'll be square," I added. "You won't owe me any-more."

"This is way more than what I owe you," she said. She studied my face for a moment, and I stood there, waiting for her verdict. She was right, this was probably stupid of me. But I was tired of playing it smart. Tired of everything.

"All right," she said finally. "But I'm not taking you from here. Get yourself to the Quik Zip, and I'll pick you up."

"Done," I told her, pulling my bag over my shoulder. "See you there."

Chapter Eight

When I slid into Olivia's front seat ten minutes later, my foot immediately hit something, then crunched it flat. Looking down, I saw it was a popcorn tub, the kind you buy at the movies, and it wasn't alone: there were at least four more rolling across the floorboards.

"I work at the Vista Ten," she explained, her engine puttering as she switched into reverse. "It pays crap, but we get all the free popcorn we can eat."

"Right," I said. Now that I thought of it, that did explain the butter smell.

We pulled out onto the main road, then merged into traffic and headed for the highway. I'd spent so much time riding with Jamie and Nate that I'd almost forgotten what it was like to be in a regular car, i.e., one that was not new and loaded with every possible gadget and extra. Olivia's Toyota was battered, the fabric of the seats nubby, with several stains visible, and there was one of those prisms hanging on a cord dangling from the rearview. It reminded me of my mother's Subaru, the thought of which gave me a pang I quickly pushed away, focusing instead on the entrance to the highway, rising up in the distance.

"So what's the deal?" Olivia asked as we merged into traffic, her muffler rattling.

"With what?"

"You."

"No deal," I said, sitting back and propping my feet on the dashboard.

She eyed my feet pointedly. I dropped them back down again. "So you just decided to cut school for the hell of it," she said.

"Pretty much."

We were getting closer, passing another exit. The one to Jackson was next. "You know," she said, "you can't just show up and hang out on campus. They're not as organized as Perkins, but they *will* kick you off."

"I'm not going to campus," I told her.

When we came over the hill five minutes later and Jackson came into view—big, sprawling, trailers lined up behind—I felt myself relax. After so many weeks of being out of place, it was nice to finally see something familiar. Olivia pulled up in front, where there was a row of faded plastic benches. Sitting on the last one was a heavyset black girl with short hair and glasses. When she saw us, she slowly got to her feet and began to shuffle in our direction.

"Oh, look at this," Olivia said loudly, rolling down her window. "Seems like *someone* should have listened to someone else who said maybe running a mile wasn't such a smart idea."

"It's not because of the running," the girl grumbled, pulling open the back door and sliding gingerly onto the seat. "I think I have the flu."

"All the books say you should start slow," Olivia continued. "But not you. You have to sprint the first day."

"Just shut up and give me some Advil, would you please?"

Olivia rolled her eyes, then reached across me and popped the glove compartment. She pulled out a bottle of pills, then chucked it over her shoulder. "This is Laney, by the way," Olivia said, banging the glove compartment shut again. "She thinks she can run a marathon."

"It's a five-K," Laney said. "And some support would be nice."

"I'm supportive," Olivia told her, turning around in her seat. "I support you so much that I'm the only one telling you this isn't a good idea. That maybe, just maybe, you could hurt yourself."

Laney just looked at her as she downed two Advils, then popped the cap back on. "Pain is part of running," she said. "That's why it's an endurance sport."

"You don't know anything about endurance!" Olivia turned to me. "One night she sees that crazy woman Kiki Sparks in one of those infomercials, talking about caterpillars and butterflies and potential and setting fitness goals. Next think you know, she thinks she's Lance Armstrong."

"Lance Armstrong is a cyclist," Laney pointed out, wincing as she shifted her weight. "That's not even a valid analogy."

Olivia harrumphed but withheld further comment as we pulled forward out of the turnaround. As she put on her blinker to turn left, I said, "Do you mind going the other way? It's not far."

"There's nothing up there but woods," she said.

"It'll only take a minute."

I saw her glance back at Laney in the rearview, but then

she was turning, slowly, the engine chugging as we headed up the hill. The parking lots gave way to more parking lots, which then turned into scrub brush. About half a mile later, I told her to slow down.

"This is good," I said as we came up on the clearing. Sure enough, there were two cars parked there, and I could see Aaron, Peyton's ex—a chubby guy with a baby face he tried to counter by dressing in all black and scowling a lot—sitting on one of them, smoking a cigarette. "Thanks for the ride."

Olivia looked over at them, then back at me. "You want to get out here?"

"Yeah," I said.

She was clearly skeptical. "How are you planning to get back?"

"I'll find a way," I said. I got out of the car and picked up my bag. She was still watching me, so I added, "Look, don't worry."

"I'm not worried," she said. "I don't even know you."

Still, she kept her eyes on me while Laney opened the back door and slid out slowly, taking her time as she made her way into the front seat. As she pulled the door shut, Olivia said, "You know, I can take you home, if you want. I mean, I'm missing third by now, anyway, thanks to Laney."

I shook my head. "No, I'm good. I'll see you at school, okay?"

She nodded slowly as I patted the roof of the car, then turned around and headed for the clearing. Aaron squinted at me, then sat up straighter. "Hey, Ruby," he called out as I approached. "Welcome back."

"Thanks," I said, hopping up on the hood beside him. Olivia had stayed where I left her, watching me from behind the wheel, but now she moved forward, turning around in the dead end, her engine put-putting. The prism hanging from her rearview caught the light for a moment, throwing sparks, and then she was sliding past, over the hill and out of sight. "It's good to be here."

*   *   *

I'd actually come looking for Peyton, who had a free second period and often skipped third to boot, spending both at the clearing. But Aaron, whose schedule was flexible due to a recent expulsion, claimed he hadn't seen her, so I settled in to wait. That had been a couple of hours ago.

"Hey."

I felt something nudge my foot. Then again, harder. When I opened my eyes, Aaron was holding out a joint, the tip smoldering. I tried to focus on it, but it kept blurring, slightly to one side, then the other. "I'm okay," I said.

"Oh, yeah," he said flatly, putting it to his own lips and taking a big drag. In his black shirt and jeans, his white skin seemed so pale, almost glowing. "You're just fine."

I leaned back, then felt my head bonk hard against something behind me. Turning slightly, I saw thick treads, sloping metal, and I could smell rubber. It took me another minute, though, to realize I was sitting against a car. There was grass beneath me and trees all around; looking up, I could see a bright blue sky. I was still at the clearing, although how I got on the ground I wasn't exactly sure.

This was because I was also drunk, the result of the pint of vodka we'd shared soon after I'd arrived. That I remembered at least partially—him pulling out the bottle from his pocket, along with a couple of orange-juice cartons someone had nicked from the cafeteria during breakfast. We'd poured some of each into an empty Zip cup, then shook them up, cocktail style, and toasted each other in his front seat, the radio blasting. And repeat, until the orange juice was gone. Then we'd switched to straight shots, each burning a little less as they went down.

"Damn," he'd said, wiping his mouth as he passed the bottle back to me. The wind had been blowing, all the trees swaying, and everything felt distant and close all at once, just right. "Since when are you such a lush, Cooper?"

"Always," I remembered telling him. "It's in my genes."

Now he took another deep drag, sputtering slightly as he held it in. My head felt heavy, fluid, as he exhaled, the smoke blowing across me. I closed my eyes, trying to lose myself in it. That morning, all I'd wanted was to feel oblivious, block out everything I'd heard about my mom from Cora. And for a while, sitting with him and singing along to the radio, I had. Now, though, I could feel it hovering again, crouching just out of sight.

"Hey," I said, forcing my eyes open and turning my head. "Let me get a hit off that."

He held it out. As I took it, my fingers fumbled and it fell to the ground between us, disappearing into the grass. "Shit," I said, digging around until I felt heat—pricking, sudden—against my skin. As I came up with it, I had to concentrate on guiding it to my mouth slowly, easing my lips around it before pulling in a big drag.

The smoke was thick, sinking down into my lungs, and

feeling it I sat back again, my head hitting the fender behind me. God, this was good. Just floating and distant, every worry receding like a wave rushing out and then pulling
back, wiping the sand clean behind it. I had a flash of myself,
walking through these same woods not so long ago, feeling
this same way: loose and easy, everything still ahead. Then
I hadn't been alone, either. I'd been with Marshall.

Marshall. I opened my eyes, squinting down at my watch
until it came into focus. That was what I needed right now—
just any kind of closeness, even if it was only for a little
while. Sandpiper Arms was only a short walk from here, via
a path through the woods; we'd done it tons of times.

"Where you going?" Aaron asked, his voice heavy as I
pushed myself to my feet, stumbling slightly before regain-
ing my footing. "I thought we were hanging out."

"I'll be back," I told him, and started for the path.

By the time I reached the bottom of Marshall's stairs, I
felt slightly more coherent, although I was sweating from the
walk, and I could feel a headache setting in. I took a moment
to smooth down my hair and make myself slightly more
presentable, then pushed on up to the door and knocked
hard. A moment later, the door creaked open, and Rogerson
peered out at me.

"Hey," I said. My voice sounded low, liquidy. "Is Marshall
home?"

"Uh," he replied, looking over his shoulder. "I don't
know."

"It's cool if he's not," I told him. "I can wait in his room."

He looked at me for a long moment, during which I felt
myself sway, slightly. Then he stepped aside.

The apartment was dark, as usual, as I moved down the hallway to the living room. "You know," Rogerson said from behind me, his voice flat, "he probably won't be back for a while."

But at that point, I didn't care. All I wanted was to collapse onto the bed, pulling the sheets around me, and sleep, finally able to block out everything that had happened since I'd woken up in my own room that morning. Just to be someplace safe, someplace I knew, with someone, anyone, familiar nearby.

When I pushed open the door, the first thing I saw was that Whitman's sampler. It caught my eye even before I recognized Peyton, who was sitting beside it, a chocolate in her hand. I watched, frozen, as she reached it out to Marshall, who was lying beside her, hands folded over his chest, and dropped it into his open mouth. This was just the simplest gesture, taking mere seconds, but at the same time there was something so intimate about it—the way his lips closed over her fingers, how she giggled, her cheeks pink, before drawing them back—that I felt sick, even before Marshall turned his head and saw me.

I don't know what I was expecting him to do or say, if anything. To be surprised, or sorry, or even sad. In the end, though, his expression said it all: I Could Care Less.

"Oh, *shit*," Peyton gasped. "Ruby, I'm so—"

"Oh my God," I said, stumbling backward out of the door frame. I put my hand to my mouth as I turned, bumping the wall as I ran back down the hallway to the front door. Vaguely, I could hear her calling after me, but I ignored this as I burst out into the daylight again, gripping the banister as I ran down to the parking lot.

"Ruby, wait," Peyton was yelling, her own steps loud on the stairs as she followed me. "Jesus! Just let me explain!"

"Explain?" I said, whirling to face her. "How in the world do you explain this?"

She stopped by the banister, hand to her heart, to catch her breath. "I tried to tell you," she gasped. "That night, at your house. But it was so hard, and then you kept saying how things had changed, anyway, so—"

Suddenly, something clicked in my brain, and I had a flash of her that night, in the foyer with Roscoe and Jamie, then of Marshall handing me back my key that last time I'd seen him. *You told me you lived in Wildflower Ridge*, she'd said, but I was sure I hadn't. I was right. He had.

"That's why you came over?" I asked. "To tell me you were sleeping with my boyfriend?"

"You never called him that!" she shot back, pointing at me. "Not even once. You just said you had a *thing*, an *arrangement*. I thought I was being nice, wanting to tell you."

"I don't need you to be nice to me," I snapped.

"Of course you don't," she replied. At the top of the stairs, I could see Rogerson just past the open door, looking down at us. We were making a scene, the last thing he wanted. "You don't need anything. Not a boyfriend, not a friend. You were always so clear about that. And that's what you got. So why are you surprised now?"

I just stood there, looking at her. My head was spinning, my mouth dry, and all I could think about was that I wanted to go someplace safe, someplace I could be alone and okay, and that this was impossible. My old life had changed and my new one was still in progress, altering by the second. There was nothing, *nothing* to depend on. And why *was* I surprised?

I walked away from her, back to the path, but as I entered the woods I was having trouble keeping on it, roots catching my feet, branches scratching me from all sides. I was so tired—of this day, of everything—even as it all came rushing back: Cora's face in the foyer that morning, Olivia's prism glinting in the sun, stepping into the familiar dimness of the apartment, so sure of what I was there for.

As I stumbled again, I started to catch myself, then stopped, instead just letting my body go limp, hitting knees first, then elbows, in the leaves. Up ahead, I could see the edge of the clearing, and Aaron looking at me, but it suddenly felt right, even perfect, to be alone. So as I lay back on the ground, the sky already spinning above me, I tried to focus again on the idea of that wave I'd thought of earlier, wiping everything clean, blue and big and wide enough to suck me in. Maybe it was a wish, or a dream. Either way, it was so real that at some point, I could actually feel it. Like a presence coming closer, with arms that closed around me, lifting me up with a scent that filled my senses: clean and pure, a touch of chlorine. The smell of water.

*　　*　　*

The first thing I saw when I opened my eyes was Roscoe.

He was sitting on the empty seat beside me, right in front of the steering wheel, facing forward, panting. As I tried to focus, I suddenly smelled dog breath—ugh—and my stomach twisted. *Shit*, I thought, bolting forward, my hand fumbling for the door handle. Just in time, though,

I saw the Double Burger bag positioned between my feet. I'd only barely grabbed it and put it to my lips before I was puking up something hot and burning that I could feel all the way to my ears.

My hands were shaking as I eased the bag onto the floor, then sat back, my heart thumping in my chest. I was freezing, even though I was now wearing a USWIM sweatshirt that looked awfully familiar. Looking outside, I saw we were parked in some kind of strip mall—I could see a dry-cleaner and a video store—and I had no idea how I'd gotten here. In fact the only thing familiar, other than the dog, was the air freshener hanging from the rearview, which said: WE WORRY SO YOU DON'T HAVE TO.

Oh my God, I thought as these things all suddenly collided. I looked down at the sweatshirt again, breathing in that water smell, distant and close all at once. Nate.

Suddenly, Roscoe let out a yap, which was amplified by the small space around us. He leaped up on the driver's-side window, nails tap-tapping, his nub of a tail wriggling around wildly. I was wondering whether I was going to puke again when I heard a pop and felt a rush of fresh air from behind me.

Immediately, Roscoe bounded into the backseat, his tags jingling. It took me considerably longer to turn myself around—God, my head was pounding—and focus enough to see Nate, at the back of his car, easing in a pile of dry-cleaning. When he looked up and saw me, he said, "Hey, you're conscious. Good."

Good? I thought, but then he was slamming the back door shut (ouch) before walking around to pull open the driver's-side door and get in behind the wheel. As he slid his keys into the ignition, he glanced over at the bag at my feet. "How you doing there? Need another one yet?"

"Another one?" I said. My voice was dry, almost cracking on the words. "This . . . this isn't the first?"

He shot me a sympathetic look. "No," he said. "It isn't."

As if to punctuate this, my stomach rolled threateningly as he began to back out of the space. I tried to calm it, as Roscoe climbed up between our two seats, sticking his head forward and closing his eyes while Nate rolled down his window, letting in some fresh air.

"What time is it?" I asked, trying to keep my voice level, if only to control the nausea.

"Almost five," Nate replied.

"Are you serious?"

"What time did you think it was?"

Honestly, I didn't even know. I'd lost track of time on the walk back to the clearing when everything went fluid. "What—?" I said, then stopped, realizing I wasn't even sure what I was about to ask. Or even where to begin. "What is Roscoe doing here?"

Nate glanced back at the dog, who was still riding high, his ears blowing back in the wind. "He had a four o'clock vet appointment," he said. "Cora and Jamie both had to work, so they hired me to take him. When I went to pick him up and you weren't at home, I figured I'd better go looking for you."

"Oh," I said. I looked at Roscoe, who immediately took this as an invitation to start licking my face. I pushed him away, moving closer to the window. "But how did you—?"

"Olivia," he said. I blinked, a flash of her driving away popping into my head. "That's her name, right? The girl with the braids?"

I nodded slowly, still trying to piece this together. "You know Olivia?"

"No," he said. "She just came up to me before fourth period and said she'd left you in the woods—at your request, she was very clear on that—and thought I should know."

"Why would you need to know?"

He shrugged. "I guess she thought you might need a friend."

Hearing this, I felt my face flush, suddenly embarrassed. Like I was so desperate and needing to be rescued that people—strangers—were actually convening to discuss it. My worst nightmare. "I was with my friends," I said. "Actually."

"Yeah?" he asked, glancing over at me. "Well, then, they must be the invisible kind. Because when I got there, you were alone."

What? I thought. That couldn't be true. Aaron had been right there in the clearing, and he'd seen me lie down. Now that I thought about it, though, it had been midday then; it was late afternoon now. If Nate was telling the truth, how long had I been there, alone and passed out? *Are you surprised?* I heard Peyton say again in my head, and a shiver ran over me. I wrapped my arms around myself, looking out the window. The buildings were blurring past, but I tried to find just one I could recognize, as if I could somehow locate myself that way.

"Look," Nate said, "what happened today is over. It doesn't matter, okay? We'll get you home, and everything will be fine."

Hearing this, I felt my eyes well up unexpectedly with hot tears. It was bad to be embarrassed, hard to be ashamed. But pitied? That was the worst of all. Of course Nate would think this could all be so easily resolved. It was how things happened in his world, where he was a friendly guy and worried so you didn't have to as he went about living his life of helpful errands and good deeds. Unlike me, so dirty and used up and broken. I had a flash of Marshall looking over his shoulder at me, and my head pounded harder.

"Hey," Nate said now, as if he could hear me thinking this, slipping further and further down this slope. "It's okay."

"It's not," I said, keeping my eyes fixed on the window. "You couldn't even understand."

"Try me."

"No." I swallowed, pulling my arms tighter around myself. "It's not your problem."

"Ruby, come on. We're friends."

"Stop saying that," I said.

"Why?"

"Because it's not true," I said, now turning to face him. "We don't even know each other. You just live behind me and give me a ride to school. Why do you think that makes us somehow something?"

"Fine," he said, holding up his hands. "We're not friends."

And now I was a bitch. We rode in silence for a block, Roscoe panting between us. "Look," I said, "I appreciate what you did. What you've done. But the thing is . . . my life isn't like yours, okay? I'm messed up."

"Everybody's messed up," he said quietly.

"Not like me," I told him. I thought of Olivia in English class, throwing up her hands: *Tell us about your pain. We're riveted!* "Do you even know why I came to live with Cora and Jamie?"

He glanced over at me. "No," he said.

"Because my mom abandoned me." My voice felt tight, but I took a breath and kept going. "A couple of months ago, she packed up and took off while I was at school. I was living alone for weeks until my landlords busted me and turned me in to social services. Who then called Cora, who I hadn't seen in ten years, since *she* took off for school and never contacted me again."

"I'm sorry." This response was automatic, so easy.

"That's not why I'm telling you." I sighed, shaking my head. "Do you remember that house I brought you to that day? It wasn't a friend's. It was—"

"Yours," he finished for me. "I know."

I looked over at him, surprised. "You knew?"

"You had the key around your neck," he said quietly, glancing at it. "It was kind of obvious."

I blinked, feeling ashamed all over again. Here at least I thought I'd managed to hide something from Nate that day, kept a part of me a secret, at least until I was ready to reveal it. But I'd been wide open, exposed, all along.

We were coming up on Wildflower Ridge now, and as Nate began to slow down, Roscoe jumped onto my seat, clambering across me to press his muzzle against the window. Without thinking, I reached up to deposit him back where he'd come from, but as soon as I touched him he sank backward, settling into my lap as if this was the most natural thing in the world. For one of us, anyway.

When Nate pulled up in front of Cora's, I could see the kitchen lights were on, and both her and Jamie's cars were in the driveway, even though it was early for either of them to be home, much less both. Not a good sign. I reached up, smoothing my hair out of my face, and tried to ready myself before pushing open the door.

"You can tell them he got his shots and the vet said everything's fine," Nate said, reaching into the backseat for Roscoe's leash. Seeing it, the dog leaped up again, moving closer, and he clipped it on his collar. "And if they want to pursue behavioral training for the anxiety thing, she has a couple of names she can give them."

"Right," I said. He handed the leash to me, and I took it, picking up my bag with the other hand as I slowly slid out of the car. Roscoe, of course, followed with total eagerness, stretching the leash taut as he pulled me to the house. "Thanks."

Nate nodded, not saying anything, and I shut the door. Just as I started up the walk, though, I heard the whirring of a window lowering. When I turned around, he said, "Hey, and for what it's worth? Friends don't leave you alone in the woods. Friends are the ones who come and take you out."

I just looked at him. At my feet, Roscoe was straining at his leash, wanting to go home.

"At least," Nate said, "that's been my experience. I'll see you, okay?"

I nodded, and then his window slid back up, and he was pulling away.

As I watched him go, Roscoe was still tugging, trying to pull me closer to the house. My instinct was to do the total opposite, even though by now I'd left, and been left, enough times to know that neither of them was good, or easy, or even preferable. Still, it wasn't until we started up the walk to those waiting bright lights that I realized this— coming back—was the hardest of all.

*   *   *

"Where the hell have you been?"

It was Cora I was braced for, Cora I was expecting to be waiting when I pushed open the door. Instead, the first thing I saw was Jamie. And he was *pissed*.

"Jamie," I heard Cora say. She was at the end of the hall, standing in the doorway to the kitchen. Roscoe, who had bolted the minute I dropped his leash, was already circling her feet, sniffling wildly. "At least let her get inside."

"Do you have any idea how worried we've been?" Jamie demanded.

"I'm sorry," I said.

"Do you even *care*?" he said.

I looked down the hallway at my sister, who had picked Roscoe up and was now watching me. Her eyes were red, a tissue in her hand, and as I realized she, like Jamie, was still in the clothes she'd had on that morning, I suddenly remembered their doctor's appointment.

"Are you *drunk?*" Jamie said. I looked at the mirror by the stairs, finally seeing myself: I looked terrible—in Nate's baggy sweatshirt—and clearly, I stank of booze and who knew what else. I looked tired and faded and so familiar, suddenly, that I had to turn away, sinking down onto the bottom stair behind me. "This is what you do, after we take you in, put you in a great school, give you everything you need? You just run off and get *wasted?*"

I shook my head, a lump rising in my throat. It had been such a long, terrible day that it felt like years ago, entire lifetimes, since I'd been in this same place arguing with Cora that morning.

"We gave you the benefit of the doubt," Jamie was saying. "We gave you *everything*. And this is how you thank us?"

"Jamie," Cora said again, louder this time. "Stop it."

"We don't need this," he said, coming closer. I pulled my knees to my chest, trying to make myself smaller. I deserved this, I knew it, and I just wanted it to be over. "Your sister, who *fought* to bring you here, even when you were stupid and resisted? *She* doesn't need this."

I felt tears fill my eyes, blurring everything again, and this time I was glad, grateful for it. But even so, I covered my face with my hand, just to make sure.

"I mean," Jamie continued, his voice bouncing off the walls, rising up to the high ceiling above us, "what kind of person just takes off, disappears, no phone call, not even caring that someone might be wondering where they are? Who *does* that?"

In the silence following this, no one said a word. But I knew the answer.

More than anyone in that room, I was aware of exactly the sort of person who did such a thing. What I hadn't realized until that very moment, though, was that it wasn't just my mother who was guilty of all these offenses. I'd told myself that everything I'd done in the weeks before and since she left was to make sure I would never be like her. But it was too late. All I had to do was look at the way I'd reacted to what Cora had told me that morning—taking off, getting wasted, letting myself be left alone in a strange place—to know I already was.

It was almost a relief, this specific truth. I wanted to say it out loud—to him, to Cora, to Nate, to everyone—so they would know not to keep trying to save me or make me better somehow. What was the point, when the pattern was already repeating? It was too late.

But as I dropped my hand from my eyes to say this to Jamie, I realized I couldn't see him anymore. My view was blocked by my sister, who had moved to stand between us, one hand stretched out behind her, toward me. Seeing her, I remembered a thousand nights in another house: the two of us together, another part of a pattern, just one I'd thought had long ago been broken, never to be repeated.

Perhaps I was just like my mother. But looking up at Cora's hand, I had to wonder whether it was possible that this wasn't already decided for me, and if maybe, just maybe, this was my one last chance to try and prove it. There was no way to know. There never is. But I reached out and took it anyway.

Chapter Nine

When I came down the next morning, Jamie was out by the pond. From the kitchen, I could see his breath coming out in puffs as he crouched by its edge, his coffee mug on the ground by his feet. It was what he did every morning, rain or shine, even when it was freezing, the grass still shiny with frost all around him. Just a few minutes spent checking on the state of the small world he'd created, making sure it had all made it through to another day.

It was getting colder now, and the fish were staying low. Pretty soon, they'd disappear entirely beneath the leaves and rocks on the bottom to endure the long winter. "You don't take them in?" I'd asked him, when he'd first mentioned this.

Jamie shook his head. "It's more natural this way," he explained. "When the water freezes, they go deep, and stay there until the spring."

"They don't die?"

"Hope not," he said, adjusting a clump of lilies. "Ideally, they just kind of . . . go dormant. They can't handle the cold, so they don't try. And then when it warms up, they'll get active again."

At the time, this had seemed so strange to me, as well as yet another reason not to get attached to my fish. Now, though, I could see the appeal of just disappearing, then laying low and waiting until the environment was more friendly to emerge. If only that was an option for me.

"He's not going to come to you," Cora said now from where she was sitting at the island, flipping through a magazine. The clothes I'd been wearing the night before were already washed and folded on the island beside her, one thing easily fixed. "If you want to talk to him, you have to take the first step."

"I can't," I said, remembering how angry he'd been the night before. "He hates me."

"No," she said, turning a page. "He's just disappointed in you."

I looked back out at Jamie, who was now leaning over the waterfall, examining the rocks. "With him, that seems even worse."

She looked up, giving me a sympathetic smile. "I know."

The first thing I'd done when I woke up that morning—after acknowledging my pounding, relentless headache—was try to piece together the events from the day before. My argument with Cora I remembered, as well as my ride to school and to Jackson. Once I got to the clearing, though, it got fuzzy.

Certain things, however, were crystal clear. Like how strange it was not only to see Jamie angry, but to see him angry at me. Or catching that glimpse of my mother's face, distorted with mine, staring back from the mirror. And finally how, after I took her hand, Cora led me silently up the stairs to my room, where she'd stripped off my clothes and stood outside the shower while I numbly washed my hair and myself, before helping me into my pajamas and my bed. I'd wanted to say something to her, but every time I tried she just shook her head. The last thing I recalled before falling asleep was her sitting on the edge of my mattress, a dark form with the light coming in the window behind her. How long she stayed, I had no idea, although I vaguely remembered opening my eyes more than once and being surprised to find her still there.

Now the door behind me opened, and Jamie came in, Roscoe tagging along at his feet. I looked up at him, but he brushed past, not making eye contact, to put his mug in the sink. "So," Cora said slowly, "I think maybe we all should—"

"I've got to go into the office," he said, grabbing his phone and keys off the counter. "I told John I'd meet him to go over those changes to the campaign."

"Jamie," she said, looking over at me.

"I'll see you later," he said, then kissed the top of her head and left the room, Roscoe following. A moment later, I heard the front door shut behind him.

I swallowed, looking outside again. From anyone else, this would be hardly an insult, if even noticeable. But even I knew Jamie well enough to understand it as the serious snub it was.

Cora came over, sliding into the chair opposite mine. "Hey," she said, keeping her eyes on me until I finally turned to face her. "It's okay. You guys will work this out. He's just hurt right now."

"I didn't mean to hurt him," I said as a lump rose in my throat. I was suddenly embarrassed, although whether by the fact I was crying, or crying in front of Cora was hard to say.

"I know." She reached over, sliding her hand onto mine. "But you have to understand, this is all new to him. In his family, everyone talks about everything. People don't take off; they don't come home drunk. He's not like us."

Like us. Funny how up until recently—like maybe even the night before—I hadn't been convinced there was an us here at all. So maybe things *could* change. "I'm sorry," I said to her. "I really am."

She nodded, then sat back, dropping her hand. "I appreciate that. But the fact is, we did trust you, and you betrayed that trust. So there have to be some consequences."

Here it comes, I thought. I sat back, picking up my water bottle, and braced myself.

"First," she began, "no going out on weeknights. Weekends, only for work, for the foreseeable future. We strongly considered making you give up your job, but we've decided to let you keep it through the holidays, with the provision that we revisit the issue in January. If we find out that you skipped school again, the job goes. No discussion."

"All right," I said. It wasn't like I was in any position to argue.

Cora swallowed, then looked at me for a long moment. "I know a lot happened yesterday. It was emotional for both of us. But you doing drugs or drinking . . . that's unacceptable. It's a violation of the agreement we arranged so you could come here, and if the courts ever found out, you'd have to go back to Poplar House. It *cannot* happen again."

I had a flash of the one night I'd stayed there: the scratchy pajamas, the narrow bed, the house director reading over the sheriff's report while I sat in front of her, silent. I swallowed, then said, "It's not going to."

"This is serious, Ruby," she said. "I mean, when I saw you come in like that last night, I just . . ."

"I know," I said.

". . . it's too familiar," she finished. Then she looked at me, hard. "For both of us. You're better than that. You know it."

"It was stupid of me," I said. "I just . . . When you told me that about Mom, I just kind of freaked."

She looked down at the salt shaker between us, sliding it sideways, then back again. "Look, the bottom line is, she lied to both of us. Which shouldn't really be all that surprising. That said, though, I wish I could have made it easier for you, Ruby. I really do. There's a lot I'd do different, given the chance."

I didn't want to ask. Luckily, I didn't have to.

"I've thought about it so much since I left, how I could have tried harder to keep in touch," she said, smoothing back a few curls with her hand. "Maybe I could have found a way to take you with me, rent an apartment or something."

"Cora. You were only eighteen."

"I know. But I also knew Mom was unstable, even then. And things only got worse," she said. "I shouldn't have trusted her to let you get in touch with me, either. There were steps I could have taken, things I could have done. I mean, now, at work, I deal every day with these kids from messed-up families, and I'm so much better equipped to handle it. To handle taking care of you, too. But if I'd only known then—"

"Stop," I said. "It's over. Done. It doesn't matter now."

She bit her lip. "I want to believe that," she said. "I really do."

I looked at my sister, remembering how I'd always followed her around so much as a kid, clinging to her more and more as my mom pulled away. What a weird feeling to find myself back here, dependent on her again. Just as I thought this, something occurred to me. "Cora?"

"Yeah?"

"Do you remember that day you left for school?"

She nodded.

"Before you left, you went back in and spoke to Mom. What did you say to her?"

She exhaled, sitting back in her chair. "Wow," she said. "I haven't thought about that in years."

I wasn't sure why I'd asked her this, or if it was even important. "She never mentioned it," I said. "I just always wondered."

Cora was quiet for a moment, and I wondered if she was even going to answer me at all. But then she said, "I told her that if I found out she ever hit you, I would call the police. And that I was coming back for you as soon as I could, to get you out of there." She reached up, tucking a piece of hair behind her ear. "I believed that, Ruby. I really did. I wanted to take care of you."

"It's all right," I told her.

"It's not," she continued, over me. "But now, here, I have the chance to make up for it. Late, yes, but I do. I know you don't want to be here, and that it's far from ideal, but . . . I want to help you. But you have to let me. Okay?"

This sounded so passive, so easy, although I knew it wasn't. As I thought this, though, I had a flash of Peyton again, standing at the bottom of that stairway. *Why are you surprised?* she'd said, and for all the wrongness of the situation, I knew she was right. You get what you give, but also what you're willing to take. The night before, I'd offered up my hand. Now, if I held on, there was no telling what it was possible to receive in return.

For a moment we just sat there, the quiet of the kitchen all around us. Finally I said, "Do you think Mom's okay?"

"I don't know," she replied. And then, more softly, "I hope so."

Maybe to anyone else, her saying this would have seemed strange. But to me, it made perfect sense, as this was the pull of my mother: then, now, always. For all the coldness, her bad behavior, the slights and outright abuse, we were still tied to her. It was like those songs I'd heard as a child, each so familiar, and all mine. When I got older and realized the words were sad, the stories tragic, it didn't make me love them any less. By then, they were already part of me, woven into my consciousness and memory. I couldn't cut them away any more easily than I could my mother herself. And neither could Cora. This was what we had in common—what made us this us.

After outlining the last few terms of my punishment (mandatory checking-in after school, agreeing to therapy, at least for a little while), Cora squeezed my shoulder, then left the room, Roscoe rousing himself from where he'd been planted in the doorway to follow her upstairs. I sat in the quiet of the kitchen for a moment, then I went out to the pond.

The fish were down deep, but after crouching over the water for a few minutes, I could make out my white one, circling by some moss-covered rocks. I'd just pushed myself to my feet when I heard the bang of a door slamming. When I turned, expecting to see Cora, no one was there, and I realized the sound had come from Nate's house. Sure enough, a moment later I saw a blond head bob past on the other side of the fence, then disappear.

Like the night before, when I'd been poised with Roscoe at the top of the walk, my first instinct was to go back inside. Avoid, deny, at least while it was still an option. But Nate had taken me out of those woods. For my own twisted reasons, I might not have wanted to believe this made us friends. But now, if nothing else, we were something.

I went inside, picked up his sweatshirt from the counter, then took in a breath and started across the grass to the fence. The gate was slightly ajar, and I could see Nate through the open door to the nearby pool house, leaning over a table. I slid through the gate, then walked around the pool to come up behind him. He was opening up a stack of small bags, then lining them up one by one.

"Let me guess," I said. "They're for cupcakes."

He jumped, startled, then turned around. "You're not far off, actually," he said when he saw me. "They're gift bags."

I stepped in behind him, then walked around to the other side of the table. The room itself, meant to be some kind of cabana, was mostly empty and clearly used for the business; a rack on wheels held a bunch of dry-cleaning, and I recognized some of Harriet's milk-crate storage system piled against a wall. There was also a full box of WE WORRY SO YOU DON'T HAVE TO air fresheners by the door, giving the room a piney scent that bordered on medicinal.

I watched quietly as Nate continued to open bags until the entire table was covered. Then he reached beneath it for a box and began pulling plastic-wrapped objects out of it, dropping one in each bag. *Clunk, clunk, clunk.*

"So," I said as he worked his way down the line, "about yesterday."

"You look like you feel better."

"Define better."

"Well," he said, glancing at me, "you're upright. And conscious."

"Kind of sad when that's an improvement," I said.

"But it is an improvement," he replied. "Right?"

I made a face. Positivity anytime was hard for me to take, but in the morning with a hangover, almost impossible. "So," I said, holding out the sweatshirt, "I wanted to bring this back to you. I figured you were probably missing it."

"Thanks," he said, taking it and laying it on a chair behind him. "It is my favorite."

"It does have that feel," I replied. "Well worn and all that."

"True," he said, going back to the bags. "But it also reflects my personal life philosophy."

I looked at the sweatshirt again. "'You swim' is a philosophy?"

He shrugged. "Better than 'you sink,' right?"

Hard to argue with that. "I guess."

"Plus there's the fact," he said, "that wearing that sweat-shirt is the closest I might get to the U now."

"I thought you had a scholarship," I said, remembering the guy who'd called out to him in the parking lot.

"I did," he said, going back to dropping things into the bags. "But that was before I quit swim team. Now I've got to get in strictly on my grades, which frankly are not as good as my swimming."

I considered this as he moved down the next row, still adding things to the bags. "So why did you quit?"

"I don't know." He shrugged. "I was really into it when I lived in Arizona, but here . . . it just wasn't that fun any-more. Plus my dad needed me for the business."

"Still, seems like a big decision, giving it up entirely," I said.

"Not really," he replied. He reached down, picking up another box. "So, was it bad when you came in last night?"

"Yeah," I said, somewhat surprised by the sudden change in subject. "Jamie was really pissed off."

"Jamie was?"

"I know. It was bizarre." I swallowed, taking a breath. "Anyway, I just wanted to say . . . that I appreciate what you did. Even if, you know, it didn't seem like it at the time."

"You weren't exactly grateful," he agreed. *Clunk, clunk, clunk.*

"I was a bitch. And I'm sorry." I said this quickly, prob-ably too quickly, and felt him look up at me again. *So em-barrassing,* I thought, redirecting my attention to the bag in front of me. "What are you putting in there, anyway?"

"Little chocolate houses," he replied.

"What?"

"Yeah," he said, tossing one to me. "See for yourself. You can keep it, if you want."

Sure enough, it was a tiny house. There were even windows and a door. "Kind of strange, isn't it?" I said.

"Not really. This client's a builder. I think they're for some open house or something."

I slid the house into my pocket as he dropped the box, which was now almost empty, and pulled out another one, which was full of brochures, a picture of a woman's smiling face taking up most of the front. QUEEN HOMES, it said. LET US BUILD YOUR CASTLE! Nate started sliding one into each bag, working his way down the line. After watching him for a moment, I reached across, taking a handful myself and starting on the ones closest to me.

"You know," he said, after we'd worked in silence for a moment, "I wasn't trying to embarrass you by showing up yesterday. I just thought you might need help."

"Clearly, I did," I said, glad to have the bags to concentrate on. There was something soothing, orderly, to dropping in the brochures, each in its place. "If you hadn't come, who knows what would have happened."

Nate didn't speculate as to this, which I had to admit I appreciated. Instead, he said, "Can I ask you something?"

I looked up at him, then slid another brochure in. "Sure."

"What was it really like, living on your own?"

I'd assumed this would be a question about yesterday, like why I'd done it, or a request for further explanation of my twisted theories on friendship. This, however, was completely unexpected. Which was probably why I answered it honestly. "It wasn't bad at first," I said. "In fact, it was kind of a relief. Living with my mom had never been easy, especially at the end."

He nodded, then dropped the box onto the floor and pulled out another one, this one filled with magnets emblazoned with the Queen Homes logo. He held it out to me and I took a handful, then began working my way up the line. "But then," I said, "it got harder. I was having trouble keeping up with bills, and the power kept getting turned off. . . ." I was wondering if I should go on, but when I glanced up, he was watching me intently, so I continued. "I don't know. There was more to it than I thought, I guess."

"That's true for a lot of things," he said.

I looked up at him again. "Yeah," I said, watching him continue to drop in magnets, one by one. "It is."

"Nate!" I heard a voice call from outside. Over his shoulder, I could see his dad, standing in the door to the main house, his phone to his ear. "Do you have those bags ready yet?"

"Yeah," he called over his shoulder, reaching down to pull out another box. "Just one sec."

"They need them now," Mr. Cross said. "We told them ten at the latest. Let's move!"

Nate reached into the new box, which was full of individually wrapped votive candles in all different colors, and began distributing them at warp speed. I grabbed a handful, doing the same. "Thanks," he said as we raced through the rows. "We're kind of under the gun here."

"No problem," I told him. "And anyway, I owe you."

"You don't," he said.

"Come on. You saved my ass yesterday. Literally."

"Well," he said, dropping in one last candle, "then you'll get me back."

"How?"

"Somehow," he said, looking at me. "We've got time, right?"

"Nate!" Mr. Cross called out, his tone clearly disputing this. "What the hell are you doing in there?"

"I'm coming," Nate said, picking up the empty boxes and beginning to stack the bags into them. I reached to help, but he shook his head. "It's cool, I've got it. Thanks, anyway."

"You sure?"

"Nate!"

He glanced over his shoulder at his dad, still standing in the doorway, then at me. "Yeah. I'm good. Thanks again for your help."

I nodded, then stepped back from the table as he shoved the last of the bags into a box, stacking it onto the other one. As he headed for the door, I fell in behind him. "Finally," Mr. Cross said as we came out onto the patio. "I mean, how hard is it—" He stopped, suddenly, seeing me. "Oh," he said, his face and tone softening. "I didn't realize you had company."

"This is Ruby," Nate said, bringing the box over to him.

"Of course," Mr. Cross said, smiling at me. I tried to reciprocate, even though I suddenly felt uneasy, remembering that night I'd seen him in this same place with Roscoe. "How's that brother-in-law of yours doing? There's some buzz he might be going public soon with his company. Any truth to that?"

"Um," I said. "I don't know."

"We should go," Nate said to him. "If they want us there by ten."

"Right." Still, Mr. Cross stayed where he was, smiling at me, as I started around the pool to the gate. I could see Nate behind him in the house. He was watching me as well, but when I raised my hand to wave, he stepped down a hallway, out of sight. "Take care," Mr. Cross said, raising his hand to me. He thought I'd been waving at him. "Don't be a stranger."

I nodded, still feeling unsettled as I got to the fence and pushed my way through. Crossing the yard, I remembered the house Nate had given me, and reached down to pull it out and look at it again. It was so perfect, pristine, wrapped away in plastic and tied with a pretty bow. But there was something so eerie about it, as well—although what, I couldn't say—that I found myself putting it away again.

*   *   *

"Okay," I said, uncapping my pen. "What does family mean to you?"

"Not speaking," Harriet replied instantly.

"Not speaking?" Reggie said.

"Yeah."

He was just staring at her.

"What? What were you going to say?"

"I don't know," he said. "Comfort, maybe? History? The beginning of life?"

"Well, that's you," she told him. "For me, family means the silent treatment. At any given moment, someone is always not speaking to someone else."

"Really," I said.

"We're passive-aggressive people," she explained, taking a sip of her coffee. "Silence is our weapon of choice. Right now, for instance, I'm not speaking to two of my sisters and one brother."

"How many kids are in your family?" I asked.

"Seven total."

"That," Reggie said, "is just plain sad."

"Tell me about it," Harriet said. "I never got enough time in the bathroom."

"I meant the silence thing," Reggie told her.

"Oh." Harriet hopped up on the stool by the register, crossing her legs. "Well, maybe so. But it certainly cuts down the phone bill."

He shot her a disapproving look. "That is not funny. Communication is crucial."

"Maybe at your house," she replied. "At mine, silence is golden. And common."

"To me," Reggie said, picking up a bottle of Vitamin A and moving it thoughtfully from one hand to the other, "family is, like, the wellspring of human energy. The place where all life begins."

Harriet studied him over her coffee cup. "What do your parents do, again?"

"My father sells insurance. Mom teaches first grade."

"So suburban!"

"Isn't it, though?" He smiled. "I'm the black sheep, believe it or not."

"Me, too!" Harriet said. "I was supposed to go to med school. My dad's a surgeon. When I dropped out to do the jewelry-design thing, they freaked. Didn't speak to me for months."

"That must have been awful," he said.

She considered this. "Not really. I think it was kind of good for me, actually. My family is so big, and everyone always has an opinion, whether you want to hear it or not. I'd never done anything all on my own before, without their help or input. It was liberating."

Liberating, I wrote down. Reggie said, "You know, this explains a *lot.*"

No kidding, I thought.

"What's that supposed to mean?" Harriet asked.

"Nothing," he told her. "So what makes you give up the silent treatment? When do you decide to talk again?"

Harriet considered this as she took a sip of coffee. "Huh," she said. "I guess when someone else does something worse. Then you need people on your side, so you make up with one person, just as you're getting pissed off at another."

"So it's an endless cycle," I said.

"I guess." She took another sip. "Coming together, falling apart. Isn't that what families are all about?"

"No," Reggie says. "Only yours."

They both burst out laughing, as if this was the funniest thing ever. I looked down at my notebook, where all I had written was *not speaking, comfort, wellspring,* and *liberating.* This project was going to take a while.

"Incoming," Harriet said suddenly, nodding toward a guy and girl my age who were approaching, deep in conversation.

". . . wrong with a Persian cat sweatshirt?" said the guy, who was sort of chubby, with what looked like a home-done haircut.

"Nothing, if she's eighty-seven and her name is Nana," the girl replied. She had long curly hair, held back at the nape of her neck, and was wearing cowboy boots, a bright red dress, and a cropped puffy parka with mittens hanging from the cuffs. "I mean, think about it. What kind of message are you trying to send here?"

"I don't know," the guy said as they got closer. "I mean, I like her, so . . ."

"Then you don't buy her a sweatshirt," the girl said flatly. "You buy her jewelry. Come on."

I put down the feather duster I was holding, standing up straighter as they came up to the cart, the girl already eyeing the rows of thin silver hoops on display. "Hi," I said to the guy, who, up close, looked even younger and dorkier. His T-shirt—which said ARMAGEDDON EXPO '06: ARE YOU READY FOR THE END?—didn't help matters. "Can I help you?"

"We need something that screams romance," the girl said, plucking a ring out and quickly examining it before putting it back. As she leaned into the row of lights overhead, I noticed that her face was dotted with faint scars. "A ring is too serious, I think. But earrings don't say enough."

"Earrings don't say anything," the guy mumbled, sniffing the incense. He sneezed, then added, "They're inanimate objects."

"And you are hopeless," she told him, moving down to the necklaces. "What about yours?"

Startled, I glanced back at the girl, who was looking right at me. "What?"

She nodded at my neck. "Your necklace. Do you sell those here?"

"Um," I said, my hand reaching up to it, "not really. But we do have some similar chains, and charms that you can—"

"I like the idea of the key, though," the girl said, coming around the cart. "It's different. And you can read it so many ways."

"You want me to give her a key?" the guy asked.

"I want you to give her a *possibility*," she told him, looking at my necklace again. "And that's what a key represents. An open door, a chance. You know?"

I'd never really thought about my key this way. But in the interest of a sale, I said, "Well, yeah. Absolutely. I mean, you could buy a chain here, then get a key to put on it."

"Exactly!" the girl said, pointing a finger at the nearby KEY-OSK, which sold keys and key accessories of all kinds. "It's perfect."

"You'll want a somewhat thick one," I told her. "But not too thick. You need it to be strong and delicate at the same time."

The girl nodded. "That's it," she said. "Just what I had in mind."

Ten minutes and fifteen dollars later, I watched them as they walked away, bag in hand, over to the KEY-OSK cart, where the girl explained what she wanted. I watched the saleswoman as she pulled out a small collection of keys, sliding them across for them to examine.

"Nice job," Harriet said, coming up beside me. "You salvaged the sale, even if we didn't have exactly what she was looking for."

"It was her idea," I said. "I just went with it."

"Still. It worked, right?"

I glanced over again at KEY-OSK, where the girl in the parka was picking up a small key as her friend and the saleswoman looked on. People were passing between us, hustling and bustling, but still I craned my neck, watching with Harriet as she slid it over the clasp, carefully, then down onto our chain. It dangled there for a second, spinning slightly, before she closed her hand around it, making it disappear.

*   *   *

I'd just stepped off the greenway, later that afternoon, when I saw the bird.

At first, it was just a shadow, passing overhead, temporarily blotting out the light. Only when it cleared the trees and reached the open sky did I see it in full. It was *huge*, long and gray, with an immense wingspan, so big it seemed impossible for it to be airborne.

For a moment, I just stood there, watching its shadow move down the street. It was only when I started walking again that it hit me.

It's herons and waterbirds you really need to worry about, Heather had said. *One swoop, and they can do some serious damage.*

No way, I thought, but at the same time I found myself picking up the pace as Cora's house came into view, breaking into a jog, then a run. It was cold out—the air was stinging my lungs, and I knew I had to look crazy, but I kept going, my breath ragged in my chest as I cut across the neighbor's lawn, then alongside Cora's garage to the side yard.

The bird was impossible to miss, standing in the shallow end, its wings slightly raised as if it had only just landed there. Distantly, I realized that it was beautiful, caught with the sun setting in the distance, its elegant form reflected in the pond's surface. But then it dipped its massive beak down into the water.

"Stop!" I yelled, my voice carrying and carrying far. "Stop it!"

The bird jerked, its wings spreading out a little farther, so it looked like it was hovering. But it stayed where it was.

For a long moment, nothing happened. The bird stood there, wings outstretched, with me only a short distance away, my heart thumping in my ears. I could hear cars passing on the street, a door slamming somewhere a few yards over. But all around us, it was nothing but still.

At any moment, I knew the bird could reach down and pluck up a fish, maybe even my fish. For all I knew I was already too late to save anything.

"Get out!" I screamed, louder this time, as I moved closer. "Now! *Get out now!*"

At first, it didn't move. But then, almost imperceptibly at first, it began to lift up, then a little farther, and farther still. I was so close to it as it moved over me, its enormous wings spread out, pumping higher and higher into the night sky, so amazing and surreal, like something you could only imagine. And maybe I would have thought it was only a dream, if Jamie hadn't seen it, too.

I didn't even realize he was standing right behind me, his hands in his pockets, and his face upturned, until I turned to watch as the bird soared over us, still rising.

"It was a heron," I told him, forgetting our silence. I was gasping, my breath uneven. "It was in the pond."

He nodded. "I know."

I swallowed, crossing my arms over my chest. My heart was still pounding, so hard I wondered if he could hear it. "I'm sorry for what I did," I said. "I'm so, so sorry."

For a moment, he was quiet. "Okay," he said finally. Then he reached a hand up, resting it on my shoulder, and together, we watched the bird soar over the roofline into the sky.

Chapter Ten

"You want buttered, or not?"

"Either is fine," I said.

Olivia eyed me over the counter, then walked over to the butter dispenser, sticking the bag of popcorn she was holding underneath it and giving it a couple of quick smacks with her hand. "Then you are officially my favorite kind of customer," she said. "As well as unlike ninety-nine percent of the moviegoing population."

"Really."

"Most people," she said, turning the bag and shaking it slightly, then adding a bit more, "have very strong views on their butter preference. Some want none—the popcorn must be dry, or they freak out. Others want it sopping to the point they can feel it through the bag."

I made a face. "Yuck."

She shrugged. "I don't judge. Unless you're one of those totally anal-retentive types that wants it in specific layers, which takes ages. Then I hate you."

I smiled, taking the popcorn as she slid it across to me. "Thanks," I said, reaching for my wallet. "What do I—?"

"Don't worry about it," she said, waving me off.

"You sure?"

"If you'd asked for butter layers, I would have charged you. But that was easy. Come on."

She came out from behind the counter, and I followed her across the lobby of the Vista 10—which was mostly empty except for some kids playing video games by the restrooms—to the box office door. She pulled it open, ducking inside, then flipped the sign in the window to OPEN before clearing a bunch of papers from a nearby stool for me to sit down. "You sure?" I said, glancing around. "Your boss won't mind?"

"My dad's the manager," she said. "Plus I'm working Saturday morning, the kiddie shift, against my will. The girl who was supposed to be here flaked out on him. I can do what I want."

"The kiddie—?" I began, then stopped when I saw a woman approaching with about five elementary school–aged children, some running ahead in front, others dragging along behind. One kid had a handheld video game and wasn't even looking where he was going, yet still managed to navigate the curb without tripping, which was kind of impressive. The woman, who appeared to be in her mid-forties and was wearing a long green sweater and carrying a huge purse, stopped in front of the window, squinting up.

"Mom," one of the kids, a girl with ponytails, said, tugging on her arm. "I want Smarties."

"No candy," the woman murmured, still staring up at the movie listings.

"But you promised!" the girl said, her voice verging on a whine. One of the other kids, a younger boy, was now on her other side, tugging as well. I watched the woman reach out to him absently, brushing her hand over the top of his head as he latched himself around her leg.

"Yes!" the kid with the handheld yelled, jumping up and down. "I made level five with the cherries!"

Olivia shot me a look, then pushed down the button by her microphone, leaning into it. "Can I help you?" she asked.

"Yes," the woman said, still staring up, "I need . . . five children and one adult for *Pretzel Dog Two*."

Olivia punched this into her register. "That'll be thirty-six dollars."

"Thirty-six?" the woman said, finally looking at us. The girl was tugging her arm again. "With the child's price? Are you sure?"

"Yes."

"Well, that's crazy. It's just a movie!"

"Don't I know it," Olivia told her, hitting the ticket button a few times. She put her hand on the tickets as the woman reached into her huge purse, digging around for a few minutes before finally coming up with two twenties. Then Olivia slid them across, along with her change. "Enjoy the show."

The woman grumbled, hoisting her bag up her shoulder, then moved into the theater, the kids trailing along behind her. Olivia sighed, sitting back and stretching her arms over her head as two minivans pulled into the lot in front of us in quick succession.

"Don't I know it," I said, remembering my mom with

her clipboard, on so many front stoops. "My mom used to say that."

"Empathy works," Olivia replied. "And it's not like she's wrong. I mean, it *is* expensive. But we make the bulk of our money on concessions, and she's sneaking in food for all those rug rats. So it all comes out even, really."

I looked over my shoulder back into the lobby, where the woman was now leading her brood to a theater. "You think?"

"Did you see that purse? Please." She reached over, taking a piece of popcorn from my bag, which I hadn't even touched. Apparently she'd noticed, next saying, "What? Too much butter?"

I shook my head, looking down at it. "No, it's fine."

"I was about to say. Don't get picky on me now."

The minivans were deboarding now, people emptying car seats and sliding open back doors. Olivia sighed, checking her watch. "I didn't really come here for the popcorn," I said. "I wanted . . . I just wanted to thank you."

"You already did," she said.

"No," I corrected her, "I *tried*—twice—but you wouldn't let me. Which, frankly, I just don't understand."

She reached for the popcorn again, taking out a handful. "Honestly," she said as another pack of parents and kids approached, "it's not that complicated. You did something for me, I did something for you. We're even. Let it go already."

This was easier said than done, though, something I considered as she sold a bunch of tickets, endured more kvetching about the prices, and directed one woman with a very unhappy toddler in the direction of the bathroom. By the time things had calmed down, fifteen minutes had passed, and I'd worked my way halfway through the popcorn bag.

"Look," I said, "all I'm saying is that I just . . . I want you to know I'm not like that."

"Like what?" she said, arranging some bills in the register.

"Like someone who ditches school to get drunk. I was just having a really bad day, and—"

"Ruby." Her voice was sharp, getting my attention. "You don't have to explain, okay? I get it."

"You do?"

"Switching schools totally sucked for me," she said, sitting back in her chair. "I missed everything about my life at Jackson. I still do—so much so that even now, after a year, I haven't really bothered to get settled at Perkins. I don't even have any friends there."

"Me neither," I said.

"Yes, you do," she said. "You have Nate Cross."

"We're not really friends," I told her.

She raised her eyebrows. "The boy drove fifteen miles to pick you up out of the woods."

"Only because you told him to," I said.

"No," she said pointedly. "All I did was let him know where you were."

"Same thing."

"Actually, it isn't," she said, reaching over and taking another piece of popcorn. "There's a big difference between information and action. I gave him the facts, mostly because I felt responsible about leaving you there with that loser in the first place. But going there? That was all him. So I hope you were sufficiently grateful."

"I wasn't," I said quietly.

"No?" She seemed genuinely surprised. "Well . . ." she said, drawing the word out. "Why not?"

I looked down at my popcorn, already feeling that butter-and-salt hangover beginning to hit. "I'm not very good at accepting help," I said. "It's an issue."

"I can understand that," she said.

"Yeah?"

She shrugged. "It's not the easiest thing for me, either, especially when I think I don't need it."

"Exactly."

"But," she continued, not letting me off the hook, "you *were* passed out in the woods. I mean, you clearly needed help, so you're lucky he realized it, even if you didn't."

There was a big crowd approaching now, lots of kids and parents. We could see them coming at us from across the parking lot like a wide, very disorganized wave.

"I want to try to make it up to him," I said to Olivia. "To change, you know? But it's not so easy to do."

"Yeah," she said, taking another handful of popcorn and tossing it into her mouth as the crowd closed in. "Don't I know it."

* * *

Everyone has their weak spot. The one thing that, despite your best efforts, will always bring you to your knees, regardless of how strong you are otherwise. For some people, it's love. Others, money or alcohol. Mine was even worse: calculus.

I was convinced it was the reason I would not go to college. Not my checkered background, or that I was getting my applications together months after everyone else, or even the fact that up until recently, I hadn't even been sure I wanted to go at all. Instead, in my mind, it would all come down to one class and its respective rules and theorems, dragging down my GPA and me with it.

I always started studying with the best of intentions, telling myself that today just might be the day it all fell into place, and everything would be different. More often than not, though, after a couple of pages of practice problems, I'd find myself spiraling into an all-out depression. When it was really bad, I'd put my head down on my book and contemplate alternate options for my future.

"Whoa," I heard a voice say. It was muffled slightly by my hair, and my arm, which I locked around my head in an effort to keep my brain from seeping out. "You okay?"

I lifted myself up, expecting to see Jamie. Instead, it was Nate, standing in the kitchen doorway, a stack of dry-cleaning over one shoulder. Roscoe was at his feet, sniffing excitedly.

"No," I told him as he turned and walked out to the foyer, opening the closet there. With Jamie hard at work on the new ad campaign, and Cora backlogged in cases, they'd been outsourcing more and more of their errands to Rest Assured, although this Saturday morning was the first time Nate had shown up when I was home. Now I heard some banging around as he hung up the cleaning. "I was just thinking about my future."

"That bad, huh?" he said, crouching down to pet Roscoe, who leaped up, licking his face.

"Only if I fail calculus," I said. "Which seems increasingly likely."

"Nonsense." He stood up, wiping his hands on his jeans, and came over, leaning against the counter. "How could that happen, when you personally know the best calc tutor in town?"

"You?" I raised my eyebrows. "Really?"

"Oh God, no," he said, shuddering. "I'm good at a lot of things, but not that. I barely passed myself."

"You did pass, though."

"Yeah. But only because of Gervais."

Immediately, he popped into my head, small and foul smelling. "No thanks," I said. "I'm not that desperate."

"Didn't look that way when I came in." He walked over, pulling out a chair and sitting down opposite me, then drew my book over to him, flipping a page and wincing at it. "God, just looking at this stuff freaks me out. I mean, how basic is the power rule? And yet why can I still not understand it?"

I just looked at him. "The what?"

He shot me a look. "You need Gervais," he said, pushing the book at me. "And quickly."

"That is just what I *don't* need," I said, sitting back and pulling my leg to my chest. "Can you imagine actually asking Gervais for a favor? Not to mention owing him any-thing. He'd make my life a living hell."

"Oh, right," Nate said, nodding. "I forgot. You have that thing."

"What thing?"

"The indebtedness thing," he said. "You have to be self-sufficient, can't stand owing anyone. Right?"

"Well," I said. Put that way, it didn't sound like some-thing you wanted to agree to, necessarily. "If you mean that I don't like being dependent on people, then yes. That is true."

"But," he said, reaching down to pat Roscoe, who had settled at his feet, "you *do* owe me."

Again, this did not seem to be something I wanted to second, at least not immediately. "What's your point?"

He shrugged. "Only that, you know, I have a lot of er-rands to run today. Tons of cupcakes to ice."

"And . . ."

"And I could use a little help," he said. "If you felt like, you know, paying me back."

"Do these errands involve Gervais?" I asked.

"No."

I thought for a second. "Okay," I said, shutting my book. "I'm in."

*   *   *

"Now," he said, as I followed him up the front steps of a small brick house that had a flag with a watermelon flying off the front, "before we go in, I should warn you about the smell."

"The smell?" I asked, but then he was unlocking the door and pushing it open, transforming this from a question to an all-out exclamation. *Oh my God*, I thought as the odor hit me from all sides. It was like a fog; even as you walked right through it, it just kept going.

"Don't worry," Nate said over his shoulder, continuing through the living room, past a couch covered with a brightly colored quilt to a sunny kitchen area beyond. "You get used to it after a minute or two. Soon, you won't even notice it."

"What *is* it?"

Then, though, as I waited in the entryway—Nate had disappeared into the kitchen—I got my answer. It started with just an odd feeling, which escalated to creepy as I realized I was being watched.

As soon as I spotted the cat on the stairs—a fat tabby, with green eyes—observing me with a bored expression, I noticed the gray one under the coatrack to my right, followed by a black one curled up on the back of the couch and a long-haired white one stretched out across the Oriental rug in front of it. They were everywhere.

I found Nate on an enclosed back porch where five carriers were lined up on a table. Each one had a Polaroid of a cat taped to it, a name written in clean block lettering beneath: RAZZY. CESAR. BLU. MARGIE. LYLE.

"So this is a shelter or something?" I asked.

"Sabrina takes in cats that can't get placed," he said, picking up two of the carriers and carrying them into the living room. "You know, ones that are sick or older. The unwanted and abandoned, as it were." He grabbed one of the Polaroids, of a thin gray cat—RAZZY, apparently—then glanced around the room. "You see this guy anywhere?"

We both looked around the room, where there were several cats but no gray ones. "Better hit upstairs," Nate said. "Can you look around for the others? Just go by the pictures on the carriers."

He left the room, jogging up the stairs. A moment later, I heard him whistling, the ceiling creaking as he moved around above. I looked at the row of carriers and the Polaroids attached, then spotted one of them, a black cat with yellow eyes—LYLE—watching me from a nearby chair. As I picked up the carrier, the picture flipped up, exposing a Post-it that was stuck to the back.

Lyle will be getting a checkup and blood drawn to monitor how he's responding to the cancer drugs. If Dr. Loomis feels they are not making a difference, please tell him to call me on my cell phone to discuss if there is further action to take, or whether I should just focus on keeping him comfortable.

"Poor guy," I said, positioning the carrier in front of him, the door open. "Hop in, okay?"

He didn't. Even worse, when I went to nudge him forward, he reached out, swiping at me, his claws scraping across my skin.

I dropped the carrier, which hit the floor, the open door banging against it. Looking down at my hand, I could already see the scratches, beads of blood rising up in places. "You little shit," I said. He just stared back at me, as if he'd never moved at all.

"Oh, man," Nate said, coming around the corner carrying two cats, one under each arm. "You went after Lyle?"

"You said to get them," I told him.

"I said to *look*," he said. "Not try to wrangle. Especially that one—he's trouble. Let me see."

He reached over, taking my hand and peering down at it to examine the scratches. His palm was warm against the underside of my wrist, and as he leaned over it I could see the range of color in his hair falling across his forehead, which went from white blond to a more yellow, all the way to almost brown.

"Sorry," he said. "I should have warned you."

"I'm okay. It's just a little scrape."

He glanced up at me, and I felt my face flush, suddenly even more aware of how close we were to each other. Over his shoulder, Lyle was watching, the pupils of his yellow eyes widening, then narrowing again.

In the end, it took Nate a full twenty minutes to get Lyle in the carrier and to the car, where I was waiting with the others. When he finally slid behind the wheel, I saw his hands were covered with scratches.

"I hope you get combat pay," I said as he started the engine.

"I don't scar, at least," he replied. "And anyway, you can't really blame the guy. It's not like he's ever been given a reason to like the vet."

I just looked at him as we pulled away from the curb. From behind us, someone was already yowling. "You know," I said, "I just can't get behind that kind of attitude."

Nate raised his eyebrows, amused. "You can't what?"

"The whole positive spin—the "oh, it's not the cat's fault

he mauled me" thing. I mean, how do you do that?"

"What's the alternative?" he asked. "Hating all creatures?"

"No," I said, shooting him a look. "But you don't have to give everyone the benefit of the doubt."

"You don't have to assume the worst about everyone, either. The world isn't always out to get you."

"In your opinion," I added.

"Look," he said, "the point is there's no way to be a hundred percent sure about anyone or anything. So you're left with a choice. Either hope for the best, or just expect the worst."

"If you expect the worst, you're never disappointed," I pointed out.

"Yeah, but who lives like that?"

I shrugged. "People who don't get mauled by psycho cats."

"Ah, but you *did*," he said, pointing at me. "So clearly, you aren't that kind of person. Even if you want to be."

After the group vet appointment—during which Lyle scratched the vet, the vet tech, and some poor woman minding her own business in the waiting room—we went back to Sabrina's and re-released the cats to their natural habitat. From there, we hit the dry-cleaners (where we collected tons of suits and dress shirts), the pharmacy (shocking how many people were taking antidepressants, not that I was judging), and One World—the organic grocery store—where we picked up a special order of a wheat-, eggs-, and gluten-free cake, the top of which read HAPPY FORTIETH, MARLA!

"Forty years without wheat or eggs?" I said as we carried it up the front steps of a big house with columns in the front. "That's got to suck."

"She doesn't eat meat, either," he told me, pulling out a ring of keys and flipping through them. When he found the one he was looking for, he stuck it in the lock, pushing the door open. "Or anything processed. Even her shampoo is organic."

"You buy her shampoo?"

"We buy everything. She's always traveling. Kitchen's this way."

I followed him through the house, which was huge and immensely cluttered. There was mail piled on the island, recycling stacked by the back door, and the light on the answering machine was blinking nonstop, the way it does when the memory is packed.

"You know," I said, "for someone so strict about her diet, I'd expect her to be more anal about her house."

"She used to be, before the divorce," Nate said, taking the cake from me and sliding it into the fridge. "Since then, it's gone kind of downhill."

"That explains the Xanax," I said as he took a bottle out of the pharmacy bag, sticking it on the counter.

"You think?"

I turned to the fridge, a portion of which was covered with pictures of various Hollywood actresses dressed in bikinis. On a piece of paper above them, in black marker, was written THINK BEFORE YOU SNACK! "Yes," I said. "She must be really intense."

"Probably is," Nate said, glancing over at the fridge. "I've never met her."

"Really?"

"Sure," he said. "That's kind of the whole point of the business. They don't have to meet us. If we're doing our job right, their stuff just gets done."

"Still," I said, "you have to admit, you're privy to a lot. I mean, look at how much we know about her just from this kitchen."

"Maybe. But you can't really *know* anyone just from their house or their stuff. It's just a tiny part of who they are." He grabbed his keys off the counter. "Come on. We've got four more places to hit before we can quit for the day."

I had to admit it was hard work, or at least harder than it looked. In a way, though, I liked it. Maybe because it reminded me of Commercial, driving up to houses and leaving things, although in this case we got to go inside, and often picked things up, as well. Plus there was something interesting about these little glimpses you got into people's lives: their coat closet, their garage, what cartoons they had on their fridge. Like no matter how different everyone seemed, there were some things that everyone had in common.

Our last stop was a high-rise apartment building with a clean, sleek lobby. As I followed Nate across it, carrying the last of the dry-cleaning, I could hear both our footsteps, amplified all around us.

"So what's the story here?" I asked him as we got into the elevator. I pulled the dry-cleaning tag where I could see it. "Who's P. Collins?"

"A mystery," he said.

"Yeah? How so?"

"You'll see."

On the seventh floor, we stepped out into a long hall lined with identical doors. Nate walked down about halfway, then pulled out his keys and opened the door in front of him. "Go ahead," he said.

When I stepped in, the first thing I was aware of was the stillness. Not just a sense of something being empty, but almost hollow, even though the apartment was fully furnished with sleek, contemporary furniture. In fact, it looked like something out of a magazine, that perfect.

"Wow," I said as Nate took the cleaning from me, disappearing into a bedroom that was off to the right. I walked over to a row of windows that looked out over the entire town, and for miles farther; it was like being on top of the world. "This is amazing."

"It is," he said, coming back into the room. "Which is why it's so weird that whoever it belongs to is never here."

"They must be," I said. "They have dry-cleaning."

"That's the only thing, though," he said. "And it's just a duvet cover. We pick it up about every month or so."

I walked into the kitchen, looking around. The fridge was bare, the counters spotless except for one bottle cap, turned upside down. "Aha," I said. "They drink root beer."

"That's mine," Nate said. "I left it there last time as an experiment, just to see if anyone moved it or threw it away."

"And it's still here?"

"Weird, right?" He walked back over to the windows, pulling open a glass door. Immediately I could smell fresh air blowing in. "I figure it's got to be a rental, or some company-owned kind of deal. For visiting executives or something."

I went into the living room, scanning a low bookcase by the couch. There were a few novels, a guide to traveling in Mexico, a couple of architectural-design books. "I don't know," I said. "I bet someone lives here."

"Well, if they do, I feel for them," he said, leaning into the open door. "They don't even have any pictures up."

"Pictures?"

"You know, of family or friends. Some proof of a life, you know?"

I thought of my own room back at Cora's—the blank walls, how I'd only barely unpacked. What would someone think, coming in and seeing my stuff? A few clothes, some books. Not much to go on.

Nate had gone outside, and was now on the small terrace, looking out into the distance. When I came to stand next to him, he looked down at my hand, still crisscrossed with scratches. "Oh, I totally forgot," he said, reaching into his pocket and pulling out a small tube. "I got something at One World for that."

BOYD'S BALM, it said in red letters. As he uncapped it, I said, "What is this, exactly?"

"It's like natural Neosporin," he explained. When I gave him a doubtful look, he added, "Marla swears by it."

"Oh, well. Then by all means." He gestured for me to stick out my hand. When I did, he squeezed some on, then began to rub it in, carefully. It burned a bit at first, then turned cold, but not in a bad way. Again, with us so close to each other, my first instinct was to pull back, like I had before. But instead, I made myself stay where I was and relax as his hand moved over mine.

"Done," he said after a moment, when it was all rubbed in. "You'll be healed by tomorrow."

"That's optimistic."

"Well, you can expect your hand to fall off, if you want," he said. "But personally, I just can't subscribe to that way of thinking."

I smiled despite myself. Looking up at his face, the sun just behind him, I thought of that first night, when he'd leaned over the fence. Then it had been impossible to make out his features, but here, all was clear, in the bright light of day. He wasn't really at all what I'd assumed or expected, and I wondered if I'd surprised him, too.

Later, after he dropped me off, I came in to find Cora at the stove, peering down into a big pot as she stirred something. "Hey," she called out as Roscoe ran to greet me, jumping up. "I didn't think you were working today."

"I wasn't," I said.

"Then where were you?"

"Everywhere," I said, yawning. She looked up at me, quizzical, and I wondered why I didn't just tell her the truth. But there was something about that day that I wanted to keep to myself, if just for a little while longer. "Do you need help with dinner?"

"Nah, I'm good. We'll be eating in about a half hour, though, okay?"

I nodded, then headed up to my room. After dropping my bag onto the floor, I went out onto my balcony, looking across the yard and the pond to Nate's house. Sure enough, a minute later I saw him carrying some things into the pool house, still working.

Back inside, I kicked off my shoes and climbed onto the bed, stretching out and closing my eyes. I was just about to drift off when I heard a jingle of tags and looked over to see Roscoe in the doorway to my room. *Cora must have turned on the oven*, I thought, waiting for him to move past me to my closet, where he normally huddled until the danger had passed. Instead, he came to the side of the bed, then sat down, peering up at me.

I looked at him for a second, then sighed. "All right," I said, patting the bed. "Come on."

He didn't hesitate, instantly leaping up, then doing a couple of quick spins before settling down beside me, his head resting on my stomach. As I began to pet him, I looked down at the scratches Lyle had given me, smoothing my fingers across them and feeling the slight rises there as I remembered Nate doing the same. I kept doing this, in fact, for the rest of the night—during dinner, before bed—tracing them the way I once had the key around my neck, as if I needed to memorize them. And maybe I did, because Nate was right: By the next morning, they were gone.

Chapter Eleven

"All I'm saying," Olivia said, picking up her smoothie and taking a sip, "is that to the casual observer, it looks like something is going on."

"Well, the casual observer is mistaken," I said. "And even if there was, it wouldn't be anyone's business, anyway."

"Oh, right. Because *so* many people are interested. All one of me."

"You're asking, aren't you?"

She made a face at me, then picked up her phone, opening it and hitting a few buttons. The truth was, Olivia and I had never officially become friends. But clearly, somewhere between that ride and the day in the box office, it had happened. There was no other explanation for why she now felt so completely comfortable getting into my personal life.

"Nothing is going on with me and Nate," I said to her, for the second time since we'd sat down for lunch. This was something else I never would have expected, us eating together—much less being so used to it that I barely noticed as she reached over, pinching a chip out of my bag. "We're just friends."

"A little while ago," she said, popping the chip into her mouth, "you weren't even willing to admit to that."

"So?"

"So," she said as the phone suddenly rang, "who knows what you'll be copping to a week or two from now? You might be engaged before you're willing to admit it."

"We are not," I said firmly, "going to be engaged. Jesus."

"Never say never," she said with a shrug. Her phone rang again. "Anything's possible."

"Do you even see him here?"

"No," she said. "But I do see him over at the sculpture, *looking* over here."

I turned my head. Sure enough, Nate was behind us, talking to Jake Bristol. When he saw us watching him, he waved. I did the same, then turned back to Olivia, who was regarding me expressionlessly, her phone still ringing.

"Are you going to answer that?" I asked.

"Am I allowed to?"

"Are you saying I make the rules now?"

"No," she said flatly. "But I certainly don't want to be rude and inconsiderate, carrying on two conversations at once." This was, in fact, exactly what I'd said, when I got sick of her constantly interrupting me to take calls. Which, now that I thought of it, was very friend-like as well, in its own way. "Unless, of course, you feel differently now?"

"Just make it stop ringing, please," I said.

She sighed, as if it was just such a hardship, then flipped open her phone, putting it to her ear. "Hey. No, just eating lunch with Ruby. What? Yes, she did say that," she said, eyeing me. "I don't know, she's fickle. I'm not even trying to understand."

I rolled my eyes, then looked over my shoulder at Nate again. He was still talking to Jake and didn't see me this time, but as I scanned the rest of the courtyard, I did spot someone staring right at me. Gervais.

He was alone, sitting at the base of a tree, his backpack beside him, a milk carton in one hand. He was also chewing slowly, while keeping his eyes steady on me. Which was kind of creepy, I had to admit. Then again, Gervais had been acting sort of strange lately. Or stranger.

By this point, I'd gotten so used to his annoying car behavior that I hardly even noticed it anymore. In fact, as Nate and I had gotten closer, Gervais had almost become an afterthought. Which was probably why, at least at first, I didn't realize when he suddenly began to change. But Nate did.

"How can you not have noticed he's combing his hair now?" he'd asked me a couple of mornings earlier, after Gervais had already taken off and we were walking across the parking lot. "*And* he's lost the headgear?"

"Because unlike some people," I said, "I don't spend a lot of time looking at Gervais?"

"Still, it's kind of hard to miss," he replied. "He looks like a totally different person."

"*Looks* being the operative word."

"He smells better, too," Nate added. "He's cut down considerably on the toxic emissions."

"Why are we talking about this again?" I asked him.

"I don't know," he said, shrugging. "When someone starts to change, and it's obvious, it's sort of natural to wonder why. Right?"

I wasn't wondering about Gervais, though. In fact, even if he got a total makeover and suddenly smelled like petunias,

I couldn't have cared less. Now, though, as I looked across the green at him, I had to admit that Nate was right—he did look different. The hair was combed, not to mention less greasy, and without the headgear his face looked completely changed. When he saw me looking at him, he flinched, then immediately ducked his head, sucking down the rest of his carton of milk. *So weird*, I thought.

". . . no, I don't," Olivia was saying now as she took another sip of her smoothie. "Because shoes are not going to make you run faster, Laney. That's all hype. What? Well, of course they're going to tell you that. They get paid on commission!"

"Who does?" Nate said, sliding onto the bench beside me. Olivia, listening to Laney, raised her eyebrows at me.

"No idea," I told him. "As you'll notice, she's not talking to me. She's on the phone."

"Ah, right," he said. "You know, that's really kind of rude."

"Isn't it?"

Olivia ignored us, picking up my chip bag and helping herself again. Then she offered it to Nate, who took a handful out, popping them into his mouth. "Those are mine," I pointed out.

"Yeah?" Nate said. "They're good."

He smiled, then bumped me with his knee. Across the table, Olivia was still talking to Laney about shoes, her voice shifting in and out of lecture mode. Sitting there with them, it was almost hard to remember when I first came to Perkins, so determined to be a one-woman operation to the end. But that was the thing about taking help and giving it, or so I was learning: there was no such thing as really getting even. Instead, this connection, once opened, remained ongoing over time.

*　　*　　*

At noon on Thanksgiving Day I was positioned in the foyer, ready to perform my assigned duty as door-opener and coat-taker. Just as the first car slowed and began to park in front of the house, though, I realized there was a hole in my sweater.

I took the stairs two at a time to my room, heading into the bathroom to my closet. When I pulled the door open, I jumped, startled. Cora was inside, sitting on the floor with Roscoe in her lap.

"Don't say it," she said, putting a hand up. "I know this looks crazy."

"What are you doing?"

She sighed. "I just needed to take a time-out. A few deep breaths. A moment for myself."

"In my closet," I said, clarifying.

"I came to get Roscoe. You know how he gets when the oven is on." She shot me a look. "But then, once I was in here, I began to understand why he likes it so much. It's very soothing, actually."

For the first time, Cora and Jamie were hosting Thanksgiving dinner, which meant that within moments, we'd be invaded by no less than fifteen Hunters. Personally, I was kind of curious to meet this extended tribe, but Cora, like Roscoe, was a nervous wreck.

"You were the one who suggested it," Jamie had said to her the week before as she sat at the kitchen table in full stress mode, surrounded by cookbooks and copies of

Cooking Light. "I never would have asked you to do this."

"I was just being polite!" she said. "I didn't think your mother would actually take me up on it."

"They want to see the house."

"Then they should come for drinks. Or appetizers. Or dessert. Something simple. Not on a major holiday, when I'm expected to provide a full meal!"

"All you have to do is the turkey and the desserts," Jamie told her. "They're bringing everything else."

Cora glared at him. "The turkey," she said, her voice flat, "is the center of the whole thing. If I screw it up, the entire holiday is ruined."

"Oh, that's not true," Jamie said. Then he looked at me, but I stayed quiet, knowing better than to get involved in this. "It's a turkey. How hard can it be?"

This question had been answered the night before, when Cora went to pick up the bird she'd ordered, which weighed twenty-two pounds. It took all three of us just to get it inside, and then it wouldn't even fit in the fridge.

"Disaster," Cora announced once we'd wrestled it onto the island. "Complete and total disaster."

"It's going to be fine," Jamie told her, confident as always. "Just relax."

Eventually, he had managed to get it into the fridge, although it meant removing just about everything else. As a result, the countertops were lined not only with all the stuff Cora had bought for the meal, but also all the condiments, breads, and cans of soda and bottled water— everything that didn't absolutely have to be refrigerated. Luckily, we'd been able to arrange to use Nate's oven for overflow—he and his dad were going to be gone all day, getting double time from clients who needed things done for their own dinners—as nothing else could fit in ours while the turkey was cooking. Still, all of this had only made Cora more crabby, to the point that I'd finally taken a loaf of bread, some peanut butter, and jelly into the enormous dining room, where I could fix myself sandwiches and eat in peace.

"You know," Jamie had said the night before, as Cora rattled around the kitchen beyond the doorway, "I think this is actually going to be a really good thing for us."

I looked at my sister, who was standing by the stove, examining a slotted spoon as if not exactly sure what to do with it. "Yeah?"

He nodded. "This is just what this house needs—a real holiday. It gives a place a sense of fullness, of family, you know?" He sighed, almost wistful. "And anyway, I've always loved Thanksgiving. Even before it was our anniversary."

"Wait," I said. "You guys got married on Thanksgiving?"

He shook his head. "June tenth. But we got together on Turkey Day. It was our first anniversary, you know, before the wedding one. It was, like, our first real date."

"Who dates on a major holiday?"

"Well, it wasn't exactly planned," he said, pulling the bread toward him and taking out a few slices. "I was supposed to go home for Thanksgiving that year. I was pumped for it, because, you know, I'm all about an eating holiday."

"Right," I said, taking a bite of my own sandwich.

"But then," he continued, "the night before, I ate some weird squid at this sushi place and got food poisoning. Seriously bad news. I was up sick all night, and the next day I was completely incapacitated. So I had to stay in the dorm, alone, for Thanksgiving. Isn't that the saddest thing you ever heard?"

"No?" I said.

"Of course it is!" He sighed. "So there I am, dehydrated, miserable. I went to take a shower and felt so weak I had to stop and rest on the way back in the hallway. I'm sitting there, fading in and out of consciousness, and then the door across from me opens up, and there's the girl that yelled at me the first week of classes. Alone for the holiday, too, fixing English-muffin pizzas in a contraband toaster oven."

I looked in at my sister, who was now consulting a cookbook, her finger marking the page, and suddenly remembered those same pizzas—English muffin, some cheap spaghetti sauce, cheese—that she'd made for me, hundreds of times.

He picked up the knife out of the jelly jar. "At first, she looked alarmed—I was kind of green, apparently. So she asked me if I was okay, and when I said I wasn't sure, she came out and felt my forehead, and she told me to come in and lie down in her room. Then she walked over to the only open convenience store—which was, like, miles away—bought me a six-pack of Gatorade, and came back and shared her pizzas with me."

"Wow," I said.

"I know." He shook his head, flipping a piece of bread over. "We spent the whole weekend together in her room, watching movies and eating toasted things. She took care of me. It was the best Thanksgiving of my life."

I glanced back at Cora again, remembering what Denise

had said about her that night at the party. Funny how it was so hard to picture my sister as a caretaker, considering that had been what she was to me, once. And now again.

"Which is not to say," Jamie added, "that other Thanksgivings can't be equally good, or even better in their own way. That's why I'm excited about this year. I mean, I love this house, but it's never totally felt like home to me. But tomorrow, when everyone's here, gathered around the table, and reading their thankful lists, it will."

I was listening to this, but still thinking about Cora and those pizzas so intently that I didn't really hear the last part. At least intially. "Thankful lists?"

"Sure," he said, pulling another piece of bread out and bringing the peanut butter closer to him. "Oh, that's right. You guys didn't do those, either, did you?"

"Um, no," I said. "I don't even know what that is."

"Just what it sounds like," he said, scooping out a glop of peanut butter and putting it on his bread. "You make a list of everything you're thankful for. For Thanksgiving. And then you share it with everyone over dinner. It's great!"

"Is this optional?" I asked.

"What?" He put down the knife with a clank. "You don't want to do it?"

"I just don't know . . . I'm not sure what I'd say," I said. He looked so surprised I wondered if he was hurt, so I added, "Off the top of my head, I mean."

"Well, that's the great thing, though," he said, going back to spreading the peanut butter. "You don't have to do it at the moment. You can write up your list whenever you want."

I nodded, as if this was actually my one hesitation. "Right."

"Don't worry," he said. "You'll do great. I know it."

You had to admire Jamie's optimism. For him, anything was possible: a pond in the middle of the suburbs, a wayward sister-in-law going to college, a house becoming a home, and thankful lists for everyone. Sure, there was no guarantee any of these things would actually happen as he envisioned. But maybe that wasn't the point. It was the planning that counted, whether it ever came to fruition or not.

Now, as Cora and I sat in the closet, we heard the doorbell ring downstairs. Roscoe perked up his ears, then yelped, the sound bouncing around the small space.

"That's me," I said, pulling off my sweater and grabbing another one off a nearby hanger. "I'll just—"

I felt a hand clamp around my leg, jerking me off balance. "Let Jamie get it," she said. "Just hang out here with me for a second. Okay?"

"You want me to get in there?"

"No." She reached over to rub Roscoe's ears before adding, more quietly, "I mean, only if you want to."

I crouched down, and she scooted over as I crawled in, moving aside my boots so I could sit down.

"See?" she said. "It's nice in here."

"Okay," I told her. "I will say it. You're acting crazy."

"Can you blame me?" She leaned back with a thud against the wall. "Any minute now, the house will be crawling with people who are expecting the perfect family Thanksgiving. And who's in charge? Me, the last person who is equipped to produce it."

"That's not true," I said.

"How do you figure? I've never done Thanksgiving before."

"You made pizzas that year, for Jamie," I pointed out.

"What, you mean back in college?" she asked.

I nodded.

"Okay, that is so *not* the same thing."

"It was a meal, and it counts," I told her. "Plus, he said it was the best Thanksgiving of his life."

She smiled, leaning her head back and looking up at the clothes. "Well, that's Jamie, though. If it was just him, I wouldn't be worried. But we're talking about his entire family here. They make me nervous."

"Why?"

"Because they're all just so well adjusted," she said, shuddering. "It makes our family look like a pack of wolves."

I just looked at her. "Cora. It's one day."

"It's Thanksgiving."

"Which is," I said, "just one day."

She pulled Roscoe closer to her. "And that's not even including the whole baby thing. These people are so fertile, it's ridiculous. You just know they're all wondering why we've been married five years and haven't yet delivered another member into the tribe."

"I'm sure that's not true," I said. "And even if it is, it's none of their business, and you're fully entitled to tell them so if they start in on you."

"They won't," she said glumly. "They're too nice. That's what so unsettling about all this. They all get along, they love me, they'll eat the turkey even if it's charred *and* raw.

No one's going to be drunk and passed out in the sweet potatoes."

"Mom never passed out in food," I said.

"That you remember."

I rolled my eyes. We hadn't talked about my mom much since the day Cora had laid down my punishment, but she also wasn't as taboo a topic as before. It wasn't like we agreed wholeheartedly now on our shared, or unshared, past. But at the same time, we weren't split into opposing camps—her attacking, me defending—either.

"I'm just saying," she said, "it's a lot of pressure, being part of something like this."

"Like what?"

"A real family," she said. "On the one hand, a big dinner and everyone at the table is the kind of thing I always wanted. But at the same time, I just feel . . . out of place, I guess."

"It's your house," I pointed out.

"True." She sighed again. "Maybe I'm just being hormonal. This medication I'm taking might be good for my ovaries, but it's making me crazy."

I made a face. Being privy to the reproductive drama was one thing, but specific details, in all honesty, made me kind of queasy. A few days before, I'd gone light-headed when she'd only just mentioned the word *uterus*.

The doorbell rang again. The promise of visitors clearly won out over the fear of the oven, as Roscoe wriggled loose, taking off and disappearing around the corner.

"Traitor," Cora muttered.

"Okay. Enough." I got out of the closet, brushing myself

off, then turned around to face her. "This is happening. So you need to go downstairs, face your fears, and make the best of it, and everything will be okay."

She narrowed her eyes at me. "When did you suddenly become so positive?"

"Just get out of there."

A sigh, and then she emerged, getting to her feet and adjusting her skirt. I shut the closet door, and for a moment we both stood there, in front of the full-length mirror, staring at our reflections. Finally I said, "Remember Thanksgiving at our house?"

"No," she said softly. "Not really."

"Me neither," I said. "Let's go."

*　　*　　*

It wasn't so much that I was positive. I just wasn't fully subscribing to such a negative way of thinking anymore.

That morning, when Cora had been in serious food-prep freak-out mode—covered in flour, occasionally bursting into tears, waving a spoon at anyone who came too close—all I'd wanted was a reason to escape the house. Luckily, I got a good one.

"Hey," Nate said from the kitchen as I eased in through his sliding-glass door, carrying the four pies stacked on two cookie sheets. "For me? You shouldn't have."

"If you even as much as nip off a piece of crust," I warned him, carrying them carefully to the stove, "Cora will eviscerate you. With an eggbeater, most likely."

"Wow," he said, recoiling slightly. "That's graphic."

"Consider yourself warned." I put the pies down. "Okay to go ahead and preheat?"

"Sure. It's all yours."

I pushed the proper buttons to set the oven, then turned and leaned against it, watching him as he flipped through a thick stack of papers, jotting notes here and there. "Big day, huh?"

"Huge," he said, glancing up at me. "Half our clients are out of town and need their houses or animals checked on, the other half have relatives visiting and need twice as much stuff done as usual. Plus there are those who ordered their entire dinners and want them delivered."

"Sounds crazy," I said.

"It isn't," he replied, jotting something else down. "It just requires military precision."

"Nate?" I heard his dad call out from down a hallway. "What time is the Chambells' pickup?"

"Eleven," Nate said. "I'm leaving in ten minutes."

"Make it five. You don't know how backed up they'll be. Do you have all the keys you need?"

"Yes." Nate reached over to a drawer by the sink, pulling out a key ring and dropping it on the island, where it landed with a clank.

"Double-check," Mr. Cross said. "I don't want to have to come back here if you end up stuck somewhere."

Nate nodded, making another note as a door slammed shut in another part of the house.

"He sounds stressed," I said.

"It's his first big holiday since we started the business," he said. "He signed up a lot of new people just for today. But he'll relax once we get out there and start getting things done."

Maybe this was true. Still, I could hear Mr. Cross muttering to himself in the distance, the noise not unlike that my own mother would make, banging around before she reluctantly headed off to work. "So when, in the midst of all this, do *you* get to eat Thanksgiving dinner?"

"We don't," he said. "Unless hitting the drive-through at Double Burger with someone else's turkey and potatoes in the backseat counts."

"That," I said, "is just plain sad."

"I'm not much for holidays," he said with a shrug.

"Really."

He raised his eyebrows. "Why is that surprising?"

"I don't know," I said. "I guess I just expected someone who was, you know, so friendly and social to be a big fan of the whole family-gathering thing. I mean, Jamie is."

"Yeah?"

I nodded. "In fact, I'm supposed to be making up my thankful list as we speak."

"Your what?"

"Exactly," I said, pointing at him. "Apparently, it's a list of the things you're thankful for, to be read aloud at dinner. Which is something we never did. Ever."

He flipped through the pages again. "Neither did we. I mean, back when we *were* a we."

I could hear Mr. Cross talking now, his voice bouncing down the hall. He sounded much more cheerful than before, and I figured he had to be talking to a customer. "When did your parents split, anyway?"

Nate nodded, picking up the key ring and flipping through it. "When I was ten. You?"

"Five," I said as the oven beeped behind me. Instantly, I thought of Roscoe, huddling in my closet. "My dad's pretty much been out of the picture ever since."

"My mom lives in Phoenix," he said, sliding a key off the ring. "I moved out there with her after the divorce. But then she got remarried and had my stepsisters, and it was too much to handle."

"What was?"

"Me," he said. "I was in middle school, mouthing off, a pain in her ass, and she just wanted to do the baby thing. So year before last, she kicked me out and sent me back here." I must have looked surprised, because he said, "What? You're not the only one with a checkered past, you know."

"I just never imagined you checkered," I told him. Which was a massive understatement, actually. "Not even close."

"I hide it well," he said easily. Then he smiled at me. "Don't you need to put in those pies?"

"Oh. Right."

I turned around, opening the oven and sliding them onto the rack, side by side. As I stood back up, he said, "So what's on your thankful list?"

"I haven't exactly gotten it down yet," I said, easing the oven shut. "Though, actually, you being checkered might make the top five."

"Really," he said.

"Oh, yeah. I thought I was the only misfit in the neighborhood."

"Not by a long shot." He leaned back against the counter behind him, crossing his arms over his chest. "What else?"

"Well," I said slowly, picking up the key he'd taken off

the ring, "to be honest, I have a lot to choose from. A lot of good things have happened since I came here."

"I believe it," he said.

"Like," I said slowly, "I'm very thankful for heat and running water these days."

"As we should all be."

"And I've been really lucky with the people I've met," I said. "I mean, Cora and Jamie, of course, for taking me in. Harriet, for giving me my job. And Olivia, for helping me out that day, and just, you know, being a friend."

He narrowed his eyes at me. "Uh-huh."

"And," I continued, shifting the key in my hand, "there's always Gervais."

"Gervais," he repeated, his voice flat.

"He's almost totally stopped burping. I mean, it's like a miracle. And if I can't be thankful for that, what can I be thankful for?"

"Gee," Nate said, cocking his head to the side, "I don't know."

"There *might* be something else," I said slowly, turning the key in my palm, end over end. "But it's escaping me right now."

He stepped closer to me, his arm brushing, then staying against mine as he reached out, taking the key from my palm and sliding it back onto the table. "Well," he said, "maybe it'll come to you later."

"Maybe," I said.

"Nate?" Mr. Cross called out. He was closer now, and Nate immediately stepped back, putting space between us just before he stuck his head around the corner. He glanced at me, giving a curt nod instead of a hello, then said, "What happened to five minutes?"

"I'm leaving right now," Nate told him.

"Then let's go," Mr. Cross said, ducking back out. A nearby door slammed and I heard his car start up, the engine rumbling.

"I better hit it," Nate said, grabbing up the stack of papers and the key ring. "Enjoy your dinner."

"You, too," I said. He squeezed my shoulder as he passed behind me, quickening his steps as he headed out into the hallway. Then the door banged behind him, and the house was quiet.

I checked on the pies again, then washed my hands and left the kitchen, turning off the light behind me. As I walked to the door that led out onto the patio, I saw another one at the end of the hallway. It was open just enough to make out a bed, the same USWIM sweatshirt Nate had lent me that day folded on top of it.

I don't know what I was expecting, as it wasn't like I'd been in a lot of guys' rooms. A mess, maybe. Some pinup in a bikini on the wall. Perhaps a shot of Heather in a frame, a mirror lined with ticket stubs and sports ribbons, stacks of CDs and magazines. Instead, as I pushed the door open, I saw none of these things. In fact, even full of furniture, it felt . . . empty.

There was a bed, made, and a bureau with a bowlful of change on it, as well as a couple of root beer bottle caps. His backpack was thrown over the chair of a nearby desk, where a laptop was plugged in, the battery light blinking. But there were no framed pictures, and none of the bits and pieces I'd expected, like Marla's fridge collage, or even Sabrina's tons of cats. If anything, it looked more like the last apartment he'd taken me to, almost sterile, with few if any clues as to who slept, lived, and breathed there.

I stood looking for a moment, surprised, before backing out and returning the door to exactly how it had been. All the way back home, though, I kept thinking about his room, trying to figure out what it was about it that was so unsettling. It wasn't until I got back to Cora's that I realized the reason: it looked just like mine. Hardly lived in, barely touched. Like it, too, belonged to someone who had just gotten there and still wasn't sure how long they'd be sticking around.

*　　*　　*

"Can I have your attention, please. Hello?"

At first, the plinking noise was barely audible. But as people began to quiet down, and then quieted those around them, it became louder, until finally it was all you could hear.

"Thanks," Jamie said, putting down the fork he'd been using to tap his wineglass. "First, I want to thank all of you for coming. It means a lot to us to have you here for our first holiday meal in our new place."

"Hear, hear!" someone in the back said, and there was a pattering of applause. The Hunters were effusive people, or so I'd noticed while letting them in and taking their coats. His mom, Elinor, was soft-spoken with a kind face; his dad, Roger, had grabbed me in a big hug, ruffling my hair like I was ten. All three of his sisters shared Jamie's dark coloring and outspokenness, whether it was about the pond (which they admired, loudly) or the recent elections (about which they disagreed, also loudly, albeit good-naturedly). And then there were children, and brothers-in-law, various uncles and cousins—so many names and relationships to remember that I'd already decided to give up trying and was just smiling a lot, hoping that compensated. It would have to.

"And now that we have you here," Jamie continued, "there's something else we'd like to share with you."

Standing at the entrance to the foyer, I was behind him, with the perfect view of his audience as he said this. The response was two-pronged: first, hopeful expressions—raised eyebrows, mouths falling open, hands to chests—followed by everyone looking at Cora at once. *Oh, shit*, I thought.

My sister turned pink instantly, then pointedly took a sip from the wineglass in her hand before forcing a smile. By then, Jamie had realized his mistake.

"It's about UMe," he said quickly, and everyone slowly directed their attention back to him. "Our new advertising campaign. It rolls out officially tomorrow, all over the country. But you get to see it here first."

Jamie reached behind a chair, pulling out a square piece of cardboard with the ad I'd seen blown up on it. I looked at Cora again, but she'd disappeared into the kitchen, her glass abandoned on a bookcase.

"I hope you like it," Jamie said, holding the picture up in front of him. "And, um, won't want to sue."

I slipped through the foyer, missing the Hunters' initial reactions, although I did hear some gasps and shrieks, followed by more applause, as I entered the kitchen where

Cora was sliding rolls into the oven, her back to me. She didn't turn around as she said, "Told you."

I glanced behind me, wondering how on earth she could have known for sure it was me. "He felt horrible," I said. "You could tell."

"I know." She shut the oven, tossing a potholder onto the island. From the living room, I could hear people talking over one another, their voices excited. Cora glanced over at the noise. "Sounds like they like it."

"Did he really think they wouldn't?"

She shrugged. "People are weird about family stuff, you know?"

"Really?" I said as I slid onto a stool by the island. "I wouldn't know a thing about that."

"Me either," she agreed. "Our family is perfect."

We both laughed at this, although not nearly loudly enough to drown out the merriment from the next room. Then Cora turned back to the oven, peering in through the glass door. "So," I said, "speaking of family. What does it mean to you?"

She looked at me over her shoulder, one eyebrow raised. "Why do you ask?"

"It's a project for school. I'm supposed to ask everybody."

"Oh." Then she was quiet for a moment, her back still to me. "What are people saying?"

"So far, different things," I told her. "I haven't made a lot of headway, to be honest."

She moved down to the stove, lifting up a lid on a pot and examining the contents. "Well, I'm sure my definition is probably similar to yours. It would have to be, right?"

"I guess," I said. "But then again, you have another family now."

We both looked into the living room. From my angle, I could see Jamie had put the blown-up ad on the coffee table, and everyone else was gathered around. "I guess I do," she said. "But maybe that's part of it, you know? That you're not supposed to have just one."

"Meaning what?"

"Well," she said, adjusting a pot lid, "I have my family of origin, which is you and Mom. And then Jamie's family, my family of marriage. And hopefully, I'll have another family, as well. Our family, that we make. Me and Jamie."

Now I felt bad, bringing this up so soon after Jamie's gaffe. "You will," I said.

She turned around, crossing her arms over her chest. "I hope so. But that's just the thing, right? Family isn't something that's supposed to be static or set. People marry in, divorce out. They're born, they die. It's always evolving, turning into something else. Even that picture of Jamie's family was only the true representation for that one day. By the next, something had probably changed. It had to."

In the living room, I heard a burst of laughter. "That's a good definition," I said.

"Yeah?"

I nodded. "The best yet."

Later, when the kitchen had filled up with people looking for more wine, and children chasing Roscoe, I looked across all the chaos at Cora, thinking that of course you would assume our definitions would be similar, since we had come from the same place. But this wasn't actually true.

We all have one idea of what the color blue is, but pressed to describe it specifically, there are so many ways: the ocean, lapis lazuli, the sky, someone's eyes. Our definitions were as different as we were ourselves.

I looked into the living room, where Jamie's mom was now alone on the couch, the ad spread out on the table in front of her. When I joined her, she immediately scooted over, and for a moment we both studied the ad in silence.

"Must be kind of weird," I said finally. "Knowing this is going to be out there for the whole world to see."

"I suppose." She smiled. Of all of them, to me she looked the most like Jamie. "At the same time, I doubt any-one would recognize me. It was a long time ago."

I looked down at the picture, finding her in the center in her white dress. "Who were these women?" I asked, point-ing at the elderly women on each side of her.

"Ah." She leaned forward, a little closer. "My great-aunts. That's Carol on the far left, and Jeannette, next to her. Then Alice on my other side."

"Was this at your house?"

"My parents'. In Cape Cod," she said. "It's so funny. I look at all those children in the front row, and they're all parents themselves now. And all my aunts have passed, of course. But everyone still looks so familiar, even as they were then. Like it was just yesterday."

"You have a big family," I told her.

"True," she agreed. "And there are times I've wished oth-erwise, if only because the more people you have, the more likely someone won't get along with someone else. The po-tential for conflict is always there."

"That happens in small families, too, though," I said.

"Yes," she said, looking at me. "It certainly does."

"Do you know who all these people are, still?" I asked.

"Oh, yes," she said. "Every one."

We were both quiet for a moment, looking at all those faces. Then Elinor said, "Want me to prove it?"

I looked up at her. "Yeah," I said. "Sure."

She smiled, pulling the photo a little closer, and I wondered if I should ask her, too, the question for my project, get her definition. But as she ran a finger slowly across the faces, identifying each one, it occurred to me that maybe this was her answer. All those names, strung together like beads on a chain. Coming together, splitting apart, but still and always, a family.

*   *   *

Despite Cora's concerns, when dinner did hit a snag, it wasn't her fault. It was mine.

"Hey," Jamie said as we cleared the table, having told Cora to stay put and relax. "Where are the pies?"

"Whoops," I said. With all the time in the closet, not to mention the chaos of turkey for eighteen, I'd forgotten all about the ones over at Nate's.

"Whoops," Jamie repeated. "As in, whoops the dog ate them?"

"No," I said. "They're still next door."

"Oh." He glanced into the dining room, biting his lip. "Well, we've got cookies and cake, too. I wonder if—"

"She'll notice," I said, answering this question for him. "I'll go get them."

It had been bustling and noisy at our house for so long

that I was actually looking forward to the quiet of Nate's house. When I stepped inside, all I could hear was the whirring of the heating system and my own footsteps.

Luckily, I'd set the timer, so the pies weren't burned, although they were not exactly warm, either. I was just starting to arrange them back on the cookie sheets when I heard a thud from the other side of the wall.

It was solid and sudden, something hitting hard, and startled me enough that I dropped one of the pies onto the stove, where it hit a burner, rattling loudly. Then there was a crash, followed by the sound of muffled voices. Someone was in the garage.

I put down the pies, then stepped out into the hallway, listening again. I could still hear someone talking as I moved to the doorway that led to the garage, sliding my hand around the knob and carefully pulling it open. The first thing I saw was Nate.

He was squatting down next to a utility shelf that by the looks of it had been leaning against the garage wall up until very recently. Now, though, it was lying sideways across the concrete floor, with what I assumed were its contents—a couple of paint cans, some car-cleaning supplies, and a glass bowl, now broken—spilled all around it. Just as I moved forward to see if he needed help, I realized he wasn't alone.

". . . *specifically* said you should check the keys before you left," Mr. Cross was saying. I heard him before I saw him, now coming into view, his phone clamped to his ear, one hand covering the receiver. "One thing. *One thing* I ask you to be sure of, and you can't even get that right. Do you even know how much this could cost me? The Chambells are half our business in a good week, easily. Jesus!"

"I'm sorry," Nate said, his head ducked down as he grabbed the paint cans, stacking them. "I'll just get it now and go straight there."

"It's too late," Mr. Cross said, snapping his phone shut. "You screwed up. *Again.* And now I'm going to have to deal with this personally if we're going to have any hope of saving the account, which will put us even more behind."

"You don't. I'll talk to them," Nate told him. "I'll tell them it was my fault—"

Mr. Cross shook his head. "No," he said, his voice clenched. "Because that, Nate, is admitting incompetence. It's bad enough I can't count on you to get a single goddamned thing right, *ever*, but I'll be damned if I'm going to have you blabbing about it to the clients like you're proud of it."

"I'm not," Nate said, his voice low.

"You're not what?" Mr. Cross demanded, stepping closer and kicking a bottle of Windex for emphasis. It hit the nearby lawnmower with a bang as he said, louder, "*Not what*, Nate?"

I watched as Nate, still hurriedly picking things up, drew in a breath. I felt so bad for him, and somehow guilty for being there. Like this was bad enough without me witnessing it. His voice was even quieter, hard to make out, as he said, "Not proud of it."

Mr. Cross just stared at him for a moment. Then he shook his head and said, "You know what? You just disgust me. I can't even look at your face right now."

He turned, then crossed the garage toward me, and I quickly moved down the hallway, ducking into a bathroom.

There, in the dark, I leaned back against the sink, listening to my own heart beat, hard, as he moved around the kitchen, banging drawers open and shut. Finally, after what seemed like forever, I heard him leave. I waited a full minute or two after hearing a car pull away before I emerged, and even then I was still shaken.

The kitchen looked the same, hardly touched, my pies right where I'd left them. Past the patio and over the fence, Cora's house, too, was unchanged, the lights all bright downstairs. I knew they were waiting for the pies and for me, and for a moment I wished I could just go and join them, stepping out of this house, and what had just happened here, entirely. At one time, this might have even come naturally. But now, I opened the garage door and went to find Nate.

He was down on the floor, picking up glass shards and tossing them into a nearby trash can, and I just stood there and watched him for a second. Then I took my hand off the door behind me, letting it drop shut.

Immediately, he looked up at me. "Hey," he said, his voice casual. *I hide it well,* I heard him say in my head. "What happened to dinner? You decide to go AWOL rather than do your thankful list?"

"No," I said. "I, um, forgot about the pies, so I had to come get them. I didn't think anyone was here."

Just like that, his face changed, and I knew he knew—either by this last sentence, or the look on my face—that I'd been there. "Oh," he said, this one word flat, toneless. "Right."

I came closer and, after a moment, bent down beside him

and started to pick up pieces of glass. The air felt strange all around me, like just after or before a thunderstorm when the very ions have been shifted, resettled. I knew that feeling. I hadn't experienced it in a while, but I knew it.

"So," I said carefully, my voice low, "what just happened here?"

"Nothing." Now he glanced at me, but only for a second. "It's fine."

"That looked like more than nothing."

"It's just my dad blowing off steam. No big deal. The shelf took the brunt of it."

I swallowed, taking in a breath. Out on the street, beyond the open garage door, an older couple in windsuits walked by, arms swinging in tandem. "So . . . does he do that a lot?"

"Pull down shelves?" he asked, brushing his hands off over the trash can.

"Talk to you like that."

"Nah," he said.

I watched him as he stood, shaking his hair out of his face. "You know," I said slowly, "my mom used to slap us around sometimes. When we were younger. Cora more than me, but I still caught it occasionally."

"Yeah?" He wasn't looking at me.

"You never knew when to expect it. I hated that."

Nate was quiet for a moment. Then he said, "Look, my dad's just . . . he's got a temper. Always has. He blows up, he throws stuff. It's all hot air."

"Has he ever hit you, though?"

He shrugged. "A couple of times when he's really lost it. It's rare, though."

I watched as he reached down, picking up the shelf and pushing it back up against the wall. "Still," I said, "it sounds like he's awfully hard on you. That stuff about you disgusting him—"

"Please," he replied, stacking the paint cans on the bottom shelf. "That's nothing. You should have heard him at my swim meets. He was the only parent to get banned from the deck entirely, for life. Not that it stopped him. He just yelled from behind the fence."

I thought back to that day in the parking lot, the guy who had called after him. "Is that why you quit?"

"One reason." He picked up the Windex. "Look, like I said, it's no big deal. I'm fine."

Fine. I'd thought the same thing. "Does your mom know about this?"

"She's aware that he's a disciplinarian," he said, drawing out this last word in such a way that it was clear he'd heard it a lot, said in a certain way. "She tends to be a bit selective in how she processes information. And anyway, in her mind, when she sent me back here, that was just what I needed."

"Nobody needs that," I said.

"Maybe not. But it's what I've got."

He headed for the door, pulling it open. I followed him inside, watching as he went to the island, picking up the key that I'd been holding earlier. I could remember so clearly turning it in my palm, the way he'd taken it from me—putting it back on the island but not on the ring—and suddenly

I felt culpable, even more a part of this than I already was.

"You could tell someone, you know," I said as he slid it into his pocket. "Even if he's not always hitting you, it's not right."

"What, and get put into social services? Or shipped off to live with my mom, who doesn't want me there? No thanks."

"So you have thought about it," I said.

"Heather did. A lot," he said, reaching up to rub his face. "It freaked her out. But she just didn't understand. My mom kicked me out, and at least he took me in. It's not like I have a lot of options here."

I thought of Heather, that day at the pond place. *I'm glad you and Nate are friends,* she'd said. "She was worried about you," I said.

"I'm fine." I couldn't help notice each time he said this. "At this point, I've only got six months until graduation. After that, I'm coaching a swim camp up north, and as long as I get into school somewhere, I'm gone."

"Gone," I repeated.

"Yeah," he said. "To college, or wherever. Anyplace but here."

"Free and clear."

"Exactly." He looked up at me, and I thought of us standing in this same spot earlier as he took that key from my hand. I'd felt so close to something then—something that, back at the yellow house or even in my first days at Cora's, I never would have imagined. "I mean, you stayed with your mom, stuck it out even though it was bad. You understand, right?"

I did. But it was more than that. Sure, being free and clear had been just what I'd wanted, so recently that it should have been easy to agree with it. But if it was still true, I wouldn't have even been there. I'd have left when I'd had the chance earlier, staying out of this, of everything.

But I hadn't. Because I wasn't the same girl who'd run to that fence the first night, thinking only of jumping over it and getting away. Somewhere, something had changed.

I could have stood there and told him this, and more. Like how glad I was, now, that the Honeycutts had turned me in, because in doing so they'd brought me here to Cora and Jamie and all the things I was thankful for, including him. And how even when you felt like you had no options or didn't need anyone, you could be wrong. But after all he'd just told me, to say this seemed foolish, if not impossible. Six months wasn't that long. And I'd been left behind enough.

You understand, right? he'd said. There was only one answer.

"Yeah," I said. "Of course I do."

Chapter Twelve

"There you are! Thank God!"

It was the day after Thanksgiving, the biggest shopping day of the year, and the mall was opening at six a.m. for door-buster specials. Harriet, however, insisted I had to be there at five thirty to get ready. This seemed a little extreme to me, but still I'd managed to rouse myself in the dark and stumble into the shower, then pour myself a big cup of coffee, which I sucked down as I walked along the greenway, a flashlight in my other hand. When I got to the mall itself, people were already lined up outside the main entrance, bundled up in parkas, waiting.

Inside, all the stores I passed were bustling—employees loading up stock, chattering excitedly—everyone in serious preparation mode, bracing for the crowds. When I got to Harriet's kiosk, it was clear she had already been there for a while: there were two Jump Java cups already on the register, a third clamped in her hand. Needless to say, she was pumped.

"Hurry, hurry," she called out to me now, waving her arms back and forth as if she could move me closer faster, by sheer force of will. "We don't have much time!"

Slightly alarmed, I looked over at Reggie, who was sitting at the Vitamin Me kiosk, a cup with a tea bag poking out of it in one hand. He took a sleepy sip, waving at me as I passed.

"You had to be here early, too?" I asked him. I couldn't imagine someone actually wanting some shark cartilage for Christmas.

He shrugged. "I don't mind it. I kind of like the bustle."

Then he smiled and looked at Harriet, who was maniacally lighting another incense stick. *Yeah*, I thought. *The bustle*.

"Okay," Harriet said, pulling me to stand next to her in front of the cart as she took another gulp of coffee. "Let's do a check and double check. We've got the low-dollar stuff on the bottom, higher on the top. Rings by the register for impulse buyers, incense burning for ambience, plenty of ones in the register. Do you remember the disaster plan?"

"Grab the cashbox and the precious gems, do a head-count, proceed to the food court exit," I recited.

"Good," she said with a curt nod. "I don't think we'll need it, but on a day like this you never know."

I glanced over at Reggie, who just shook his head, stifling a yawn.

"You know," Harriet continued, studying the kiosk, "as I'm looking at this now, I think maybe we should switch the earrings and bracelets. They don't look right. In fact—"

"Harriet. They're great. We're ready," I told her.

She sighed. "I don't know," she said. "I still feel like I'm missing something."

"Could it be, maybe, the true meaning of the holiday season?" Reggie called out from his kiosk. "In which we focus on goodwill and peace on earth, and not on making as much money as possible?"

"No," Harriet said. Then she snapped her fingers, the sound loud, right by my ear. "Hold on!" she said. "I can't believe I almost forgot."

She bent down beneath the register, pulling out the plastic bin where she kept all her stock. As she picked through the dozens of small plastic bags, finally pulling one out and opening it, I looked at my watch. It was 5:51. When I looked back at Harriet, she was fastening a clasp around her neck, her back to me.

"Okay," she said. "I made these a couple of weeks back, just fooling around, but now I'm wondering if I should put them out. What do you think?"

When she turned around, the first thing I saw was the key. It was silver and delicate, dotted with red stones, and hung from a braided silver chain around her neck. Instantly, I was aware of my own key, which was bulkier and not nearly as beautiful.But even so, seeing this one, I understood why I'd gotten so many comments on it. There was something striking about a single key. It was like a question waiting to be answered, a whole missing a half. Useless on its own, needing something else to be truly defined.

Harriet raised her eyebrows. "Well?"

"It's—"

"You hate it, don't you," she decided, before I could even finish. "You think it's tacky and derivative."

"It's not," I said quickly. "It's beautiful. Really striking."

"Yeah?" She turned to the mirror, reaching up to touch

the key, running her finger over it. "It kind of is, isn't it? Unique, at any rate. You think they'll sell?"

"You made more?"

She nodded, reaching into the box again. As she laid more bags out on the counter, I counted at least twenty, none of them the same: some keys were smaller, some bigger, some plain, others covered in gemstones. "I got inspired," she explained as I examined them one by one. "It was kind of manic, actually."

"You should definitely put them out," I told her. "Like, right now."

In record time, we'd slapped on price tags and organized a display. I was just putting the last necklace on the rack when the clock hit six and the doors opened. At first, the sound was distant, but then, like a wave, it got louder and louder as people spilled into sight, filling the long, wide corridor between us. "It's on," Harriet said. "Here we go."

We sold the first key necklace twenty minutes later, the second, a half hour after that. If I hadn't been there to see it myself, I never would have believed it, but every single customer who came by paused to look at them. Not everyone bought, but clearly they drew people's attention. Over and over again.

The day passed in a blur of people, noise, and the Christmas music overhead, which I only heard in bits and pieces, whenever the din briefly died down. Harriet kept drinking coffee, the key necklaces kept selling, and my feet began to ache, my voice getting hoarse from talking. The zinc lozenges Reggie offered up around one o'clock helped, but not much.

Still, I was grateful for the day and the chaos, if only because it kept my mind off what had happened the day before with Nate. All that evening, after I'd taken the pies back and watched them get devoured, then helped Cora load the dishwasher before collapsing onto my bed, I'd kept going over and over it in my head. It was all so unsettling: not only what I'd seen and heard, but how I'd responded afterward.

I never would have thought of myself as someone who would want to help or save anybody. In fact, this was the one thing that bugged me so much about Nate in the first place. And yet, I was surprised, even disappointed, that at that crucial moment—*You understand, right?*—I'd been so quick to step back and let the issue drop, when, as his friend, I should have come closer. It wasn't just unsettling, even. It was shameful.

At three o'clock, the crowds were still thick, and despite the lozenges, I'd almost totally lost my voice. "Go," Harriet said, taking a sip of her umpteenth coffee. "You've done more than enough for one day."

"Are you sure?" I asked.

"Yes," she replied, smiling at a young woman in a long red coat who was buying one of the last key necklaces. She handed over the bag, then watched the woman disappear into the crowd. "That's fifteen we've sold today," she said, shaking her head. "Can you even believe it? I'm going to have to go home and stay up all night making more. Not that I'm complaining, of course."

"I told you," I said. "They're beautiful."

"Well, I have you to thank for them. Yours was the

inspiration." She picked up one trimmed with green stones. "In fact, you should take one. It's the least I can do."

"Oh, no. You don't have to."

"I want to." She gestured at the rack. "Or I can make you one special, if you prefer."

I looked at them, then down at my own necklace. "Maybe later," I said. "I'm good for now."

Outside, the air was crisp, cool, and as I headed toward the greenway and home, I reached up, running my hand over my own necklace. The truth was, lately I'd been thinking about taking it off. It seemed kind of ridiculous to be carrying around a key to a house that was no longer mine. And anyway, it wasn't like I could go back, even if I wanted to. More than once, I'd even gone so far as to reach up to undo the clasp before stopping myself.

On that first night, when Nate and I had met, he had asked me, *What's it to?* and I'd told him, nothing. In truth, though, then and now, the key wasn't just to that lock at the yellow house. It was to me, and the life I'd had before. Maybe I'd even begun to forget it a bit over the last few weeks, and this was why it was easier to imagine myself without it. But now, after what had happened the night before, I was thinking maybe having a reminder wasn't such a bad idea. So for now, it would stay where it was.

* * *

After everything that had happened on Thanksgiving, I'd thought things might be a little awkward for the ride on the first day back at school. And they were. Just not in the way I was expecting.

"Hey," Nate said as I slid into the front seat. "How's it going?"

He was smiling, looking the same as always. Like nothing out of the ordinary had happened. But then to him, I supposed that it hadn't. "Good," I said, fastening my seat belt. "You?"

"Miserable," he announced cheerfully. "I've got two papers and a presentation due today. I was up until two last night."

"Really," I said, although actually, I knew this, as I'd been awake until about the same time, and I could see the lights from his room—two small squares, off to the right—breaking up the dark that stretched between our two houses. "I've got a calculus test that I have to pass. Which means, almost certainly, that I won't."

As soon as I said this, I expected Gervais to chime in from the backseat, agreeing with this, as it was the perfect setup to slam me. When I turned around, though, he was just sitting there, quiet and unobtrusive, the same way he had been for the last couple of weeks. As if to compensate for his silence, though, I was seeing him more and more. At least once a week, I caught him watching me at lunch, the way he had that one day, and whenever I passed him in the hallways he was always giving me these looks I couldn't figure out.

"What?" he said now, as I realized I was still looking strangely at him.

"Nothing," I replied, and turned back.

Nate reached for the radio, cranking it up, and then we

were turning out into traffic. Everything actually felt okay, wholly unchanged, and I realized maybe I'd overreacted, thinking they would have. The bottom line was, I knew something I hadn't the week before, and we were friends—at least for another six months or so. I didn't have to get all wrought up about what was going on with his dad; I'd never wanted anyone to get involved with me and my domestic drama. Maybe what we had now, in the end, was best—to be close but not too close, the perfect middle ground.

Half a block from school, Nate pulled into the Quik Zip for gas. As he got out to pump it, I sat back in my seat, opening the calc book in my lap. About half a page in, though, I heard a noise from behind me.

By this point, I was well acquainted with Gervais's various percussions, but this wasn't one I was used to. It was more like an intake, a sudden drawing in of breath. The first one I ignored; the second, barely noted. By the third, though, I was starting to think he might be having an attack of some sort, so I turned around.

"What are you doing?" I asked him.

"Nothing," he said, instantly defensive. But then, he did it again. "The thing is—"

He was interrupted by Nate opening his door and sliding back behind the wheel. "Why is it," he said to me, "that whenever I'm in a hurry I always get the slowest gas pump in the world?"

I glanced at Gervais, who had hurriedly gone back to his book, his head ducked down. "Probably the same reason you hit every red light when you're late."

"And lose your keys," he added, cranking the engine.

"Maybe it's the universe conspiring against you."

"I have had a run of bad luck lately," he agreed.

"Yeah?"

He glanced over at me. "Well, maybe not all bad."

Hearing this, I had a flash of us in the kitchen that day, his hand brushing against mine as he reached for the key lying in my palm. As Nate turned back to the road, I suddenly did feel awkward, in just the way I'd thought I would. Talk about bad luck. Maybe this wouldn't be so easy after all.

* * *

For me, December was all about work. Working for Harriet, working on my applications, working on calculus. And when I wasn't doing any of these things, I was tagging along with Nate on his job.

Logically, I knew the only way to stay in that middle ground with Nate was to let space build up between us. But it wasn't so easy to stop something once it had started, or so I was learning. One day you were all about protecting yourself and keeping things simple. The next thing you know, you're buying macaroons.

"Belgian macaroons," Nate corrected me, pulling two boxes off the shelf. "That's key."

"Why?"

"Because a macaroon you can buy anywhere," he replied. "But these, you can only find here at Spice and Thyme, which means they are gourmet and expensive, and therefore suitable for corporate gift-giving."

I looked down at the box in my hand. "Twelve bucks is a lot for ten macaroons," I said. Nate raised his eyebrows. "*Belgian* macaroons, I mean."

"Not to Scotch Design Inc.," he said, continuing to add boxes to the cart between us. "In fact, this is the very low end of their holiday buying. Just wait until we get to the nut-and-cheese-straw towers. *That's* impressive."

I glanced at my watch. "I might not make it there. My break is only a half hour. If I'm even a minute late, Harriet starts to have palpitations."

"Maybe," he said, adding a final box, "you should buy her some Belgian macaroons. For ten bucks, they might cure her of that entirely."

"I somehow doubt the solution is that easy. Or inexpensive."

Nate moved back to the head of the cart, nudging it forward past the chocolates into the jelly-bean section. Spice and Thyme was one of those huge gourmet food stores designed to feel small and cozy, with narrow aisles, dim lighting, and stuff stacked up everywhere you turned. Personally, it made me feel claustrophobic, especially during Christmas, when it was twice as crowded as usual. Nate, however, hardly seemed bothered, deftly maneuvering his cart around a group of senior citizens studying the jelly beans before taking the corner to boxed shortbreads.

"I don't know," he said, glancing at the list in his hand before beginning to pull down tins decorated with the face of a brawny Scotsman playing a bagpipe. "I think that what Harriet needs might be simpler than she thinks."

"Total organization of her house, courtesy of Rest Assured?" I asked.

"No," he said. "Reggie."

"Ah," I said as the senior citizens passed us again, squeezing by the cart. "So you noticed, too."

"Please." He rolled his eyes. "It's kind of flagrant. What does she think all that ginkgo's about?"

"That's what I said," I told him. "But when I suggested it to her, she was shocked by the idea. *Shocked.*"

"Really," he said, pulling the cart forward again. "Then she must be more distracted than we even realize. Which, honestly, I'm not quite sure is possible."

We jerked to a stop suddenly, narrowly missing a collision with two women pushing a cart entirely full of wine. After some dirty looks and a lot of clanking, they claimed their right of way and moved on. I said, "She said she was too busy for a relationship."

"Everyone's busy," Nate said.

"I know. I think she's really just scared."

He glanced over at me. "Scared? Of Reggie? What, she thinks he might force her to give up caffeine for real or something?"

"No," I said.

"Of what, then?" he asked.

I paused, only just now realizing that the subject was hitting a little close to home. "You know, getting hurt. Putting herself out there, opening up to someone."

"Yeah," he said, adding some cheese straws to the cart, "but risk is just part of relationships. Sometimes they work, sometimes they don't."

I picked up a box of cheese straws, examining it. "Yeah," I said. "But it's not all about chance, either."

"Meaning what?" he asked, taking the box from me and adding it to the rest.

"Just that, if you know ahead of time that there might an issue that dooms everything—like, say, you're incredibly controlling and independent, like Harriet—maybe it's better to acknowledge that and not waste your time. Or someone else's."

I looked over at Nate, who I now realized was watching me. He said, "So being independent dooms relationships? Since when?"

"That was just one example," I said. "It can be anything."

He gave me a weird look, which was kind of annoying, considering he'd brought this up in the first place. And anyway, what did he want me to do, just come out and admit it would never work between us because it was too hard to care about anyone, much less someone I had to worry about? It was time to get back to the theoretical, and quickly. "All I'm saying is that Harriet won't even trust me with the cashbox. So maybe it's a lot to ask for her to give over her whole life to someone."

"I don't think Reggie wants her life," Nate said, nudging the cart forward again. "Just a date."

"Still," I said, "one can lead to the other. And maybe, to her, that's too much risk."

I felt him look at me again, but I made a point of checking my watch. It was almost time to go. "Yeah," he said. "Maybe."

Ten minutes later—and one minute late—I arrived back at Harriet's, where, true to form, she was waiting for me. "Am I glad to see you," she said. "I was starting to get nervous. I think we're about to have a big rush. I can just kind of feel it."

I looked down the middle of the mall, which was busy but not packed, and then the other way at the food court, which looked much the same. "Well, I'm here now," I said, sticking my purse in the cabinet under the register. As I did, I remembered the thing I'd bought for her, pulling it out. "Here," I said, tossing it over. "For you."

"Really?" She caught it, then turned the box in her hand. "Macaroons! I love these."

"They're Belgian," I said.

"All right," she replied, tearing them open. "Even better."

* * *

"Come on, Laney! Pick up the pace!"

I looked at Olivia, then in the direction she was yelling, the distant end of the mall parking lot. All I could see were a few cars and a Double Burger wrapper being kicked around by the breeze. "What are you doing, again?"

"Don't even ask," she told me. This was the same thing she'd said when I'd come across her, ten minutes earlier, sitting on the curb outside the Vista 10 box office on this unseasonably warm Saturday, a book open in her lap. "All I can say is it's not my choice."

"Not your—" I said, but then this sentence, and my concentration, were interrupted by a *thump-thump* noise. This time when I turned, I saw Laney, wearing a purple tracksuit, rounding the distant corner of Meyer's Department Store at a very slow jog, headed our way.

"Finally," Olivia said, pulling a digital kitchen timer out from beneath her book and getting to her feet. "You're going to have to go faster than that if you want me to sit out here for another lap!" she yelled, cupping her hands around her mouth. "You understand?"

Laney ignored her, or just didn't hear, keeping her gaze straight as she kept on, *thump-thump, thump-thump*. As she got closer I saw her expression was serious, her face flushed, although she did give me a nod as she passed.

Olivia consulted the stopwatch. "Eight minutes," she called out as Laney continued on toward the other end of the mall. "That's a sixteen-minute mile. Also known as *slow*."

"Still training for the five-K, huh?" I asked as a mall security guard rolled by, glancing at us.

"Oh, she's beyond training now," Olivia replied, sitting down on the curb again and setting the timer beside her. "She's focused, living and breathing the run. And yes, that *is* a direct quote."

"You're supportive," I said.

"No, I'm realistic," she replied. "She's been training for two months now, and her times aren't improving. At all. If she insists on doing this, she's just going to embarrass herself."

"Still," I said, looking at Laney again, who was still plodding along. "You have to admit, it's kind of impressive."

Olivia harrumphed. "What is? Total denial?"

"Total commitment," I said. "You know, the idea of discovering something that, for all intents and purposes, goes against your abilities, and yet still deciding to do it anyway. That takes guts, you know?"

She considered this as the security guard passed by, going the other way. "If she's so gutsy, though, why is it that she usually quits at about the two-mile mark, then calls me to come pick her up?"

"She does that?" I asked.

"Only about every other time. Oh, wait. Is that not supportive, though?"

I sat back, ignoring this, planting my hands on the pavement behind me. It wasn't like I was some expert on the meaning of being supportive. Was it being loyal even against your better judgment? Or, like Olivia, was it making your displeasure known from the start, even when someone didn't want to hear it? I'd been thinking about this more and more since Nate's and my discussion at Spice and Thyme. Maybe he was someone who lived in the moment, easily able to compartmentalize one part of his life from another. But to me, the Nate I was spending more and more time with was still the same one who was going home to a bad situation with his dad and who planned to get out as soon as he could—both of these were reasons I should have kept away, or at least kept my distance. Yet if anything, I kept moving closer, which just made no sense at all.

Now, I looked over at Olivia, who was squinting into the distance, the timer still counting down in her lap. "Do you remember," I asked, "how you said that when you first came from Jackson, it was hard for you, and that's why you never bothered to talk to anyone or make friends?"

"Yeah," she said, sounding a bit wary. "Why?"

"So why did you, then?" I asked, looking at her. "I mean, with me. What changed?"

She considered this as a minivan drove by, pulling up on the other side of the box office. "I don't know," she said. "I guess it was just that we had something in common."

"Jackson."

"Yeah, that. But also, not being like everyone else at Perkins. You know, having some part that's different, and yet shared. I mean, with me it's my family, my economic standing. You, well, you're a lush and a delinquent—"

"Hey," I said. "That was just one day."

"I know, I'm just kidding," she said, waving me off with her hand. "But neither of us exactly fit the mold there."

"Right."

She sat back, brushing her braids away from her face. "My point is, there are a lot of people in the world. No one ever sees everything the same way you do; it just doesn't happen. So when you find one person who gets a couple of things, especially if they're important ones . . . you might as well hold on to them. You know?"

I looked down at the stopwatch sitting on the curb between us. "Nicely put," I said. "And all in less than two minutes."

"Conciseness is underrated," she said easily. Then she looked over my shoulder, suddenly raising her hand to wave to someone behind me. When I turned, I was surprised to see Gervais, in his peacoat standing in front of the box office. Seeing me, his face flushed, and he hurriedly grabbed his ticket from under the glass and darted inside.

"You know Gervais?" I asked her.

"Who, extra salt, double–lic whip? Sure. He's a regular." I just looked at her. "That's his concession order," she explained. "Large popcorn, no butter, extra salt, and two packs of licorice whips. He hits at least one movie a week. The boy likes film. How do you know him?"

"We ride to school together," I said. So Gervais had a life outside of carpool. It wasn't like it should have been surprising, but for some reason, it was.

Just then, I heard a buzzing: her phone. She pulled it out of her pocket, looked at the screen, then sighed. Laney. "I'd say I told you so," she said. "But it's not like I get any satisfaction from this."

I watched as she flipped it open, hitting the TALK button and saying she'd be there in a minute. Then she picked up her book and got to her feet, brushing herself off. "Still," I said, "you have to get something, though."

"From what? "

"From this." I gestured around me. "I mean, you are out here timing her. So you can't be totally opposed to what she's doing."

"No, I am." She pulled her keys out of her pocket, shoving the book under her arm. "But I'm also a sucker. Clearly."

"You are not," I said.

"Well, then, I don't know the reason," she said. "Other than she's my cousin, and she asked, so I'm here. I try not to go deeper than that. I'll see you around, okay?"

I nodded, and then she was walking away, across the lot to her car. Watching her, I kept thinking of what she'd said earlier about having things in common, and then of Nate and me in his garage on Thanksgiving, when I'd told him about my mom and our history. Clearly, sharing something could take you a long way, or at least to a different place than you'd planned. Like a friendship or a family, or even just alone on a curb on a Saturday, trying to get your bearings as best you can.

*　*　*

It wasn't just me that was feeling out of sorts. Even the weather was weird.

"You have to admit," Harriet said, shaking her head as we stepped out into the employee parking lot later that night, "this is very strange. When has it ever been seventy-seven degrees a week before Christmas?"

"It's global warming," Reggie told her. "The ice caps are melting."

"I was thinking more along the lines of the apocalypse," she said.

He sighed. "Of course you were."

"Seriously, though, who wants to Christmas-shop when it feels like summer?" she asked as we started across the lot. "This *cannot* be good for sales."

"Do you ever think about anything but business?" Reggie said.

"The apocalypse," she told him. "And occasionally coffee."

"You know," he said, "I'm aware that you're kidding, but that's still really—"

"Good night," I called out as I peeled off toward the greenway. They both waved, still bickering. This, however, was not strange in the least; it was the way I always left them.

Often, Harriet gave me a ride home, as she hated me taking the greenway in the dark, but as the weather had grown oddly warm I'd been insisting on walking instead, just to make the most of the unseasonable weather while it lasted. On my way back to Cora's, I passed several bicyclists, two runners, and a pack of kids on scooters, all with the same idea. Weirdest of all, though, was what I saw at home when I walked in the front door: Jamie, at the bottom of the stairs, wearing his bathing suit and swim fins, a towel thrown over his shoulder. It might not have been a sign of the apocalypse, but it seemed pretty close.

At first, it was clear that I'd surprised him: he jumped, flustered, before quickly recovering and striking a casual pose. "Hey," he said, like he hung out in swimgear in the foyer every day. "How was work?"

"What are you—?" I began, then stopped as Cora appeared at the top of the stairs, a pair of shorts pulled over her own suit.

"Oh," she said, stopping suddenly, her face flushing. "Hi."

"Hi," I said slowly. "What's going on?"

They exchanged a guilty look. Then Cora sighed and said, "We're going pool jumping."

"You're what?"

"It's seventy-five degrees! In December!" Jamie said. "We have to. We can't help ourselves."

I looked up at my sister again. "It is pretty nice out," she said.

"But the neighborhood pool doesn't even have water in it," I said.

"That's why we're going to Blake's," Jamie told me. "You want to come?"

"You're sneaking into Nate's pool?"

Cora bit her lip as Jamie said, "Well, technically, it's not really sneaking. I mean, we're neighbors. And it's right there, heated, with nobody using it."

"Do you have permission?" I asked.

He looked up at Cora, who squirmed on the step. "No," she said. "But I saw Blake earlier and he said he and Nate were taking off for an overnight business thing. So . . ."

". . . you're just going to jump their fence and their pool," I finished for her.

Silence. Then Jamie said, "It's seventy-five degrees! In December! Do you know what this means?"

"The apocalypse?" I asked.

"What?" he said. "No. God. Why would you—"

"She's right, you know," Cora said, coming down the stairs. "We're not exactly setting a good example."

"It was your idea," Jamie pointed out. Cora flushed again. "Your sister," he said to me, "is a serious pool jumper. In college, she was always the first to go over the fence."

"Really," I said, turning to look at her.

"Well," she replied, as if about to justify this. Then she just said, "You know, it's seventy-five degrees. In December."

Jamie grabbed her hand, grinning. "That's my girl," he said, then pointed at me. "You coming?"

"I don't have a bathing suit," I told him.

"In my closet, bottom right-hand drawer," Cora said. "Help yourself."

I just shook my head, incredulous, as they started through the kitchen. Cora was laughing, Jamie's flippers slapping the floor, and then they were outside, the door swinging shut behind them.

I wasn't going to go and certainly didn't plan to swim. But after sitting on my bed in the quiet for a few moments, I did go find a suit of Cora's, pull on some sweatpants over it, and head downstairs, crossing the yard to where I could hear splashing just beyond the fence.

"There she is," Jamie said as I slipped through. He was in the shallow end, next to Roscoe, who was on the deck, barking excitedly, while Cora was underwater, swimming down deep, her hair streaming out behind her. "Couldn't resist, huh?"

"I don't think I'm coming in," I said, walking over and sitting down on the edge, my knees pulled to my chest. "I'll just watch."

"Ah, that's no fun," he said. Then, with Roscoe still barking, he dove under, disappearing. As he swam the length of the pool, the dog ran alongside, following him.

I looked over at Cora, who was now bobbing in the deep end, brushing her hair back from her face. "You know," I said, "I never would have figured you for a lawbreaker."

She made a face at me. "It's not exactly a felony. And besides, Blake owes us."

"Really? Why?" I asked, but she didn't hear me, or chose not to answer, instead diving under again to join Jamie, who was circling along the bottom.

As they emerged a moment later, laughing and splashing each other, I kicked off my shoes, then rolled up my sweatpants and dunked my feet in the water. It was warm, even more so than the air, and I leaned back on my palms, turning my face up to the sky. I hadn't been swimming since the last time we'd lived in a complex with a pool, around ninth grade. In the summer, I would spend hours there, staying in until my mom had to come get me when dark was falling.

Jamie and Cora stayed in for about a half hour, dunking each other and playing Marco Polo. By the time they climbed out, it was past ten, and even Roscoe—who'd been barking nonstop—was exhausted. "See," Jamie said as they toweled off, "one dip, no harm done."

"It is nice," I agreed, moving my feet through the water.

"You coming back with us?" Cora asked as they walked behind me, heading for the fence.

"In a minute. I think I'll hang out a little while longer."

"Might as well make the most of it," Jamie said as Roscoe trotted behind him. "After all, it won't be like this forever."

Then they were gone, through the fence, where I could hear their voices fading as they crossed the yard. I waited until it had been quiet for a few minutes before slipping off my sweatpants. Then, with one last quick look around me to make sure I was alone, I jumped in.

It was startling, at first, being back in a pool after so long not swimming. Just as quickly, though, all the instinct came back, and before I knew it I was moving steadily to the other side, the water filling my ears. I don't know how many laps I'd done, back and forth, only that I had hit such a rhythm that at first, I didn't even notice when a light clicked on in the house. By the time the second one came on, it was too late.

I froze, sinking down below the pool's edge, as a figure

moved through the now-bright living room. After it crossed back once, then again, I heard a door slide open. *Shit*, I thought, then panicked, taking a deep breath and submerging myself.

Which, as it turned out, was not the smartest move, as became apparent when I looked up through the shifting blue water above to see Nate staring down at me. By that time, my lungs were about to explode, so I had no choice but to show myself.

"Well, well," he said as I sputtered to the surface. "What's this all about?"

I swam to the edge, just to do something, then ran a hand over my face. "Um," I said. "Actually—"

"Cora and Jamie were pool jumping, huh?" he said. I just looked at him, confused, until he pulled one flipper, then another, from behind his back. "They're not exactly slick about it," he said, dropping them on the deck beside his feet. "These were right there on that chair. Last time they left a swimming noodle."

"Oh," I said. "Yeah. I guess we're busted."

"No big deal." He crouched down by me, dipping his hand in the water. "It's good someone's getting some use out of this thing. My dad's always complaining about how much it costs to heat it."

"You don't swim at all anymore?"

"Not really," he said.

"You must miss it, though."

He shrugged. "Sometimes. It was a good escape. Until, you know, it wasn't."

I thought of what he'd said, about his dad getting banned but still yelling from the fence. "You should come in," I said. "It's really warm."

"Nah, I'm okay." He sat on a nearby chair. "You go ahead, though."

I bobbed there for a second, neither of us talking. Finally I said, "So I thought you were out of town on a business thing."

"Change of plans," he said. "It was decided I should come home early."

"Decided," I repeated.

He looked up, then gave me a tired smile. "It's been a long day, let's just say that."

I'll bet, I thought. Out loud, I said, "All the more reason to take a dip. I mean, it's December. Seventy-five degrees. You know you want to."

I honestly didn't think he'd agree with this; I was just talking. But then he nodded slowly, and pushed himself to his feet. "All right," he said. "I'll be back in a sec."

As he disappeared inside, it occurred to me that maybe this was not the smartest idea. After all, I was trying to keep my distance and now, with this invitation, had narrowed the space we were in considerably. Before I could figure out how to change this, though—or even if I wanted to—he was coming back outside, now in trunks, and walking across the patio. Needless to say, this was distracting. That first night, I hadn't really seen him shirtless, and now I could focus on little else. All the more reason, I realized, to backtrack, but before I could he was stretching his arms overhead and diving in, hitting the water with barely a splash and disappearing below.

You swim, I thought, having a flash of that sweatshirt as he came to the surface, then closer toward me with a breast-stroke that looked effortless. When he emerged, shaking his head and sending droplets flying, I said, "Nice form."

"Thanks," he said, bobbing in front of me. "Years of training."

Suddenly, I was so aware of how close we were to each other, with only the water between us. I looked down: beneath the surface my skin looked so pale, almost blue, my necklace lying across it. When I glanced up again, he was looking at it, too, and after meeting my gaze for a second he reached over, catching it in one hand to lie flat on his palm.

"How many of those key necklaces do you think Harriet has sold since Thanksgiving?" he asked.

"I don't know," I said. "A lot."

"I saw a girl at Jump Java today wearing one. It was so weird."

"I'll be sure to tell Harriet you said that," I said. "She'll be overjoyed."

"I don't mean it like that." He turned his palm, letting the key fall loose, and it slowly floated back down to rest against me again. "It's just that I associate them with you, and this one. You know? It was the first thing I noticed about you that night we met."

"Even before I was jumping the fence?"

"Okay." He smiled. "Maybe the second."

All around us, the neighborhood was quiet, the sky

spread out wide and sprinkled with stars overhead. I could feel him right there in front of me, and I thought of what Jamie had said earlier: *It won't be like this forever.* That was true, and also the reason I should have climbed out right then, as well as why I knew I would stay.

He was still watching me, both of us bobbing, and I could feel the water around me, pressing in, pulling back. Then, slowly, Nate was moving closer, leaning in, and despite all I'd told myself, and all I wanted to believe I was and wasn't capable of, I stayed where I was as he kissed me. His lips were warm, his skin wet, and when he drew back, I felt myself shiver, unaccustomed to anyone being so close, and yet still not ready for him to pull away.

"Are you cold?" he asked.

I was about to shake my head, say it wasn't that at all, but before I could, I felt his hand close over mine. "Don't worry," he said, "it's warmer the deeper you go." Then, to prove it, he went under, and I took a deep breath, the biggest I could, and let him pull me down with him.

*   *   *

I already knew Jamie liked holidays. There were the matching blue shirts, for one thing, not to mention the thankful lists. But even armed with this knowledge, I still was not fully prepared for how he approached Christmas.

"Just stand still, okay?" Cora said, making a face as she stuffed the pillow farther up under his jacket. "Stop wriggling around."

"I can't," Jamie replied. "This long underwear is a lot itchier than I thought it would be."

"I told you to just wear your boxer shorts."

"Santa doesn't wear boxers!" he said, his voice rising slightly as she yanked the wide black belt of his costume tight over the pillow, holding it in place. "If I'm going to do this, I want to be authentic about it."

"I seriously doubt," Cora said, pushing herself to her feet, "that the Santa police do an underwear check. Now where's your beard?"

"On the bed," he told her. Then he saw me. "Hey, Ruby! So what do you think? Pretty great, right?"

This wasn't exactly the first word that had come to mind at seeing him in a full-on Santa outfit: red suit, black boots, and big white wig, which to me looked itchier than any underwear could ever be. But in the interest of family, I decided to play along.

"Yeah," I agreed as Cora reached over his head, fastening his beard. "Are you going to a party or something?"

"No," he said. Cora stepped back, hands on her hips, examining her work. "It's Christmas Eve."

"Right," I said slowly. "So this is for . . ."

"Walking around the neighborhood!" he finished for me. I just looked at Cora, who simply shook her head. "My dad always dressed up like Santa on Christmas Eve," he explained. "It was a family tradition."

"Which we did not have a lot of," Cora added. "And Jamie knows that, which is why he's made it a personal mission to make up for it now."

Jamie looked from her to me, then back at her again. Even in the full costume, wig and all, he still looked so boyish, like *Santa: The Early Days.* "I know, it's a little over the top," he said. "It's just . . . we always made a big deal of Christmas at my house. I guess it's kind of rubbed off on me."

Even without the Santa outfit, this was an understatement. All month long, Jamie had thrown himself into getting ready for Christmas: stringing up an elaborate light show out front, putting Advent calendars in practically every room, dragging home the biggest tree he could find, which we then decorated with a mix of brand-new ornaments and homemade ones from Hunter holidays past. Between all this and working at the mall, I'd frankly been over the holidays weeks ago. But as with most things involving Jamie, I'd gone along anyway, allowing myself to be dragged to the neighborhood tree-lighting ceremony, watching the Charlie Brown Christmas special over and over again, even holding Roscoe down while Jamie outfitted him in an elaborate harness of jingle bells.

"Here," he said now, reaching behind him to the bed to pick up a red elf's hat. "For you."

"Me?"

"Yeah. So we'll match, when we go out."

I looked at Cora again, but this time she avoided my eyes, busily putting away her blusher, which she'd used to give Jamie his festive red cheeks. "Where," I said slowly, "are we going?"

"To hand out gifts in the neighborhood," he said, like this was obvious. "They're all in the foyer, ready to go. Come on!"

He brushed past me, his own hat in hand, and bounded down the stairs, his boots thumping on the carpet. I narrowed my eyes at Cora until she finally turned to face me.

"I'm sorry," she said, looking like she meant it. "But I did it last year."

And that was how I ended up out in Wildflower Ridge, at eight o'clock on Christmas Eve, with Jamie in his Santa suit, and Roscoe in his jingle bells, spreading good cheer. Or, looking at it another way, walking in the cold—which had returned with a vengeance—and interrupting people from their own family celebrations while scaring the occasional motorist.

After the first couple of houses, we worked out a system: I rang the bell, then let Jamie stay front and center, hanging back with Roscoe until the door was opened, and pitching in when needed to help hand out the gifts, which were mostly stuffed animals and boxes of mini candy canes. Aside from a few weird looks—and some people who were clearly home but chose to ignore us—people seemed happy to see us, especially the kids, and after about an hour and three blocks, our stuff was mostly gone.

"We've got enough for maybe two more stops," Jamie said as we stood on the corner by Nate's house, having paused for Roscoe, bells jingling, to relieve himself against a mailbox. "So which ones do you think? You want to take something to Nate?"

I looked over at the Cross house, dark except for a couple of lights in the back. "I don't know," I said. "He might not be your target audience. Maybe we should go a little younger."

"I'll do that," he said, reaching into his almost-empty sack. "But you go ahead and bring him some candy canes. I'll meet you back here. All right?"

"Okay," I said, handing over Roscoe's leash. He took it,

then tossed his sack over his shoulder—the Santa police would have approved—and started across the street to a house with brightly lit snowflakes on either side of the front steps.

I slid the box of candy canes in my pocket, then headed up Nate's walk, taking a deep breath of cool air. The truth was, I'd thought about getting him a Christmas gift. I had even picked out more than one before stopping myself, not sure even after that night in the pool that I was ready or able to make such a grand gesture. But in the days since, I'd also realized that with Nate, everything just came so easily, as easily as letting him take my hand and pull me beneath the surface. Maybe it was impossible for someone to share everything with you, but I was beginning to think what we had was enough. And anyway, it was Christmas, a time above all for hope, or so I'd been told. He'd given me so much, and now, here, I was finally ready to reciprocate. So I stepped up to the door and rang the bell.

The moment he opened the door, I knew something was wrong. It was just the look on his face—surprised, even alarmed—followed immediately by the way he eased the door a bit more shut, the same move I'd once mastered with the Jehovah's and landlords. "Ruby," he said, his voice low. "Hey. What are you doing here?"

Right that moment, I heard his dad: loud, bellowing, barely muffled from behind a nearby wall. I swallowed, then said, "Jamie was just handing out stuff, for Christmas—"

"It's not a good time," he said as there was a bang, or a thud, discernible. "I'll call you a little later, okay?"

"Are you all right?" I asked him.

"I'm fine."

"Nate—"

"I am. But I've got to go," he said, easing the door closed a bit more. I could barely see him now. "I'll talk to you tomorrow."

I didn't get a chance to answer this, as the door was already shutting with an audible click. I just stood there, my mouth dry, wondering what I should do. *I'm fine*, he'd said. I reached out, putting my hand on the knob and turning it. Here I was, finally ready to let him in, and it was me locked out.

"Hey!" Jamie called from behind me. I turned. He and Roscoe were across the street, coming closer. "Are they there?"

Say something, I thought, but even as I tried to form the words, any words, I remembered that day in the garage, how he'd asked me to keep this quiet. *You understand.* Did I want to be the Honeycutts, stepping in and ruining everything, even if I thought it was for the best? Jamie was coming up the walk, Roscoe pulling ahead. I had to decide, now.

"They're not home," I said, stepping off the porch. The box of candy canes was still in my pocket, and I slid my fingers in, cupping them around it. It felt almost like a hand, resting in mine. "Let's just go."

Chapter Thirteen

I was up until way late, but not waiting for Santa. Instead, I lay on my bed, watching the lights from Nate's pool dance across the trees, the same way I had that first night. More than once, I thought about sneaking over again to find him and see if he was okay. But then I'd remember him shutting the door in my face, the click of the latch catching, and stay where I was.

The next morning, I got a new backpack, some CDs, a few books, and a laptop. Cora got her period.

"I'm fine, I'm fine," she sputtered when, shortly after we'd opened gifts, I found her sitting on her bed, crying. "Really."

"Honey." Jamie came over, sitting beside her and sliding his arm over her shoulder. "It's okay."

"I know." Her voice was still choked as she reached up, wiping her eyes with the back of her hand. "It's just, I really had a feeling it had happened this month. Which I know is so stupid . . ."

"You're not stupid," Jamie said softly, smoothing a hand over her head.

". . . but I just started thinking how great it would be to find out today and be able to tell you guys, and how it would be the best gift ever—" She drew in a long, shaky breath, her eyes welling up again. "But it didn't happen. I'm not pregnant. Again."

"Cora."

"I know," she said, waving her hand. "It's Christmas, we have a wonderful life, roof over our head, things so many people want. But I want this. And no matter what I do, I can't get it. It just . . ." She trailed off, wiping her eyes again. This time, Jamie didn't say anything.

"Sucks," I finished for her.

"Yeah," she said, looking up at me. "It *sucks*."

I felt so helpless, the way I always did when I saw Cora upset about the baby issue. It was the one thing that could take her from zero to emotional in less than five minutes, the single tender spot in her substantial personal armor. The previous month she'd finally agreed to a little pharmaceutical help, via an ovulation drug, which made her hot and emotional, liable to be sweating or weeping or both at any given moment. Not a good mix, especially during the holidays. And now, it was all for nothing. It did suck.

"We'll just try again," Jamie was saying now. "It was just the first month. Maybe the second time will be the charm."

Cora nodded, but I could see she was hardly convinced as she reached up, running her finger over the gift I'd given her that morning: one of Harriet's key necklaces, a silver one lined with red stones. I'd been strangely nervous as she opened the box, worried she wouldn't like it, but the minute she slid it out into her hand, her eyes widening, I knew I'd scored. "It's beautiful," she said, looking up at me. "It's like yours!"

"Kind of," I said. "But not completely."

"I love it," she told me, reaching up immediately to put it on. She brushed her hair over her shoulders. "What do you think? Does it look good?"

It had, and did now, as she rested her head on Jamie's shoulder, curling into him. She still had one hand around the key. The necklace looked different on her than on me, but you could see some similarities. You just had to know where to look.

Just then, the doorbell rang. Roscoe, who'd been snoozing at the foot of the bed, perked up his ears and let out a yap. "Was that the door?" Jamie asked.

"It was," Cora said as Roscoe hopped down, bolting from the room. A moment later, we heard him barking from the foyer as the bell sounded again. "Who would show up on Christmas?"

"I'll find out," I said, although as I quickly got up, heading for the stairs, I was hoping I already knew. The bell rang again when I was halfway down, then once more as I approached the door. When I got to the door and looked through the peephole, though, Nate wasn't there. Nobody was. Then it chimed again—so weird—so I just opened it.

It was Gervais. Too short for the peephole, he was standing on the front step, in his glasses, peacoat, and scarf, with what looked like a brand-new scooter parked on the walk behind him. "Hi," he said.

I just looked at him. "Hey," I said slowly. "What are you—?"

"I have a proposition for you," he said, all business. "Can I come in?"

"Um," I said. Behind me, Roscoe had stopped barking but was still trying to nudge past me. "We're kind of busy, actually—"

"I know." He reached up, adjusting his glasses. "This will only take a minute."

I still didn't really want to let him in. But in the spirit of the holiday, I stepped aside. "Shouldn't you be with your family?" I asked as he shut the door behind him.

"We finished Christmas hours ago," he told me. "My dad already took down the tree."

"Oh." Now we were just standing there, together, in the foyer. "Well," I said, "we're still kind of doing things, so—"

"Do you think you'll be prepared for your next big calculus exam?"

I just looked at him. "What?"

"Your next exam. It's in March and counts for half your grade, right?"

"How do you know that?"

"Will you be prepared for it?"

Upstairs, I heard Cora laughing. A good sign. "Define prepared," I said.

"Scoring a ninety or higher."

"No," I said. Which was, sadly, the truth. Even with all my studying and preparation, calculus was still the one thing that could take me from zero to panicked in less than thirty seconds.

"Then you should let me help you," Gervais said.

"Help me?"

"I'm very good at calculus," he explained, pushing up his glasses. "Not only doing it, but explaining it. I'm tutor-

ing two people in my class at the U right now. And that's
college-level calc, not that easy-schmeezy kind you're doing."

Easy-schmeezy, I thought. He hadn't changed entirely.
"You know," I said, "that's a very nice offer. But I think I'll
be okay."

"It's not an offer," he said. "It's a proposition."

Suddenly, I had a flash of him in the car that day, drawing in his breath. Plus the staring at lunch in the green,
and the weird way he'd acted at the Vista 10. *Oh, God*, I
thought, finally getting it. Nate was right. He *liked* me. This
was just what I needed. "You know," I said, reaching behind
him for the door, "you're a nice kid, Gervais, but—"

"It's about Olivia," he said.

I stopped, mid-sentence, not sure I was hearing him
right. "What?"

He coughed. Then blushed. "Olivia Davis," he said.
"You're friends with her, aren't you?"

"Yes," I said slowly. "Why?"

"Because," he said. He coughed again. "I, um, like her.
Kind of."

"You like *Olivia*?"

"Not like that," he said quickly. "I just . . ."

I waited. It seemed like a long time passed.

". . . I want to be her friend," he finished.

This was kind of sweet, I had to admit. Also surprising.
Which brought me to my next question. "Why?"

"Because," he said as if it was simple, obvious. When
it became clear this was not the case, he added, "She talks
to me."

"She talks to you," I repeated.

He nodded. "Like, at the theater. And when she sees me in the hall at school, she always says hello. Nobody else does that. Plus, she likes the same movies I do."

I looked down at him, standing there before me in his heavy coat and glasses. Sure, he was annoying, but it did have to be hard for him. No matter how smart you were, there was a lot you couldn't learn from books. "Then just be friends with her," I said. "You don't need me for that."

"I do, though," he said. "I can't just go up and talk to her. But if I was, you know, helping you with your calculus at lunch or something, then I could just hang out with you guys."

"Gervais," I said slowly. "I think that's really sweet—"

"Don't say no," he pleaded.

"—but it's also deceptive."

He shook his head, adamant. "It's not, though! I don't like her that way. I just want to be friends."

"Still, it would be like I'm setting her up. And friends don't do that."

Never in a million years would I have thought I would be offering up a primer on friendship, much less to Gervais Miller. Even less likely? That I would feel sorry for him after I did so. But as he regarded me glumly, then stepped back to the door, I did.

"All right," he said, his voice flat. Defeated. "I understand."

I watched him as he turned the knob, pulling the door open. Once again, I found myself torn as to what to do, but this time, the stakes weren't so high. Maybe I couldn't do anything for Nate. But I could help someone.

"How about this," I said. He turned back to me slowly. "I'll hire you."

"Hire me?"

"As a tutor. I pay what everyone else pays, you do what you do. If it just so happens we meet during lunch and Olivia is there, then so be it. But she is not part of the deal. Understood?"

He nodded vigorously, his glasses bobbing slightly. "Yes."

"All right then," I said. "Merry Christmas."

"Merry Christmas," he replied, stepping outside and starting down the stairs. Halfway there, he turned back to me. "Oh. I'm twenty dollars an hour, by the way. For the tutoring."

Of course he was. I said, "Am I going to pass calculus?"

"It's guaranteed," he replied. "My method is proven."

I nodded, and then he continued down the steps, grabbing his helmet from his scooter and pulling it on. Maybe this was a big mistake, one among many. But sometimes, we all need a little help, whether we want to admit it or not.

*   *   *

"Come in, come in," Jamie said as yet another group came bustling in, their chatter rising up to the high ceiling of the foyer. "Welcome! Drinks are in the back, and there's tons of food. Here, let me take your coat. . . ."

I leaned back against the doorjamb of the laundry room, where I'd been hiding out with Roscoe ever since Jamie and Cora's post-Christmas, pre–New Year holiday open house began. Officially, it was my job to keep the ice bucket full and make sure the music was audible, but other than doing this on a most perfunctory level, I wasn't exactly mingling.

Now, though, as Jamie, with his arms full of coats, glanced around him, I knew I should show myself and offer to help him stow them upstairs. Instead, I slid down into a sitting position, my back to the dryer, nudging the door shut with my foot. Roscoe, who'd been exiled here for his own mental well-being, immediately hopped up from his bed and came over to join me.

It had been two days since Christmas, and I hadn't seen or talked to Nate. Once, this would have seemed impossible, considering our very proximity—not to mention how often we crossed paths, intentionally or otherwise. Maybe it was just that school was out, we weren't riding together, and we were both busy with our respective jobs, where things hadn't slowed down, even after Christmas. But even so, I had the distinct feeling he was avoiding me.

This was surprising, but even more shocking was the fact that it was bothering me so much. After all, this was what I'd wanted once—more space between us, less connection. Now that I had it, though, I felt more worried about him than ever.

Just then, the door opened. "One second, I just have to grab another roll of—" Cora was halfway inside, still talking to someone over her shoulder, when she stopped in mid-stride and sentence, seeing me and Roscoe on the floor. "Hey," she said slowly. "What's going on?"

"Nothing," I said. She shut the door as Roscoe got up, wagging his tail. "Just taking a breather."

"But not in the closet," she said.

"This was closer."

She reached over the washing machine, pulling down a

roll of paper towels. "Already a spill on the carpet," she said, tearing them open. "Happens every year."

"Sounds like it's going well otherwise, though," I said as some people passed by in the hallway outside, their voices bouncing off the walls.

"It is." She turned back to me, the towels in her arms. "You should come out, have some food. It's not that bad, I promise."

"I'm a little low on cheer," I told her.

She smiled. "You've been a real trooper, I have to say. Christmas with Jamie is like an endurance trial. My first year I almost had a total breakdown."

"It's just weird," I said. "I mean, last year . . ." I trailed off, realizing I didn't even remember what I'd done last year for the holidays. I had a vague recollection of delivering luggage, maybe a company party at Commercial. But like everything else from my old life, this was distant, faded. "I'm just tired, I guess."

"Just make an appearance," she said. "Then you can come back here, or hit the closet for the rest of the day. All right?"

I looked up at her, dubious, as she extended her hand to me. But then I let her pull me to my feet and followed her out into the hallway. Two steps later, as we entered the kitchen, we were ambushed.

"Cora! Hello!" I jumped, startled, as a petite woman in a flowing, all-white ensemble, her dark hair pulled back at her neck, suddenly appeared in front of us, a wineglass in one hand. "Happy holidays!"

"Happy holidays," Cora replied, leaning forward to

accept a kiss—and a shadow of a lipstick stain—on her cheek. "Barbara, this is my sister, Ruby. Ruby, this is Barbara Starr."

"You have a sister?" Barbara asked. She was wearing several multicolored beaded necklaces that swayed and clacked across her chest each time she moved, as she did now, turning to face me. "Why, I had no idea!"

"Ruby just came to live with us this year," Cora explained. To me, she said, "Barbara is an author. Best-selling, I might add."

"Oh, stop," Barbara replied, waving her hand. "You'll embarrass me."

"She was one of my very first clients," Cora added. "When I was working in a family law practice, just out of school."

"Really," I said.

"I got divorced," Barbara explained, taking a sip of her wine. "Which is never fun. But because of your sister, it was the *best* divorce I've ever had. And that's really saying something."

I looked at Cora, who shook her head almost imperceptibly, making it clear I should not ask what exactly this meant. Instead, she said, "Well, we should probably go check on the food, so . . ."

"Everything is just wonderful. I love the holidays!" Barbara said, sighing. Then she smiled at me and said, "Is the rest of your family here, as well? I'd just love to meet your mother."

"Um," I said, "actually—"

"We're not really in touch with our mom these days,"

Cora told her. "But we *are* lucky to have so many great friends like you here today. Would you like some more wine?"

"Oh," Barbara said, looking at her glass, then at us. "Well, yes. That would be lovely."

Cora eased the glass from her hand—still smiling, smiling—then passed it off to me, touching the small of my back with her other hand. As I took this cue, moving forward, I looked back at her. Barbara was talking again, her hands fluttering as she made some point, but my sister, even as she nodded, was watching me. Awfully smooth, I thought. But then again, she'd been away from my mom a lot longer than I had. Practice does make perfect, or close to it.

Glass in hand, I made my way through the crowd, which had grown considerably since the last time I'd checked the ice and music. Jamie was still in the foyer, answering the door and taking coats, when I finally reached the bar area to get the white wine.

"Macaroons!" I heard him say suddenly. "You shouldn't have."

I turned around. Sure enough, there was Nate, in jeans and a blue collared shirt, his hands in his pockets. His dad was beside him, shrugging off his jacket and smiling as Jamie admired his offering. "They're Belgian," Mr. Cross said. "*Very* expensive."

"I'll bet," Jamie replied, clapping Nate on the shoulder. "Now, let me get you a drink. What's your poison, Blake? We've got beer, Scotch, wine . . ."

He gestured toward the bar, and as they all turned, Nate's eyes met mine. Mr. Cross lifted a hand, waving at me, but I just picked up the glass, quickly folding myself back into the crowd.

When I returned to the spot where I'd left Cora and Barbara, however, they were both gone, a couple of Jamie's UMe.com employees—easily identified by their so-nerdy-they're-cool glasses, expensive jeans, and vintage T-shirts—in their place, jabbering about Macs. I turned slowly, scanning the crowd for Barbara. Instead, I came face-to-face with Nate.

"Hey," he said. "Merry Christmas."

I swallowed, then took in a breath. "Merry Christmas."

There was a pause, which then stretched to an awkward pause, even as someone laughed behind us.

"So I brought you a present," he said, reaching behind him and pulling out a wrapped parcel from his back pocket.

"Let me guess," I said. "Macaroons."

"No," he replied, making a face as he held it out to me. "Open it up."

I looked down at the gift, which was wrapped in red paper decorated with little Christmas trees, and thought of myself standing at his door that night, my own small offering in hand. "You know," I said, nodding to the glass of wine I was still holding, "I should probably—"

"Never delay opening a gift," Nate said, reaching to take the glass from me, putting it on a nearby counter. "Especially one that's already belated."

Emptyhanded, I had no choice but to take it from him, turning it over in my hands and running a finger under the tape. Two women passed by us, chattering excitedly, their heels clacking, as it fell open to reveal a T-shirt. On the front, in that same familiar block lettering: USWIM.

"Your personal philosophy," I said.

"Well," he said, "I looked for one that said 'If you expect the worst you'll never be disappointed,' but they were all out."

"I'll bet." I looked up at him. "This is really nice. Thank you."

"No problem." He leaned back against the wall behind him, smiling at me, and I had a flash of us in the pool together, how he'd grabbed my hand and pulled me under. The memory was so close, I could see every bit of it. But just as clearly, there was the other night, how his face had looked, retreating through the crack in that door. Two opposite images, one easing me closer, another pushing away. "So," he said, "how was your Christmas?"

"How was yours?" I replied, and while I didn't mean for there to be an edge in my voice, even I could hear it. So could he. His face immediately changed, the smile not disappearing, but seeming to stretch more thin. I cleared my throat, then looked down at the shirt again. "I mean, you had to expect I'd ask."

Nate nodded, glancing across the kitchen to the living room, where I could see his dad was talking to a stout woman in a red Christmas sweater. "It was fine," he said. "A little stressful, as you saw."

"A little?" I asked.

"It's not a big deal, okay?"

"Sure seemed that way."

"Well, it wasn't. And it's ancient history."

"It was three days ago," I pointed out.

"So the holidays suck. That's not exactly a news flash, is it?" He ducked his head, a shock of hair falling across his face as the same women passed back by in a cloud of perfumed hand soap, leaving the powder room. When they were gone, he said, "Look, I'm sorry I couldn't talk to you that night. But I'm here now. And I brought a gift. That's got to count for something, right?"

I looked back down at the shirt. *You swim*, I thought. Like he'd said, it was better than sinking. Maybe this was just part of staying afloat. "I don't have anything for you, though."

"Not even Belgian macaroons?"

I shook my head.

"That's all right. They're actually pretty overrated."

"Really."

He nodded, glancing over across the party again, then reached down, sliding his hand around my free one and tugging me a bit down the hallway, around the corner. There, out of sight, he leaned against the wall, gently looping his arms around my waist and pulling me closer. "Okay," he said, his voice low. "Let's try this again. Merry Christmas, Ruby."

I looked up at him, taking in the line of his chin, his eyes and long lashes, the way his fingers were already brushing a bit of my hair off my face, entwining themselves in the strands there. So nearby now, after the distance before. But he was here.

"Merry Christmas," I said, and it was this closeness I tried to concentrate on—not that it might be fleeting, a feeling I knew too well—as he leaned down and put his lips to mine, kissing me, as around the corner the party went on without us, noisy and continuous and completely unaware.

*   *   *

"Cora," I said as we pulled up outside the mall, "we really don't have to do this."

"We do," she replied, cutting the engine. "Like I said, desperate times call for desperate measures."

"That's just my point, though," I said as she pushed open her door to climb out and I reluctantly did the same. "I'm not desperate."

She just looked at me as I came around the back of the car, then hoisted her purse over one shoulder. "First," she said, "I gave you money for clothes. You bought four things."

"Seven, actually," I pointed out.

"Then," she continued, ignoring this, "for Christmas, I gave you gift cards, with which you bought nothing."

"I don't need anything!"

"And so really, you have given me no choice but to take you shopping by force." She sighed, then reached up, dropping her sunglasses down from their perch on her head to cover her eyes. "Do you even realize how happy the average teenage girl would be in your shoes? I have a credit card. We're at the mall. I want to buy you things. It's like adolescent nirvana."

"Well," I said as we passed two moms pushing strollers, "I guess I'm not the average teenage girl."

She looked over at me as we approached the entrance. "Of course you're not," she said more quietly. "Look, I know this is kind of weird for you. But we have the money, and it's something Jamie and I want to do."

"It's not weird," I told her. "Just unnecessary."

"You know," she said as the automatic doors to Esther Prine, the upscale department store, slid open in front of us, "it's okay to accept things from people. It doesn't make you weak or helpless, even if that is how Mom felt about it."

This was a bit too reminiscent of the ground I'd been forced to cover during my first (and hopefully only) therapy session a few weeks earlier, so instead of responding, I stepped inside. As always, I was temporarily blinded by the gleaming white tile of the store, as well as the polished-to-a-high-sheen jewelry cases. To our left, a guy in a tuxedo was playing Pachelbel by the escalators. It was always kind of odd to be talking about my mother, anyway, but in this setting, it bordered on surreal.

"It's not about Mom," I said as Cora gestured for me to follow her up to the next floor. "Or not just about her. It's a big change. I'm not used to . . . We didn't have much these last few years."

"I know," she replied. "But that's just what I'm saying. In some ways, that was a choice, too. There were things Mom could have done to make things easier for you and for herself."

"Like get in touch with you," I said.

"Yes." She cleared her throat, looking out over cosmetics as we rose up higher, then higher. "But it goes even further back than that. Like with Dad, and the money he tried to give her. But she was so stubborn and angry, she wouldn't take it."

"Wait," I said as we finally reached the top, and she stepped off into Juniors. "I thought Dad never gave her any money. That he dodged her for child support, just disappeared."

Cora shook her head. "Maybe he did later, once he moved to Illinois. But those early years, right after he moved out? He tried to do the right thing. I remember."

Maybe this shouldn't have surprised me. After all, by now I knew my mom had kept so much secret, tweaking her history and my own. Cora was not what I'd been led to believe, so why would my father be, either? Thinking this, though, something else occurred to me. Something that also didn't belong in the polished world of Esther Prine, and yet I had to bring it in, anyway.

"Cora," I said as she drifted over to a table of sweaters, running her hand over them, "do you know where Dad is?"

In the pause that followed, I saw my entire life changing again, twisted and shifting and different. But then she turned around to face me. "No," she said softly as a salesgirl drifted past, pushing a rack of flimsy dresses. "I've thought about looking for him, though, many times. Mostly because Jamie's been really insistent about it, how easy it would be. But I guess I'm sort of afraid still."

I nodded. This, if nothing else, I could understand. There were so many levels to the unknown, from safe to dangerous to outright nebulous, scariest of all.

"You never know, though," she said. "Maybe we can do it together. Strength in numbers and all that."

"Maybe," I said.

She smiled at me, a bit tentatively, then looked back

at the sweaters. "Okay, now—down to business. We're not leaving here until you have at least two new outfits. And a jacket. And new shoes."

"Cora."

"No arguments." She hoisted her purse over her shoulder, then pushed on into Juniors, disappearing between two racks of jeans. After a moment, all I could see was her head bobbing in and out of the displays, her expression caught in the occasional mirror, focused and determined. At first, I stayed where I was, out in the open aisle as the salegirl passed by once more, smiling at me. But then I looked for Cora again and couldn't spot her right away, which was enough to make me force myself forward, in after her.

Chapter Fourteen

"Wow," Nate said. "You look great."

This was exactly the kind of reaction I'd been hoping to avoid, especially considering Cora had assured me repeatedly that my new clothes did not necessarily look that, well, new. Apparently she was wrong.

"It's just a jacket," I told him, pulling my seat belt over my shoulder. As I did so, I glanced at Gervais, who was studying me, as well. "What?"

"Nothing," he said, shrinking back a little bit in his seat.

I sighed, shaking my head, then looked over at Nate, who was just sitting behind the wheel, a half smile on his face. "So what's the occasion for the makeover? Got a hot date for Valentine's or something?"

"Nope," I said, and he laughed, shifting into gear and pulling away from the curb. As we came up to the stop sign at the end of the street, though, he reached over, squeezing my knee, and kept his hand there as we turned onto the next street.

It was February now, which meant Nate and I had been doing whatever it was we were doing—dating, making out, spending most of our free time together—for over a month. And I had to admit, I was happy about it, at least most of the time. But regardless of how well we were getting to know each other, there was always the issue with his dad, the one part of himself he still held back and kept from me. It was only a single thing, but somehow it counted for a lot. Like even when things were as good as they could be, they could only be good enough.

Such as Valentine's Day, which was less than twenty-four hours away. Normally, I'd be happy to have a boyfriend (or something close to it) on the very day you're made to be *very* aware when you don't. But even as Nate hinted at his big plans for us—which, by the sound of it, were secret, detailed, and still in development—I couldn't completely just relax and enjoy it. Rest Assured had run a special promotion for gift baskets and flower delivery for its customers, and the response had been overwhelming. As a result, they were booked fully for that day, just like on Thanksgiving, and I'd not forgotten how that had turned out.

"It's going to be fine," Nate had assured me the night before, out by the pond, when I'd brought this up. We'd taken to meeting there sometimes in the evening, between our respective homework and work schedules, if only for a few moments. "I'll do deliveries all afternoon, be done by seven. Plenty of time for what I have in mind."

"Which is what?" I asked.

"You'll see." He reached over, brushing my hair back from my face. Behind him I could see the lights from the pool flickering over the fence, and even as he leaned in, kissing my temple, I was distracted, knowing that he was supposed to be over there, assembling gift baskets and that any moment his dad might wander out and find him gone. This must have been obvious, as after a moment he pulled back. "What's wrong?"

"Nothing."

"You look worried."

"I'm not."

"Look," he said, his expression serious, "if this is about my gift . . . just relax. I'm not expecting anything phenomenal. Just, you know, super great."

I just looked at him, regretting once again that in a moment of weakness a few days earlier, I'd confessed to Olivia—who then had of course told Nate—that I was stressing about finding the right thing for him for Valentine's. Her loyalty aside, though, the truth was that having dropped the ball at Christmas, it seemed especially important to deliver something good here, if not phenomenal.

"It's not about your gift," I told him.

"Then what is it?"

I shrugged, then looked past him again, over at the pool house. After a moment, he turned and glanced that way as well, then back at me, finally getting it. "It's fine, okay? I'm off the clock," he said. "All yours."

But that was just the thing. Even in these moments—sitting by the pond with his leg linked around mine, or riding in the car with his hand on my knee—I never felt like I had all of Nate, just enough to make me realize what was missing. Even stranger was that with anyone else I'd ever been with—especially Marshall—what I was given, as well as what I gave, had always been partial, and yet that had still been plenty.

Now, we pulled into the Perkins lot, and Gervais jumped

out, bolting for the building as always. As soon as the door shut behind him, Nate leaned across the console between us and kissed me. "You do look great," he said. "So what made you finally break down and spend those gift cards?"

"I didn't. Cora ambushed me and took me to Esther Prine. I was powerless to resist."

"Most girls I know would consider that wish fullfill-ment, not torture."

I sat back, shaking my head. "Why does everyone keep saying that? Who says just because I'm a girl I'm hardwired to want to spent a hundred and eighty bucks on jeans?"

Nate pulled away, holding up his hands. "Whoa there," he said. "Just making an observation."

"Well, don't." I looked down at my lap and those ex-pensive jeans, not to mention the shoes I had on with them (suede, not on sale) and my jacket (soft leather, some la-bel I'd never even heard of). Who was this person in these fancy clothes, at this expensive school, with a for-all-in-tents-and-purposes boyfriend who she was actually worried wasn't opening up to her enough emotionally? It was like I'd been brainwashed or something.

Nate was still watching me, not saying anything. "Sorry," I said finally. "It's just . . . I don't know. Everything feels overwhelming right now, for some reason."

"Overwhelming," he repeated.

It was times like these that I knew I should just come clean and tell him that I worried about him. Having the courage to do that was the part of me *I* was still holding back. And I was always aware of it, even as, like now, I did it once again.

"Plus," I said, sliding my knee so it rested against his, "there's this issue of your gift."

"My gift," he repeated, raising an eyebrow.

"It's just so all-encompassing," I said with a sigh, shaking my head. "Huge. And detailed . . . I mean, the flow charts and spread sheets alone are out of control."

"Yeah?" he said.

"I'll be lucky if I get it all in place by tonight, to be honest."

"Huh." He considered this. "Well. I have to admit, I'm intrigued."

"You should be."

He smiled, then reached over, running a hand over my jacket. "This is pretty cool," he said. "What's the inside look like?"

"The inside . . ." I said, just as he slid his hand over my shoulder, easing off one sleeve. "Ah, right. Well, it's equally impressive."

"Yeah? Let me see." He nudged it off over the other shoulder, and I shook my head. "You know, it is. This sweater is pretty nice, too. Who makes it?"

"No idea," I said.

I felt his hand go around my waist, then smoothly move up my back to the tag. "Lanoler," he read slowly, ducking his head down so his lips were on my collarbone. "Seems well made. Although it's hard to tell. Maybe if I just—"

I glanced outside the car, where people were walking past to the green, coffees in hand, backpacks over shoulders. "Nate," I said. "It's almost first bell."

"You're so conscientious," he said, his voice muffled by

my sweater, which he was still trying to ease off. "When did that happen?"

I sighed, then looked at the dashboard clock. We had five minutes before we'd be officially late. Not all the time we wanted, but maybe this, too, was too much to ask for. "Okay," I told him as he worked his way back around my neck, his lips moving up to my ear. "I'm all yours."

*   *   *

When I got home that afternoon, I saw Jamie seated at the island with his laptop. As he heard me approach, he quickly leaped up, grabbing a nearby loaf of bread and holding it in front of him as if struck by a sudden desire to make a sandwich.

I raised my eyebrows. "What are you doing?"

He exhaled loudly. "I thought you were Cora," he said, tossing the bread down. "Whew! You scared me. I've worked too hard on this for her to find out about it now."

As he sat back down, I saw that the island was covered with piles of CDs, some in their cases, others scattered all over the place. "So this is your Valentine's Day gift?"

"One of them," he said, opening a case and taking out a disk. "It'll be, like, the third or fourth wave."

"Wave?"

"That's my V-day technique," he explained, sliding the disk into the side of his laptop. I heard a whirring, then some clicks, and the screen flickered. "Multiple gifts, given in order of escalating greatness, over the entire day. So, you know, you begin with flowers, then move to chocolates, maybe some balloons. This'll come after that, but before the gourmet dinner. I'm still tweaking the order."

"Right," I said glumly, sitting down across from him and picking up a Bob Dylan CD.

He glanced over at me. "What's wrong? Don't tell me you don't like Valentine's Day. *Everyone* likes Valentine's Day."

I considered disputing this, but as he'd said the same thing about Thanksgiving, Christmas, and New Year's, I figured it wasn't worth the argument. "I'm just kind of stuck," I said. "I need to get something for someone. . . ."

"Nate," he said, hitting a couple of buttons on the laptop. I looked up at him. "Ruby, come on. We're not that *dense*, you know. Plus half the house does look out at the pond, even at night."

I bit my lip, turning the CD case in my hands. "Anyway," I said, "I want it to be, like, this great gift. But I can't come up with anything."

"Because you're overthinking it," he said. "The best gifts come from the heart, not a store."

"This from the man who buys in waves."

"I'm not buying this," he pointed out, nodding at the laptop. "I mean, I bought the CDs, yeah. But the idea is from the heart."

"And what's the idea?"

"All the songs Cora loves to sing, in one place," he said, sounding pleased with himself. "It wasn't easy, let me tell you. I wrote up a list, then found them online or at the record store. For the really obscure ones, I had to enlist this guy one of my employees knows from his Anger Management class who's some kind of music freak. But now I finally have them all. 'Wasted Time,' 'Frankie and Johnny,' 'Don't Think Twice, It's All Right' . . ."

"'Angel from Montgomery,'" I said quietly.

"Exactly!" He grinned. "Hey, you can probably help me, now that I think of it. Just take a look at the list, and see if I'm missing anything."

He pushed a piece of paper across to me, and I glanced down at it, reading over the familiar titles of the songs my mom had always sung to me, listed in block print. "No," I said finally. "This is pretty much all of them."

"Great." He hit another button, taking out the CD and putting it on the counter as I pushed out my chair, getting to my feet. "Where you headed?"

"Shopping," I said, pulling my bag over my shoulder. "I have to find something phenomenal."

"You will," he replied. "Just remember: the heart! Start there, and you can't go wrong."

I remained unconvinced, however, especially once I got to the mall, where there were hearts everywhere: shaped into balloons and cookies, personalized on T-shirts, filled with chocolate and held by fuzzy teddy bears. But even after going into a dozen stores, I still couldn't find anything for Nate.

"Personally," Harriet said as I slumped onto her stool an hour later for a much-needed rest, "I think this holiday is a total crock, completely manufactured by the greeting-card companies. If you really love someone, you should show it every day, not just one."

"And yet," Reggie said, from his kiosk, "you are not averse to running a two-for-one Valentine's Day special on bracelets and assorted rings."

"Of course not!" she said. "I'm a businesswoman. As

long as the holiday exists, I might as well profit from it."

Reggie rolled his eyes and went back to stacking daily multis. "I just want to get something good," I said. "Something that *means* something."

"Just try to forget about it for a while," she replied, adjusting a rack of pendants. "Then, out of nowhere, the perfect gift will just come to you."

I looked at my watch. "I have about twenty-six hours. Not exactly a lot of time for inspiration to strike."

"Oh." She took a sip of her coffee. "Well, then I'd get him some of those macaroons you bought me at Christmas. Those you can't go wrong with."

In the end, though, it didn't come to that, although what I did end up with was almost as pathetic: a gift card to PLUG, the music store. It wasn't phenomenal, not even decent, and as I left the mall feeling thoroughly defeated, all I could hope was that Harriet was right, and I'd come up with something better in the short time I had remaining.

The next morning, though, this still hadn't happened, a fact made even more obvious when I came down for breakfast and walked right into Jamie's first wave. Four dozen roses in varying colors were arranged in vases all around the kitchen, each tied with a big white bow. Cora was at the counter, reading the card off of one of them, her face flushed, as I helped myself to coffee.

"He *always* overdoes it on Valentine's," she said, although she looked kind of choked up as she tucked the card into her purse. "The first year we were married, he got me a new car."

"Really," I said.

"Yep. Totally overwhelmed me." She sighed, picking up her mug. "It was so sweet, but I felt terrible. All I'd gotten him was a gift card."

I swallowed. "I have to go."

What I needed, I decided as I headed down the walkway to Nate's car ten minutes later, was to just stop thinking about Valentine's Day altogether. Which seemed easy, at least until I opened the car door and found myself face-to-face with a huge basketful of candy and flowers.

"Sorry," Nate said from somewhere behind the tiny balloons that were poking out of the top of it. "We're a little cramped in here. Do you mind holding that in your lap?"

I picked up the basket, then slid into the seat, pulling the door shut behind me. The instant it was closed, the smell of roses was overpowering, and as I shifted in my seat I saw why: the entire back was piled with baskets of assorted sizes, stacked three deep. "Where's Gervais?" I asked.

"I'm here," I heard a muffled voice say. A huge bunch of baby's breath shifted to one side, revealing his face. "And I think I'm having an allergic reaction."

"Just hang in there for a few more minutes," Nate told him, opening his window as we pulled away from the curb. His phone rang, rattling the console, and I peered around the flowers in my lap to look at him as he grabbed it, putting it to his ear. "Yeah," he said, slowing for the next light. "I'm on my way to school right now, so in ten or so I'll start down the list. Lakeview first, then over to the office complex. Right. Okay. Bye."

"You're not going to school today?" I asked as he hung up.

"Duty calls," he said, shutting his phone. "My dad got

a little overambitious with the response to the special, so we're pretty booked. We'll be lucky to get it all done, even with the two of us going all day."

"Really," I said quietly.

"Don't worry," he said as his phone rang again. "I'll be done in plenty of time for our thing tonight."

But this wasn't what I was worried about, and I wondered if he knew it. It was hard to tell, since he was talking to his dad again as he pulled up in front of Perkins Day, and Gervais and I extracted ourselves to disembark. As he headed off, sneezing, I put the basket I'd been holding back on the seat, then stood by the open door, waiting for Nate to hang up. Even as he did, he was already shifting back into gear, moving on.

"I gotta go," he said to me, over the flowers. "But I'll see you tonight, okay? Seven, at the pond. Don't be late."

I nodded and shut the door. He already had his phone back to his ear as he pulled into traffic. As he drove off, all I could see were a bunch of heart-shaped balloons in the back window, bobbing and swaying, first to one side, then back again.

*   *   *

Jamie and Cora were out for dinner—in the midst of a wave, no doubt—so I was alone, sitting at the kitchen table, my stupid gift card in hand, when the clock over the stove flipped to seven o'clock.

I stood up, sliding it into my pocket, then ran a hand through my hair as I stepped out onto the patio, Roscoe rousing himself from his dog bed to follow along behind me. Outside, the air was cold, the lights from Nate's pool and house visible over the fence.

Call it a bad feeling. Or just the logical conclusion to an unavoidable situation. But I think I knew, even before that first fifteen minutes passed with no sign of him, that he wasn't just late, something was wrong. Before my fingers— even jammed into the pockets of my new jacket—began to get numb, before Roscoe abandoned me for the warmth of the house, before another set of lights came up from the opposite side, lighting up the trees briefly before cutting off and leaving me in darkness again. It was eight fifteen when I saw Cora appear in the patio doorway, cupping a hand over her eyes. A moment later, she stuck her head out.

"Are you okay?" she said. "It's freezing out there."

"How was dinner?" I asked her.

"Fantastic." She glanced behind her at Jamie, who was walking into the kitchen with one of those leftover containers shaped into a swan. "You should hear this CD he made for me. It's—"

"I'll be in soon," I told her. "Just a couple more minutes."

She nodded slowly. "Okay," she said. "Don't wait too long, though."

But I already had. And not just that hour and fifteen minutes, but every moment that had passed since Thanksgiving, when I should have told Nate I couldn't just stand by and worry about him. Instead, though, I had let months pass, pushing down my better instincts, and now, sitting out in the February chill, I was getting exactly what I deserved.

When I finally went inside, I tried to distract myself

with homework and TV, but instead I kept looking over at Nate's house, and his window, which I could see clearly from my own. Behind the shade, I could see a figure moving back and forth. After a little while, it stopped, suddenly so still that I wondered if it was really anyone at all.

It was over an hour later when the phone rang. Cora and Jamie were downstairs, eating wave-two chocolates out of the box and listening to her CD, their voices and the music drifting up to me. I didn't even look at the caller ID, lying back on my bed instead, but then Jamie was calling my name. I looked at the receiver for a minute, then hit the TALK button. "Hello?"

"I know you're probably pissed," Nate said. "But meet me outside, okay?"

I didn't say anything, not that it mattered. He'd hung up, the dial tone already buzzing in my ear.

Billie Holiday was playing as I went downstairs and back outside, retracing my steps across the grass, which felt stiff and ungiving beneath my feet. This time, I didn't sit, instead crossing my arms over my chest as Nate emerged from the shadows. He had one hand behind his back, a smile on his face.

"Okay," he said, before he'd even gotten to me, "I know that me being over two hours late was not *exactly* the surprise you were expecting. But today was crazy, I just now got home, and I'll make it up to you. I promise."

We were in the swath of darkness between the lights from his house and those of Cora's, so it was hard to make out all the details of his face. But even so, I could tell there was something off: a nervous quality, something almost jittery. "You've been home," I told him. "I saw your light was on."

"Yeah, but we had stuff to do," he said easily, although now he was slowing his steps. "I had to put things away, get the accounts all settled. And then, you know, I had to wrap this."

He pulled his hand out from behind his back, extending a small box to me, tied with a simple bow. "Nate," I said.

"Go ahead," he told me. "It won't make it all better. But it might help a little bit."

I took the box but didn't open it. Instead, I sat down on the bench, holding it between my knees, and a moment later he came and sat down beside me. Now closer, I could see his neck was flushed, the skin pink around his collar. "I know you've been home for a couple of hours," I said quietly. "What was going on over there?"

He slid one leg over the bench, turning to face me. "Nothing. Hey, we've got two hours left of Valentine's Day. So just open your gift, and let's make the most of it."

"I don't want a gift," I said, and my voice sounded harsher than I meant it to. "I want you to tell me what happened to you tonight."

"I got held up dealing with my dad," he replied. "That's all."

"That's all," I repeated.

"What else do you want me to say?"

"Do you understand how worried I've been about you? How I've sat over here all night, looking at your house, wondering if you're okay?"

"I'm fine," he said. "I'm here now. With you, on Valentine's Day, which is the only place I've wanted to be all day. And now that I *am* here, I can think of a million things I'd rather talk about than my dad."

I shook my head, looking out over the water.

"Like," he continued, putting his hands on either side of me, "my gift, for instance. Word on the street is that it's phenomenal."

"It's not," I said flatly. "It's a gift card, and it sucks."

He sat back slightly, studying my face. "Okay," he said slowly. "So maybe we shouldn't talk."

With this, I could feel him moving closer, and then his lips were on my ear, moving down my neck. Normally, this was enough to push everything away, at least temporarily, the sudden and indisputable closeness that made all other distance irrelevant. Tonight, though, was different. "Stop," I said, pulling back and raising my hands between us. "Okay? Just stop."

"What's wrong?"

"What's wrong?" I repeated. "Look, you can't just come here and tell me everything's fine and kiss me and just expect me to go along with it."

"So," he said slowly, "you're saying you don't want me to kiss you."

"I'm saying you can't have it both ways," I told him. "You can't act like you care about someone but not let them care about you."

"I'm not doing that."

"You are, though," I said. He looked away, shaking his head. "Look, when we first met, you practically made a practice of saving my ass. That night at the fence, coming to pick me up at Jackson—"

"That was different."

"Why? Because it was me, not you?" I asked. "What, you think just because you help people and make their lives easier that you're somehow better and don't need help yourself?"

"I don't."

"So it's just fine that your dad yells at you and pushes you around."

"What happens between me and my dad is private," he said. "It's a family thing."

"So was my living alone in that place you called a slum," I told him. "Are you saying you would have left me there if I had told you to? Or in the clearing that day?"

Nate immediately started to say something in response to this, then let out a breath instead.

Finally, I thought. *I'm getting through.*

"I don't understand," he said, "why these two things always have to be connected."

"What two things?" I said.

"Me and my dad, and me and everyone else." He shook his head. "They're not the same thing. Not even close."

It was that word—*always*—that did it, nudging a memory loose in my brain. Me and Heather, that day over the fish. *You never know*, she'd said, when I'd told her one more friend would hardly make a difference. The sad way he looked at her, all those mornings walking to the green, so many rumors, and maybe none of them true. "So that's why you and Heather broke up," I said slowly. "It wasn't that she couldn't take what was happening. It was not being able to help you."

Nate looked down at his hands, not saying anything. Here I'd thought Heather and I were so different. But we, too, had something in common, all along.

"Just tell someone what's going on," I said. "Your mom, or—"

"I can't," he said. "There's no point. Don't you understand that?"

This was the same thing he'd asked me, all those weeks ago, and I'd told him yes. But now, here, we differed. Nate might not have thought that whatever was happening with his dad affected anything else, but I knew, deep in my heart, that this wasn't true. My mother, wherever she was, still lingered with me: in the way I carried myself, the things that scared me, and the way I'd reacted the last time I'd been faced with this question. Which was why this time, my answer had to be no.

But first, I lifted my hand, putting it on his chest, right over where I'd noticed his skin was flushed earlier. He closed his eyes, leaning into my palm, and I could feel him, warm, as I slowly pushed his shirt aside. Again, call it a bad feeling, a hunch, or whatever—but there, on his shoulder, the skin was not just pink but red and discolored, a broad bruise just beginning to rise. "Oh, Jesus," I said, my voice catching. "Nate."

He moved closer, covering my hand with his, squeezing it, and then he was kissing me again, sudden and intense, as if trying to push down these words and everything that had prompted them. It was so hungry and so good that I was almost able to forget all that had led up to it. But not quite.

"No," I said, pulling back. He stayed where he was, his mouth inches from mine, but I shook my head. "I can't."

"Ruby," he said. Even as I heard this, though, breaking my heart, I could see his shirt, still pushed aside, the reason undeniable.

"Only if you let me help you," I said. "You have to let me in."

He pulled back, shaking his head. Over his shoulder, I could see the lights of the pool flickering—otherworldy, alien. "And if I don't?" he said.

I swallowed, hard. "Then no," I told him. "Then go."

For a moment, I thought he wouldn't. That this, finally, more than all the words, would be what changed his mind. But then he was pushing himself to his feet, his shirt sliding back, space now between us, everything reverting to how it had been before. *You don't have to make it so hard,* I wanted to say, but there was a time I hadn't believed this, either. Who was I to tell anyone how to be saved? Only the girl who had tried every way not to be.

"Nate," I called out, but he was already walking away, his head ducked, back toward the trees. I sat there, watching him as he folded into them, disappearing.

A lump rose in my throat as I stood up. The gift he'd brought was still on the bench, and I picked it up, examining the rose-colored paper, the neatly tied bow. So pretty on the surface, it almost didn't matter what was inside.

When I went back in the house, I tried to keep my face

composed, thinking only of getting up to my room, where I could be alone. But just as I started up the stairs, Cora came out of the living room, where her CD was still playing—Janis Joplin now—the chocolate box in her hands. "Hey, do you want—?" she said, then stopped suddenly. "Are you all right?"

I started to say yes, of course, but before I could, my eyes filled with tears. As I turned to the wall and sucked down a breath, trying to steady myself, I felt her come closer. "Hey," she said, smoothing my hair gently off my shoulder. "What's wrong?"

I swallowed, reaching up to wipe my eyes. "Nothing."

"Tell me."

Two words, said so easily. But even as I thought this, I heard myself doing it. "I just don't know," I said, my voice sounding bumpy, not like mine, "how you help someone who doesn't want your help. What do you do when you can't do anything?"

She was quiet for a moment, and in that silence I was bracing myself, knowing the next question would be harder, pulling me deeper. "Oh, Ruby," she said instead, "I know. I know it's hard."

More tears were coming now, my vision blurring. "I—"

"I should have known this CD would remind you of all that," she said. "Of course it would—that was stupid of me. But Mom's not your responsibility anymore, okay? We can't do anything for her. So we have to take care of each other, all right?"

My mother. Of course she would think that was what

I was talking about. What else could there be? What other loss would I ever face comparable to it? None. None at all.

Cora was behind me, still talking. Through my tears, I could hear her saying it was all going to be okay, and I knew she believed this. But I was sure of something, too: it's a lot easier to be lost than found. It's the reason we're always searching, and rarely discovered—so many locks, not enough keys.

Chapter Fifteen

"So as you can see," Harriet said, moving down the kiosk with a wave of her hand, "I work mostly in silver, using gemstones as accents. Occasionally I've done things with gold, but I find it's less inspiring to me."

"Right," the reporter replied, scribbling this down as her photographer, a tall guy with a mustache, repositioned one of the key necklaces on the rack before taking another shot. "And how long have you been in business at this location?"

"Six years." As the woman wrote this down, Harriet, a nervous expression on her face, glanced over at Vitamin Me, where I was standing with Reggie. I flashed her a thumbs-up, and she nodded, then turned back to the reporter.

"She's doing great," Reggie said, continuing work on his pyramid of omega-3 bottles, the centerpiece of his GET FISH, GET FIT display. "I don't know why she was so nervous."

"Because she's Harriet," I told him. "She always nervous."

He sighed, adding another bottle to the stack. "It's the caffeine. If she'd give it up, her whole life would change. I'm convinced of it."

The truth was, Harriet's life *was* changing, though coffee had nothing to do with it. Instead, it was the KeyChains—as she'd taken to calling them since Christmas—which were now outselling everything else we carried, sparking some-what of a local phenomenon. Suddenly we had shoppers coming from several towns over, seeking them out, not to mention multiple phone calls from people in other states, asking if we did mail order (yes) or had a Web site (in the works, up any day). When she wasn't fielding calls or re-quests, Harriet was busy making more keys, adding shapes and sizes and different gems, as well as experimenting with expanding the line to bracelets and rings. The more she made, the more she sold. These days, it seemed like every girl at my school was wearing one, which was kind of weird, to say the least.

This reporter was from the style section of the local pa-per, and Harriet had been getting ready all week, making new pieces and working both of us overtime to make sure the kiosk looked perfect. Now, Reggie and I watched as—at the reporter's prompting—she posed beside it, a KeyChain studded with rhinestones around her neck, smiling for the camera.

"Look at her," I said. "She's a superstar."

"That she is," Reggie replied, adding another bottle to his stack. "But it's not because she's suddenly famous. Harriet's always been special."

He said this so easily, so matter-of-factly, that it kind of broke my heart. "You know," I said to him as he opened an-other box, "you could tell her that. How you feel, I mean."

"Oh, I have," he replied.

"You have? When?"

"Over Christmas." He picked up a bottle of shark-cartilage capsules, examining it, then set it aside. "We went down to Garfield's one night after closing, for drinks. I had a couple of margaritas, and the next thing I knew . . . it was all out."

"And?"

"Total bust," he said, sighing. "She said she's not in a relationship place right now."

"A relationship place?" I repeated.

"That's what she said." He emptied the box, folding it. "The KeyChains are selling so well, she's got to focus on her career, maybe expanding to her own store someday. Eye on the ball, and all that."

"Reggie," I said softly. "That sucks."

"It's okay," he replied. "I've known Harriet a long time. She's not much for attachments."

I looked over at Harriet again. She was laughing, her face flushed, as the photographer took another picture. "She doesn't know what she's missing."

"That's very nice of you to say," Reggie replied, as if I'd complimented his shirt. "But sometimes, we just have to be happy with what people can offer us. Even if it's not what we want, at least it's something. You know?"

I nodded, even though it was exactly what I didn't believe, at least not since Nate and I had argued on Valentine's Day. The space I'd once claimed to want between us was now not just present, but vast. Whatever it was we'd had—something, nothing, anything—it was over.

As a result, so was my involvement in the carpool, which I'd decided to opt out of after a couple of very silent and very awkward rides. In the end, I'd dug out my old bus schedules, set my alarm, and decided to take advantage of the fact that

my calculus teacher, Ms. Gooden, was an early bird who offered hands-on help before first bell. Then I asked Gervais
to pass this information along to Nate, which he did. If Nate
was surprised, he didn't show it. But then again, he wasn't
letting on much these days, to me or anyone.

I still had the gift he'd given me, if only because I couldn't
figure out a way to return it that wasn't totally awkward.
So it sat, wrapped and bow intact, on my dresser, until I
finally stuffed it into a drawer. You would think it would
bother me, not knowing what was inside, but it didn't, really. Maybe I'd just figured out there were some things you
were better off not knowing.

As for Nate himself, from what I could tell, he was always working. Like most seniors in spring semester—i.e.,
those who hadn't transferred from other schools with not-
so-great grades they desperately needed to keep up in order
to have any chance at college acceptance—he had a pretty
light schedule, as well as a lot of leeway for activities. While
most people spent this time lolling on the green between
classes or taking long coffee runs to Jump Java, whenever
I saw Nate, either in the neighborhood or at school, he
seemed to be in constant motion, often loaded down with
boxes, his phone pressed to his ear as he moved to and from
his car. I figured Rest Assured had to be picking up, business-
wise, although his work seemed even more ironic to me
than ever. All that helping, saving, taking care. As if these
were the only two options, when you had that kind of home
life: either caring about yourself and no one else, like I had,
or only about the rest of the world, as he did now.

I'd been thinking about this lately every time I passed

the HELP table, where Heather Wainwright was set up as usual, accepting donations or petition signatures. Ever since Thanksgiving, I'd sort of held it against her that she'd broken up with Nate, thinking she'd abandoned him, but now, for obvious reasons, I was seeing things differently. So much so that more than once, I'd found myself pausing and taking a moment to look over whatever cause she was lobbying for. Usually, she was busy talking to other people and just smiled at me, telling me to let her know if I had any questions. One day, though, as I perused some literature about saving the coastline, it was just the two of us.

"It's a good cause," she said as I flipped past some pages illustrating various stages of sand erosion. "We can't just take our beaches for granted."

"Right," I said. "I guess not."

She sat back, twirling a pen in her hand. Finally, after a moment, she said, "So . . . how's Nate doing?"

I shut the brochure. "I wouldn't really know," I said. "We're kind of on the outs these days."

"Oh," she said. "Sorry."

"No, it's okay," I said. "It's just . . . it got hard. You know?"

I wasn't expecting her to respond to this, really. But then she put her pen down. "His dad," she said, clarifying. I nodded, and she smiled sadly, shaking her head. "Well, I hate to tell you, but if you think keeping your distance makes it easier not to worry . . . it doesn't. Not really."

"Yeah," I said, looking down at the brochure again. "I'm kind of getting that."

"For me, the worst was just watching him change, you know?" She sighed, brushing her hair back from her face.

"Like with quitting swim team. That was his entire world. But in the end, he gave it up, because of this."

"He gave you up, too," I said. "Right?"

"Yeah." She sighed. "I guess so."

Across the green, there was a sudden burst of laughter, and we both looked in its direction. As it ended, she said, "Look, for what it's worth, I think I could have tried harder. To stick by him, or force the issue. I kind of wish I had."

"You do?"

"I think he would have done it for me," she said. "And that's been the hardest part of all of this, really. That maybe I failed him, or myself, somehow. You know?"

I nodded. "Yeah," I said. "I do."

"So," a dark-haired girl with a ponytail said to Heather, sliding into the empty seat beside her. "I just spent, like, a half hour working on Mr. Thackray, and he's finally agreed to let us plug our fund-raiser again this afternoon during announcements. I'm thinking we should write some new copy, though, to really make an impact, like . . ."

I started to move down the table, our conversation clearly over. "Take care, Ruby," Heather called after me.

"You, too," I told her. As she turned back to the girl, who was still talking, I reached into my pocket, pulling out the few dollars' change from my lunch and stuffing it into the SAVE OUR BEACHES! jar. It wasn't much, in the grand scheme of things. But it made me feel somewhat better, nonetheless.

Also slightly encouraging was the fact that while I hadn't been of help to Nate, I didn't have to look far to find someone who *had* benefited from my actions. Not now that Gervais was front and center, at my picnic table, every weekday from 12:05 to 1:15.

"Again," he said to me, pointing at the book with his pencil, "remember the power rule. It's the key to everything you're trying to do here."

I sighed, trying to clear my head. The truth was, Gervais was a good tutor. Already, I understood tons more than I had before he'd begun working with me, stuff even my early-morning help sessions couldn't make sense of. But there were still distractions. Initially, it had been me worrying about how he'd interact with Olivia, whether he'd act so goopy or lovesick she'd immediately suspect something, and rightfully blame me. As it turned out, though, this wasn't an issue at all. If anything, I was a third wheel now.

"The power rule," Olivia recited, flipping her phone open. "The derivative of any given variable (x) to the exponent (n) is equal to product of the exponent and the variable to the (n–1) power."

I just looked at her. "Exactly right," Gervais said, beaming. "See? Olivia gets it."

Of course she did. Olivia was apparently a whiz at calculus, something she had neglected to mention the entire time we'd been sharing our lunch hour. Now that Gervais had joined us, though, they were in math heaven. That is, when they weren't talking about one of the other myriad, inexplicable things they had in common, including but not limited to a love of movies, the pros and cons of various college majors, and, of course, picking on me.

"What exactly is going on with you two?" I'd asked her

recently after one of Gervais's visits, which I had spent alternately struggling with the power rule and sitting by, open-mouthed, as they riffed on the minute details of a recent sci-fi blockbuster, down to the extra scenes after the credits.

"What do you mean?" she asked. We were crossing the green. "He's a nice kid."

"Look, I have to be honest," I told her. "He likes you."

"I know."

She said this so simply, so matter-of-factly, that I almost stopped walking. "You know?"

"Sure. I mean, it's kind of obvious, right?" she said. "He was always hanging around the theater when I was working. Not exactly slick."

"He wants to be friends with you," I told her. "He asked me to help him do it."

"Did you?"

"No," I said. "But I did tell him he could help me with my calculus at lunch. And that you might, you know, be there."

I kind of spit this last part out, as I was already bracing myself for her reaction. To my surprise, though, she seemed hardly bothered. "Like I said," she said with a shrug, "he's a nice kid. And it's got to be tough for him here, you know?"

Ah, I thought, remembering back to what she'd said to me about having things in common. Who knew Gervais would count, too? "Yeah," I said. "I guess you're right."

"Plus," she continued, "he knows nothing is going to happen between us."

"Are you *sure* he knows that?"

Now she stopped walking, narrowing her eyes at me. "What?" she said. "Do you think I'm not capable of being clear?"

I shook my head. "No. You are."

"That's right." She started walking again. "We both know the limits of this relationship. It's understood. And as long as we're both comfortable with that, nobody gets hurt. It's basic."

Basic, I thought. *Just like the power rule.*

Calculus aside, I had surprised myself by not only keeping up my end of the deal I'd made with Jamie but actually feeling slightly confident as I sent off my applications back at the end of January. Because of ongoing worries about my GPA, I'd done all I could to strengthen the rest of my material, from my essays to my recommendations. In the end, I'd applied to three schools: the U, Cora's alma mater and one town over; a smaller, more artsy college in the mountains called Slater-Kearns; and one long shot, Defriese University, in D.C. According to Mrs. Pureza, my guidance counselor, all three were known to take a second look at "unique" students like myself. Which meant I might actually have a chance, a thought that at times scared the hell out of me. I'd been looking ahead to the future for so long, practically my entire life. Now that it was close, though, I found myself hesitant, not so sure I was ready.

There was still a lot of the year to go, though, which I reminded myself was a good thing whenever I surveyed what I had done so far on my English project. One day, in a burst of organization I'd hoped would lead to inspiration, I'd spread out everything I had on the desk in my room: stacks of notes, Post-its with quotes stuck up on the wall above, the books I'd used as research—pages marked—piled on either side. Lately, after dinner or when I wasn't working, I'd sit down and go through it bit by bit waiting for that spark.

So far, no luck. In fact, the only thing that ever made me feel somewhat close was the picture of Jamie's family, which I'd taken from the kitchen and tacked up on the wall, right at eye level. I'd spent hours, it felt like, sitting there looking over each individual face, as if one of them might suddenly have what I was searching for. *What is family?* For me, right then, it was one person who'd left me, and two I would have to leave soon. Maybe this was an answer. But it wasn't the right one. Of that, I was sure.

Now, I heard Harriet call my name, jerking me back to the mall, and the present. When I looked up, she was waving me over to the kiosk, where she was standing with the reporter.

"This is my assistant, Ruby Cooper," she said to the reporter as I walked up. "She had on that necklace the day I hired her, and it was my inspiration."

As both the photographer and the reporter immediately turned their attention to my key, I fought not to reach up and cover it, digging my hands into my pockets instead. "Interesting," the reporter said, making a note on her pad. "And what was *your* inspiration, Ruby? What compelled you to start wearing your key like that?"

Talk about being put on the spot. "I . . . I don't know," I said. "I guess I just got tired of always losing it."

The reporter wrote this down, then glanced at the photographer, who was still snapping some shots of the necklaces. "I think that ought to do it," she said to Harriet. "Thanks for your time."

"Thank you," Harriet said. When they'd walked away, she whirled around to face me. "Oh my God. I was a nervous wreck. You think I did all right?"

"You were great," I told her.

"Better than," Reggie added. "Cool as a cuke."

Harriet sat down on her stool, wiping a hand over her face. "They said it will probably run on Sunday, which would be huge. Can you imagine if this gives us an even bigger boost? I can barely keep up with orders as it is."

This was typical Harriet. Even the good stuff meant worrying. "You'll do fine," Reggie said. "You have good help."

"Oh, I know," Harriet said, smiling at me. "It's just . . . a little overwhelming, is all. But I guess I can get Rest Assured to do more, too. Blake's been pushing me to do that anyway. You know, shipping, handling some of the Web site stuff, all that. . . ."

"Just try to enjoy this right now," Reggie told her. "It's a good thing."

I could understand where Harriet was coming from, though. Whenever something great happens, you're always kind of poised for the universe to correct itself. Good begets bad, something lost leads to found, and on and on. But even knowing this, I was surprised when I came home later that afternoon to find Cora and Jamie sitting at the kitchen table, the phone between them. As they both turned to look at me, right away I knew something was wrong.

"Ruby," Cora said. Her voice was soft. Sad. "It's about Mom."

* * *

My mother was not in Florida. She was not on a boat with Warner or soaking up sun or waiting tables in a beachside pancake joint. She was in a rehab clinic, where she'd ended up two weeks earlier after being found unconscious by a maid in the hotel where she'd been living in Tennessee.

At first, I was sure she was dead. So sure, in fact, that as Cora began to explain all this, I felt like my own heart stopped, only beating again once these few words—*hotel, unconscious, rehab, Tennessee*—unscrambled themselves in my mind. When she was done, the only thing I could say was, "She's okay?"

Cora glanced at Jamie, then back at me. "She's in treatment," she said. "She has a long way to go. But yes, she's okay."

It should have made me feel better now that I knew where she was, that she was safe. At the same time, the thought of her in a hospital, locked up, gave me a weird, shaky feeling in my stomach, and I made myself take in a breath. "Was she alone?" I asked.

"What?" Cora said.

"When they found her. Was she alone?"

She nodded. "Was . . . Should someone have been with her?"

Yes, I thought. *Me*. I felt a lump rise up in my throat, sudden and throbbing. "No," I said. "I mean, she had a boyfriend when she left."

She and Jamie exchanged another look, and I had a flash of the last time I'd come back to find them waiting for me in this same place. Then, I'd caught a glimpse of myself in the mirror and seen my mother, or at least some part of her—bedraggled, half-drunk, messed up. But at least someone had been expecting me. No one was picking up my mom from the side of the road, getting her home safe. It was probably only coincidence—a maid's schedule, one room, one day—that got her found in time.

And now she was found, no longer lost. Like a bag I'd given up for good suddenly reappearing in the middle of the night on my doorstep, packed for a journey I'd long ago forgotten. It was odd, considering I'd gotten accustomed to her being nowhere and anywhere, to finally know where my mother was. An exact location, pinpointed. Like she'd crossed over from my imagination, where I'd created a million lives for her, back into this one.

"So what . . ." I said, then swallowed. "What happens now?"

"Well," Cora replied, "the initial treatment program is ninety days. After that, she has some decisions to make. Ideally, she'd stay on, in some kind of supported environment. But it's really up to her."

"Did you talk to her?" I asked.

She shook her head. "No."

"Then how did you hear?"

"From her last landlords. The hospital couldn't find anyone to contact, so they ran a records search, their name came up, and they called us." She turned to Jamie. "What was their name? Huntington?"

"Honeycutt," I said. Already they'd popped into my head, Alice with her elfin looks, Ronnie in his sensible plaid. *Stranger danger!* she'd said that first day, but how weird that they were now the ones that led me back not only to Cora but to my mother, as well.

I felt my face get hot; suddenly, it was all too much. I looked around me, trying to calm down, but all I could see was this clean, lovely foyer, in this perfect neighborhood, all the things that had risen up in my mother's absence, settling into the space made when she left.

"Ruby," Jamie said. "It's all right, okay? Nothing's going to change. In fact, Cora wasn't even sure we should tell you, but—"

I looked at my sister, still seated, the phone in her hands. "But we did," she said, keeping her eyes steady on me. "That said, you have no obligation to her. You need to know that. What happens next with you and Mom, or even if anything does, is up to you."

As it turned out, though, this wasn't exactly true. We soon found out that the rehab place where my mother was staying—and which Cora and Jamie were paying for, although I didn't learn that until later—had a strong policy of patient-focused treatment. Simply put, this meant no outside contact with family or friends, at least not initially. No phone calls. No e-mails. If we sent letters, they'd be kept until a date to be decided later. "It's for the best," Cora told me, after explaining this. "If she's going to do this, she needs to do it on her own."

At that point, we didn't even know if my mom would stay in the program at all, as she hadn't exactly gone willingly. Once they resuscitated her at the hospital, the police found some outstanding bad-check warrants, so she'd had to choose: rehab or jail. I would have had more faith if she'd gone of her own accord. But at least she was there.

Nothing's going to change, Jamie had said that day, but I'd known even then this wasn't true. My mother had always been the point that I calibrated myself against. In knowing where she was, I could always locate myself, as well. These months she'd been gone, I felt like I'd been floating, loose and boundaryless, but now that I knew where she was, I kept waiting for a kind of certainty to kick in. It didn't. Instead, I was more unsure than ever, stuck between this new life and the one I'd left behind.

The fact that this had all happened so soon after Nate and I had fallen out of touch seemed ironic, to say the least. At the same time, though, I was beginning to wonder if this was just how it was supposed to be for me, like perhaps I wasn't capable of having that many people in my life at any one time. My mom turned up, Nate walked away, one door opening as another clicked shut.

As the days passed, I tried to forget about my mom, the way I'd managed to do before, but it was harder now. This was partly because she wasn't lost anymore, but there was also the fact that everywhere I went—school, work, just walking down the street—I saw people wearing Harriet's KeyChains, each one sparkling and pretty, a visible reminder of this, my new life. But the original was there as well—more jaded and rudimentary, functional rather than romantic. It fit not just the yellow house but another door, deep within my own heart. One that had been locked so tight for so long that I was afraid to even try it for fear of what might be on the other side.

Chapter Sixteen

"So basically," Olivia said, "you dig a hole and fill it with water, then throw in some fish."

"No," I said. "First, you have to install a pump system and a skimmer. And bring in rocks and plants, and do something to guard it against birds, who want to eat the fish. And that's not even counting all the water treatments and algae prevention."

She considered this as she leaned forward, peering down into the pond. "Well," she said, "to me, that seems like a lot of trouble. Especially for something you can't even swim in."

Olivia and I were taking a study break from working on our English projects, ostensibly so I could introduce to her to Jamie, who'd been out puttering around the pond, the way he always did on Saturday mornings. When we'd come out, though, he'd been called over to the fence by Mr. Cross, and now, fifteen minutes later, they were still deep in discussion. Judging by the way Jamie kept inching closer to us, bit by bit—as well as the fact that Nate's dad seemed to be doing all the talking—I had a feeling he was trying to extricate himself, although he'd had little luck thus far.

"Then again," Olivia said, sitting back down on the bench, "with a spread like this, you could have a pond *and* a pool, if you wanted."

"True," I agreed. "But it might be overkill."

"Not in this neighborhood," she said. "I mean, honestly. Did you see those boulders when you come in? What is this supposed to be, Stonehenge?"

I smiled. Over by the fence, Jamie took another step backward, nodding in that all-right-then-see-you-later kind of way. Mr. Cross, not getting the hint—or maybe just choosing not to—came closer, bridging the gap again.

"You know, he looks familiar," Olivia said, nodding toward them.

"That's Nate's dad," I told her.

"No, I meant your brother-in-law. I swear, I've seen him somewhere."

"He donated some soccer fields to Perkins," I told her.

"Maybe that's it," she said. Still, she kept her eyes on them as she said, "So Nate lives right there, huh?"

"I told you we were neighbors."

"Yeah, but I didn't realize he was right behind you, only a few feet away. Must make this stalemate—or breakup— you two are in the midst of that much harder."

"It's not a stalemate," I told her. "Or a breakup."

"So you just went from basically hanging out constantly, pretty much on the verge of dating, to not speaking and totally ignoring each other for no reason," she said. "Yeah. *That* makes sense."

"Do we have to talk about this?" I asked as Jamie took another definitive step backward from Mr. Cross, lifting his hand. Mr. Cross was still talking, although this time he stayed where he was.

"You know," Olivia said, "it's pretty rare to find someone

you actually *like* to be with in this world. There are a lot of annoying people out there."

"Really?"

She made a face at me. "My point is, clearly you two had something. So maybe you should think about going to a little trouble to work this out, whatever it is."

"Look," I said, "you said yourself that relationships only work when there's an understanding about the limits. We didn't have that. So now we don't have a relationship."

She considered this for a moment. "Nice," she said. "I especially like how you explained that without actually telling me anything."

"The bottom line is that I just get where you're coming from now, okay?" I said. "You don't want to waste your time on anything or anyone you don't believe in, and neither do I."

"You think that's how I am?" she asked.

"Are you saying it's not?"

Jamie was crossing the yard to us, finally free. He lifted a hand, waving hello. "I'm not saying anything," Olivia replied, leaning back again and shaking her head. "Nothing at all."

"Ladies," Jamie said, ever the happy host as he came up to the bench. "Enjoying the pond?"

"It's very nice," Olivia said politely. "I like the skimmer."

I just looked at her, but Jamie, of course, beamed. "Jamie, this is my friend Olivia," I said.

"Nice to meet you," he said, sticking out his hand.

They shook, and then he crouched down at the edge of the pond, reaching his hand down into the water. As he scooped some up, letting it run over his fingers, Olivia suddenly gasped. "Oh my God. I know where I know you from!" she said. "You're the UMe guy!"

Jamie looked at her, then at me. "Um," he said. "Yeah. I guess I am."

"You recognize him from UMe?" I asked.

"Hello, he's only on the new sign-in page, which I see, like, ten million times a day," she said. She shook her head, clearly still in shock. "Man, I can't believe this. And Ruby never even said anything."

"Well, you know," Jamie said, pushing himself back to his feet, "Ruby is not easily impressed."

Unlike Olivia, who now, as I watched, incredulous, began to actually gush. "Your site," she said to Jamie, putting a hand to her chest, "saved my *life* when I had to switch schools."

"Yeah?" Jamie said, obviously pleased.

"Totally. I spent every lunch in the library on my UMe page messaging with my old friends. And, of course, all night, too." She sighed, wistful. "It was, like, my only connection with them."

"You still had your phone," I pointed out.

"I can check my page on that, too!" To Jamie she said, "Nice application, by the way. Very user friendly."

"You think? We've had some complaints."

"Oh, please." Olivia flipped her hand. "It's easy. Now, the friends system? *That* needs work. I hate it."

"You do?" Jamie said. "Why?"

"Well," she said, "for starters, there's no way to search through them easily. So if you have a lot, and you want to reorganize, you have to just keep scrolling, which takes forever."

I thought of my own UMe.com page, untouched all these months. "How many friends do you have, anyway?" I asked her.

"A couple of thousand," she replied. I just looked at her. "What? Online, I'm popular."

"Obviously," I said.

Later, when Olivia had gone—taking with her a promotional UMe.Com messenger bag packed with UMe.com stickers and T-shirts—I found Jamie in the kitchen, marinating some chicken for dinner. As I came in, the phone began to ring: I went to grab it, but after glancing at the caller ID, he shook his head. "Just let the voice mail get it."

I looked at the display screen, which said CROSS, BLAKE. "You're screening Mr. Cross?"

"Yeah," he said with a sigh, dribbling some olive oil over the chicken and shaking the pan slightly. "I don't want to. But he's being really persistent about this investment thing, so . . ."

"What investment thing?"

He glanced up at me, as if not sure whether or not he wanted to expound on this. Then he said, "Well, you know. Blake's kind of a wheeler-dealer. He's always got some grand plan in the works."

I thought of Mr. Cross that morning, practically stalking Jamie in the yard. "And he wants to do a deal with you?"

"Sort of," he said, going over to the cabinet above the stove and opening it, then rummaging through the contents.

After a minute, he pulled out a tall bottle of vinegar. "He says he wants to expand his business and is looking for silent partners, but really I think he's just short on cash, like last time."

I watched him add a splash of vinegar, then bend down and sniff the chicken before adding more. "So this has happened before."

He nodded, capping the bottle. "Last year, a few months after we moved in. We had him over, you know, for a neighborly drink, and we got to talking. Next thing I know, I'm getting the whole epic saga about his hard financial luck—none of which was his fault, of course—and how he was about to turn it all around with this new venture. Which turned out to be the errand-running thing."

Roscoe came out of the laundry room, where he'd been enjoying one of his many daily naps. Seeing us, he yawned, then headed for the dog door, vaulting himself through it, and it shut with a *thwack* behind him.

"Did you see that?" Jamie said, smiling. "Change is possible!"

I nodded. "It is impressive."

We both watched Roscoe go out into the yard and lift his leg against a tree, relieving himself. Never had a simple act resulted in such pride. "Anyway," Jamie said, "in the end I gave him a check, bought in a bit to the business. It wasn't that much, really, but when your sister found out, she hit the roof."

"Cora did?"

"Oh, yeah," he said. "She's been off him from the start, for some reason. She claims it's because he always talks about money, but my uncle Ronald does that, too, and him she loves. So go figure."

I didn't have to, though. In fact, I was pretty sure I knew exactly why Cora didn't like Mr. Cross, even if she herself couldn't put her finger on it.

"Anyway," Jamie said, "now Blake's scrambling again, I guess. He's been hounding me about this new billing idea and the money ever since Thanksgiving, when I asked him about borrowing his oven. I keep putting him off, but man, he's tenacious. I guess he figures since I'm a sucker, he can pull me in again."

I had a flash of Olivia on the curb, using this same word. "You're not a sucker. You're just nice. You give people the benefit of the doubt."

"Usually to my detriment," he said as the phone rang again. We both looked at it: CROSS, BLAKE. The message light was already beeping. "However," he continued, "other times, people even surpass my expectations. Like you, for instance."

"Does this mean you're going to give me a check?" I asked.

"No," he said flatly. I smiled. "But I am proud of you, Ruby. You've come a long way."

Later, up in my room, I kept thinking about this, the idea of distance and accomplishment. The further you go, the more you have to be proud of. At the same time, in order to come a long way, you have to be behind to begin with. In the end, though, maybe it's not how you reach a place that matters. Just that you get there at all.

*   *   *

Middle-school girls, I had learned, moved in packs. If you saw them coming, the best thing to do was step aside and save yourself.

"Look, you guys! These are the ones I was telling you about!" a brown-haired girl wearing all pink, clearly the leader of this particular group, said as they swarmed the kiosk, going straight for the KeyChains. "Oh my God. My brother's girlfriend has this one, with the pink stones. Isn't it great?"

"I like the diamond one," a chubby blonde in what looked like leather pants said. "It's the prettiest."

"That's not a diamond," the girl in pink told her as their two friends—twins, by the look of their matching red hair and similar features—moved down to the bracelets. "Otherwise, it would be, like, a million dollars."

"It's diamonelle," Harriet corrected her, "and very reasonably priced at twenty-five."

"Personally," the brunette said, draping the pink-stoned one across her V-necked sweater, "I like the plain silver. It's classic, befitting my new, more streamlined, eco-chic look."

"Eco-chic?" I said.

"Environmentally friendly," the girl explained. "Green? You know, natural metals, non-conflict stones, minimal but with big impact? All the celebrities are doing it. Don't you read *Vogue*?"

"No," I told her.

She shrugged, taking off the necklace, then moved down the kiosk to her friends, who were now gathered around the rings, quickly dismantling the display I'd just spent a good twenty minutes organizing. "You would think," I said to Harriet as we watched them take rings on and off, "that they could at least try to put them back. Or pretend to."

"Oh, let them make a mess," she said. "It's not that big a deal cleaning it up."

"Says the person who doesn't have to do it."

She raised her eyebrows at me, walking over to take her coffee off the register. "Okay," she said slowly. "You're in a bad mood. What gives?"

"I'm sorry," I said as the girls finally moved on, leaving rings scattered across the counter behind them. I went over and began to put them away. "I think I'm just stressed or something."

"Well, it kind of makes sense," Harriet said, coming over to join me. She put an onyx ring back in place, a red one beside it. "You're in your final semester, waiting to hear about college, the future is wide open. But that doesn't necessarily have to get you all bent out of shape. You could look at it as, you know, a great opportunity to embrace stepping out of your comfort zone."

I stopped what I was doing, narrowing my eyes at her as she filled out another row of rings, calm as you please. "Excuse me?" I said.

"What?"

I just looked at her, waiting for her to catch the irony. She didn't. "Harriet," I said finally, "how long did you have that HELP WANTED sign up before you hired me?"

"Ah," she said, pointing at me, "but I *did* hire you, right?"

"And how long did it take you to leave me alone here, to run the kiosk myself?"

"Okay, so I was hesitant," she admitted. "However, I

think you'll agree that I now leave you fairly often with little trepidation."

I considered pointing out that the *fairly* and *little* spoke volumes. Instead I said, "What about Reggie?"

She wiped her hands on her pants, then moved down to the KeyChains, adjusting the pink one on the rack. "What about him?"

"He told me what happened at Christmas," I said. "What was it you said? That you weren't in a 'relationship place'? Is that anywhere near your comfort zone?"

"Reggie is my friend," she said, straightening a clasp. "If we took things further and it didn't work out, it would change everything."

"But you don't know it won't work out."

"I don't know it *will*, either."

"And that's reason enough to not even try," I said. She ignored me, moving down to the rings. "You didn't know that hiring me would work out. But you did it anyway. And if you hadn't—"

"—I'd be enjoying a quiet moment at my kiosk right now, without being analyzed," she said. "Wouldn't that be nice!"

"—you never would have made the KeyChains and seen them be so successful," I finished. "Or been able to enjoy my company, and this conversation, right now."

She made a face at me, then walked back over and hopped up on her stool, opening up the laptop she'd recently bought to keep up with her Web site stuff. "Look. I know in a perfect, utterly romantic world, I'd go out with

Reggie and we'd live happily ever after," she said, hitting the power button. "But sometimes you just have to follow your instincts, and mine say this would not be a good thing for me. All right?"

I nodded. Really, considering everything I'd just gone through, Harriet was someone I should be trying to emulate, not convince otherwise.

I moved back to the rings, reorganizing them the way I had originally, in order of size and color. I was just doing another quick pass with the duster when I heard Harriet say, "Huh. This is weird."

"What is?"

"I'm just checking into my account, and my balance is kind of off," she said. "I know I had a couple of debits out, but not for this much."

"Maybe the site's just delayed," I said.

"I knew I shouldn't have signed on for this new system with Blake. I just feel better when I sign every check myself, you know?" She sighed, then picked up her phone and dialed. After a moment, she closed it. "Voice mail. Of course. Do you know Nate's number, offhand?"

I shook my head. "No. I don't."

"Well, when you see him, tell him I need to talk to him. Like, soon. Okay?"

I wanted to tell her I wouldn't be seeing him, much less delivering messages. But she was already back on the computer, scrolling down.

Harriet wasn't the only one not resting assured, or so I found out when I got home and found Cora in the foyer, wiping up the floor with a paper towel. Roscoe, who usually could not be prevented from greeting me with a full body attack, was conspicuously absent.

"No way," I said, dropping my bag on the floor. "He's mastered the dog door."

"We lock it when we're not here," she told me, pushing herself to her feet. "Which is usually no problem, but someone didn't bother to show up to walk him today."

"Really?" I said. "Are you sure? Nate's usually really dependable."

"Well, not today," she replied. "Clearly."

It was weird. So much so that I wondered if maybe Nate had taken off or something, as that seemed to be the only explanation for him just blowing off things he usually did like clockwork. That night, though, his lights were on, just like always, as were the ones in the pool. It was only when I really looked closely, around midnight, that I saw something out of the ordinary: a figure cutting through the water. Moving back and forth, with steady strokes, dark against all that blue light. I watched him for a long time, but even when I finally turned out the light, he was still swimming.

Chapter Seventeen

That weekend, there was only one thing I should have been thinking about: calculus. The test that pretty much would decide the entire fate of both my GPA and my future was on Monday, and according to Gervais—whose method was proven—it was time to shift into what he called "Zen mode."

"I'm sorry?" I'd said the day before, Friday, when he'd announced this.

"It's part of my technique," he explained, taking a sip of his chocolate milk, one of two he drank each lunch period. "First, we did an overview of everything you were supposed to learn so far this year. Then, we homed in on your weaknesses therein, pinpointing and attacking them one by one. Now, we move into Zen mode."

"Meaning what?" I asked.

"Admitting that you are powerless over your fate, on this test and otherwise. You have to throw out everything that you've learned."

I just looked at him. Olivia, who was checking her UMe page on her phone, said, "Actually, that is a very basic part of Eastern cinema tradition. The warrior, once taught, must now, in the face of his greatest challenge, rely wholly on instinct."

"Why have I spent weeks studying if I'm now supposed to forget everything I've learned?" I said. "That's the stupidest thing I've ever heard."

Olivia shrugged. "The man says his method is proven."

Man? I thought.

Gervais said, "The idea isn't to forget everything. It's that by now, you should know all this well enough that you don't *have* to actively think about it. You see a problem, you know the solution. It's instinct."

I looked down at the practice sheet he'd given me, problems lined up across it. As usual, with just one glance I felt my heart sink, my brain going fuzzy around the edges. If this was my instinct talking, I didn't want to hear what it was saying.

"Zen mode," Gervais said. "Clear your head, accept the uncertainty, and the solutions appear. Just trust me."

I was not convinced, and even less so when he presented me with his instructions for my last weekend of studying. (Which, incidentally, were bullet-pointed and divided into headings and subheadings. The kid was nothing if not professional.) Saturday morning, I was supposed to do a final overview, followed in the afternoon by a short series of problems he'd selected that covered the formulas I had most trouble with. Sunday, the last full day before the test, I wasn't supposed to study at all. Which seemed, frankly, insane. Then again, if the goal was to forget everything by Monday morning, this did seem like the way to do it.

Early the next morning, I sat down on my bed and started my overview, trying to focus. More and more, though, I found myself distracted, thinking about Nate, as I had been pretty much nonstop—occasional calculus obsessions aside—since I'd seen him swimming a couple of nights earlier. In the end, both Harriet and Cora had heard from Mr. Cross, who was wildly apologetic, crediting Harriet's account and offering Cora a free week's worth of walks to compensate. But in the days since, whenever I'd seen Nate across the green or in the halls at school, I couldn't help but notice a change in him. Like even with the distance between us, something about him—in his face or the way he carried himself—was suddenly familiar in a way I hadn't felt before, although how, exactly, I couldn't say.

After two hours of studying, I felt so overwhelmed that I decided to take a break and quickly run over to get my paycheck from Harriet. As soon as I stepped off the greenway, I saw people everywhere—lined up on the curb that ran alongside the mall, gathered in the parking lot, crowded at the base of a stage set up by the movie theater.

"Welcome to the Vista Five-K!" a voice boomed from the stage as I worked my way toward the main entrance, stepping around kids and dogs and more runners stretching and chatting and jogging in place. "If you're participating in the race, please make your way to the start line. Ten minutes to start!"

The crowd shifted as people headed toward the banner— VISTA 5K: RUN FOR YOUR LIFE!—strung between the parking lot and the mall entrance. Following them, I kept an eye out for Olivia but didn't see her—just runners of all shapes and sizes, some in high-tech lycra bodysuits, others in gym shorts and ratty T-shirts.

Inside the mall, it was much quieter, with few shoppers

moving between stores. I could still hear the announcer's voice from outside, along with the booming bass of the music they were playing, even as I walked from the entrance down to the kiosk courtyard, where I found Harriet and Reggie standing at Vitamin Me.

"I'm not doing the fish oil," she was saying as I walked up. "I'm firm on that."

"Omega-threes are crucial!" Reggie told her. "It's like a wonder drug."

"I didn't agree to wonder drugs. I agreed to take a few things, on a trial basis. Nobody said anything about fish."

"Fine." Reggie picked up a bottle, shaking some capsules into a plastic bag. "But you're taking the zinc and the B-twelve. Those are deal breakers."

Harriet shook her head, taking another sip of coffee. Then she saw me. "I thought you might turn up," she said. "Forget vitamins. Money is crucial."

Reggie sighed. "That kind of attitude," he said, "is *precisely* why you need more omega-threes."

Harriet ignored this as she walked over to her register, popping it open and taking out my check. "Here," she said, handing it over to me. "Oh, and there's a little something extra in there for you, as well."

Sure enough, the amount was about three hundred bucks more than I was expecting. "Harriet," I said. "What is this?"

"Profit-sharing," she said, then added, "And a thank-you for all the work you've put in over the last months."

"You didn't have to do this," I said.

"I know. But I got to thinking the other day, after we

had that talk. You were right. The KeyChains, all that. I couldn't have done it without you. Literally."

"That's not why I said that," I told her.

"I know. But it made me think. About a lot of things."

She looked over at Reggie, who was still adding things to her bag. Now that I thought of it, she had been awfully receptive to that zinc. And what was that about a few things, on a trial basis? "Wait," I said, wagging my finger between his kiosk and ours. "What's going on here?"

"Absolutely nothing," she replied, shutting the register.

I raised my eyebrows.

"Fine. If you must know, we just had drinks last night after work, and he convinced me to try a few samples."

"Really."

"Okay, maybe there was a dinner invitation, too," she added.

"Harriet!" I said. "You changed your mind."

She sighed. Over at Vitamin Me, Reggie was folding the top of her bag over neatly, working the crease with his fingers. "I didn't mean to," she said. "Initially, I just went to tell him the same thing I said to you. That I was worried about it not working out, and what that would do to our friendship."

"And?"

"And," she said, sighing, "he said he totally understood, we had another drink, and I said yes to dinner anyway."

"What about the vitamins?"

"I don't know." She flipped her hand at me. "These things happen."

"Yeah," I said, looking over at Reggie again. He'd been

so patient, and eventually he, too, got what he wanted. Or at least a chance at it. "Don't I know it."

By the time I went to the bank, ran a couple of errands, and then doubled back around to the greenway, the Vista 5K was pretty much over. A few runners were still milling around, sipping paper cups of Gatorade, but the assembled crowd had thinned considerably, which was why I immediately spotted Olivia. She was leaning forward on the curb, looking down the mall at the few runners left that were slowly approaching the finish line.

"No Laney yet?" I asked.

She shook her head, not even turning to look at me. "I figure she's dropped out, but she has her phone. She should have called me."

"Thanks to everyone who came out for the Vista Five-K!" a man with a microphone bellowed from the grandstand. "Join us next year, when we'll run for our lives again!"

"She's probably collapsed somewhere," Olivia said. "God, I *knew* this was going to happen. I'll see you, okay?"

She was about halfway across the street when I looked down the mall again and saw something. Just a tiny figure at first, way off in the distance.

"Olivia," I called out, pointing. "Look."

She turned, her eyes following my finger. It was still hard to be sure, so for a moment we just stood there, watching together, as Laney came into sight. She was going so slowly, before finally coming to a complete stop, bending over with her hands on her knees. "Oh, man," Olivia said finally. "It's her."

I turned around, looking at the man on the stage, who

had put down his microphone and was talking to some woman with a clipboard. Nearby, another woman in a Vista 5K T-shirt was climbing a stepladder to the clock, reaching up behind it.

"Wait," I called out to her. "Someone's still coming."

The woman looked down at me, then squinted into the distance. "Sorry," she said. "The race is over."

Olivia, ignoring this, stepped forward, raising her hands to her mouth. "Laney!" she yelled. "You're almost done. Don't quit now!"

Her voice was raw, strained. I thought of that first day I'd found her here with her stopwatch, and all the complaining about the race since. Olivia was a lot of things. But I should have known a sucker wasn't one of them.

"Come on!" she yelled. She started clapping her hands, hard, the sound sharp and single in the quiet. "Let's go, Laney!" she yelled, her voice rising up over all of us. *"Come on!"*

Everyone was staring as she jumped up and down in the middle of the road, her claps echoing off the building behind us. Watching her, I thought of Harriet, doubtfully eyeing those vitamins as Reggie dropped them into the bag, one by one, and then of me with Nate on the bench by the pond the last time we'd been together. *And if I don't?* he'd asked, and I'd thought there could be only one answer, in that one moment. But now, I was beginning to wonder if you didn't always have to choose between turning away for good or rushing in deeper. In the moments that it really counts, maybe it's enough—more than enough, even—just to be there. Laney must have thought so. Because right then, she started running again.

When she finally finished a few minutes later, it was hard to tell if she was even aware that the crowds had thinned, the clock was off, and the announcer didn't even call her time. But I do know that it was Olivia she turned to look for first, Olivia she threw her arms around and hugged tight, as that banner flapped overhead. Watching them, I thought again of how we can't expect everybody to be there for us, all at once. So it's a lucky thing that really, all you need is someone.

*　　*　　*

Back home, I sat down with my calculus notes, determined to study, but within moments my mind wandered past the numbers and figures and across the room to the picture of Jamie's family, still up on the wall over my desk. It was the weirdest thing—I'd studied it a thousand times, in this same place, the same way. But suddenly, all at once, it just made sense.

What is family? They were the people who claimed you. In good, in bad, in parts or in whole, they were the ones who showed up, who stayed in there, regardless. It wasn't just about blood relations or shared chromosomes, but something wider, bigger. Cora was right—we had many families over time. Our family of origin, the family we created, as well as the groups you moved through while all of this was happening: friends, lovers, sometimes even strangers. None of them were perfect, and we couldn't expect them to be. You couldn't make any one person your world. The trick was to take what each could give you and build a world from it.

So my true family was not just my mom, lost or found;

my dad, gone from the start; and Cora, the only one who had really been there all along. It was Jamie, who took me in without question and gave me a future I once couldn't even imagine; Olivia, who did question, but also gave me answers; Harriet, who, like me, believed she needed no one and discovered otherwise. And then there was Nate.

Nate, who was a friend to me before I even knew what a friend was. Who picked me up, literally, over and over again, and never asked for anything in return except for my word and my understanding. I'd given him one but not the other, because at the time I thought I couldn't, and then proved myself right by doing exactly as my mother had, hurting to prevent from being hurt myself. Needing was so easy: it came naturally, like breathing. Being needed by someone else, though, that was the hard part. But as with giving help and accepting it, we had to do both to be made complete—like links overlapping to form a chain, or a lock finding the right key.

I pushed out my chair, and headed downstairs, through the kitchen and out into the yard. I knew this was crazy, but suddenly it seemed so crucial that I somehow tell Nate I was sorry, reach out to him and let him know that I was here.

When I got to the gate, I pulled it open, then peered in, looking for him. But it was Mr. Cross I saw a moment later, walking quickly through the living room, his phone to his ear. Immediately I stepped back, around the fence, hiding as he slid open the glass door and came out onto the patio.

"I told you, I've been out of town all day," he was saying as he crossed by the pool, over to the garage. "He was supposed to be doing pickups and check-ins. Did he come by and get the cleaning today?" He paused, letting out a breath. "Fine. I'll keep looking for him. If you see him, tell him I want him home. Now. Understood?"

As he went back inside, all I could hear, other than my breathing, was the bubbling of the nearby pump, pushing the water in and out, in and out. I thought of Nate swimming laps that night, his dark shadow moving beneath the trees, how long it had been since I'd seen him alone in the pool.

Mr. Cross was inside now, still looking as his pace quickened, moving faster, back and forth. Watching him, I had a flash of Nate at school the last time I'd seen him, suddenly realizing why his expression—distant, distracted—had been so familiar. It was the same one on my mother's face the last time I'd seen her, when I walked into a room and she turned, surprised.

And this was why, as Mr. Cross called his name again, I knew his searching was useless. There's just something obvious about emptiness, even when you try to convince yourself otherwise. Nate was gone.

Chapter Eighteen

"Here," Jamie said. "For luck."

I watched him as he slid his car keys across the table toward me. "Really?" I said. "Are you sure?"

"Positive," he replied. "It's a big day. You shouldn't have to start it on the bus."

"Wow," I said, slipping them into my pocket. "Thanks."

He sat down across from me, pouring himself his usual heaping bowl of cereal, which he then drowned with milk. "So," he said, "what's your state of mind. Confident? Nervous? Zen?"

I made a face at him. "I'm fine," I told him. "I just want to get it over with."

His phone, which was on vibrate, suddenly buzzed, skipping itself sideways across the table. Jamie glanced at the caller ID and groaned. "Jesus," he said, but answered anyway. Still, his voice was curt, not at all Jamie-like, as he said, "Yes?"

I pushed out my chair, taking my own bowl to the sink. As I passed him, I could hear a voice through the receiver, although the words were indistinguishable.

"Really," Jamie said, and now he sounded concerned. "When was the last time you saw him? Oh. Okay, hold on, I'll ask her." He moved the phone away from his ear. "Hey, have you talked to Nate lately? His dad's looking for him."

I knew it, I thought. Out loud, I said, "No."

"Did you see him this weekend?"

I shook my head. "Not since school on Friday."

"She hasn't seen him since Friday," Jamie repeated into the phone. "Yeah, absolutely. We'll definitely let you know if we do. Keep us posted, okay?"

I opened the dishwasher, concentrating on loading in my bowl and spoon as he hung up. "What's going on?" I asked.

"Nate's gone AWOL, apparently," he said. "Blake hasn't seen him since Friday night."

I stood up, shutting the dishwasher. "Has he called the police?"

"No," he said, taking a bite of cereal. "He thinks he probably just took off for the weekend with his friends— you know, senioritis or whatever. Can't have gone far, at any rate."

But I, of course, knew this wasn't necessarily true. You could get anywhere on foot, especially if you had money and time. And Nate hadn't had a fence to jump. He'd just walked out. Free and clear.

And I was too late. If I'd just gone over there that night I'd seen him swimming, or talked to him on Friday at school, maybe, just maybe, I might have been able to help. Now, even if I wanted to go after him, I didn't know where to start. He could be anywhere.

It was weirder than I'd expected, driving myself to school after so many long months of being dependent on someone else. Under any other circumstances, I probably would have enjoyed it, but instead it felt almost strange to be sitting in traffic in the quiet of Jamie's Audi, other cars on all sides of me. At one light, I glanced over to see a woman in a minivan looking at me, and I wondered if to her I was just a spoiled teenage girl in an expensive car, a backpack on the seat beside her, blinker on to turn in to an exclusive school. This was unnerving for some reason, so much so that I found myself staring back at her, hard, until she turned away.

Once at school, I started across the green, taking a deep breath and trying to clear my head. Because of my certainty that Nate had taken off—even before I knew it for sure—I'd actually ended up following Gervais's Zen-mode plan, if only because I'd been too distracted to study the night before. Now, though, calculus was the last thing on my mind, even as I approached my classroom and found him waiting outside the door for me.

"All right," he said. "Did you follow my pre-test instructions? Get at least eight hours sleep? Eat a protein-heavy breakfast?"

"Gervais," I said. "Not right now, okay?"

"Remember," he said, ignoring this, "take your time on the first sets, even if they seem easy. You need them to prime your brain, lay the groundwork for the harder stuff."

I nodded, not even bothering to respond this time.

"If you find yourself stumbling with the power rule, remember that acronym we talked about. And write it down on the test page, so you can have it right in front of you."

"I need to go," I said.

"And finally," he said as, inside, my teacher Ms. Gooden was picking up a stack of papers, shuffling them as she prepared to hand them out, "if you get stuck, just clear your head. Envision an empty room, and let your mind examine it. In time, you will find the answer."

He blurted out this last part, not very Zen at all, as he rushed to fit it in as the bell rang. Even in my distracted state, as I looked at him I realized I should be more grateful. Sure, we'd had a deal, and I had paid him his twenty bucks an hour when he invoiced me (which he did on a biweekly basis on preprinted letterhead, no joke). But showing up like this, for a last-minute primer? That was above the call of duty. Even for a multipronged, proven method like his.

"Thanks, Gervais," I said.

"Don't thank me," he replied. "Just go get that ninety. I don't want you messing up my success rate."

I nodded, then turned to go into my classroom, sliding into my seat. When I looked back out the door, he was still standing there, peering in at me. Jake Bristol, who was sitting beside me looking sleepy, leaned across the aisle, poking my shoulder. "What's up with you and Miller?" he asked. "You into jailbait or something?"

I just looked at him. Jerk. "No," I said. "We're friends."

Now, Ms. Gooden came down the aisle, smiling at me as she slid a test, facedown, onto the desk in front of me. She was tall and pretty, with blonde hair she wore long, twisting it back with a pencil when she got busy filling up the board with theorems. "Good luck," she said as I turned it over.

At first glance, I felt my heart sink, immediately overwhelmed. But then I remembered what Gervais had said, about taking my time and priming my brain, and picked up my pencil and began.

The first one was easy. The second, a little harder, but still manageable. It wasn't until I got to the bottom of the front page that I realized that somehow, I was actually doing this. Carefully moving from one to the next, following Gervais's advice, jotting the power rule down in the margin: *The derivative of any given variable (x) to the exponent (n) is equal to product of the exponent and the variable to the (n–1) power.* I could hear Olivia saying it in my head, just as I heard Gervais's voice again and again, telling me the next step, and then the one following, each time I found myself hesitating.

There were ten minutes left on the clock when I reached the last problem, and this one did give me pause, more than any of the others. Staring down at it, I could feel myself starting to panic, the worry rising up slowly from my gut, and this time, no voices were coming, no prompting to be heard. I glanced around me at the people on either side still scribbling, at Ms. Gooden, who was flipping through *Lucky* magazine, and finally at the clock, which let me know I had five minutes left. Then I closed my eyes.

An empty room, Gervais had said, and at first I tried to picture white walls, a wood floor, a generic anywhere. But as my mind began to settle, something else came slowly into view: a door swinging open, revealing a room I recognized. It wasn't one in the yellow house, though, or even Cora's, but instead one with high glass windows opposite, a bedroom to the side with a dry-cleaned duvet, sofas that had hardly been used. A room empty not in definition, but in feeling. And finally, as my mind's eye moved across all of these, I saw one last thing: a root-beer cap sitting square on a countertop, just where someone had left it to be found.

I opened my eyes, then looked back down at the one blank spot on my paper, the problem left unsolved. I still had three minutes as I quickly jotted down an answer, not thinking, just going on instinct. Then I brought my paper to the front of the room, handed it in, and pushed out the door onto the green, heading toward the parking lot. I could just barely hear the bell, distant and steady, as I drove away.

* * *

In a perfect world, I would have remembered not only where the apartment building was, what floor to take the elevator to, but also the exact number of the unit. Because this was my world, however, I found myself on the seventh floor, all those doors stretching out before me, and no idea where to begin. In the end, I walked halfway down the hallway and just started knocking.

If someone answered, I apologized. If they didn't, I moved on. At the sixth door, though, something else happened. No one opened it, but I heard a noise just inside. On instinct—call it Zen mode—I reached down and tried the knob. No key necessary. It swung right open.

The room was just as I'd pictured it earlier. Sofas undisturbed, counter clutter-free, the bottle cap just where it had been. The only difference was a USWIM sweatshirt hanging over the back of one of the island stools. I picked it up, putting it to my face as I breathed in the smell of

chlorine, of water. Of Nate. And then, with it still lingering, I looked outside and found him.

He was standing on the balcony, hands on the rail, his
back to me, even though it was cold, so cold I could feel the
air seeping through the glass as I came closer. I reached for
the door handle to pull it open, then stopped halfway, suddenly nervous. How do you even begin to return to someone, much less convince them to do the same for you? I had
no idea. More than ever, though, right then I had to believe
the answer would just come to me. So I pulled the door
open.

When Nate turned around, I could tell I'd startled him.
His face was surprised, only relaxing slightly when he saw it
was me. By then, I'd already noticed the marks on his cheek
and chin, red turning to blue. There comes a point when
things are undeniable and can't be hidden any longer. Even
from yourself.

"Ruby," he said. "What are you doing here?"

I opened my mouth to say something in response to
this. Anything, just a word, even if it wasn't the perfect one.
But as nothing came, I looked at the landscape spread out
behind him, wide and vast on either side. It wasn't empty,
not at all, but maybe this could inspire you as well, because
right then, I knew just what to say, or at least a good place
to start, even if only because it was what Cora had said to
me back when all this began.

"It's cold," I said, holding out my hand to him. "You
should come inside."

Chapter Nineteen

Nate did come in. Getting him to come back with me, though, was harder.

In fact, we'd sat on the couch in that apartment for more than two hours, going over everything that had happened, before he finally agreed to at least talk to someone. This part, at least, I didn't even have to think about. I'd picked up his phone and dialed a number, and by the time we got back to my house, Cora was already waiting.

They sat at the kitchen table, me hanging back against the island, as Nate told her everything. About how when he'd first moved back, living with his dad had been okay—occasionally, he had money problems and issues with creditors, but when he took out his stress on Nate it was infrequent. Since the fall, though, when Rest Assured began to struggle, things had been getting worse, culminating in the months since Christmas, when a bunch of loans had come due. Nate said he had always planned to stick it out, but after a particularly bad fight a few nights earlier—the end result of which were the bruises on his face—he'd had enough.

Cora was amazing that day. She did everything—from just listening, her face serious, to asking careful questions, to calling up her contacts at the social-services division to answer Nate's questions about what his options were. In the end, it was she who dialed his mom in Arizona, her voice calm and professional as she explained the situation, then nodded supportively as she handed the receiver over to Nate to do the rest.

By that night, a plane ticket was booked, a temporary living arrangement set. Nate would spend the rest of the school year in Arizona, followed by working the swim-camp job in Pennsylvania he'd already set up through the summer. Come fall, he'd head off to the U, where he'd recently gotten in early admission, albeit without his scholarship due to quitting swim team midyear. Still, it was his hope that the coach might be open to letting him try for alternate, or at least participate in practices. It wasn't exactly what he'd planned, but it was something.

Mr. Cross was not happy when he found out about all this. In fact, at first he insisted that Nate return home, threatening to get the police involved if he didn't. It wasn't until Cora informed him that Nate had more than enough cause to press charges against him that he acquiesced, although even then he made his displeasure known with repeated phone calls, as well as making it as difficult as he could for Nate to collect his stuff and move in with us for the few days before he left town.

I did my best to distract Nate from all this, dragging him to movies at the Vista 10 (where we got free popcorn and admission, thanks to Olivia), hanging out with Roscoe, and taking extended coffee trips to Jump Java. He didn't go back to Perkins, as Cora had arranged for him to finish the little bit of work he had left via correspondence or online, and every afternoon as I came up the front walk, I was nervous, calling out to him the minute I stepped in the door. I finally understood what Jamie and Cora had gone through with me those first few weeks, if only from the relief I felt every time I heard his voice responding.

All the while, though, I knew he soon wouldn't be there. But I never talked to him about this. He had enough to worry about, and what mattered most was that I was just there for him, however he needed me to be. Still, the morning of his flight, when I came downstairs to find him in the foyer, his bags at his feet, I felt that same twist in my stomach.

I wasn't the only one upset. Cora sniffled through the entire good-bye, hugging him repeatedly, a tissue clutched in her hand. "Now, I'll call you tonight, just to make sure you're getting settled in," she told him. "And don't worry about things on this end. It's all handled."

"Okay," Nate said. "Thanks again. For everything."

"Don't be a stranger, all right?" Jamie told him, giving him a bear hug and a back slap. "You're family now."

Family, I thought as we pulled out of the driveway. The neighborhood was still asleep, houses dark as we drove out past those big stone pillars, and I remembered how I'd felt, coming in all those months ago, with everything so new and different.

"Are you nervous?" I asked Nate as we pulled out onto the main road.

"Not really," he replied, sitting back. "It's all kind of surreal, actually."

"It'll hit you eventually," I told him. "Probably at the exact moment it's too late to come back."

He smiled. "But I am coming back," he said. "I just have to survive Arizona and my mother first."

"You think it'll be that bad?"

"I have no idea. It isn't like she chose for me to come there. She's only doing this because she has to."

I nodded, slowing for a light. "Well, you never know. She might surprise you," I said. He did not look convinced, so I added, "Either way, don't decide to pack it in the first night, or jump any fences. Give it a few days."

"Right," he said slowly, looking over at me. "Any other advice?"

I switched lanes, merging onto the highway. It was so early, we had all the lanes to ourselves. "Well," I said, "if there's some annoying neighbor who tries to make nice with you, don't be a total jerk to them."

"Because you might need them later," he said. "To take you out of the woods, or something."

"Exactly."

I felt him look at me but didn't say anything as we came up to the airport exit. As I took it, circling around, I could see a plane overhead—just a sliver of white, heading up, up, up.

At the terminal, even at this early hour, there were a fair amount of people, heading off, arriving home. The sun was coming up now, the sky streaked with pink overhead as we unloaded his stuff, piling it on the curb beside him. "All right," I said. "Got everything?"

"Think so," he said. "Thanks for the ride."

"Well, I did kind of owe you," I said, and he smiled. "But there is one more thing, actually."

"What's that?"

"Even if you do make tons of new friends," I told him, "try not to forget where you came from, okay?"

He looked down at me. "I seriously doubt that could happen."

"You'd be surprised," I told him. "New place, new life. It's not hard to do."

"I think," he said, "that I'll have plenty to remind me."

I hoped this was true. Even if it wasn't, all I could do was hand over what I could, with the hope of something in return. But of course, this was easier said than done. Ever since Christmas, I'd been trying to come up with the perfect gift for Nate, something phenomenal that might come close to all he'd given me. Once again, I thought I had nothing to offer. But then I looked down and realized I was wrong.

The clasp of my necklace was stubborn at first, and as I took the key to the yellow house off and put it into my pocket, I noticed how worn it was. Especially in comparison to the bright, shiny new one to Jamie and Cora's, which I slid onto the chain in its place. Then I took Nate's hand, turning it upward, and pressed the necklace, with Cora's key on it, into his palm.

"Well," I said, "just in case."

He nodded, wrapping his hand around the necklace, and my hand, as well. This time, I let my palm relax against his, feeling the warmth there and pressing back, before stepping in closer. Then I reached up, sliding my hand behind his neck and pulling him in for a kiss, closing that space between us once and for all.

In the weeks since, Nate and I had been in constant contact, both by phone and on UMe.com. My page, long inactive, was now not only up and running but full of extras, thanks to Olivia, who helped me set it up and tweaked it on a regular basis. So far, I'd only accrued a few friends—her, Nate, Gervais, as well as Jamie, who sent me more messages than anyone—although I had lots of photos, including a couple Nate had sent of him at his new job, lifeguarding at a pool near his mom's house. He was swimming every day now, working on his times and getting back into shape; he said it was slow progress, but he was seeing improvements, bit by bit. Sometimes at night in my room when I couldn't sleep, I imagined him in the pool, crossing its length again and again, stroke by even stroke.

In my favorite picture, though, he's not in the water but posing in front of a lifeguard stand. He's smiling, the sun bright behind him, and has a whistle around his neck. If you look really closely, you can see there's another, thinner chain behind, with something else dangling from it. It was hard to make it out, exactly. But I knew what it was.

Chapter Twenty

"Ruby? You about ready?"

I turned, looking over my shoulder at Cora, who was standing in the door to the kitchen, her purse over her shoulder. "Are we leaving?" I asked.

"As soon as Jamie finds the camcorder," she replied. "He's determined to capture every moment of this milestone."

"You have to document important family events!" I heard Jamie yell from somewhere behind her. "You'll thank me later."

Cora rolled her eyes. "Five minutes, whether he finds it or not. We don't want to be late. Okay?"

I nodded, and she ducked back inside, the door falling shut behind her, as I turned back to the pond. I'd been spending a lot of time out there lately, ever since the day a couple of months earlier when I'd come home from work to find her and Jamie huddled over something in the foyer.

"Jamie. Put it down."

"I'm not opening it. I'm just looking."

"Would you stop?"

I came up right behind them. "What are you guys doing?"

Cora jumped, startled. "Nothing," she said. "We were just—"

"You got a letter from the U," Jamie told me, holding up what I now saw was an envelope. "I brought it in about an hour ago. The anticipation has been *killing* us."

"It was killing Jamie," Cora said. "I was fine."

I walked over to where they were standing, taking the envelope from him. After all I'd heard and read about thick and thin letters, this one was, of course, neither. Not bulky, not slim, but right in the middle.

"It only takes a page to say no," Jamie told me as if I'd said this aloud. "It is only one word, after all."

"Jamie, for God's sake!" Cora swatted him. "Stop it."

I looked at the envelope again. "I'm going to take it outside," I said. "If that's okay."

Jamie opened his mouth to protest, but Cora put her hand over it. "That's fine," she said. "Good luck."

Then it was April. The grass had gone from that nubby, hard brown to a fresh green, and the trees were all budding, shedding pollen everywhere. A nice breeze was blowing as I walked out to the pond, the envelope dangling from my hand. I walked right up to the edge, where I could see my reflection, then tore it open.

I was just about to unfold the pages within when I saw something, out of the corner of my eye, moving quickly, so quickly I almost doubted it. I stepped closer, peering down into the murky depths, past the rocks and algae and budding irises, and there, sure enough, I saw a flash of white blurring past. There were others as well, gold and speckled and black, swimming low. But it was the white one, my fish, that I saw first. I took a deep breath and tore the letter open.

Dear Ms. Cooper, it began. *We are pleased to inform you . . .*

I turned around, looking back at the kitchen door where, unsurprisingly, Jamie and Cora were both standing, watching me. Jamie pushed it open, then stuck his head out. "Well?" he said.

"Good news," I said.

"Yeah?" Beside him, Cora put her hand to her mouth, her eyes widening.

I nodded. "And the fish are back. Come see."

Now, in mid-June, they were even more present, circling around the lilies and water grasses. Above them, in the water's surface, I could see my reflection: my hair loose, black gown, cap in one hand. Then a breeze blew across the yard, rustling the leaves overhead and sending everything rippling. Beside me, sitting on the grass, Roscoe closed his eyes.

As always, when I saw myself, it was weird to be without my necklace. Even now, I was still very aware of its absence, the sudden empty space where for so long I'd always seen something familiar. A few days earlier, though, I'd been digging through a drawer and come across the box Nate had given me for Valentine's Day. The next time we spoke, I mentioned this, and he told me to open it. When I did, I saw that once again he'd known what I needed, even before I did. Inside was a pair of key-shaped earrings—clearly Harriet's work—studded with red stones. I'd been wearing them every day since.

I looked across the yard, the trees swaying overhead, to Nate's house. I still called it that, a habit that I had yet to break, even though neither he nor his dad had lived there for a while. Mr. Cross had put it up for sale in May, just after a lawsuit was filed by several Rest Assured clients who had began to notice, and question, various discrepancies on their accounts. The last I'd heard, he was still in business, but just barely, and renting an apartment somewhere across town. The new owners of the house had small children and used the pool all the time. On warm afternoons, from my window, I could hear them laughing and splashing.

As for me, thanks to Gervais's method, I'd made a ninety-one on my calc test—guaranteeing my own spot at the U—and soon would be walking across the green at Perkins Day, taking my diploma from Mr. Thackray, officially a high-school graduate. In the lead up to the ceremony, I'd received endless paperwork and e-mails about getting tickets for family, and all the rules and regulations about how many we were allowed to reserve. In the end, I'd taken four, for Cora and Jamie, Reggie and Harriet. Not all family, but if there was one thing I'd learned over these last few months, it was that this was a flexible definition.

At least, that was the final thesis of my English project, which I'd handed in during the last week of classes. We'd each had to get up in front of the class and do a presentation that showcased our research and findings, and for mine, I'd brought in two pictures. The first was of Jamie's extended tribe, which I put up while I explained about the different definitions I'd gathered, and how they all related to one another. The second was more recent, from the eighteenth birthday party Cora had thrown me at the end of May. I'd told her not to make a fuss, but of course she'd ignored me, insisting that we had to do something, and that I should invite anyone I wanted to celebrate with me.

In the picture, we're all posing by the pond, one big group. I'm in the center, with Cora on one side, Olivia on the other. You can see Jamie, slightly blurred from running back into the shot after setting the timer on the camera— he's standing by Harriet, who is looking at me and smiling, and Reggie, who is of course looking at her. Next to them you can see Laney, smiling big, and then Gervais, the only one eating, a plate of cake in his hand. Like the first one, which I'd studied all these months, it is not a perfect picture, not even close. But in that moment, it was exactly what it was supposed to be.

It was also, like the one of Jamie's family, already changing, even if that day we hadn't known it yet. That came a couple of weeks later, when I was leaving for school one morning and found my sister sitting on her bed, crying.

"Cora?" I dropped my backpack, then came over to sit beside her. "What's wrong?"

She drew in a big, shuddering breath, shaking her head, clearly unable to answer. By then, though, I didn't need her to; I'd already seen the pregnancy-test box on the bedside table. "Oh, Cora," I said. "It's okay."

"I—I—" she said, sobbing through the words.

"What's going on?" Jamie, who had just come up the stairs, said as he came into the room. I nodded at the test box, and his face fell. "Oh," he said, taking a seat on her other side. "Honey. It's all right. We've got that appointment next week—we'll see what's going on—"

"I'm fine," Cora sputtered as I grabbed her some tissues. "I really am."

I reached over, taking her hand so I could put the tissues into it. She was still holding the test stick, so I took it from her as she drew in another breath. It wasn't until after I put it down on the bed beside me that I actually looked at it.

"Are you, though?" Jamie was saying, rubbing her shoulders. "Are you sure?"

I stared at the stick again, double-checking it. Then tripling. "Yeah," I said, holding it up, the plus sign more than clear as Cora dissolved in tears again. "She's positive."

She was also sick as a dog, morning and night, as well as so tired she couldn't stay up much past dinner. Not that I'd heard her complain, even once.

All of this had got me thinking, and a few days before my birthday, I'd sat down at my desk to write a letter, long overdue, to my own mother, who was still in rehab in Tennessee. I wasn't sure what I wanted to say, though, and after sitting there for a full hour, with nothing coming, I'd just photocopied my acceptance letter from the U and slid it inside the envelope. It wasn't closure, by any means, but it was progress. If nothing else, now we knew where to find each other, even if only time would tell if either of us would ever come looking.

"Got it! Let's go!" I heard Jamie yell from inside. Roscoe perked up his ears, and I watched him run, tags jingling, across the grass to the house.

It was only then, when I knew I was alone, at least for the moment, that I reached under my gown into the pocket of my dress. As I pulled out my key from the yellow house, which I'd kept on my bureau since the day Nate left, I traced the shape one last time before folding my hand tightly around it.

Behind me, Cora was calling again. My family was waiting. Looking down at the pond, all I could think was that it is an incredible thing, how a whole world can rise from what seems like nothing at all. I stepped closer to the edge, keeping my eyes on my reflection as I dropped the key into the water, where it landed with a splash. At first, the fish darted away, but as it began to sink they circled back, gathering around. Together, they followed it down, down, until it was gone.

Turn the page for a preview
of Sarah Dessen's next book,

along
for the
ride

one

THE EMAILS ALWAYS began the same way.

Hi Auden!!

It was the extra exclamation point that got me. My mother would call it extraneous, overblown, exuberant. To me, it was simply annoying, just like everything else about my stepmother, Heidi.

I hope you're having a great last few weeks of classes. We are all good here! Just getting the last few things done before your sister-to-be arrives. She's been kicking like crazy lately. It's like she's doing the karate moves in there! I've been busy minding the store (so to speak) and putting a few final touches on the nursery. I've done it all in pink and brown; it's gorgeous. I'll attach a picture so you can see it.

Your dad is busy as always, working on his book. I figure I'll see more of him burning the midnight oil when I'm up with the baby!

I really hope you'll consider coming to visit us once

you're done with school. It would be so much fun, and
make this summer that much more special for all of us.
Just come anytime. We'd love to see you!

Love,
Heidi (and your dad, and the baby to be!)

Just reading these missives exhausted me. Partially it was the excited grammar—which was like someone yelling in your ear—but also just Heidi herself. She was just so . . . extraneous, overblown, exuberant. And annoying. All the things she'd been to me, and more, since she and my dad got involved, pregnant, and married in the last year.

My mother claimed not to be surprised. Ever since the divorce, she'd been predicting it would not be long before my dad, as she put it, "shacked up with some coed." At twenty-six, Heidi was the same age my mother had been when she had my brother Hollis, followed by me two years later, although they could not be more different. Where my mother was an academic scholar with a smart, sharp wit and a nationwide reputation as an expert on women's roles in Renaissance literature, Heidi was . . . well, Heidi. The kind of woman whose strengths were her constant self-maintenance (pedicures, manicures, hair highlights), knowing everything you never wanted to about hemlines and shoes, and sending entirely too chatty e-mails to people who couldn't care less.

Their courtship was quick, the implantation (as my mother christened it) happening within a couple of months. Just like that, my father went from what he'd been for years—husband of Dr. Victoria West and author of one well-received novel, now more known for his interdepartmental feuds than his long-in-progress follow-up—to a new husband and father to be. Add all this to his also-new position as head of the creative writing department at Weymar College, a small school in a beachfront town, and it was like my dad had a whole new life. And even though they were always inviting me to come, I wasn't sure I wanted to find out if there was still a place for me in it.

Now, from the other room, I heard a sudden burst of laughter, followed by some clinking of glasses. My mother was hosting another of her graduate student get-togethers, which always began as formal dinners ("Culture is so lacking in this culture!" she said) before inevitably deteriorating into loud, drunken debates about literature and theory. I glanced at the clock—ten-thirty—then eased my bedroom door open with my toe, glancing down the long hallway to the kitchen. Sure enough, I could see my mom sitting at the head of our big butcher-block kitchen table, a glass of red wine in one hand. Gathered around her, as usual, were a bunch of male graduate students, looking on adoringly as she went on about, from the little bit I could gather, Marlowe and the culture of women.

This was yet another of the many fascinating contradictions about my mom. She was an expert on women in literature but didn't much like them in practice. Partly, it was because so many of them were jealous: of her intelligence (practically Mensa level), her scholarship (four books, countless articles, one endowed chair), or her looks (tall and curvy with very long jet-black hair she usually wore loose and wild, the only out-of-control thing about her). For these reasons, and others, female students seldom came to these gatherings, and if they did, they rarely returned.

"Dr. West," one of the students—typically scruffy, in a cheap-looking blazer, shaggy hair, and hip-nerdy black eyeglasses—said now, "you should really consider developing that idea into an article. It's fascinating."

I watched my mother take a sip of her wine, pushing her hair back smoothly with one hand. "Oh, God no," she said, in her deep, raspy voice (she sounded like a smoker, although she'd never taken a drag in her life). "I barely even have time to write my book right now, and that at least I'm getting paid for. If you can call it payment."

More complimentary laughter. My mother loved to complain about how little she got paid for her books—all academic, published by university presses—while what she termed "inane housewife stories" pulled in big bucks. In my mother's world, everyone would tote the collected works of Shakespeare to the beach, with maybe a couple of epic poems thrown in on the side.

"Still," Nerdy Eyeglasses said, pushing on, "it's a brilliant idea. I could, um, coauthor it with you, if you like."

My mother lifted her head and her glass, narrowing her eyes at him as a silence fell. "Oh, my," she said, "how very sweet of you. But I don't do coauthorship, for the same reason I don't do office mates or relationships. I'm just too selfish."

I could see Nerdy Eyeglasses gulp, even from my long vantage point, his face flushing as he reached for the wine bottle, trying to cover. Idiot, I thought, nudging the door back shut. As if it was that easy to align yourself with my mom, form some quick and tight bond that would last. I would know.

Ten minutes later, I was slipping out the side door, my shoes tucked under my arm, and getting into my car. I drove down the mostly empty streets, past quiet neighborhoods and dark storefronts, until the lights of Ray's Diner appeared in the distance. Small, with entirely too much neon and tables that were always a bit sticky, Ray's was the only place in town open twenty-four hours, 365 days a year. Since I hadn't been sleeping, I'd spent more nights than not in a booth there, reading or studying, tipping a buck every hour on whatever I ordered until the sun came up.

The insomnia started when my parents' marriage began to fall apart three years earlier. I shouldn't have been surprised: their union had been tumultuous for as long as I could remember, although they were usually arguing more about work than about each other.

They'd originally come to the U straight out of grad school, when my dad was offered an assistant professorship there. At the time, he'd just found a publisher for his first novel, *The Narwhal Horn*, while my mom was pregnant with my brother and trying to finish her dissertation. Fast-forward four years, to my birth, and my dad, riding a wave of critical and commercial success—*NYT* best seller list, National Book Award nominee—was heading up the creative writing program, while my mom was, as she liked to put it, "lost in a sea of diapers and self-doubt." When I entered kindergarten, though, my mom came back to academia with a vengeance, scoring a visiting lectureship and a publisher for her dissertation. Over time, she became one of the most popular professors in the department, was hired on for a full-time position, and banged out a second, then a third book, all while my father looked on. He claimed to be proud, always making jokes about her being his meal ticket, the breadwinner of the family. But then my mother got her endowed chair, which was very prestigious, and he got dropped from his publisher, which wasn't, and things started to get ugly.

The fights always seemed to begin over dinner, with one of them making some small remark and the other taking offense. There would be a small dustup—sharp words, a banged pot lid—but then it would seem resolved . . . at least until about ten or eleven, when suddenly I'd hear them start in again, about the same issue. After a while I figured out that this time lag occurred because they were waiting for me to fall asleep before really going at it. So I decided, one night, not to. I left my door open, my light on, took pointed, obvious trips to the bathroom, washing my hands as loudly as possible. And for a while, it worked. Until it didn't, and the fights started up again. But by then my body was used to staying up way late, which meant I was now awake for every single word.

I knew a lot of people whose parents had split up, and everyone seemed to handle it differently: complete surprise, crushing disappointment, total relief. The common denominator, though, was always that there was a lot of discussion about these feelings, either with both parents, or one on one separately, or with a shrink in group or individual therapy. My family, of course, had to be the exception. I did get the sit-down-we-have-to-tell-you-something moment. The news was delivered by my mother, across the kitchen table as my dad leaned against a nearby counter, fiddling with his hands and looking tired. "Your father and I are separating," she informed me, with the same flat, businesslike tone I'd so often heard her use with students as she critiqued their work. "I'm sure you'll agree this is the best thing for all of us."

Hearing this, I wasn't sure what I felt. Not relief, not crushing disappointment, and again, it wasn't a surprise. What struck me, as we sat there, the three of us, in that room, was how little I felt. Small, like a child. Which was the weirdest thing. Like it took this huge moment for a sudden wave of childhood to wash over me, long overdue.

I'd been a child, of course. But by the time I came along, my brother—the most colicky of babies, a hyperactive toddler, a "spirited" (read "impossible") kid—had worn my parents out. He was still exhausting them, albeit from another continent, wandering around Europe and sending only the occasional e-mail detailing yet another epiphany concerning what he should do with his life, followed by a request for more money to put it into action. At least his being abroad made all this seem more nomadic and artistic: now my parents could tell their friends Hollis was hanging out at the Eiffel Tower smoking cigarettes, instead of at the Quik Zip. It just sounded better.

If Hollis was a big kid, I was the little adult, the child who, at three, would sit at the table during grown-up discussions about literature and color my coloring books, not making a peep. Who learned to entertain myself at a very early age, who was obsessive about school and grades from kindergarten, because academia was the one thing that always got my parents' attention. "Oh, don't worry," my mother would say, when one of their guests would slip with the *F*-word or something equally grown-up in front of me. "Auden's very mature for her age." And I was, whether that age was two or four or seventeen. While Hollis required constant supervision, I was the one who got carted everywhere, constantly flowing in my mom's or dad's wake. They took me to the symphony, art shows, academic conferences, committee meetings, where I was expected to be seen and not heard. There was not a lot of time for playing or toys, although I never wanted for books, which were always in ample supply.

Because of this upbringing, I had kind of a hard time relating to other kids my age. I didn't understand their craziness, their energy, the rambunctious way they tossed around couch cushions, say, or rode their bikes wildly around cul-de-sacs. It did look sort of fun, but at the same time, it was so different from what I was used to that I couldn't imagine how I would ever partake if given the chance. Which I wasn't, as the cushion-tossers and wild bike riders didn't usually attend the highly academic, grade-accelerated private schools my parents favored.

In the past four years, in fact, I'd switched schools three times. I'd only lasted at Jackson High for a couple of weeks before my mom, having spotted a misspelling *and* a grammatical error on my English syllabus, moved me to Perkins Day, a local private school. It was smaller and more academically rigorous, although not nearly as much as Kiffney-Brown, the charter school to which I transferred junior year.

Founded by several former local professors, it was elite—a hundred students, max—and emphasized very small classes and a strong connection to the local university, where you could take college-level courses for early credit. While I had a few friends at Kiffney-Brown, the ultra-competitive atmosphere, paired with so much of the curriculum being self-guided, made getting close to them somewhat difficult.

Not that I really cared. School was my solace, and studying let me escape, allowing me to live a thousand vicarious lives. The more my parents bemoaned Hollis's lack of initiative and terrible grades, the harder I worked. And while they were proud of me, my accomplishments never seemed to get me what I really wanted. I was such a smart kid, I should have figured out that the only way to really get my parents' attention was to disappoint them or fail. But by the time I finally realized that, succeeding was already a habit too ingrained to break.

My dad finally moved out at the beginning of my sophomore year, renting a furnished apartment right near campus in a complex mostly populated by students. I was supposed to spend every weekend there, but he was in such a funk—still struggling with his second book, his publication (or lack of it) called into question just as my mom's was getting so much attention—that it wasn't exactly enjoyable. Then again, my mom's house wasn't much better, as she was so busy celebrating her newfound single life, and academic success, that she had people over all the time, students coming and going, dinner parties every weekend. It seemed like there was no middle ground anywhere, except at Ray's Diner.

I'd driven past it a million times but had never thought of stopping until one night when I was heading back to my mom's around two A.M. My dad, like my mom, didn't really keep close tabs on me. Because of my school schedule— one night class, flexible daytime seminar hours, and several independent studies—I came and went as I pleased, with little or no questioning, so neither of them really noticed that I wasn't sleeping. That night, I glanced in at Ray's, and something about it just struck me. It looked warm, safe almost, populated by people who at least I had one thing in common with. So I pulled in, went inside, and ordered a cup of coffee and some apple pie. I stayed until sunrise.

The nice thing about Ray's was that even once I became a regular, I still got to be alone. Nobody was asking for more than I wanted to give, and all the interactions were short and sweet. If only all relationships could be so simple, with me always knowing my role exactly.

Back in the fall, one of the waitresses, a heavyset older woman whose name-tag said JULIE, had peered down at the application I was working on as she refilled my coffee cup.

"Defriese University," she read out loud. Then she looked at me. "Pretty good school."

"One of the best," I agreed.

"Think you'll get in?"

I nodded. "Yeah. I do."

She smiled, like I was kind of cute, then patted my shoulder. "Ah, to be young and confident," she said, and then she was shuffling away.

I wanted to tell her that I wasn't confident, I just worked really hard. But she had already moved onto the next booth, chatting up the guy sitting there, and I knew she didn't really care anyway. There were worlds where all of this—grades, school, papers, class rank, early admission, weighted GPAs—mattered, and ones where they didn't. I'd spent my entire life squarely in the former, and even at Ray's, which was the latter, I still couldn't shake it.

Being so driven, and attending such an unorthodox school, meant that I'd missed out on making all those senior moments that my old friends from Perkins Day had spent this whole last year talking about. The only thing I'd even considered was prom, and then only because my main competition for highest GPA, Jason Talbot, had asked me as a sort of peace offering. In the end, though, even that hadn't happened, as he canceled last minute after getting invited to participate in some ecology conference. I told myself it didn't matter, that it was the equivalent of those couch cushions and cul-de-sac bike rides all those years ago, frivolous and unnecessary. But I still kind of wondered, that night and so many others, what I was missing.

I'd be sitting at Ray's, at two or three or four in the morning, and feel this weird twinge. When I looked up from my books to the people around me—truckers, people who'd come off the interstate for coffee to make another mile, the occasional crazy—I'd have that same feeling that I did the day my mother announced the separation. Like I didn't belong there, and should have been at home, asleep in my bed, like everyone else I'd see at school in a few hours. But just as quickly, it would pass, everything settling back into place around me. And when Julie came back around with her coffeepot, I'd push my cup to the edge of the table, saying without words what we both knew well—that I'd be staying for a while.

*　*　*

My stepsister, Thisbe Caroline West, was born the day before my graduation, weighing in at six pounds, fifteen ounces. My father called the next morning, exhausted.

"I'm so sorry, Auden," he said, "I hate to miss your speech."

"It's all right," I told him as my mother came into the kitchen, in her robe, and headed for the coffeemaker. "How's Heidi?"

"Good," he replied. "Tired. It was a long haul, and she ended up having a Caesarean, which she wasn't so happy about. But I'm sure she'll feel better after she gets some rest."

"Tell her I said congratulations," I told him.

"I will. And you go out there and give 'em hell, kid." This was typical: for my dad, who was famously combative, anything relating to academia was a battle. "I'll be thinking about you."

I smiled, thanked him, then hung up the phone as my mother poured milk into her coffee. She stirred her cup, the spoon clanking softly, for a moment before saying, "Let me guess. He's not coming."

"Heidi had the baby," I said. "They named her Thisbe."

My mother snorted. "Oh, good Lord," she said. "All the names from Shakespeare to choose from, and your father picks *that* one? The poor girl. She'll be having to explain herself her entire life."

My mom didn't really have room to talk, considering

she'd let my dad name me and my brother: Detram Hollis was a professor my dad greatly admired, while W. H. Auden was his favorite poet. I'd spent some time as a kid wishing my name was Ashley or Katherine, if only because it would have made life simpler, but my mom liked to tell me that my name was actually a kind of litmus test. Auden wasn't like Frost, she'd say, or Whitman. He was a bit more obscure, and if someone knew of him, then I could be at least somewhat sure they were worth my time and energy, capable of being my intellectual equal. I figured this might be even more true for Thisbe, but instead of saying so I just sat down with my speech notes, flipping through them again. After a moment, she pulled out a chair, joining me.

"So Heidi survived the childbirth, I assume?" she asked, taking a sip off her coffee.

"She had to have a Caesarean."

"She's lucky," my mom said. "Hollis was eleven pounds, and the epidural didn't take. He almost killed me."

I flipped through another couple of cards, waiting for one of the stories that inevitably followed this one. There was how Hollis was a ravenous child, sucking my mother's milk supply dry. The craziness that was his colic, how he had to be walked constantly, and even then screamed for hours on end. Or there was the one about my dad, and how he . . .

"I just hope she's not expecting your father to be of much help," she said, reaching over for a couple of my cards and scanning them, her eyes narrowed. "I was lucky if he changed a diaper every once in a while. And forget about him getting up for night feedings. He claimed that he had sleep issues and had to get his nine hours in order to teach. Awfully convenient, that."

She was still reading my cards as she said this, and I felt the familiar twinge I always experienced whenever anything I did was suddenly under her scrutiny. A moment later, though, she put them aside without comment.

"Well," I said as she took another sip of coffee, "that was a long time ago. Maybe he's changed."

"People don't change. If anything, you get more set in your ways as you get older, not less." She shook her head. "I remember I used to sit in our bedroom, with Hollis screaming, and just wish that once the door would open, and your father would come in and say 'Here, give him to me. You go rest.' Eventually, it wasn't even your dad I wanted, just anybody. Anybody at all."

She was looking out the window as she said this, her fingers wrapped around her mug, which was not on the table or at her lips but instead hovering just between. I picked up my cards, carefully arranging them back in order. "I should go get ready," I said, pushing my chair back.

My mother didn't move as I got up and walked behind her. It was like she was frozen, still back in that old bedroom, still waiting, at least until I got down the hallway. Then, suddenly, she spoke.

"You should rethink that Faulkner quote," she said. "It's too much for an opening. You'll sound pretentious."

I looked down at my top card, where the words—" The past isn't dead. It isn't even past"—were written in my neat block print. "Okay," I said. She was right, of course. She always was. "Thanks."

* * *

I'd been so focused on my last year of high school and beginning college that I hadn't really thought about the time in between. Suddenly, though, it was summer, and there was nothing to do but wait for my real life to begin again.

I spent a couple of weeks getting all the stuff I needed for Defriese, and tried to pick up a few shifts at my tutoring job at Huntsinger Test Prep, although it was pretty slow. I seemed to be the only one thinking about school, a fact made more obvious by the various invitations I received from my old friends at Perkins to dinners or trips to the lake. I wanted to see everyone, but whenever we did get together, I felt like the odd person out. I'd only been at Kiffney-Brown for two years, but it was so different, so entirely academic, that I found I couldn't really relate to their talk about summer jobs and boyfriends. After a few awkward outings, I began to beg off, saying I was busy, and after a while, they got the message.

Home was kind of weird as well, as my mom had gotten some research grant and was working all the time, and when she wasn't, her graduate assistants were always showing up for impromtu dinners and cocktail hours. When they got too noisy, and the house too crowded, I'd head out to the front porch with a book and read until it was dark enough to go to Ray's.